TRAITEUR'S

RING

WITHDRAWN

By
Jeffrey Wilson

JournalStone
San Francisco

JournalStone books may be ordered through booksellers or by contacting:

JournalStone
199 State Street
San Mateo, CA 94401
www.journalstone.com

ISBN: 978-1-936564-17-0   (sc)
ISBN: 978-1-936564-18-7   (dj)
ISBN: 978-1-936564-19-4   (ebook)

Library of Congress Control Number: 2011932592

Printed in the United States of America
JournalStone rev. date: September 9, 2011

Cover Design: Denise Daniel
Cover Art: Joey Adams

Edited by: Whitney L.J. Howell

Photography Credits, Back Cover: US Nave/John P. Curtis and Eric S. Logsdon – (Works have been modified) http://creativecommons.org/licenses/by-sa/3.0/us/

DEDICATION

For Wendy, whose love and support allowed me to turn a dream into reality; Jack and Emma who keep me young; and Connor whose imagination and creativity make him my favorite author.

And for the men and women of U.S. Naval Special Warfare, those of you I know and those of you I have yet to meet– thank you for your service.

Thanks to Chris Payne and the entire staff at JournalStone Publishing for including me in their exciting venture. The JournalStone editing staff took great care and patience in their editing process taking my book and turning it into Novel.

SEE OTHER JOURNALSTONE PUBLISHED BOOKS!

Ghosts of Coronado Bay

That Which Should Not Be

Shaman's Blood

Imperial Hostage

The Pentacle Pendant

The Jokers Club

Duncan's Diary, Birth of a Serial Killer

The only easy day was yesterday

-US Navy SEAL mantra

PRELUDE

He could see the men who moved silently in the shadows just beyond the tree line. He saw them not with his eyes, though he suspected a little effort would reveal the shapes that moved slowly and so very quietly just a short distance into the thick brush. He saw them with the other eyes, the ones inside his other mind. The men were light skinned, all but one of them, and they wore clothing and equipment of men from far away. And guns, of course. Always, it seemed, there were the guns.

He knew he could hear them, too. They moved all but silently. If he tried he could hear their thoughts. For a moment, he listened to the hearts of the quiet men that watched his village, and that short time told him enough. The men from far away meant no harm to the village. They sought the others - the bad men - who passed through here more and more frequently these days. In a way that made them friends, he supposed. He thought briefly of sending a heart message to them, to calm them and give them peace. The large one in particular seemed to need that. He decided not to only because he didn't think they could understand it. And, anyway, they meant only to watch them for a while and to see if the bad men came. Then, they would move on.

He had been a Seer for seventy-one changes of the sun now, ever since his father's father placed the ring on the third finger of his right hand. He quietly spun the ring on his worn, dark finger, as he had so often when he felt something coming. The ring did not give the power, he knew, but helped him use it. The power came from inside and was the reason he wore the ring so young. His father didn't have the mind's eye, at least not enough to protect the people, and so his father's father had slipped the ring on his hand when he was barely as tall as a harvest basket.

Why do these thoughts fill me now? Perhaps the next one is close.

He shifted his weight as he squatted over his thin mat of leaves and fruit from the jungle and let go of the ring. He got tired much sooner these days, and his hips ached as he worked over his medicines. He put the thoughts of the far-away men out of his mind for a moment and ground the smooth rock over the berries and leaves in the pestle, smoothing the paste out to the sides. He would need a little bit more for the new mother. Her wounds would heal without the medicine, but the pain would be easier with his help.

He felt the far-away men move softly away and deeper into the jungle. The Seer closed his eyes and sent a small heart message to the thin man, who he knew to be the leader. He gave him the way to the path that would take him and his men to the camp a few miles away where the bad men made loud noise and desecrated the living jungle. He urged him quietly in that direction and, then, set back to his task of making the medicine paste.

As he stretched his back, his other mind's eye saw a flash of images from the days to come. They were ugly and loud, and he thought they meant pain for his people and for him. He sighed. For hundreds and hundreds of seasons they had been the keepers of the living jungle. Bad things came and went, but always they went on. The other mind gave him no vision, but still he felt perhaps the end would come this time. He would try and pass the knowledge if he could. The other mind had always been a responsibility so much more than a power. He supposed he had come to love them both. His eye told him there would be another with a seer's mind. He would come to them in the last hour.

The Seer stretched his back again and rose on frail legs to carry his paste to the new mother. If the end came, then it was just the cycle of things.

The thought sounds of the far-away men faded off into the distance.

CHAPTER

1

He simultaneously raised a closed fist and sank his body deeper down into the bush. He listened. He could hear the jungle sounds and his own breathing, but not a sound from the four men behind him. There had been something, though. He felt it more than heard it, but he knew there had been something.

Cautiously, Chris raised his head up until his eyes were just above the gnarled root and thick leaves into which he had melted. He moved just his eyes, his head still, and peered in a small arc around him. Even with his trained and blooded eyes, he could barely make out the other four SEALs behind him – except for Auger's left ass cheek where he cocked himself sideways because of the shrapnel still in his hip. It was a nice souvenir from their tour in Afghanistan last fall that apparently still bothered him more than he admitted.

Nothing else caught his eye.

Had it been a sound or more of a feeling?

I'm starting to sound like Ben.

He didn't believe in that shit much back home in Virginia Beach. But he listened more to his superstitious, Cajun SEAL medic here in the bush when they deployed.

Chris looked back at Ben now and pointed at him and, then, tapped his ear and raised a hand palm up.

You hear anything?

The SEAL shook his head slowly.

Chris, then, tapped his temple and put his palm up again, a grin now on his face.

You feel anything in that radar head of yours, Ben?

The face broke into its own grin behind the cammo war paint. His SEAL medic gave him a thumbs-down and, then, flipped him a middle finger.

Chris smiled and rose softly and gestured his men to continue their quiet patrol. He knew the ragged band of Al Qaeda assholes were out here somewhere. The predator over flights had shown glimpses of them, but the thick jungle made the unmanned aerial reconnaissance almost useless. They would find them. He paused a moment. He felt suddenly consumed by an almost unbearable need to swing his trailing companions about thirty degrees to the left. Why not? Maybe he had some Cajun in him, right?

They moved through the thick brush with some difficulty, but after about seventy yards the ground cover thinned suddenly, and the young SEAL officer found himself staring at a wide path cut through the jungle.

No shit?

He raised a fist again and, then, settled his men into the thick brush beside the trail. The trail had been used recently, his trained eyes knew. They would watch awhile, maybe the rest of the day.

Theirs was a game of patience.

Chris relaxed his body so he wouldn't cramp up and, then, silently pulled a can of Skoal from the front pocket of his combat vest. He slipped a pinch in behind his lower lip and gestured behind him to his men.

We're going to be here awhile.

They would need to make contact with the folks from the village behind them. Perhaps tomorrow they could bring some medical supplies and trinkets with them and find a 'terp who could help them talk to the village leaders.

Hearts and minds, right?

Then maybe they could get some intel on who else passed this way. From the look of the path, someone came through here regularly and in fairly large numbers.

The SEAL team settled in and watched and waited.

CHAPTER

2

Ben Morvant settled back into the homemade chair and accepted the can of Copenhagen snuff from Reed.

"Thanks, bro," he said and snapped the can with a flick of his wrist to pack the fine tobacco before opening the can and taking a generous pinch. Ben almost never dipped at home anymore, but deployments were, well, just different. He tossed the can back to his best friend and fellow frogman. Reed caught it without looking and slipped it into a cargo pocket of his cammies. Then, he went back to cleaning the receiving bolt of his M-4 rifle with a worn and dirty green toothbrush. Ben breathed deeply of the familiar smell of Hoppes gun cleaner without thinking.

"'Least we don't have the fucking moon dust shit settling on everything here, like we did in Iraq," Reed said. "Don't have to clean shit every time you wake up."

"Yeah," Ben said and waited. There would be more from Reed, something else to bitch about.

"Course, here everything is so fuckin' hot and wet my ass is chafing," Reed continued and Ben smiled. "It's a wonder everything doesn't corrode all to shit. It's a miracle we can keep the electronics working, especially the laptops."

"Yeah. This place sucks ass," Ben said with exaggerated angst. He stifled his grin.

"Yeah, it does," Reed went on, slipping the receiving bolt back into the frame of his rifle. "And another thing – how come we're out here on our own away from the support folks? What the fuck? They can't spring a few bucks for gas to exfil us during the day? How come...." He stopped when he looked up and saw the laughing smile on Ben's face. "Oh, fuck you, Ben," he said, but he couldn't contain his own grin. "What – you love it here, dude? You gonna build a retirement shack here in the African fuckin' boonies?"

"Nah, but I'll tell ya." Ben leaned forward and spit into the dirt beside his wooden chair. "You bitch more than any Frog I know, dude."

"Yeah, well maybe I'm just more observant about the world's injustices," Reed grinned back.

"Maybe you're just a whiner-baby," Ben said.

Reed laughed. "Yeah, maybe. Or I've just been doin' it too long."

Ben stood and stretched his back. "You don't know how to do nothing else, man."

"True," Reed conceded.

They both turned as Chris approached with Auger's tall dark frame shadowing him from behind. "Hey, guys," he said.

"Hey, bro," Ben answered for both of them.

The lieutenant held out his hand, and Reed fumbled for his can of tobacco and tossed it to him. "Thought you quit, man," he said as their officer caught it one-handed.

"Nah," Chris answered with a grin as he took a generous pinch and put it behind his lip. "Just quit buying it," he said with a smile and tossed the can back.

"Perfect," Reed said.

"Talked to the Head Shed," Chris said, referring to the command element of the task force which made the operational decisions for the team. Ben watched his officer stretch out in the dirt, leaning back against the side of the homemade chair. "We're a go to take a 'terp to that little village and see what we can find out."

"Cool," Reed said. "Then, what?"

"Our discretion with the usual standing order," the officer answered.

"Kill or Capture – blah, blah, blah," Ben said.

"Yeah," Chris answered. "Intel guys think there are some big players in this ragged little band of assholes we been hunting," he bent forward and spit. "Get some of these dudes and close up their little shop here, and we can head back uptown for a few days."

"Nice," Reed said. "Get to somewhere with a chow hall and an exchange so I can restock the shit you quit buying."

Chris got up and laughed. "Next sleeve is on me," he said and clapped Reed on the back. "Rest up tonight. If we get good intel from the village, we may just keep on and hit the bad guys tomorrow night."

"Sooner the better, L.T.," Auger said, a big confident smile spreading across his dark chiseled face. "Reed, give me a dip."

"God damn it," Reed grumbled and fished the can from his cammies again. "You guys living clean is costing me a fortune."

Ben watched the two bicker like old women and tried to shake a strange and foreboding feeling. He knew better than to ignore it, his Grandma taught him that the hard way, but no sense dwelling on a bad feeling he couldn't define. He reached for his own rifle and the bottle of Hoppes cleaner.

Better to just be ready.

* * *

Ben followed behind Chris and felt his finger tap the trigger guard of his rifle. The 'terp walked ahead of Chris, and Reed followed a few yards back. The other two SEALs had melted into the jungle around the small village just in case it turned less friendly than it looked. Lash would be watching closely through his sniper rifle's high-power sight, Ben knew. Everything happened as they had briefed early that morning after the Head Shed had approved their plan.

The interpreter who shuffled ahead of Chris was local and had worked with them before, yet even he seemed to know very little about the primitive community. The villagers had been here for centuries, he had told them, and kept completely to themselves. He said the village had a powerful *Ashe* – a spiritual power controlled by their leader, a very old and very wise man. The 'terp seemed a little frightened which had made Ben feel strange. He felt strange again now, like something alive shifted around inside him, and struggled with a weird sense – not of déjà vu – but more of premonition. He shifted his heavy gear on his shoulders and felt the tug of something. Something strong.

Gammy had an old Indian word for this feeling.

He tried to remember the word but couldn't come up with it. His eyes darted back and forth as he scanned the village for signs of danger. His gaze met only the silent curious stares of the villagers who stopped what they were doing to watch the strange men who walked into their lives. Even that seemed odd or maybe a little surrealistic. He realized what bothered him about the dark faces of the people around them was the lack of surprise.

Like they knew we were coming.

Unlike the other locals he had met here, who wore strange combinations of ragged western clothes mixed with homemade sandals or bare feet; these people were right out of an old movie or a National Geographic magazine. They dressed scantily in handmade grey cloth which contrasted with their elaborate and brightly colored necklaces and head gear. The men had simple bands of grey cloth around their biceps and most held long staffs. For the most part, the women squatted on the ground, their chins resting on their knees as they watched them pass.

"These people give me the fucking creeps," Reed mumbled from behind him. Ben didn't answer. He actually felt a paradoxical calm settle over him and relaxed his grip on his M-4. He felt something strange, no doubt, but it wasn't danger he sensed.

Not now. Not yet.

It comes later.

The second voice, still his own, made him shudder, and for a second the feeling of premonition nearly choked him.

"Whadya think, Ben?" Chris asked without turning around.

"Dunno," Ben answered and shook off the superstitious feelings. "I think they're not surprised to see us."

"Yeah," Chris agreed and looked around.

"Dey be surprised by nuddin" the interpreter said softly. "Dey leader see ever 'tin. Dey know we comin' afore we know."

"Maybe he should come work with us. We could use that kind of help," Reed chuckled from behind him.

"You sure could," Ben agreed. "You usually don't know what we did even after we did it."

They both laughed.

The interpreter stopped at a small, but powerfully built, man who stood with one hand on his hip and the other on a heavily laden long pole which stretched back over his shoulder. The 'terp said a few things in what sounded like a different gibberish from what they usually talked, and the half-naked man pointed and made a sound like "Gah."

"Da leader be dis way," the 'terp said, leading them on through the village.

Ben tried to penetrate the wall of jungle encircling the village with his eyes, hoping to see Auger or Lash. But his SEAL buddies were easily concealed by the dense brush. The tingly feelings he remembered from growing up with his Traiteur Grandma in the bayou west of New Orleans had left him, and he tried to concentrate on the job.

"Creepy shit, man," Reed said as he sped up beside him.

Ben just nodded at his best friend and tried to grin.

The old man squatted in front of a flat basket, woven from long strips of what looked like thin branches. Three clumps of different colored pastes were pushed to the sides, and in the middle of the basket the man stirred together varying amounts of the three into what became an orange oatmeal-looking clump. Ben knew immediately this was the village elder and that he healed, as well as led.

He had stirrings of home, of late nights peering down from his loft bedroom while his Gammy spoke in a strange tongue to the old man who came at night. The two would laugh and argue in the hybrid language of French, Native

American, and English while mixing their own Traiteur potions. This seemed a lot like that, and he felt for a moment like the mesmerized child he had been then.

The 'terp spoke to the man, who looked up and replied in a similar clipped gibberish. One word jumped out as familiar, and Ben felt the childhood pull again. The 'terp turned to Chris.

"He welcome you here and say he knows you coming. He say you good men and dat you like da gagrow dat kill da evil tings around da living jungle, so you be friends to dem."

Ben smiled when he saw the lieutenant put his cupped right hand over his heart – a habit from Iraq.

"Tell him we are his friends, and we wish to help his people. We have medicine to share and would like his help to find the evil men who lurk in his jungle and wish harm to good people. We hope he can help us find them."

"What mean lurk?" the interpreter asked.

"Live – just say live," Chris said with a little impatience.

The 'terp and the old man spoke again.

"He wanna know'd if you find da road he send to you two days ago. Da one he help you find wit da heart message."

What the hell is that supposed to mean?

Ben noticed that his leader's mouth had fallen open.

"What the hell does that mean, he sent it to me? What the fuck is a heart message?"

The 'terp shrugged, and Chris shifted uncomfortably.

"Tell him we found a road two days ago, yes. Tell him evil men use that road. We want to know if those bad men, men with guns, have come to his village."

The old man nodded and shifted back on his heels before the interpreter began to speak. Then, he listened and answered before he had finished.

"He say de evil come here, and he know dey man dat kill man. He say dey bad for living jungle also. Dey promise bad tings to village if he talk to you, but he not afraid."

"Does he know where they are? When were they last here?"

While the interpreter spoke, Ben felt the old man's eyes on him and looked up. The wrinkled and leathery face split into a wide grin over brown teeth.

I am glad it is you as the Living Jungle told me. You have great Ashe which you will need. The bad time cannot be stopped, but you can help us in ways your Grandmother understood.

A chill ran up Ben's spine and gripped around his throat. The voice in his head had been clear and not his own. He flashed briefly to another night in the bayou – a terrible night best forgotten. The old man's eyes left his, and he turned to the interpreter to answer. When he did, the cold that ran through Ben's chest evaporated slowly.

Get a grip, bro. Jesus. This creepy place is making your mind do somersaults. That was not real, and there are some memories best left buried.

The interpreter was speaking again.

"He say evil men be here yesterday and leave da same hour. He say da road go to dem, and it take two or tree hours for a hunting man to go to it. Or maybe four hours for a ole man like he be."

The old man nodded and laughed and winked at Ben who smiled uncomfortably.

Chris was all business.

"Tell him he should tell no one he told us this. Tell him we will make the evil leave his jungle, we promise. Then, tell him we have medicines with us and that Ben is our doctor who can help him take care of anyone in the village who may be sick."

The old man laughed aloud, again before the 'terp even got started. Then, he smiled and answered back.

"He say you to go in peace, and he believe you good men. He say you doctor more power than he know, but you medicine very weak, and he no need it. Then, he say you take his medicine dat he make for you friend who hide in da jungle. He say it make him ass feel better."

The old man scraped the paste into a flat leaf, rolled it up like a little green envelope, and handed it to Ben. He took it and felt himself bow a little and nodded.

"Tell him thank you," Ben said and slipped the leaf pouch of medicine into his cargo pants pocket. The old man spoke again. Another word jumped out at Ben, and he grabbed the interpreter's arm.

"What was that word? Something'wata'. What does that mean?"

The interpreter nodded to the old man and, then, turned to Ben.

"Mami Wata be da water serpent. She give medicine men dey healing power. He say water serpent strong in you and dat you soon find you be having many udder power also."

Ben heard the words from far away. His eyes locked on the old man whose own eyes danced with youth and power from the frame of old and tired skin. The old man still nodded so Ben nodded back.

"He say you go now and take you friend from da jungle wall wit you. He say you stop evil men today."

Ben and Chris nodded to the old man while Reed continued the nervous visual sweep of the village as he had throughout the conversation with the old man. Then, they all turned and left and the old man hugged his knees and watched them go.

I will see you when the loud and ugly time comes for my people. I will see you at the end time, Ben. Then, you will learn so much. I am glad the Living Jungle sent you.

Ben shook the voice out of his head and followed Chris and Reed back into the jungle. He turned for a moment and swept his gaze over the quiet and peaceful village. He felt certain something bad was coming here – something big and powerful.

He hoped they could stop it.

They were SEALs, after all.

* * *

The jungle became dark very quickly. Ben was accustomed to the speed with which the sun set in the Iraqi desert, but nothing matched the suddenness with which the dense jungle swallowed up the last ray of light with the dusk. He sat back against a thick and gnarled tree, his knees pulled up, and scooped what the folks the DoD contracted to package their MRE's had ludicrously named "Jambalaya." He usually avoided that particular "Meal-Ready-to-Eat," just on principle, but as the choice tonight was that or "Captain's Country Chicken" – which tasted like total ass – he shoveled the bland rice into his mouth with the green plastic fork that came with it. The packet of powdered Gatorade went into his pocket for later, and he sipped plain water instead.

Ben looked around at the darkening jungle and reflexively confirmed his night vision goggles (NVG's) were hanging from the left side of his kit. Then, he finished his packaged meal and set about taking inventory of his kit for ammo and other supplies. They would move out in a few hours, once the Al Qaeda camp settled in from their own evening meal. He and Lash had scouted ahead earlier, creeping up slowly on the camp to confirm the place and distance, scout good fields of fire and retreat, and establish a potential rally point. Most importantly, they had come up with a rough tally of opposing forces. They had counted perhaps fifteen or sixteen men and boys, ranging from hardened and well-armed soldiers to young teen-agers who looked too frail to even hoist up their weapons. There were at least ten serious fighters he guessed. Then, they had pulled back, briefed their friends, and settled in to wait.

Reed slept curled in a fetal position at Ben's feet and Auger flipped through a paperback book a few yards away, then looked up into the jungle canopy and cursed the darkness which rapidly engulfed them. He shoved the book back into the cargo pocket of his cammies, tipped his hat forward over his eyes, and crossed his arms across his chest. In moments his breathing slowed and deepened. With Chris and Lash patrolling quietly around their hide on watch, Ben sat basically alone. He adjusted the earpiece from his headset so he wouldn't miss any calls from the guys on watch, and then settled back himself. He knew he couldn't possibly sleep, but perhaps if he could get his mind to stop flying between the past and his bizarre feelings from the village, he could at least get a little rest before they hit the camp.

Ben closed his eyes and instead of fighting the memories chasing him, he just let them float around his mind. He drifted to happier thoughts of his grandmother and his early life in the boonies of Louisiana. They were mostly happy times, and, except for the few troubling memories he had convinced himself were merely bad dreams, his thoughts of Gammy were all good. He loved her very much and believed he chose his specialty training as a combat medic almost as a tribute to her memory.

She would be happy to know I'm now a Traiteur of sorts myself.

And more at times.

Ben didn't remember falling asleep but he woke up to a gentle nudge and Reed's hushed whisper.

"Gotta head out, bro."

He felt on the ground beside him for his helmet and put it on his head, then reached without fumbling to the point on his kit where he knew his NVG's would be. He snapped them into place on his helmet, swung the binocular-like eyepieces to his eyes, and turned the device on. Instantly the thick, ink-like blackness came alive with trees and his fellow Frogmen, all in eerie green and grey.

Ben got to his feet and re-slung his rifle into a combat position across his chest. He pulled the slide back half an inch and checked to see a chambered round, shoved the MRE remnants into a cargo pocket, and followed Reed to where Chris, Auger, and Lash waited. His footsteps were loud and metallic, magnified by the volume enhancement of his head set. He heard Chris's voice in both his head set and his other ear.

"Set?"

The four other SEALs nodded, and they moved out into the jungle in single file, Chris in the lead and Auger in trail. It took only moments before the distracting feelings disappeared, and he settled into the familiar mindset of a combat operation. His mind ran through scenarios of the encounter to come. He checked off his plans for each of them, all the time scanning the grey-green jungle around them through his NVGs as they moved nearly silently towards their objective.

They made it to the rally point in just over half an hour. Chris used hand signals to move the other four SEALs out toward their positions as they had briefed at the rest area. They would remain silent until Lash called back with his survey and Chris gave the go. Then they would hit the camp under the cover of confusion provided by concussion grenades from four corners.

Ben turned left after Auger and moved low and silent along the periphery of the camp. He couldn't see the Al Qaeda fighters yet, but he could hear them as he circled around behind Auger. When he had paced off to the halfway point he stopped and watched Auger continue around his arc. He glanced at his watch from beneath the NVGs, covering the face with his hand to prevent any light from escaping. He waited for a minute and thirty seconds then belly crawled slowly towards the edge of the camp.

What he saw confused him at first and, then, frightened him.

The camp looked virtually empty. Only two fighters remained, their faces aglow in the unmasked fire burning under a pot in the center of the clearing. They were boys and likely not much in the way of fighters. But it hardly mattered. The body nailed to the tree near where they sat remained motionless, and Ben doubted he was alive. He didn't recognize the short, thin boy from the village, but he knew from the grey cloth around his waist and the matching arm band at his bicep where he had come from.

Both the boy's legs bent impossibly forward at the knees and below the knees they had turned swollen and black. The eyelids were propped open with sticks over motionless eyes and blood, black in the green-grey world of the NVGs, had poured over the chin and chest where the boys tongue had been cut out.

Ben closed his eyes tightly. Then, he tried hard to focus.

He squeezed the button on the cord running from the radio in the front of his vest to his headset. He whispered into the mike at his lips.

"Lead – Three. Hold. Hold."

There was a pause, and he pictured Chris furrowing his brow and trying to figure out what the hell the problem could be.

"Viper team, hold." Another pause. "Go, three."

"Dry site. Rally site fast," Ben whispered.

"Rog," came Chris's voice. The others confirmed in his earpiece.

"Two."

"Four."

"Five."

Ben pulled silently back until he felt himself a safe distance into the brush and, then, moved quickly but quietly back to the rally point. Auger overtook him on the way but said nothing.

Moments later the five SEALs huddled together and spoke in hushed whispers which were metallic but clear in their headsets.

"They're gone, boss," Ben said. "All but two kids. It looks like they tortured some young boy from the village to death, and now they're gone."

"Fuck," Chris said and wiped his face. "You sure, Ben?"

"Yeah, man," Ben answered without hesitation. "I never seen anyone else out here dressed like them villagers."

"Shit," Lash said quietly.

"They went to hit the village," Reed said, a real pain in his voice. "They're gonna slaughter those people."

"We don't know that," Auger said, his deep voice tight and strained.

"Yeah, we do," Chris said. "We gotta get the fuck back there."

"It'll be light by the time we get there," Lash said calmly.

"I don't give a shit," Chris said. "I don't want us to have killed those poor people. We gotta head back there now." He pressed a thumb into his right temple and, then, looked around at his team. "Is everyone okay with that?"

"Fuck yeah," Lash said. The others nodded.

"Okay," Chris said. "Fast, but quiet. Lash on point then two-by-two, okay?"

The SEALs all nodded, and Lash moved out at a quick pace. Chris and Auger pushed out to the left with Reed and Ben to the right. Ben kept ten yards or so between him and his best friend and moved swiftly through the thick brush a few yards in from the road. He listened for Lash and tried to keep himself back, his mind racing and urging him to move faster than was safe.

He knew what they were headed for.

We won't make it.

I will see you at the end time, Ben.

He moved towards the old man's voice which echoed in his mind.

CHAPTER

3

They moved through the jungle much more quickly than on the way to the target, the noise of their passage loud in Ben's headset, but still nearly imperceptible without them, he knew.

Nearly.

In different circumstances, it would not have been quiet enough. But desperation had settled into the mission now, and they could only hope the enemy was as ragged and undisciplined as they looked.

The jungle suddenly began to lighten, and Ben saw the trees begin to emerge in his peripheral vision without his NVGs. Just shadows now, but in a few minutes the light would grow. They would have no choice but to slow down. He could see the movement of branches and broad, bushy leaves through his NVGs that marked where Reed moved through the brush to his left.

The crack of a rifle shattered the quiet of the jungle, and like in an old movie, it was followed by the *"caw-caw"* of birds nearby. Instinctively, Ben dropped low and remained motionless. His eyes scanned to and fro. Then, his headset crackled, and he heard Chris's strained and whispered voice.

"Two – Lead – Position?"

"Half click past the turn from the road and five mikes from target."

"Viper team – lead. That's the rally, then. Fall in on Lash."

"Three," Ben choked into his microphone with a gravelly whisper.

"Four."

"Five."

He heard the calm voices of his friends and felt a momentary sense of inadequacy. His heart didn't pound in his chest because he was afraid for himself, though. His mind's eye saw quite clearly the chaos and horror the Al Qaeda fighters would be wreaking on the peaceful village.

And, we did that to them.

He swallowed the bile taste rising in his throat at the thought. He stood up and, only half crouched, began to move double time through the brush along the road, his ears listening for Reed's position a few yards off his left side. He could hear the static-filled heavy breathing from his friend in his headset. Ben glanced down at the GPS on his wrist – only another hundred yards to the turn then a half a kilometer into the jungle to Lash.

Twelve minutes. Plus five more to the village.

Way too fucking long.

"Hurry," Lash's voice said in his earpiece. "I hear screams." A bolt of lightning went through Ben, and he pushed the thoughts from his past out of his head. He moved left and joined up with Reed who swung his NVGs up and looked at him with eyes grey in the jungle morning's soft light. Ben just nodded, and they turned left together. After a glance at the GPS, they moved quickly towards Lash. Ben didn't know if Reed's dark expression was because of the undisciplined noise their haste created and the danger associated with it or from the feelings he shared about what was assuredly happening in the village. Both, he decided.

They arrived at Lash's crouched position beside a large, gnarled tree just as Chris and Auger emerged to their right. Ben noticed Auger still favored his left leg a little and for a moment thought about the thick paste wrapped in a jungle leaf in his cargo pocket. Then, he pictured the old man, young eyes in an ancient face, and knew he would likely be dead by the time they got to the village. The five SEALs crouched together and caught their collective breath. Chris spoke, and they leaned in a like a football team, the quarterback calling out the last play of the game.

"Simplicity, okay?" Chris somehow looked them all in the eye at the same time. "Lash, up the middle and hold a position outside the ville. Snipe anything that's a threat to us or the villagers, and take any squirters that come your way. Reed and Ben, up the left and halfway around the arc. Auger and me, up the right. Four corners and, then, we hit together on my call, 'kay?"

"Rog," Ben said.

"Yep," Auger said.

"Capture? Kill?" Reed asked flatly.

Chris rubbed his eyes briefly.

"If we can take one or two crows for intel that's icing on the cake, but this mission is now about saving those villagers. You smoke anything threatening those people, understood?"

"You bet," Reed said.

Lash picked up his long sniper rifle and slung his M-4 by his side. Then, he moved off quickly and quietly through the thick brush. Chris and Auger did the same, but angled to the right. Ben looked at Reed.

"Ready?" he asked.

Reed flashed the broad grin Ben loved the most about him.

"Fuck, yeah," he said. "Easy day."

They moved off together through the thick jungle.

*   *   *

There were only rare gunshots. They would be unnecessary against the peaceful and primitive village, he guessed. The screams, however, cut into him like a sharp, hot knife and ran up his neck, exploding like white light in the back of his head. The screams were from women and children, he thought. He crawled into position at the very edge of the clearing and peered through the brush. Nothing in his past life or his life as a Navy SEAL prepared him for the horror that greeted him.

Twenty yards away, a younger fighter, his dirty pants around his knees, raped a woman who lay impassively spread-eagled atop a pile of dead bodies. A dark pool of blood spread slowly out from beneath them as the boy grunted on top of her. Beside her in the dirt, the woman stretched out a hand which held the arm of the dead and bloody toddler beside her.

Farther away, two fighters had lined four men up on their knees, their back to their captors. One at a time, the Al Qaeda fighters screamed something at the men in a strange tongue, waited a moment for a reply, and, then, brought a large, rusty machete down onto the center of their heads, splitting them open like melons with an explosion of blood and gray matter that seemed to delight the younger fighters watching from the sides. Moments later, the four villagers were dead and the man with the machete let out a sickening and animal like squeal of laughter. He was soaked in blood from his face to his tennis shoe-clad feet.

Ben pulled his M-4 into position and settled the floating red dot through his sight on the back of the rapist's head. He flicked off the safety with his right thumb and began to squeeze tension onto the trigger.

Wait – wait for Chris's call or you might get us all killed.

He squeezed his eyes tight and felt the burn of salty sweat. Then, he refocused through his gun-sight. The boy rose off the half-naked and moaning woman, pulled up his pants with one hand, and reached with the other for a long-handled knife. Ben felt the tension in his trigger increase.

Come on, Chris. Come on, Goddammit.

Ben was about to fire anyway when his earpiece crackled out with Chris' voice.

"Viper team – Go! Go!"

Ben squeezed the trigger in cadence to the second "Go" from his leader and friend, and the rapist's head exploded in a puff of pink, his lifeless body crumpling straight down into a heap on the ground. The half-naked woman looked up in surprise and, then, simply shut her eyes slowly, her hand still in that of her dead child.

Ben felt himself sob.

He reached for a concussion grenade, a non-lethal distraction which would spread confusion and panic but, hopefully, not seriously injure any of the innocents, and he pulled the pin and tossed it deep into the village just as he heard two other explosions from his comrades. His grenade went off with a bang. He heard the pop of a smoke grenade, and eerie orange smoke filled the village.

Ben jumped to his feet and moved swiftly into the clearing, his rifle up and aimed, sweeping back and forth as he moved. He kept his shoulders hunched forward, just as he had a hundred times. The good and bad guys would be easy to distinguish, and he moved swiftly through the orange smoke as he heard the angry screams of the Al Qaeda fighters, the older men hollering orders no doubt to the panicky teen-agers they led. Ben heard a few sporadic rifle shots as the enemy fired blindly into the jungle. Then, he heard the more familiar crack of the SEAL's M-4s and screams, this time not from women or children.

Ben saw a shadowy figure move towards him through the orange glow, and his mind identified it as a bad guy. Without hesitation he squeezed twice with his trigger finger and watched the teen-aged fighter collapse to the ground. He swept over the body and kicked the rifle away from the dead, outstretched hand and kept moving. As he cleared the smoke he moved right, conscious that he moved towards where he remembered the old man being, and continued his sweep back and forth. Two more targets ran towards him, rifles clutched uselessly in hands that pumped as they ran in a panic. He dropped them both without thought or feeling.

Ben's gut tightened as his boots splashed through a deep puddle of dark blood stretched out from another pile of dead bodies, but he ignored the feeling and pushed on. He heard an almost rhythmic cadence of deep, burping explosions he knew to be Lash's sniper rifle dispatching targets that popped into his view from his hide in the jungle.

"Five – Coming towards you!"

Reed's voice was in his earpiece. Three cracks from an M-4 and, then, "Got him."

The thatched lean-to came into view. Smoke rose innocuously from a smoldering fire. Ben made out the thin, frail body of the old man, hunched over but moving on the mat where he had met him.

Moving and alive.

Ben swept the area around them through the sight of his rifle. His mind screamed in protest at the number of mutilated and motionless bodies around him, but he saw no targets and moved towards the village elder. As the image became clear, Ben felt a vice grip his throat and stifled another sob.

The old man cradled a small girl no more than two years old in his lap. The girl's hands shook in what looked like a seizure, and with horror, Ben saw her head was soaked in blood from a deep machete wound that started beneath her left eye and extended across the top of her head. Little arcs of arterial bleeding sprayed out across the old man's face from the wound, and he could see bleeding grey brain matter in the wide split in her head. In a state-side trauma center, at best she would have no meaningful recovery. Here – well, here the girl would be gratefully dead in moments.

Ben's rifle dropped to his side, and his shoulders sagged. He shuffled slowly towards the old man, the baby's body trembling in the village elder's lap like Jell-O. He reached in his kit for a morphine syringe. He could at least offer comfort – he could remove the pain. The old man's eyes remained closed, and he continued to chant. His frail body swayed back and forth slowly. Ben knelt beside him in the dirt and reached out a hand to the touch the man's shoulder.

I'm glad you are here, Ben.

The voice sounded so crystal clear in his head that his hand stopped before it reached the man's shoulder. But the man still rocked and chanted. His lips moved but not in time to the voice in his head. It felt like watching an old Japanese movie dubbed badly in English.

We have only a moment, Ben.

Ben dropped the morphine syringe into the dirt, his body suddenly not his own. For a moment that feeling seemed so strong he believed he might, in fact, be at home in his bed in Virginia Beach, his arms around Christy, with the horror around him being nothing but a terrible dream. He watched with surrealistic fascination as the old man stretched a thin, wrinkled hand out over the wound in the girl's head. Then, the old eyes popped open, and Ben felt shock at the milky-white appearance of those eyes. They did not seem covered in a white film so much as filled from the inside with a swirling white smoke. The chanting stopped, and the old man's jaw clenched tight. Ben's own eyes widened as the dark hand seemed suddenly engulfed in a golden light which spread out from the fingers and encircled the girl's mutilated head.

The golden light began to sparkle as if it came from a million invisible fireflies. The glow now engulfed the man's thin arm nearly to the elbow, and in addition to the flickering, golden light, the girl's face now seemed bathed in a faint and pulsating bluish glow.

Ben stared with a far-away fascination as the light sparkled from inside the ragged and gory wound. He watched the deeper edges of split-open brain seemed to pull slowly together. As the tissue edges found each other, the bluish glow turned into a white light emanating now from the wound itself. As he watched, the wound slowly repaired itself, the arcs of blood disappearing in a puff of light. As the process sped up, the light became so bright he raised a hand against it. The brightness felt painful in his head, but he couldn't bring himself to pull his burning eyes away. Finally, the golden sparkles and the white light reached a crescendo that became unbearable. He closed his eyes tightly. Dark spots and a photo negative image of the girl's open head danced in his mind's eye. He felt a momentary heat and something tight in his chest. Suddenly, he realized a humming sound he had not even noticed before had abruptly stopped.

Ben opened his eyes and looked into the smiling face of the cooing little girl, her skin soft and healthy across her unmarked head. Her eyes sparkled up at him, and her mouth smiled.

"Gah, Dah eh!" she said.

Ben smiled back. The old man's hands were slack and grey across her chest. He moaned, and Ben tore his fascinated eyes from the healed little girl to look at him. A huge, deep gash ran from beneath the old man's left eye up across his head. Bloody gray brain matter was exposed in the wound. As Ben reached for him, blue light exploded from the wound, and the lethal gash disappeared. Then, the eyes opened, and the man smiled at him, the eyes clear, brown, and full of youth.

You see, Ben?

Yes.

That is the power of the Seer's mind's eye. It is a power we share, Ben. You are a seer, too, just like your grandmother.

A Traiteur?

If you like. But it is much more than a healer. You will see. You will come to know.

How?

The elder smiled a brown-toothed smile at him but didn't answer. The little girl cooed and squirmed in his lap. Then, the old man looked for a moment in the direction the bullet came from.

The high velocity round from the Al Qaeda AK-47 tore out the old man's throat in an explosion of dark muscle and skin, bright red blood, and white cartilage. He collapsed backwards into the dirt, his arms spread wide.

Ben heard himself scream and, then, raised his rifle instinctively to his shoulder and swept it in the direction the old man had looked. Just as he locked on target, the Al Qaeda fighter arched his back and collapsed, the sound of Reed's rifle crack reaching Ben's ears.

Ben dropped his rifle and scrambled frantically to the old man's side. His right hand fumbled in his cargo pocket for his medical blow-out kit, but as he bent over the elder, the old man grabbed his wrists with surprising strength and pulled them up between them. Ben's right hand came up without the battle dressings he had fumbled for, and he struggled against the vice-like grip.

The old man's lips were already blue and dark bloody bubbles formed and popped from the obscene and impossibly large hole in his throat. The face had begun to turn grey, and Ben saw an ocean of blood begin to form like a halo around the old man's head. The ashen lips didn't move, but the words came anyway.

The Ashe is in you. It is in you, Ben, not the ring.

"What are you talking about," Ben cried out, his eyes rimmed with tears and his vision blurred. "What does that mean?" He felt his fingers tingle with numbness under the incredibly strong grip.

The power was always there, Ben. Just as your grandmother knew it was. The power is you, not the ring. The ring can organize it. The ring can focus it. But the power is in you.

Ben felt the grip on his right hand relax and looked down as the old man reached over to the third finger of his own weathered right hand. He spun the black, shiny ring off of the middle finger and, then, grasped Ben's right hand again. The wrinkled old hands fumbled for a moment and, then, slipped the dark ring effortlessly onto Ben's middle finger.

The power is already in you. Use it to help us. Help our people.

Ben felt warmth spread up his right arm. He realized it must be the feeling coming back into his arm as the old man's hand let go of him and fell into the dirt. He looked at the wrinkled old face where the sometimes white and usually young eyes now looked dry, staring upward at nothing.

No gold light.

No fireflies.

Just a dead, very old man with his throat shot out.

The crackle in his ear from his earpiece startled him for a moment, but then brought him back to where he was.

"Lead – Clear."

"Two – Clear."

Ben scanned quickly around and saw nothing but dead bodies and dissipating orange smoke. He keyed his mike with his left hand, and his eyes fell on his right middle finger.

"Three, clear," he said. The ring had turned a grayish bone color somehow. Ben was certain it had been a deep and shiny black only moments ago. He touched it with his left hand, and it felt smooth and warm. For a moment, he believed it might be vibrating softly.

"Four – Clear," he heard in his earpiece and in the air around him. He looked up and saw Reed who looked down at him with clouded eyes. "You okay, bro?"

"Five – Clear," he heard Auger's strained voice in his earpiece.

Ben cleared his throat.

"Yeah," he managed to choke out.

He heard a soft cooing and saw the little girl who smiled and reached out to him. Tears filled his eyes, and he reached for her, scooped her into his arms and held her against his neck. He rose with her and turned to his best friend.

"Let's get the fuck out of here," he said.

CHAPTER

4

They had one prisoner and five survivors, including the little girl that clung to Ben's neck. The prisoner looked to be no more than fifteen, and Ben doubted he could provide any real intel. But as he approached the group, he resisted the urge to unload his M-4 into the terrified face anyway. The other four survivors included three women, two young and one very old, and a middle-aged man who wept and rocked back and forth, his arms spread wide as his eyes scanned the piles of dead relatives around him.

The two younger women sat cross-legged and slack-jawed, obviously in shock. The older woman stared up in the sky and chanted. He recognized one of the young women as the rape victim he had saved – the one with the dead toddler. Ben saw no one he felt comfortable turning the little girl over to just yet. He and Reed joined their friends.

"Reed, grab Lash, and give us some security," Chris said.

"Aye, aye," Reed said. His voice sounded thick and not the always up-and-ready SEAL that Ben knew.

Reed moved off in the direction Lash approached from, and the two of them spoke. Then, they moved in opposite directions towards the jungle at the edges of the village.

"Ben, take a look at Auger's leg while I call the Head Shed and get some marching orders and get us a ride the fuck out of here," Chris rubbed his face with both hands. "We probably need to go snatch those other two assholes from their camp, too."

Ben barely heard the last part, his eyes and attention now on Auger's blood-stained left leg. He reached for the medical bag hanging off his kit and set the little girl gently on the ground beside them.

"Just a minute, baby girl," he said with a smile.

"Dah, eh!" she answered and smiled back.

Ben squatted down in front of Auger who looked down with a wry smile.

"Somethin' you need, Ben?"

"Let me have a look, Auger," Ben said. "No macho bullshit." He used both hands to tear a larger hole from the bloody one already a few inches above Auger's knee. "What happened?"

"Ricochet, I think," Auger said, wincing when Ben touched the ragged tear.

Ben saw only a little bit of swelling around the small, bloody hole and didn't think there was a lot of bleeding inside Auger's leg. There was no exit wound, so he figured the bullet fragment was still somewhere deep in his friend's thigh. He had his fellow Frogman run through different ranges of motion, making a little more blood dribble out. But otherwise the wound seemed pretty unremarkable. He felt for pulses behind the knee, which felt normal and asked Auger if the lower part of his leg felt normal or if it had pins and needles.

"Normal," Auger told him.

"Seems okay, I guess," Ben said and shook out a sterile dressing. "You'll need to take some antibiotics when we get back, and we'll have the surgeon look at you, okay?"

Auger nodded. "Whatever you say, Doc," he said. "Just burns like a bitch. Same damn side as the ass cheek I hurt in Iraq."

Ben suddenly remembered the paste filled leaf in his cargo pocket. A part of his brain – the Traiteur part he knew – told him it would help. Since the scientific part couldn't think of a way it would hurt, he fumbled the broad folded leaf out of his pocket and opened it. He smeared a thick glob onto the sterile dressing.

"Hey, what the hell is that shit?" Auger asked and pulled his leg away.

"It'll help with the pain and speed up healing," Ben said. That actually felt true, and he smeared the paste onto the wound and began to wrap the leg in Gauze.

"You ain't turning all Voodoo on me, are you Doc?" Auger grinned.

"No," Ben chuckled back.

At least I don't think so.

Ben felt a tingling, almost like a subtle vibration in his right hand. He looked down and saw the ring had turned a deep and rich blue, the surface now looked polished and shiny.

Fuckin' mood ring or something. It changes when my temperature or moisture or something changes.

It still gave him a little chill and for a moment he thought about pulling the ring off. Then, he looked around at the massacred village, and across the clearing he could still see the motionless dark and wrinkled feet of the old man who so passionately seemed to need Ben to wear the damned thing. He sighed and decided he could suffer with it a little longer.

Respect for the dead.

Ben finished wrapping Auger's leg and stood in time to see Chris striding towards them. He reached down, scooped up the little girl, and turned to face their officer. The little girl grabbed at his ear and giggled.

"You okay?" Chris said to Auger.

"Yeah," Auger answered and flexed his leg at the knee. "Actually, the burning is gone already."

"Nice work, Ben" Chris said and patted Ben on the back.

Ben only nodded and looked at the ring – a dark orange now.

"Okay, here's the deal," Chris said. "We got the MEDEVAC helo that was standing by at the forward refueling point about fifteen minutes out. We're gonna exfil back to base…"

"Fuck, yeah," Auger exclaimed.

"…AFTER," Chris continued and gave a wry look at Ben, "we get those other two assholes." He put his hand on Ben's shoulder. "You and Auger stay here with the prisoner and the survivors. Wait for me, Lash, and Reed to get back with the other two bad guys. Then, we'll call for the exfil."

Ben looked around.

"You want us to make these people sit here surrounded by all their dead family members?"

Chris frowned. "No, I guess not." He thought for a moment. "Okay. Let's pull everyone back to the road, and you guys wait there. Then, we'll go back to our little camp for the exfil. Cool?"

"Yeah," Ben said. That sounded a lot better. Not just for the survivors, but he needed almost desperately to get out of this village.

Chris squeezed the transmit button on his vest and spoke into the boom mike by his lips. "Two – Five – Pull back, and rally with us at the road. Viper Lead." He turned to Ben and Auger. "Let's go," he said and reached gently down to help the older woman to her feet. "Come on, dear," he said slowly, as if speaking slowly would fix his foreign words.

Together the three SEALs helped the traumatized villagers to their feet and, then, Chris jerked their prisoner roughly to his by the plastic flex cuffs that held his hands behind his back.

"If we run into any trouble," Chris said turning to Ben, "the call sign for the helo is Voodoo forty-one, and they're on channel three."

"Rog," Ben answered.

Voodoo. Huh. How fitting.

They slowly moved the survivors and the captured killer out of the horrible death scene around them and towards the road. Ben held the little girl snuggly against him with one arm, the feel of her smooth face on his neck a mystery and a comfort. His other hand held firmly to the pistol grip of his M-4 rifle.

As they entered the jungle from the edge of the clearing, Ben took one last look at the gut-wrenching horror scene. He looked over to where the fire still smoldered by the old man's corpse and shuddered. He had lots of shit to sort out when he had a minute to breathe. Ben looked down at the ring on his right hand.

He doubted he would ever be able to tell his friends what he had seen.

* * *

A stiff wind whipped through the door-less cabin of the UH-60 Special Operations Helicopter, and the moving breeze provided a needed relief from the heavy, stagnant air of the early afternoon jungle. The four adult villagers sat on the single metal bench seat in the rear of the helicopter and clung to the cargo netting in abject terror. The other SEALs sat at the four corners of the two wide openings on either side, their legs dangling out onto the skids, each lost in their own thoughts. Ben sat at the front of the cabin on the floor, surrounded by their gear and packs, between the two helmeted aircrew guys who scanned the jungle tops over their fifty caliber machine guns. He thought this would be less scary for the little girl who sat between his outstretched legs, but she looked completely unconcerned. She pulled at the pockets of Ben's pants and looked up at him frequently to smile and bounce up and down with excitement. Ben kept a hand around her and looked past her to the prisoners who sat blind-folded in the center of the cabin, cross-legged and flex-cuffed to the floor. His eyes watched the unbroken and desolate jungle rush by beneath them, but he didn't really see it.

Ben felt total relief and happiness at being pulled out of their little hide in the jungle. They had been there alone for ten days, and he would be happy to have hot food and a rack to sleep in, even if it was in the hot, corrugated tin airplane hangar they had converted into a crude barracks back at the Joint Special Operations Task Force base. That crude little shit-hole would be like the Marriott to them for a day or so. As a SEAL, he was used to going from comfortable beds to sleeping for a few days in a hollowed-out tree. But this was different. After this morning, he needed to be around other people and out of the miserable jungle for a while, at least. He needed things that felt like home – like satellite TV and real food.

Mostly, I want some fruit. Fruit and some fresh vegetables.

Ben looked at the little girl between his outstretched legs. She clapped her hands and smiled up at him again. He tickled her cheek and, then, twirled her earlobe with his fingers, making her giggle. Then, she leaned over and lay down with her head in his lap, her eyes heavy. Moments later, she was asleep, and Ben leaned his head back and watched the jungle again, his mind drawn back to the Louisiana bayou, his grandmother's ramble-shack house, and the magic and mystery the memories held.

He steered clear of the bad nights and thought instead of warm spring days and Gammy's wonderful food. He thought of hot summer evenings and the folks who visited at all hours of day and night and looked to the local Traiteur to fix their aches and pains.

That was how the nightmare days came, wasn't it? The man who wanted more than Gammy could (would?) offer. The man with the horrible, bloody wounds and the wild, yellow eyes.

Ben sprinted away from the thoughts and focused on the jungle rushing by. He realized he really needed to be at home for a while. Not just in Virginia Beach and Christy's warm embrace in their Chicks Beach condo, but maybe Louisiana.

Who would you visit, bro? You got no friends or kin left there. Gammy's with God, and everyone else got the hell out when they could.

Ben sighed and quietly stroked the soft hair of the little sleeping girl in his lap. He just needed a little break was all.

Ben felt the helo pull up and to the right, a signal they approached their base in the middle of nowhere. He strained to see out the port-side door without shifting too much for fear of waking the sleeping child and caught a glimpse of the run down, converted airport that was home – or at least home away from home. A few folks walked around the compound, and he could see the security details in their Humvees, patrolling around the tall barbed-wire fence. But otherwise the camp looked almost empty.

Daytime. Ours is a night job. Everyone is sleeping from last night's work and resting up for the night ahead.

They were like vampires. He remembered how strange it had seemed to come home from the deserts of Iraq with less sun on his skin than when he left. Christy had told him he looked pale and anemic. Ben smiled at the thought of her – her dark eyes and pretty smile. He realized he would be able to call her that day, once they got settled in – another luxury of being out of that shitty little hide in the woods. They would have plenty of time before they were called to summarize their op at the nightly intel brief. As the officer, Chris would have to meet with the team commander and fill him in, but they would have the day to unwind until darkness fell and their fellow warriors came back to life.

The helicopter arched its nose up to slow their descent before settling onto the broken concrete ramp. Ben watched his friends unsnap their safety lanyards from the helicopter as they landed, and Auger and Reed knelt beside the villagers who looked wide-eyed out at the row of dark helicopters they now joined. Lash came up behind the prisoners and pulled a folded knife from his kit, quickly cutting the flex cuffs holding them to the floor. He and Chris grasped them by the remaining flex cuffs that secured their hands behind their back and held them firmly to the ground. Ben scooped the girl up in his arms, and Reed and Auger helped the frightened and confused villagers step out of the helo. The whining sound of the turbine slowed and dropped in pitch, and the spinning blades slowly came to a stop overhead.

Ben saw several guys in the digital cammies of their Army cousins approach and recognized one as the surgeon assigned to the Joint Task Force.

"Hey, doc," he said as the man approached.

"Hey, man," the surgeon returned. "Whatcha got there?"

Ben hugged the girl. "A beautiful little girl who has seen some wicked serious bad shit."

The surgeon's face tightened. "I'm sure," he said. "Is she hurt?"

Ben hesitated for a moment. What the hell was he supposed to say? That her head had been split open with a machete this morning, but she's quite alright now, thank you?

"She took a little blow to the head, but doesn't seem too much worse for wear," he said instead. The surgeon reached out for her, and Ben had an overwhelming urge to hold her to his chest and take off for the hills. Instead, he kissed her cheek and handed her to the surgeon who held her gently.

"'Bout the same age as my little boy," he said.

"Yeah," Ben said, not sure what else to say. The little girl reached for Ben, but didn't cry. He tickled her earlobe again and smiled. "I'll come see ya in a little bit, baby girl," he said. Then, he watched as the surgeon and his two medics helped the other four villagers into a waiting ambulance and drove off.

The three "crows", or prisoners, were being searched one last time beside the helicopter before being led blindfolded to a waiting truck. Ben decided it would be best for everyone if he stayed as far from them as possible. So he set to the task of pulling their gear out of the Blackhawk.

"Hey, Ben, let me help you out, man," a voice said beside him as arms reached past him and pulled a backpack out. Ben looked over to see Tim Schousse. The SEAL was clean and well shaved, clad in tan cargo pants and a black Dierks Bentley T-shirt. Seeing his smiling face made Ben realize how tired, sore, and filthy he was. He scratched the ten days' worth of beard on his own cheek and sighed.

"Thanks, dude," he said and slung a sea bag full of supplies onto his back and followed Tim to a waiting open-backed Humvee.

"Heard you guys smoked a bunch of shitheads," Tim said.

"Yeah," Ben answered quietly.

Not enough and not in time.

"Head Shed is chattering it up. Nice work."

Ben said nothing, but tossed the sea bag into the back of the truck. The two headed back towards the helo where Reed pulled more gear out and onto his back.

"Shower and, then, hot food," Reed shouted over his shoulder as he hustled past him with two rucksacks and a grin.

"Nice," Ben said.

That sounded about right.

Then, I'll head over to the clinic and check on my little girl.

He grabbed two ammo cans and his own backpack and headed double-time towards the Humvee with a new-found energy.

CHAPTER

5

Reed looked at his buddy and wondered again just what had smacked him and left him so sullen and distracted. The op at the village had been a bitch, had gone to shit in a hurry in fact, and the massacre had sunk in deep with him, as well. But they had all been in the shit before and had seen some terrible things in Iraq and Afghanistan. They were hardened SEALs, right? Reed felt horror at what men could do to other human beings, and he felt terrible sadness when they couldn't stop it, but it is what it is.

The world can suck, but they had the privilege of sometimes making it right when it did. But Ben seemed haunted by something more – something personal. He walked beside his former roommate in silence as they headed to the crumbling building that now served as a chow hall. Ben's eyes looked darker than usual.

Reed had always thought of Ben as a weird son-of-a-bitch. He was different for sure, but then maybe that was why they became such close friends so quickly. Ben had joined the platoon right from BUD/S, the initial phase of SEAL training, and Reed had only briefly met him before that. They crossed each other's paths in California, and Ben had actually finished the Basic SEAL training ahead of him. But because his medical training took over a year, Reed made it to their east coast team ahead of him and liked to call Ben the rookie. Ben never argued about the status, which they both knew to be bullshit, and he liked that about him, too.

They were night and day in their personalities, and Reed thought now about how good that was. There were a lot of cookie-cutter team members, and Ben was very different. That made him fun. They had become like "P-and-Q" as his mother used to tell him when he was little.

But not right now.

Reed broke the now-unbearable silence.

"You call Christy yet?" he asked.

Ben jumped a little, as if startled back from very far away.

"Huh?" he said and seemed a little embarrassed.

"Christy, dude," Reed said with a chuckle that he didn't feel. "You remember her? The chick with no taste who sleeps with you instead of me?"

That got a grin.

"Yeah, her," Ben said. "What about her?"

"You call her yet?"

"Nah," Ben said. "Too early back home. I don't wanna wake her. She won't be able to get back to sleep."

Reed nodded and searched his mind for something else to say – not usually a problem when he was with Ben.

"Starving," he said.

"Yeah," Ben replied.

They walked in silence, and Reed figured maybe his friend needed that more than idle bullshit chatter.

Real friends know when to shut the hell up.

He watched Ben absently twirl a ring on the middle finger of his right hand and realized he had never seen Ben wear jewelry before. The ring was a deep purple and looked to be made of polished stone.

"Christy give you that to help you remember she's back home so you don't fuck up?" he asked.

"What are you talking about?" Ben asked. His voice sounded a little annoyed at being brought back again from wherever he kept going.

"The ring, dude," Reed said and gestured towards his friend's right hand. "Never noticed it before. Christy give it to you?"

There was a weird, long pause, and Ben opened his mouth, shut it again, and turned to his friend with a blank look.

"Yeah," he said finally and shoved his hands into his pants pockets. "Christy gave it to me before we left." Then, he gave a half-assed smile and looked down at the ground, his mind flying back off to wherever it had been.

Reed felt sudden concern that something might really be wrong with Ben. He had never seen him like this in the several years they had been friends and roommates. SEALs didn't think much about post-traumatic stress disorder or PTSD, and they talked about it even less, but he wondered if maybe it looked like this. He started to ask Ben if he was alright and, then, thought better of it and instead walked beside him in silence.

The chow hall was pretty crowded as usual for this time of day. Their compound held only a small number of people: Army Rangers, a Delta detachment, the pilots from the 160th for the helos, and two platoons of SEALs, as well as intel and support staff. It was a few hundred people – small for the task they had been given to root out and destroy the growing Al Qaeda network in this part of Eastern Africa. The chow hall was smaller still, though, and had only a single line to a row of metal serving dishes over small heating elements. Past the line stood a station of water and sodas and a few bowls of fruit and salad. Not much, but way better than MREs.

Ben and Reed went through the line without talking, except to return greetings from several folks who passed by on their way to the long rows of folding tables. Reed felt himself growing more uncomfortable with Ben's uncustomary silence and by the time they stopped by to grab drinks and fruit, he found himself unable to bear it. He led them to the end of a long table. The other end was filled with Rangers, talking in the hushed voices of Special Forces warriors.

"So," he started and took a huge bite of some kind of meat over some kind of rice. "Pretty crazy, huh?"

He watched Ben take his own half-hearted bite and nod.

"Yeah, crazy," he agreed.

"Dude, what was the deal with that old man?"

"Whaddya mean?" Ben answered and looked more than a little uncomfortable.

Reed watched his best friend closely as he spoke, searching for signs.

"I mean, he was a strange dude is all," he said. He took another bite of his food. "Were you there when he got smoked?"

Ben put down his bite and sighed. He looked a little more like himself, and Reed thought he might open up a little.

"Yeah," he said. "I got there just before. He was taking care of the little girl when I got there, and I tried to help him." He stopped and looked at Reed as if summing him up – making a decision maybe. He smiled a small, sad little smile and, then, dropped his food to his plate. "I don't know, bro," he said. "I don't know what it is about him that is so haunting. Did you…" he paused and his brow furrowed like he didn't know how to say it. "Did you, kind of feel like – I don't know – like he was trying to communicate with you somehow?"

"What, you mean like when we met him in the morning?" Reed tried hard to understand what Ben was talking about.

"Yeah," Ben's eyes studied him closely, and Reed tried to take the question seriously but felt unsure of what Ben was really asking him.

"I couldn't understand half of what the 'terp said," he replied with a chuckle, trying to lighten his best friend's heavy mood, "much less the gibberish the old man was using."

Ben sighed. "Yeah, I guess," he said. Not the answer he seemed to be looking for.

"Look, bro," Reed said and leaned in to talk softly. "What's up? What's got ya?"

"I don't know," Ben answered, but Reed knew he did. "Been here too long I guess. Jesus, that was horrible – that massacre. And, then, the old man, just – I don't know. And, the little girl. I mean, what will happen to her now?"

That's it. It's the little girl.

Ben was the "take in the stray" type – always had been. He had always known his buddy to be more sensitive than most. He was a helluva shooter, a born sniper, and a perfect SEAL. The other side of his personality, though, always seemed so stark in contrast. This time it just showed itself on the job was all.

"Look, bro," Reed said. "I know how much it sucks, but we saved her life, dude. I wish we could have saved them all, but shit, man – sometimes it just is what it is, you know?"

Ben nodded, and his eyes looked wet.

"We're the good guys, man. We'll make sure the survivors are taken care of, but what else can we do? You and Christy," he paused and looked at Ben carefully, "you guys are great. She is way too fuckin' good for you, but she loves you, man. Maybe you're just kind of feeling that settle down thing? Maybe just wondering about making it real and having your own kids, you know?"

His friend smiled at him, but his eyes looked a little far away.

"That could be it," he said.

Reed scooped up another big spoonful of meat and rice – pretty tasty, actually.

"Yeah," Reed said, relieved to have sorted it out. "Let's eat and work out, and then it'll be time to call her."

Talking to his girl will fix this.

"Okay," Ben dug into his own plate. "I gotta stop by the clinic and check on the little girl first, okay?"

"Sure," Reed answered, losing a few grains of brown rice down his chin. "I'll go with you, alright?"

Ben nodded.

At least he didn't say "my" girl that time.

CHAPTER

6

The comfort of having a mattress under Ben's back, no matter how thin, outweighed much of the heaviness in his heart. Reed had been right, he realized as he stretched luxuriously out in his rack separated from his teammates by a series of camouflaged poncho liners hanging from the low ceiling. Talking to Christy had washed away so much of the weirdness for him that he now had trouble distinguishing between what actually happened and what was just crazy Cajun imagination. It wouldn't be the first time that his bayou childhood and genetic predisposition for weirdness made him see ghosts where none existed.

The downside of his longer than usual call home was the deep longing he now felt to be there. His team was away more time than they spent back at the beach – with training evolutions and operational assignments – and he had never minded that. He loved coming home to Christy, but he loved his brothers in the teams just as much, and the balance had always worked.

Something changed for me in that village.

The something expressed itself as a new and overwhelming desire to be home and alone on a beach somewhere with Christy. Ben had thought about marriage before. He'd been with Christy for well over four years, and he had never once strayed like some of his team mates seemed to do. But he had never seen the need to change an already perfect situation. Christy had never once pushed for it, seeming to understand their situation perhaps even better than he did. But for the last couple of years, they had always talked about the future as if it would always be there for them together.

"Maybe it's time," he mumbled under his breath and rolled onto his side. His eyes grew heavy, and he let them close. But he kept his mind focused solidly on images of Christy and their life together. He allowed a brief picture of the little girl, sound asleep and wrapped in clean, warm blankets in the clinic. He ignored the other, darker images that peeked in from his mind's peripheral vision and built himself a nice dream about being with Christy – alone, naked, and sweaty on a nice island resort somewhere.

He traveled more than he slept.

At first, his travels took him right where he wanted, and he made love slowly and gently to Christy, her soft moaning breath in his ear.

But, then, he traveled to new places, and he traveled with a companion.

The awake part of his mind thought about the Christmas Ghosts who traveled with Ebenezer in the book his Gammy loved to read him every winter. This seemed very much like that, though the old man, his split-open head glistening and wet and his smile full of brown teeth, looked nothing like the ghosts of Christmas past, present, or future.

And, there was no snow where they went.

Ben followed the old man, whose skin seemed tighter and his muscles firmer than he remembered, through a thick grove of trees. The brush wrapping around their legs was obscured by a ground fog that reminded Ben more of white smoke billowing from a witch's cauldron. The fog swirled, rising and falling, much like that.

He heard the old man's voice in his head.

We're almost there.

Where?

Home. Home as it used to be and must be again.

Ben felt a chill and realized suddenly he wore only the black running shorts and brown T-shirt he had worn to bed. His bare feet were wet and cold.

Is this a dream or is it real?

It is both. Dreams are the reality that hides from us. But you knew that. Your Gammy taught you that. You are a Seer, and you know how to find what is hidden. I will help you remember that strength.

Ben felt a new chill not related to the cold and followed the old man who moved with remarkable speed through the jungle, his feet light.

He seemed to move with the agility of the deer from back home – which brought a bad memory he was too late to stop.

Ben felt more than saw a flash image of his Gammy standing still in a clearing in the woods, her eyes closed and her arms outstretched. He remembered how the doe had come slowly to her, unafraid, as if called. He remembered how it nuzzled at her hand and how Gammy had opened her eyes and smiled at him for a moment. He had been amazed. They both looked so beautiful, and he wanted to be quiet so as not to disturb Gammy's peaceful communion with nature. But, then, there had been a flash of steel in the early morning light, and blood had sprayed across her chest and arms as the deer fell dead at her feet, its throat cut in a wide deep arc. His Gammy still smiled at him as the blood dripped from her chin and the long, curved blade in her hand.

He fell behind and pushed the image from his head to catch up with the village elder who now stood still in front of a thick tangle of jungle vine that formed a wall before him. When Ben reached him, the old man looked back at him over his shoulder and flashed his brown-toothed smile from beneath the gaping and gore-filled wound in his head and face. Then, he flashed his own blade, a dull, worn machete. With a single, powerful slice, he cut away the wall of vines and moved into the open clearing beyond.

A pleasant smell of cooking meat (just like the venison he and Gammy had eaten later the night he had learned new things about her – something about that memory bothered him, too, but he had other fish to fry right now) floated to him on thin tendrils of smoke from the low fires on the far side of the village. From the long, low houses of bamboo and thick broad leaves covered in mud, he saw brightly colored cloth which flapped from poles secured to the sides with thick ropes made of twisted vine. Other than the "*caw, caw*" of jungle birds and the soft breeze fluttering the flag-like cloth and leaves, the village remained quiet and still. No blood, no bodies, no massacre – but also no people.

Where are your people?

Our people are not here. This place is as things should be, not as they are. You will help our people come home. They are the keepers of the living jungle, and without them the living jungle cannot survive. Without you, they cannot survive.

Ben wanted to make the elder understand how he wished he could make this real again. But there was nothing left.

Your people are gone. I am so sorry, but they are gone. Only an old man and a few women and a baby are left. Everyone else is dead and gone.

The old man turned and faced him. His skin glowed with a bluish light, and the fireflies flickered in his open throat. His head wound had again miraculously healed, but the gaping wound from the AK-47 round now stared at Ben and spit black blood over the old man's chest.

The spirits of the people live in the jungle, and the others remain from view. You must help our people. Help them so they will be more than this.

A horrible smell made Ben look past the old man. The village behind him now held bloated bodies, bellies swollen from gas produced by intestinal bacteria unchecked in death. Some of the bodies, mostly the children, had split open and spilled their contents into the dirt. Millions of insects buzzed around the corpses, feeding on the misfortune. Small animals and birds tore gently, unhurried at the bodies. A few feet away, a small animal, like a cat only bigger, shook its head violently from side to side until a long piece of grey flesh pulled free from a young girl's face. Then, the cat darted off to the edge of the clearing, the ragged piece of bloody meat trailing behind it in the dirt.

Ben's eyes filled with tears, and his stomach heaved.

Then, he sat up in his rack and realized the *"caw, caw"* of the jungle birds was actually his own, high-pitched sobs. He tried to slow his breathing and relax his death grip on the sleeping bag he slept on. He swung his legs out of his bunk and rested his face in his hands, elbows on knees. What the hell could he possibly do? It was over. They were dead. His team may certainly be to blame, but it was over.

It is what it is, Reed's voice reminded him.

"What the hell can I fuckin' do?" He sobbed as softly as possible, not wanting to be heard by his teammates on the other side of the thin poncho liners than hung like shrouds around him. "What can I do?"

You will know. You are a Seer.

Ben forced the old man's voice violently from his head and lay back down, his breath slowing but still shuddered by sobs. He cried like that for a while, thoughts of the massacre and of his little girl in his head. He cried until he fell back into a restless sleep.

* * *

Ben woke to the stirrings of his teammates and stretched his sore back. The images from the night had faded slowly as he had slept, and it felt now like what it most certainly was – a stress-related nightmare.

Stress and guilt.

Ben swung himself up out of the rack and rolled his head to stretch out the tight knots in his neck. He looked down at his right hand and saw the ring had turned a crimson red. It no longer looked polished and shiny, but rough and, well – angry, maybe. He twirled it with his other hand and felt warm tingling in his fingertips.

"Headin' to chow. Ya wanna go?"

Ben looked up at Lash who was already dressed in tan cargo pants and a black T-shirt. His face was freshly shaved, and he looked rested.

"Sure," Ben answered with a yawn.

"You look like shit, bro," Lash said. "You need to shower first? Your feet are fuckin' gross."

Ben looked down, and his eyebrows arched in surprise at the sight of his bare feet, black with dirt to above his ankles. He also saw scratches and bug bites all over both calves.

"What up, dude? You go out hikin' last night?"

Ben looked at him not sure what to say. "Went to the head and didn't wear my boots," he said.

"What, did ya hike to Djibouti for your leak?" Lash laughed at him. Then, he shook his head. "Clean up, and we'll wait for you. Out front in ten?"

"Sure," Ben replied.

What the hell? From the scratches and dirt he could only guess he had been sleep walking. That crazy dream must have had him up wandering around in camp.

Lucky I didn't get shot by a sentry.

He looked again at his ring and saw it had turned a nice midnight blue and regained its shiny, polished appearance.

Ben double-timed to the head and took a short shower, just enough to hose the dirt off, and pulled on his own cargo pants and a "Hot Tuna's Bar and Grill" T-shirt. He dashed to the front of their broken down hangar-turned-barracks where a half dozen SEALs waited for him, including Reed who he was glad to see.

"Hey, bro," Reed said and clapped him on the back. "Feel better?" he said in a hushed, conspiratorial whisper.

"Yeah, thanks," Ben answered uncomfortably. "Just needed a good night's sleep, I think." He held back a wry chuckle at how untrue that seemed.

Ben found it easier than he expected to keep the memories of last night's dream-journey out of his mind, especially when surrounded by his teammates. By halfway through his breakfast (real eggs!) he felt like himself. He remembered he was no stranger to burying bad thoughts and dreams after all, though he had gotten a little out of practice after the last few, very happy years. He suspected he owed that mostly to Christy. He felt a sudden and out-of-character desire (more like a need, actually) to call her. He decided he would call after checking on the little girl.

"Well, he's like a witch doctor or somethin'. Right, Ben?" Auger slapped him on the shoulder and brought him into the banter of his fellow SEALs.

"Whaddya mean?" he asked.

"That Voodoo shit you put in my wound. What the hell was that stuff? Your grandma teach you that?"

Voodoo shit? What the….Oh right! The paste the old man made.

"Worked did it?"

"Worked?" Auger laughed. "Are you fuckin' kiddin' me? That stuff is crazy! The damn wound is healed up. Hell, my ass doesn't even hurt anymore."

Ben felt his head swim a little. Voices buzzed in the back of his head, but far away like in another room. He couldn't make them out. He forced a grin onto his face.

"I can make your ass hurt again," L.J. from Bravo platoon said.

"Dude, I'm not fuckin' kidding. My ass has ached from that shrapnel they left in me in Iraq and, no bullshit, it feels normal now. What was that stuff, Ben?"

Ben felt all eyes turn to him and again an uncustomary anxiety grabbed at him.

"Old family recipe," he said as casually as he could. "Just didn't want to hear the whining anymore."

The group laughed and like sharks with blood in the water turned their attention to razzing Auger for being a whiner. Ben didn't feel surprised that the paste had helped, just surprised he didn't feel surprised.

Like being at home. Powerful Ashe. Powerful Voodoo shit.

And, maybe a new power? He spun the ring on his finger absently and realized it felt very warm. He looked down and saw it had turned a faint burnt orange color.

The power is in you, Ben. Your Grandma knew, and I think you always knew also.

Ben pushed the old man's voice away and turned to Auger.

"We still need to see the surgeon after breakfast, okay?" Ben said. "You need antibiotics, and we need an X-ray to see what fragments might still be in there."

"Saw the surgeon yesterday when we got back, and he said it looked like just a little cut – not even deep enough for stitches he said." Auger looked at him as if he expected him to say something, but Ben had no idea what to say. "He put me on antibiotics already," Auger finished.

Ben nodded.

A little cut?

Ben had stuck his finger deep into Auger's leg when he had treated him at the village. He would never stitch a bullet wound because of the infection risk. But Auger had a bleeding hole in his leg and certainly had a bullet in there somewhere – no exit wound. What the fuck?

"Let's look at it again later in the box anyway," Ben said, referring to the little closet they used as a clinic in their barracks. The guys had come to call it the doc-in-the-box. "We'll clean it up again to be sure, okay?'

"Sure," Auger said, but kind of shook his head a little. "After PT, okay? We can go for a run and, then, look at it."

Auger hadn't volunteered for a run since his injury in Iraq, and Ben knew it was because his hip hurt much worse than he would admit.

"Great," he said. He decided he would use their archaic little X-ray machine to take a picture and look for the bullet anyway. "I gotta stop by the clinic first and, then, we can run."

"I'm in," Lash said. "Haven't had a nice run since we went down range."

"I'll go," Reed said.

"Don't be ridiculous, dude," Lash said with a twinkle in his eye. "You can't go fast enough or far enough to keep up with real Frogmen," he said with a wink at Ben.

"Fuck you," Reed said with a laugh. "I mean, you may be right, but fuck you."

A few minutes later, Ben headed off in the direction of the camp clinic where he could talk to the surgeon and check on his little girl. She had been asleep when he saw her last night, curled up on a stack of blankets at the top of a cot. He had stroked her face and left, not wanting to wake her and not knowing what he really had to offer her anyway. Now, he hoped she would be awake, and he felt confused at his excitement to see her.

She's a link to things I don't understand, but that feel so familiar.

Ben wondered if that familiarity was because of his strange past or because of the strong ties he felt to the villagers. That tie, he suspected, was just a manifestation of the burning guilt his whole team shared in an unspoken way. Whatever – he decided he would do what he could (though he had no idea what that would be) to make sure the survivors, and especially the little girl, were all taken care of.

The medical spaces filled a hanger that was in much better condition than the one converted into a barracks for the Navy SEALs and Army Special Forces Operators. Roughly square, they had actually brought in Sea Bees to build hard walls to separate the mini-recovery area from a small operating room and an even smaller X-ray room. The recovery area held twelve cots arranged in two rows and above each the Sea Bees had constructed crossbeams to support monitors, IV poles, needed supplies, and equipment. At the end of the rows were four sets of two saw horses where stretchers could rest for the initial management of bad trauma patients. So far, they had not had to use any of that advanced surgical capability on this deployment, thank God.

What struck Ben, however, was that all of the cots were empty.

Where are my people?

"Hey," he hollered out to the young Army medic across the large open room. His voice sounded harsher than he intended, but he continued on without pause anyway. "Where the hell are our villagers? Where's the little girl?"

The medic looked up, confused at first. Then, his voice seemed to register understanding.

"Oh," he said. "You mean the natives?"

Natives?

He wasn't sure why that irritated him so bad, but the word pissed him off for sure.

"They're not —'natives' – they're human beings, dickhead. They're also the only survivors of a whole village of peaceful people slaughtered by a bunch of AQ assholes, and they watched everyone they knew and loved hacked to death, raped, and mutilated. Now where the fuck are they?"

Ben realized his voice had reached a feverous pitch he had never intended and felt his face flush. The young medic seemed unsure what to do, and for a minute Ben thought he might bolt for the door. Then, he took a long, shaky breath and held out an arm as Ben approached.

"Take it easy, sir," he said, though as Ben was an enlisted SEAL, the "sir" was completely inappropriate. "I didn't mean nothing, okay? Anyway, I'm not sure where they went. Doc Gilliam said he was getting them some place more comfortable is all. Just hold on a minute, and I'll find out where they went, okay"

With that, he nearly sprinted out the door at the end of the recovery area, and Ben felt bad that he had over reacted. A few minutes later, the Army surgeon came in the same door, although the medic remained conspicuously absent.

"Whaddya say, man," the surgeon said and stretched out a hand. Ben shook it. "You hangin' in there?"

"Sure," Ben said, now really embarrassed. "Just looking for our survivors, sir."

"Of course," the surgeon said. "I wanted them somewhere more comfortable and private," he said. "Come with me."

Ben followed the digital cammie-clad doctor out the back door. Behind the hangar was a wooden squaw hut constructed by the Sea Bees. On the thin wooden door someone had wood-burned a medical caduceus with a lightning bolt and a sword through it and a Green Beret on top – the symbol of Special Forces Medical. Next to it were burned the names of the three Army officers who used the building as their quarters and office. Ben realized the Colonel and his two partners (an anesthesiologist and an ER doc) had given up their quarters to the survivors from the village.

"Where are you guys, stayin', sir?" Ben asked.

"We tossed some cots into the OR for now," the Colonel said. "No big deal. We're hoping not to use that room anyway, right?"

"Right," Ben agreed. He felt touched the three men had given up their little bit of comfort in the shithole they all lived in for the survivors. "That was pretty right on, sir."

The surgeon waved a dismissive hand and seemed embarrassed. "No biggie."

The surgeon tapped lightly on the door and, then, cracked it open a little. "Hello?" he hollered in. "You guys got a visitor." He looked back at Ben and shrugged. "They don't speak English," he said, stating the blatantly obvious.

Ben nodded and walked in.

It took a moment for his eyes to adjust to the dim light. In the center of the room, the survivors had arranged blankets and sheets pulled from the nearby beds and they sat together cross legged in the nest-like pile. Ben's little girl sat between the outstretched legs of the young woman who he remembered had lost her own child before he had been able to kill her rapist.

Too little, too late.

The little girl reached up at him.

"Gah, deh, eh," she said and looked for all the world like she thought her babble meant something. To Ben it sounded no different than any baby chatter he had ever heard, a thought that made him feel a little more normal.

"Hey there, sweetie." His voice conveyed the choked up smile that also spread across his face. His eyes felt suddenly wet, and he felt very little like the steely-eyed killer he was paid to be.

"DAH!" the girl announced and grabbed the middle of his face. She cooed, and Ben laughed.

"You have fans," the Colonel said. His voice sounded surprised.

"Yeah, well she and I bonded at the village and on the way in. I guess I became the mama duck for this little duckling." He nuzzled her neck with his nose.

"I don't mean her," the surgeon said.

"Huh?" Ben turned to look at the doctor to figure out what the hell he was talking about and, then, followed the Army officer's gaze.

The adult villagers had all shifted to their knees, the old woman clearly with some difficulty. Their arms were all outstretched and raised, their palms up towards the ceiling. Their heads were bowed forward, but four sets of dark eyes stared at him, wide-eyed, from under wrinkled brows.

"What the hell?" Ben whispered.

The large, middle-aged man made a noise that sounded like a word wrapped in a cough. The eight eyes closed tightly, and together they began a melodic chant. Ben stood and stared at them for a moment, the little girl in his arms clinging to his neck.

"They do this every time you come in here?" Ben asked the surgeon without looking back. He felt unable to pull his eyes away from the four villagers on the floor.

"We haven't disturbed them all that much," the Colonel said. "But they have always been quiet and, I don't know – stoic, maybe." He stepped forward next to Ben. "I've never seen them do this before."

"Da, da, Bad eh," the little girl said and grabbed Ben's ear hard enough to hurt a little. He barely felt it as he watched the strange scene in front of him. The man and three women continued to chant in unison, eyes closed and arms up and out. Then, the man's head snapped up, and his eyes popped open. Ben felt himself startle a little. The man smiled at him and dropped his arms as the women continued their chant. Ben tried to smile back.

The man stood up with surprising grace and fluidity, and in a blink he stood toe-to-toe with Ben who shifted uncomfortably despite the man's disarming smile. The man pulled Ben's right hand free from beneath the little girl, and he had to shift her weight into his left arm to keep from dropping her. Then, the man bent over at the waist and pulled Ben's hand to his face. The bare-chested villager stared for a moment at the ring on Ben's middle finger which sparkled back at him with a bright golden shine that nearly glowed. Then, he pressed his lips to the ring.

Ben stepped back in surprise when the man suddenly stood bolt upright, his face turned up to the ceiling.

"Ganada day not tai!" he shouted, and the three women popped to their feet, suddenly chattering and smiling, surrounded Ben, and each pulled at his arms and shirt. He held the girl close, not sure what else to do.

"Wow," the surgeon said from behind him. "They seem to like you, huh?'

"Yeah," Ben said. He felt a little dizzy, and his right hand tingled with pins and needles, but not at all like when your hand falls asleep from lying on it funny. More like little bolts of electricity shooting up from where he had perhaps inadvertently put his middle finger in a wall socket. He felt claustrophobic as the four adult villagers chattered, laughed, and pawed at his arms and body. He stepped backwards towards the door but the four moved with him. For a moment he felt a little like he couldn't take a breath.

"Stop," he hollered out louder than he intended.

In unison, the villagers dropped to their knees, the old woman with a muted grunt. Their eyes dropped to the floor, their arms again outstretched and palms up. The large man made a grunting sound, and they again began a soft and melodic chant.

"Jesus," Ben breathed and stepped around the women behind him to get away and closer to the door. He looked down at the ring, which as he watched shifted from the gold of a moment ago to a deep purple. As it did, the little electric shocks disappeared. He tightened his grip on the little girl. His eyes glued to the strange chanting people in front of him, he stepped with a heel onto the Colonel's foot and nearly stumbled. "Shit,...sorry."

"No problem," the surgeon replied, his voice hollow. "Did you do something miraculous at that village?"

"No," Ben answered as images of the little girl's injuries and healing, the old man's voice in his head, and the horrible pictures of the rape and torture of the village flashed on the screen of his mind. "I barely did anything, and what we did do was too damn late for most of them."

You are a Seer; you will know what to do.

But he didn't. He had no clue what he could do other than get these survivors, the end of their people, somewhere safe. What would happen to them then, he had no idea.

Ben looked into the big, dark eyes of the beautiful little girl he held, and she smiled at him and leaned into him. What would happen to her? With a lot of luck she could maybe have a long life working food service at a camp in Djibouti. Nice fucking life that would be, huh?

He kissed her gently on the cheek and, then, touched one of the women gently on the shoulder. She looked up at him with a face full of awe, her mouth open.

"Please," he said and leaned down to hand the child to her. The woman took the girl and smiled at him with a nod. Ben wiped tears from his cheek. "I'm so sorry," he said, but knew she didn't understand.

With great effort he turned to the doctor, who watched him with unmasked concern.

"You sure you're, okay?" he asked

"Yeah," Ben answered. "Let's get out of here."

He felt the silent stares on him as he pushed through the door, but didn't turn around, even when the cough-like grunt announced the chanting should continue.

CHAPTER

7

The heat and humidity made Ben wish they had run before breakfast, but he stretched his stride out anyway and enjoyed the feel of his body cowboying up to his demands. The grueling pace melted away much of his stress and anxiety. As he ran, with Reed puffing along beside him, he went over the encounter with the survivors in his head. He realized that, as usual, he had over reacted to the unusual behavior. His own strange past, full of its myth of magic and mystery, often made him side his view towards the occult when things were even a little out of the mainstream. Not exactly superstitious, he knew himself well enough to admit that, given a choice, he usually leaned towards the supernatural explanation. Only later would his left brain succumb to the logic of the right and show him the often obvious, and boring, scientific explanation.

As they started up a gentle dirt slope back toward their barracks, Ben picked up the pace and fell in beside Auger who pounded the ground into submission with his large legs, smiling a pain-free smile.

"You the man, Ben," he grinned. "My leg feels great – even my hip."

Ben smiled back and pulled a pace ahead of him, just a stride behind Lash, who he decided he would sprint past at the very end.

In this case, the obvious explanation for the behavior of the survivors required very little logic or smarts. He and his team had come into their primitive village where terrible men did horrible things to them and in only a few minutes, using tools that would mystify them, had completely destroyed their tormentors. Ben had saved a little girl and one of the women personally.

No real mystery how these simple folks might show awe and deference to us. They would have responded the same had Chris or Lash or any of us come in.

And, what about the man kissing the ring?

Respect for their lost elder and spiritual leader, that's all. No mystery there.

Ben lengthened his stride and closed on Lash as they started the last quarter mile to the finish.

"Comin' up on your six, Lash," Auger called out.

Lash glanced over his shoulder and grinned. Then, he broke into a full sprint.

"Nuh-uh, doc," he hollered as he pulled ahead.

Ben kicked in his own sprint and held the distance but couldn't close it. Lash was an animal.

A moment later they walked in circles together and waited for their teammates to join them one by one, Reed pulling up last.

"One day," Ben grinned at Lash.

"Maybe," Lash said. "If I lose a leg or something."

Ben laughed.

He felt so much better. The run had cleared his head and set things right around him again. He looked at the ring on his hand which held a calm orange tint. Ben pulled the mouthpiece from his camel back to his lips and took a long draw of warm water. He swallowed some and, then, swished and spit the rest into the dirt.

Ben and the other four SEALs walked slowly around the tin hangar and stretched out their muscles as they cooled down. Auger slapped Ben on the back.

"Way to go, Ben," he said.

"I didn't catch him," Ben said looking ruefully at Lash.

"Who gives a shit about that?" Auger said. "I'm talking about my leg, bro. You need to keep some of that smelly ass paste available all the time, okay?"

"Sure," Ben said. He noticed Auger showed not even the slightest hint of a limp. "Wanna head to the box to look at that thing again?"

"Let's do it after I hit some weights, okay?" Auger asked.

"Nah," Ben said. "Let's do it now, dude. It'll need to be cleaned up from your run and, anyway, I want to call home before it gets too much later."

Ben knew it would be nearly midnight at home already, but even though he had a brief call only a couple of hours ago, he desperately wanted to hear Christy's voice.

"Alright," Auger said with a six-year-old pout in his voice. He followed Ben into the barracks.

"The box" was a room the size of a very small walk-in closet where Ben kept his medical gear and a short treatment table where he would hook up electrical stimulation and heating units to treat his fellow SEALs for the aches and pains that came with their hard life. He also had a small, compact X-ray unit that sent images to a lap top computer. The entire X-Ray unit sat just outside the box in the main room of the barracks, completely unshielded by lead. OSHA would have them all locked up, but as far as he knew they didn't make site visits to bum-fuck Africa for safety violations. And, anyway he had only snapped a few pictures since they had been here, and the unit was a good ten feet from the nearest bunk.

Auger hopped effortlessly up onto the treatment table, and Ben turned sideways to be able to fit between the table and the wall.

"Let's see," he said and began to unwind the gauze dressing that covered the bullet hole above Auger's left knee.

"No problem," Auger said.

As he peeled away the last layer of gauze, Ben's eyes widened. Above Auger's knee – where he remembered the ragged bullet hole from yesterday – he saw only a small pink discoloration, soft and almost imperceptible. No cut, no hole – nothing. Ben pressed his fingers over the spot.

"Feel that?" he asked.

"Sure," Auger said. "But it doesn't hurt or anything," he said and turned his leg slightly so he could see. "Hey," he said. "Where's the cut?"

Ben shook his head and pursed his lips. "No cut," he said absently. He had seen lots of strange things during his fifteen years with Gammy in the Louisiana bayou, but certainly nothing stranger than this.

"Jesus, Ben," Auger said. "You need to patent that paste shit and sell it, dude. We could retire to an island somewhere, open a dive shop, and live a life of style." Auger leaned back on the table.

"Why the hell would I take you with me?" Ben asked as he pressed his finger deep into the tissues behind Auger's knee. "That doesn't hurt?" he asked. He pressed even harder in the area where he thought the bullet fragment should have ended up.

"Nope," Auger answered.

What the hell?

"Let's just get an X-ray to make sure we didn't leave something in there," Ben said.

"Sure," Auger said and hopped off the table.

Ben positioned his teammate against the wall outside the box and turned him slightly before positioning the X-ray plate at the level of his knee. He turned on the lap top which sat on a small desk made out of boxes, opened the radiology program, and plugged the cable from the X-ray plate into the USB port. After a moment the screen announced it was ready, and Ben aimed the X-ray cone at Auger's knee and pressed a button while telling him to "stay still." Then, he sat down in front of the lap top, vaguely aware of Auger leaning in over his shoulder. The image slowly constructed itself on the screen in sections.

"That my knee?" Auger asked.

"Yeah," Ben said absently as he stared at the image. The bones looked pristine, but more importantly, there was no bullet fragment. In fact, he saw not even a hint of the little hazy "dust trail" of tiny fragments that always followed a bullet into the soft tissues. Nothing. Nada.

Ben pressed a thumb into his temple as he stared at the stone cold normal image on the screen. He knew damn well there had been a hole in Auger's knee yesterday. Hell, he had pushed his own fingertip into it. After his deployment-heavy years in the teams he knew damn well what a bullet hole looked like and ricochet or not, Auger had one only twenty four hours ago. Even if he allowed himself to believe the magic witch-doctor paste could heal the wound, where the hell was the fragment that had torn into Auger's leg? There had been no exit wound, so it had to be inside his leg.

Had to be, but wasn't.

On a whim, Ben looked up at Auger. "Stand back at the wall again."

"Everything okay?" Auger asked. Ben could tell he was concerned Ben had seen something wrong.

"Yeah, yeah, it looks perfect, man – right as rain." He positioned Auger against the wall again and raised the plate to the level of his hip and stuck it back to the Velcro-covered wall he had created to support it. "Let's just get a quick picture of your hip. I want to make sure that ashtray sized fragment didn't move somewhere dangerous."

He didn't know if he would be able to tell if the giant, twisted piece of metal was somewhere dangerous. But that was a fragment he had seen before, and he just needed to see it was there.

But it wasn't.

Ben stared in shock at the normal X-ray picture of Auger's hip. The fragment the surgeons in Iraq had felt would be safer to leave in place in the SEAL's body had completely vanished. Ben realized his throat felt dry because his mouth hung open.

"Everything okay, Ben?" Auger's voice had the hint of worry again.

"Uh, yeah," Ben said and forced a smile onto his face. "Yeah, it looks great."

Auger walked over to him, and Ben clicked the program closed as casually as he could.

"What are you not telling me, bro? Do I have a problem? Am I gonna have to have an operation?"

Auger was a giant, fit Navy SEAL and tough as nails. But his voice had the quality of a kid who wanted to know if he would need a shot at the doctor's office.

"Dude, nothing, I swear." Ben said as he stood up and clapped Auger on the shoulders. "Your hip just looks way better than I expected, that's all."

"Yeah?" Auger asked, still suspicious.

"Yeah," Ben said with a laugh. "I swear to God." Auger seemed to relax. "You're just an amazing healer, man. I've never seen nothing like it."

"Well," Auger said, his face that of the kid just told he was the smartest in the class. "I've always been kind of a quick healer."

"You still are," Ben replied, not sure what else to say.

"We done?"

"Yep, all done. You can stop the antibiotics. You're all healed up."

"Well, I told you I'm a fast healer," Auger stood smiling, full of himself at this amazing fact. "You wanna go lift?"

"Nah, I wanna call Christy. I'll catch up with you guys later for chow before the brief."

"'Kay." Auger headed out of the barracks.

Ben watched him walk away. No sign of the limp that had become so familiar since Al Anbar Province. Nothing.

What the fuck?

He turned and clicked on the icon for the X-ray program again and stared at the image, certain he had lost his mind.

Then, he closed the lap top and pushed the mystery out of his head. He had seen things almost as strange, and sometimes much more frightening, in the moonlight back home.

This is nothing.

Ben forced away the worried curiosity and focused instead on his call to Christy as he followed Auger out of the barracks.

* * *

The connection was as clear as if he called her from the base in Virginia Beach only a few miles from their town house. That made it easier, somehow – how close she sounded.

"Well, you definitely sound better than yesterday – or last night, or however the time difference works," Christy said. Ben closed his eyes and could see her twisting her hair with her free hand, like she did when they talked at home on the couch. He could almost smell her.

"I love you, Baby," he breathed in the imaginary smell. Christy laughed on the other end.

"Okay, now I am worried," she said with a smile he could hear. "You have now officially told me you love me more times during this call than you did the entire month before you left."

"Guess I miss you,"

"I miss you too, Ben. What's different this time?"

He thought a moment.

"Me, I guess," he said honestly. "I think maybe I'm ready to move on with us."

Again, he could hear the smile.

"To where, Ben? I love you already. We have a great life."

Ben took a deep breath and jumped into the cold, wet sand emotions tended to be for him.

"Ever think about kids?" he asked.

There was a long pause, and for a moment he felt a little panic.

"All the time," she said, and Ben breathed a sigh of relief. "Every time I look at you, it seems."

"Me, too," he said, unsure what came next.

"Maybe we should talk about this when you're home," Christy said. "Didn't you make a rule about never making relationship decisions when you're deployed? Something about clear heads and wide eyes?"

He smiled.

"Yeah, well that was a long time ago when I was still scared to death of you.

"Scared of me?" she chuckled. "Big, steely-eyed SEAL man like you? How is that possible?"

"I want to tell you about someone," he said suddenly.

"Okay," Christy said.

And, he did. He told her, as best he could, about the little girl. On the open line he could give her no real details, but the advantage of people in love who really know each other seemed to be how much could be presented without really saying anything. In their own special coded language, developed over many long calls from half a world away, he told her about the girl and all that she had lost. As he did, he realized warm tears streamed down his face and dripped from his chin. He ended with his fear that her life, at least a real and happy life she had once known, was pretty much over.

"So, what are you saying, honey?" Christy asked softly. "Are you asking me something?"

Ben stopped and thought a moment. Was he asking her something? He hadn't thought so, but a faraway voice in his head told him he was, that he had digested on it in his subconscious since they had been back, and talking to Christy allowed it to find its way out.

"I don't know", but he thought he did. Could it even be done? Was it possible? There would be assloads of legal and political implications, wouldn't there? "What if I am? How would you feel about that?"

The pause was short.

"It would be hard, Ben. Really hard."

He swallowed and closed his eyes.

"But it could be wonderful, too. I look at you, and I see the father of my children, you know. I always have." Ben smiled again. "This would be a tough first step towards a family, but hearing the way you sound when you talk about her, the softness in you that only I really know is there…"

He laughed out loud at that.

"…makes me think it could be a good thing for us." She paused again, and he knew enough about her to let her. "How old is she, Ben?"

"I don't know," he said. "I'm a guy and not good at that. Old enough to walk a little but not very well and to make nonsense words, but not quite talk."

"So more than one and probably less than two," Christy said. He knew she wasn't really talking to him, so he didn't respond. "Certainly less than two."

Ben waited.

"Would it even be possible?" Christy asked.

He realized there was some excitement in her voice. "I don't know," he said honestly. "I'm not sure I realized I was thinking about it until just now when we talked about it." He took a deep breath and closed his eyes. "Do you want me to run it through our JAG?" he asked, referring to the military lawyers that all the units had, mostly for operational questions about international law. Ben figured Lieutenant Commander Chalk could find out the answers for him if he asked.

"Yes," Christy said. "I really think I do."

Ben's smile swallowed him whole.

"You know I want to marry you, right?"

Christy laughed the sweet wind-chime-on-the-beach laugh he loved about her.

"I knew that way before you did, my friend – but very classy proposal."

He laughed.

"I love you," he said again.

"I love you, too."

They talked about nothing in a way that said everything for another ten minutes, and then Ben told her goodbye with a promise that the moment he got any information from the JAG he would call her.

"No matter what time," she announced.

"No matter what time," he agreed.

He hung up and headed for the gym to lift for an hour. The exercise would help him sleep for a while before he had to get up for chow and the nightly intel and tasking briefs.

He hoped, as they all did every night he supposed, that he would be going out tonight.

For him it felt very personal now.

* * *

He thought he had dreamed, though he couldn't remember of what, and he stole a glance at his feet. He felt relief that they looked clean. Ben punched off the alarm on his watch and rubbed his face. He felt rested, actually. He stared at the steel beams high above his bunk and tried to imagine what he had dreamed. He remembered nothing except a soft voice saying, "Goodbye, father." Without any context, the words seemed a little haunting but not particularly frightening.

Ben arched his back and felt a comfortable tightness in his legs and hips from his run and workout earlier. He glanced again at his watch – almost five-thirty. He had showered before lying down to get the few extra minutes, and now he lay quietly on his back and thought about Christy.

Were they really thinking about adopting this little girl? Holy shit! That seemed at once so natural but scary and so – grown up. He smiled. No fear at the thought of marrying Christy he realized. In fact, he felt tremendous excitement at the thought. Bringing home the little girl might make it strange and rushed, but he had no doubts about his future with her.

Goodbye, father.

What does that mean?

He heard and felt the stirring in the room before he heard the hushed voices of his teammates coming back in from the shower trailer. Ben swung his feet out of the rack and pulled on his cargo pants and a black under-armor T-shirt. He slipped his feet into a soft pair of camp shoes and shuffled for the door with a toothbrush in his hand. When he pulled back the poncho liner wall, Reed grinned at him.

"Chow – you comin'?"

Ben shook his head. "Gotta do something," he said. "Bring me something back?"

"Sure," Reed said. "Whatcha want?"

"Whatever you're getting," Ben answered and clapped his friend on the back. Reed looked worried. "I'm fine, bro," he said.

"Okay," Reed shrugged. "I'll meet you here in an hour. That'll give you time to eat before the brief."

"Thanks, dude," Ben shuffled past him to the shower trailer to brush his teeth.

A few minutes later, Ben headed across the compound towards the medical hangar. He had shoved his toothbrush and toothpaste into a cargo pocket, suddenly too excited to take the time to drop them off at his rack. The little girl (she really needed a name badly – he would talk to Christy about that first thing in the morning) represented more than just a child he felt bonded to for reasons that were not all that mysterious. She was a connection now to his future and to Christy. Ben smiled and rounded the corner of the medical hangar.

He saw the three officers standing in front of their wooden hutch, and he felt a belt tighten around his heart.

Something's wrong.

Ben felt himself pick up the pace to a near jog. He couldn't shake the dread that grabbed at him. Maybe it was the old woman. Maybe she had a heart attack or something.

God, please let my baby girl be alright. Please. Anything else would just be too much unfairness.

You are a Seer, Ben. You can know what you want to know. All is as it must be.

Ben didn't want to know, not that way at least, and he jogged up to the three medical officers. The ER doc, a major, looked up at him, and his eyes reflected confusion more than tragedy.

"Hey," Ben breathed as casually as his pounding heart would allow. "What's up? How are my folks?"

You already know.

He could no longer tell if he heard the old man's voice or his own.

"Gone," the major said and spit some Skoal into the dirt.

Ben looked at him for a moment without speaking. Had he heard him right?

"Gone?" he said. "Gone where? Where did they send them?" He felt a panic growing inside and realized just how much he wanted the little girl to come home with him. "Who the hell decided that?" His face felt hot.

"I don't think you understand," the surgeon said as he took him by the elbow and lead him a few paces away from the ER Doc major. "Nobody sent them anywhere. They just left."

"Left?" Ben's wide eyes conveyed clearly how ridiculous he thought that sounded. He gestured around them with a flourish. "How in the fuck do five indigent civilians clothed in animal skins leave this place?

Getting out would be just as hard as getting in. Who the hell took them out of here?"

"Ben," the Colonel said gently. "Believe me, I know how crazy this sounds. We have a perimeter of concertina wire guarding a berm, guarding a wall, protected by eight points of elevated sentry towers with overlapping fire. There is a double gate at one point only, guarded even more heavily by a security detail. We have helos in the air almost constantly, and it's the middle of the friggin' day." The doctor rubbed his face with both hands. "Nonetheless, those villagers are gone. Vanished."

"What do you mean vanished?" Ben said suspiciously.

"I mean no one saw them leave this building much less the Goddamn compound. I came to check on them a couple hours after you left, and they were gone. We have searched the compound, and mind you there ain't really many places to hide here. They are nowhere in this camp. They vanished."

"Impossible," Ben said and shook the hand from his arm. He headed to the door of the hutch.

"Yep," the surgeon called after him. "But those mysterious people have disappeared unless you bump into some invisible bodies in there."

Ben opened the door and entered the now very well lit room. The nest of blankets and bed sheets had been returned to the cots in a disorganized way that made him suspect it was his people who had done it, unsure how to put them exactly. The room looked spotless.

And empty.

But not completely.

Ben could feel a presence of some sort hanging like a cloud in the room. Invisible – like humid air, but just as real and palpable. He closed his eyes and took a long, deep breath. For a moment, he felt something, a buzzing in the air and a tingle that ran up his right arm from his warm middle finger. He felt more than saw a flash of blue light, and then the jungle appeared in his mind's eye – like a flash on a screen at a slide show. He thought he saw his little girl, looking back over the shoulder of the village woman who carried her. Before he could really see her, though, the image disappeared.

Ben opened his eyes and looked around the clearly empty room. The smell of the jungle faded quickly, and the tingling in his hand and arm stopped. He looked down at the ring which seemed almost to pulse with orange light, but then it faded to a deep and shiny purple.

There was no trace of his people here. Not a shred of cloth – nothing. They were gone, and his little girl and his hopes for her with them.

They are the keepers of the Living Jungle, Ben. You know this. There is no life for them apart from the Living Jungle. They could no more survive away from it than you could away from your lungs. They have gone where they must always go.

How?

You know how if you will let yourself know. Help them, Ben. Restore them to their place in the web that is all things. You have the power in you to protect them. They need you for that. They can do the rest.

"I know nothing about this," Ben mumbled. "I need a psychiatrist is what I need."

Ben turned and left the room. The Colonel waited for him outside, but the other two physician officers had left.

"I'm sorry I can't tell you more, man," he said.

"Are we searching for them?" Ben asked.

"I don't know," the surgeon said honestly. "I imagine it will come out at the intel brief."

"Yeah, thanks," he managed to mumble as he walked away.

He shuffled back towards the barracks, his left hand unconsciously spinning the ring on his right middle finger. What could he do? They were gone. Ben wished he had not told Christy about the girl. She had seemed so excited and so drawn to him through the idea. She would be crushed, he thought. He felt a tear trickle down his cheek.

I'm the one who's crushed.

He looked at his watch. The intel brief would begin in less than an hour. He decided to go to the TOC, the Tactical Operations Center, beforehand to see what he could find out. He couldn't possibly wait an hour.

The TOC was the one place on the compound where the task force commander insisted on uniforms, so Ben jogged back to his rack in the barracks and pulled on some cammies. Properly dressed, he hustled across the former taxiway to the low, concrete building with a cluster of satellite dishes on top. Once inside the outer door, he punched in the memorized code for the inner door and entered the real nerve center of the task force.

The room was a stark contrast of homemade plywood table tops on which sat state-of-the-art computers and electronic communications equipment. Only a few of the work spaces were filled at this hour – the real work began when the sun went down. But Ben saw who he was looking for at a corner table.

The Chief Petty Officer stared at his lap top screen which appeared dark to Ben from his angle. The man had ear buds in his ears, despite the rule against it, and bopped up and down to what Ben knew would be old school country music. Ben looked past him into the real work center through the open double doors beyond him, where a dozen large plasma screen TVs tracked tons of data points and satellite feeds. A few officers manned posts, but mostly the other room was quiet. Ben placed both hands on the Intelligence Lead Chief Petty Officer's shoulders and felt him jump beneath his grip. The man looked up at him and smiled over round glasses.

"Hey, bro," the Chief said as he pulled the ear buds from his ears and shoved them in a pocket. "What's happenin'?"

"You're the man who's supposed to know," Ben looked again into the Operations room to see if anyone was listening.

"Yeah, I guess," Chief Bateman said. "What do you need to know?"

Ben sat down in the folding metal chair beside the Chief.

"What's up with the missing survivors?" he asked pointedly.

"Whoa, shit," Bateman said and rolled his eyes upwards. "That's gonna be the theme of the day at the brief." The Chief rocked his chair back on two legs. "How do five, primitive, scantily dressed natives—

God, I hate that word

—disappear from a Joint SpecWar base in the middle of the day without anyone seeing shit?"

The Chief stared at him as if he thought Ben might give him an answer, and he felt his right leg begin to tap up and down on his heel, dissipating the uncomfortable energy.

"I don't know," he said finally.

But I think I'm supposed to.

"Yeah, well, you and everyone," Bateman said. "I don't guess you'll be surprised to find it's got the Head Shed bound up in a shit storm. Especially them Ranger boys, what as they's supposed to be providing security and all."

Ben forced a laugh. In other circumstances it might even feel funny. "I bet," he said. "Are we searching for them?"

"Keepin' an eye out for them, but not really searching. Guess they figure if they don't want our help then that's their business, you know? They don't know nothing, probably have no fucking clue even where they are, much less us, so no real security leak."

"I guess," Ben looked down at his feet. He tried to get his arms around the idea that his little girl was gone for good. He would never see her again.

You will, and you must. The Living Jungle—

Ben squeezed his eyes shut which seemed to force the haunting force from his head in mid-sentence. He was done with the Living Jungle bullshit. He felt bad for the shit they had brought on the village, but Goddammit, enough was enough. He refused to let his guilt spin up his Cajun imagination anymore. He spun the ring on his right middle finger but couldn't quite bring himself to pull it off.

"You okay?" Bateman asked, and Ben looked up.

"Yeah", and thought he might be. "See you at the brief."

"Sure thing, man," the Chief popped his ear buds back in.

"Enough," Ben mumbled as he headed for the door. He didn't relish telling Christy, which he decided he should do right away so she wouldn't have time to get herself more excited or worried or whatever emotions she might be having. In the end this might be better. As noble as it might be to reach out to this little girl he felt pulled to, her presence in their life might actually serve as a constant reminder of the horror at the village and his guilt at having been part of bringing it about.

"We'll start our own family," he announced to himself as he headed for the barracks and a quick stop at the bank of phones. "It is definitely time."

CHAPTER

8

Reed watched his best friend and fellow Frogman check his gear and load extra magazines into the ammo pouches hanging from his vest. Ben looked like the SEAL he knew and with much relief, Reed saw the cloud that had worried him seemed gone. When they had been tasked at the ops brief to go on this mission, he had watched Ben carefully for his reaction. Ben had voiced what they all felt when he had muttered, "Fuckin'-A."

Now, he watched the familiar ritual as Ben wrapped green riggers tape around the tops of his boots to prevent them from catching on anything while they worked. His blood type (A-POS) and NKDA (for no known drug allergies) was written in block letters on the tape, just in case any medical provider needed to know and missed the same lettering on the sleeves of his brown T-shirt.

The intel had been great, provided from the crows they had taken off the target only a day and a half ago and confirmed with satellite imagery. The hit tonight would be on a cluster of concrete buildings at the edge of a small town an hour's flight from their forward operating base. The target was the half dozen Al Qaeda shit-heads that the Head Shed and higher authority believed represented the true command element for the rag tag groups of terrorists that infected this area like a disease.

"The head of the Serpent," the task force commander had announced with obvious pleasure. He had looked at the five of them and added, "and the likely command authority for the slaughter at the village."

After that, Reed didn't think the whole remaining task force could have kept the five of them from this op.

The op was huge, at least for a special operations mission, and involved the Ranger Battalion providing perimeter security and control of the surrounding town while two groups of SEALs and one group of Green Berets hit the three target structures.

"Capture or kill," the commander had announced. "But bear in mind, please, that these guys can probably provide some real intel data to other operations throughout this part of this shitty continent."

The rest of the brief had filled in the exact details and timing of the mission, including exfil plans and evacuation plans for casualties. Reed had slapped Ben on the back and enjoyed the big goofy grin he got in return.

High value target, an overwhelming elite force, good intel and support, and – why the hell not – a little bit of payback.

This was why they had become SEALs.

Ben squeezed the back of his neck as Reed secured his own gear and slung his short, M-4 Rifle over his shoulder. He chambered a round into his 9 millimeter SigSauer pistol and slipped it into the holster on his right leg as Ben began to check over his gear from behind.

"Shit-hot op for us, huh?" Ben asked him. The voice was calm and cool, and he thought he heard a smile in the tone.

"Yep," he answered. "Nothing wrong with a little payback, I say."

"Yeah," Ben said. His voice sounded chilling to Reed, but for reasons he more than understood. They had all been affected by the village, but Ben clearly more than the rest of them. When the intel guys had mentioned the survivors' disappearance at the late afternoon brief, Reed had watched his friend with true concern. The total lack of expression told him that Ben already knew about the disappearance, which explained why he failed to show up to claim the dinner he had brought back for him from the chow hall.

Reed's own reaction to the news was vastly different. He worried for the survivors, of course. But what he felt more than the loss was relief and guilt for feeling that way. Reed truly believed his best friend needed to put the events at the village behind him, and that didn't seem possible with his bond to the little girl, especially while she was in camp with them.

Reed selected a few grenades, both lethal and concussion, and slipped them into his kit and thought there was more to his relief than just concern for Ben. He turned to check over his buddies gear and thought about how much those people freaked him out. He felt terrible for what had happened, but from the moment they had first entered the village, he'd had a weird and creepy feeling about the villagers. He would never say it out loud, of course, but he knew he was a little afraid of them. It was the way he felt afraid of anything occult or supernatural. He was a blue-steel, fearless Navy SEAL, but he didn't go to horror movies about the Devil or any of that shit. He had been terrified by that sort of thing since childhood, and even heavily ritualistic church stuff just gave him a chill.

"Let's grab a Gatorade and have a dip," Ben said after he slapped him on the back to signal his gear looked good to him.

"Sure," Reed said and followed his friend out of the cage that held their combat gear. He absently patted the front of his kit to triple check that he placed extra magazines there for both his rifle and pistol. He had a feeling he would need them tonight, a thought that filled him with anticipation more than fear.

Reed wondered just how he had come to love his best friend so much when such a big part of Ben's personality seemed to be the very things that creeped him out about the villagers and the occult in general. Ben had told him only a few sketchy details of his past – how he grew up in some fucking swamp with a grandmother who was supposed to have some special, Voodoo healing powers or something. Reed absolutely hated that shit, and from anyone else it would have guaranteed he could not hang out with them. He somehow was able to look past it (by ignoring it and not thinking about it at all for the most part) in Ben. The teams were filled with his "brothers," but Ben felt like real blood.

You can pick your friends, but I guess you're stuck with your relatives.

He sucked down the lemony Gatorade and then pulled a can of Kodiak snuff from his cargo pocket. Ben poked him and held out his hand. Reed tossed it to his friend who packed a huge pinch between his front teeth and lip, tossed it back, and squatted in the dirt, leaning back against the crumbling old building.

"Thanks, bro," he said.

"Yeah," Reed answered. He tried to think of something smart-ass to say, but came up with nothing. He put in his own dip and enjoyed the initial burn of the tobacco on the inside of his lip. Ben bent forward and spilled a big puddle of brown spit into the dirt between them.

They dipped in silence for a few minutes, Ben's eyes cloudy and far away. Reed forced his mind to the task at hand, and he reviewed the infil and exfil procedures for the coming mission, hoping that's where Ben's mind was, as well.

"Hope the core leadership is in the house to the southwest," Reed said, visualizing in his mind the house that their team would be hitting. "Love to get them guys in my sights and watch them cry like babies when we take them off the X."

Ben looked at him, and the eyes sent a chill up Reed's spine. A fire flickered somewhere behind the cold gaze.

"The men who are responsible for killing my people can never be dead enough," Ben said, his face stoic. The look made Reed swallow hard, and he felt himself fill up with a whole new set of worries.

"Of course," he said and watched his friend carefully, "if we can take them off target and get them to the interrogators we could really get some shit hot gouge from them." His friend's face didn't change much, except for the tick of an almost evil grin in the corner of his mouth.

"Of course," Ben said and then rose up from his squatted position.

Reed opened his mouth to say something, but realized he had no idea what and snapped his mouth closed again. He rose up next to his friend. But before he could think of what to say, the door beside them opened, and Auger, Chris, and Lash came out.

"Hey, guys," Chris said as he swung his night vision goggles down, checked them, and swung them back up on top of his helmet. "We're third chalk. Let's get the roll call and load up in the bird."

"Hooyah," Ben said and turned from Reed and led the group towards the picnic table fifty yards away on which Jackson from Charlie platoon stood, a growing group of special operators around him waiting for the roll call.

Reed decided he would stay right beside his friend tonight.

He needed to protect him from things more internal than external he suspected.

CHAPTER

9

Ben leaned back against the side of the doorway in which he sat, the wind whipping his legs as they dangled out of the Blackhawk helicopter. He watched through his night vision goggles as the dark jungle whipped past beneath them. Now and again the glow from a campfire or the soft lights from a small cluster of buildings would light up white in the otherwise green and grey world he watched through the NVGs.

Bored with the monotonous scene a few hundred feet below them, Ben scanned around at his teammates who all sat relaxed but pensive in the helo. Reed looked back at him through his own goggles, like two mini-telescopes poking out of his face from beneath his green helmet, and gave him a thumbs up. Ben tried to grin and waved back, flipped his NVGs up onto the top of his helmet, and enjoyed the total darkness of the blacked-out helicopter. He could hear the other helos flying nearby, but without the night vision could not see a single glow to mark their position.

Ben leaned his helmeted head back against the doorway and fumbled in the front pouch of his kit, high on his chest. He felt blindly inside with his shooting finger, the glove cut away, and found the iPod he kept there. The IT guy for the task force, a Navy second class, had wired the earphone jack from his iPod directly into his headset a month ago, and he found he felt much more relaxed on the infils with a little music. He pushed the play button, and his right ear filled instantly with the sounds of Eric Clapton singing about the loss of his little boy. Ben hoped there were truly no tears in Heaven. He had found enough here, both in the nightmares of his youth, as well as the last few days in this shitty country.

The little girl's face filled his mind's eye in the blackness. Her face smiled at him as her imaginary fingers pulled at his nose and she cooed, "Gah deh, eh," at him. Ben felt tightness in his chest at the picture and wondered where she was and, more importantly, how she was. He dreaded his next call to Christy almost as much as he needed it. Ben gripped his M-4 tightly.

Get your friggin' head in the game, bro.

He needed to be a professional – now more than ever. This was a big op, and these guys were not a bunch of teenagers led by a small group of washed-up tribal militia. These guys were top-of-the-food-chain and would have real security. His team had learned a few times in Iraq that the religious zealots protecting the serpent's head would fight to the death and had no problem dying if it meant they could take a few of the Great Satan Infidels with them. He had seen Mujahedeen surround themselves with suicide bombers who wore explosive vests twenty four hours a day. He really needed to get iced and try to focus.

Ben ran through the timeline and plan for the breach of their building again. He felt his mind drift back to the villagers and sighed.

I just wish I knew they were alright. I need to know my little girl is safe. Send them a heart message if you must.

Ben felt struck, not by the sound of the elder's voice in his head (he almost expected it), but by the fact that he knew exactly what that meant. He closed his eyes and reached his mind out. For a moment, he felt a little like he floated up in the air inside the helicopter, and he could almost feel his words as they swirled around him and drifted out the door. Ben opened his eyes and for a moment saw a cloud of tiny bluish fireflies bouncing beside him, just outside the door of the helicopter. Then the lights, his heart message he knew, spread out and away from them and dove down towards the jungle below.

I am here, Jewel. I am here, and I am thinking of you. I want for you to be safe.

He had no idea when he had decided her name was Jewel, but it fit perfectly – his little Jewel from the jungle. He felt the band around his heart again. Another feeling filled his head like hot water and spread out over his body. He didn't hear it – he actually felt it inside of him.

I'm home, father. I am safe in our home until you come for me.

Ben gasped at the sensation of the words as they rattled around inside his head and chest. He had no time to absorb it, however.

"Five minutes," the voice in his headset cut out Clapton's instrumental blues, and Ben leaned out the doorway. In the distance, he thought he might see a small glow but he couldn't be sure. He snapped his NVG's back into place, but saw nothing new. Around him he could feel the stir as his teammates checked their gear and weapons one last time. Ben felt around his own kit for grenades and magazines and checked his pistol in proper place on his right thigh. Then, he pulled his rifle from its combat position on his chest to a point just below his right armpit. Last, he slipped a finger into the small pouch with his iPod and clicked it off. He was ready.

The plan called for an offset fly-by by half the force to mask the hover of the two breacher team helos as they fast roped into the jungle a kilometer from the target. Those helos would similarly cover the insertion of the rangers just at the perimeter on the side of the village farthest from the three target buildings. Helicopter activity might be concerning but was common enough to hopefully not be alarming to the targets. Ben watched the grey-green images of his fellow SEALs as they got into position for the insertion. Chris would be the rope master and sat now with his feet against a large green bag which contained the thick, coiled rope for his side of the helicopter while Jackson from Charlie platoon sat in the same position on the other side.

"Two minutes."

Ben flexed and relaxed the muscles in his upper body and then pulled a second pair of leather gloves over his combat gloves to protect his hands as he slid down the large rope. He would be second out behind Reed and then Lash, Auger, and finally Chris would follow. Five other SEALs from Charlie would simultaneously fast rope down from the other side of the bird. The entire insertion would take only a few seconds.

"One minute."

Ben reached across himself and unhooked his safety lanyard from the metal cleat beside the door. He folded the lanyard one-handed and tucked it into a belt loop on his pants and then shifted his body towards Reed who already stood half way up on one knee in the doorway.

The helicopter nosed up sharply and then settled into a hover as Chris kicked hard and sent the rope bag out the door. Reed grabbed the rope with both hands and slipped out the door into the darkness. At the same time Ben grabbed the rope in a two-handed grip close to his chest, counted one-one thousand, and followed Reed out with Auger's shoulder already against his back.

Ben looked down the rope through his NVGs to make sure he didn't come too close to Reed and seeing he had plenty of room, relaxed his grip a little to increase the speed of his slide. Reed landed just before him and moved quickly to the left, then dropped down on his belly. Ben hit a second later and moved right, took a few paces and dropped onto his own belly on the soft jungle floor and began to scan his side of the perimeter over the sight of his rifle. He felt rather than saw the other three SEALs spread out behind him before the crash of the rope as it was cut away from the helicopter. Seconds later the beat of the rotors faded away, and the silence engulfed them. It was strange after the hour of turbine whine and spinning blades from their ride in. Ben continued his slow scan of his section of the jungle around them and saw nothing.

The heart of the evil is here, Ben. Stop them here, and help us be reborn.

Ben shook his head, and the old man's voice faded away. He squeezed his eyes tightly and then scanned his sector carefully. The three minutes passed like ten.

"Viper lead – clear." Chris's voice seemed a loud interruption in his right ear.

"Two," Lash followed.

"Three, clear," Ben said.

"Four."

"Five."

There was another pause, and Ben knew that Chris checked in with the other two team leaders. Ben continued his scan through his NVGs. A soft sound, barely more than a breeze in leaves came to him. Not a breeze, though, he felt sure. It sounded almost sing-song, and he strained to hear it better. He closed his eyes, thinking he would give his mind only the sound to think on for a moment. It seemed for the world like a whisper – or more like lots of whispers. They were high-pitched, like children whispering in the dark.

–watching–

That word seemed so clear.

"Ghost and Mustang are clear." Chris's voice startled him back, and he nervously and quickly scanned his sector again.

Goddammit, keep your head in the game. Focus on the job before you get the whole team killed.

"Up on me. I have point. Two-by-two," Chris's magnified whisper commanded. Ben rose to his feet and spread out from Reed and followed their leader through the jungle towards the target. Twelve minutes and they would be in position.

Ben used every bit of mental energy he possessed to stay on his job. At times, he had to force away the childlike whispers that seemed now to come from all around him. After a few moments no more thoughts or images sneaked into his mind. He scanned his sector of the jungle as they moved silently and swiftly to the edge of the village. His mind finally wrapped completely around the task at hand, and in what felt like moments, he took a knee a few yards right of Reed and peered at the three small buildings set off from the rest of the village. The grey image in his NVGs looked blurred by the white light that seeped out from beneath the doorways and through the windows.

Shitty light discipline. They have no idea the hell that is about to rain down on them.

He could hear far away muffled conversation and laughter. The building closest to them was their target, and he re-ran the breach plan in his head as they waited for the other two teams to swing around into their positions and check in. Then, they would confirm that the Rangers had the village, and they would go.

He tightened his hold, not in fear but excitement, on the pistol grip of his rifle. He and Reed would come in from the back while Chris and Auger came in the front. Lash would enter from the rooftop doorway that all these little houses seemed to have (and satellite imagery had confirmed would be on this house) after clearing the roof. In Iraq that had always been a two-man job as there seemed always to be fighters asleep on the roof. Here that seemed uncommon, and a predator fly-over only a short time ago confirmed no thermal images on the roof.

"Mustang and Ghost are ready," Chris's voice whispered loud in his right ear. "Positions."

Ben and Reed moved quickly but silently towards the back of the house, rifles up and ready, and eyes scanning around through NVGs. To his right, he saw Lash move to the wall without any windows and take a knee to assemble the long, telescoping pole with large nubs on the sides that would serve as his ladder. Seconds later he disappeared over the ledge of the roof.

Ben and Reed knelt on either side of the back door, and Ben watched as Reed quickly placed a small, shaped charge of explosives over the door knob. Aware that his pulse pounded in his ears a little, Ben took a couple of long, slow, deep breaths to a four count – tactical breathing just like the Navy had taught him. By the time Reed nodded at him the pounding had disappeared and the hint of tunnel vision had dissipated, as well.

They waited for what seemed like forever.

"Viper – go, go, go," Chris's voice hissed in his headset.

They both turned their heads as Reed pressed a button on the small box in his hand, and the charge exploded with a dull WHUMP! Then they were both on their feet and crashed through the destroyed doorway just as another muffled explosion marked their teammates entry through the front door.

Ben moved left and spun on his left foot to clear the corner behind him without thinking. His mind registered the man seated on the floor, his AK-47 assault rifle in his lap. The face showed total surprise, and the man made no attempt to raise his rifle. Nonetheless, his front quarter still uncleared, Ben squeezed twice on the trigger of his rifle. He then spun forward without waiting to see the results and moved deeper into the room.

Ben shut out the panicked hollering – the words were meaningless to him anyway – and worked his scan around the room. A robed figure with long dark hair sprinted away from him towards the front of the house, and Ben shot him twice in the back. The man dropped to his knees and kneeled there, arms up over his head, and Ben's mind filled suddenly with the face of Little Jewel. Behind her, he saw clearly the piles of bodies in the smoke-filled village. Ben squeezed the trigger again, and the kneeling man's head collapsed on one side in a puff of red and white mist. He pitched forward onto what remained of his face.

Desecraters of the Living Jungle.

He stepped over the body and moved forward only vaguely aware of Reed to his right. He knew Reed shouted something at him, but it sounded like anger rather than fear or concern, and he continued to move forward.

"Three – we need prisoners!" the voice sounded harsh, but Ben couldn't seem to make Chris's words matter.

"Two's on the stairs," Lash's voice announced in his right ear.

Ben moved farther left, away from the stairs in the center of the room to open up Lash's field of fire.

Then his head exploded.

At first, he thought he had been hit by enemy fire, but after a second he realized what he felt in his head seemed more like a horrible noise, piercing and painful, and he wondered where it came from. He nearly dropped his weapon to grab his head with both hands. Instead, he dropped to a knee and steadied himself, his weapon somehow still up at his shoulder though he could barely see to fire.

*LEFT—HORRIBLE—DIE—SATAN—WHY?—NOW—RUN—
OUT—DOWN—HAND—GOD—CLOSE—HEAD—GOD—HEART—
FOOT—NOW—NOW—OUT—GOD—GUN—CHEST—STAIRS—GOD—
WINDOW—KNEE—RIGHT—DOOR—GRENADE—DOOR—GOD—
SATAN—*

Grenade?

Ben squeezed his eyes shut which seemed only to make the white light brighter, but made some sense of the one word that seemed to matter, more from the tone of the foreign sounding voice than the word itself.

"Grenade!" he screamed out to his team, and his vision cleared. He scanned madly about the room. He saw his teammates dropping to the deck at his call and then in the far right corner spotted the owner of the word.

The man pulled his arm back, and Ben flipped the selector on his rifle with his right thumb from single-shot to three-shot auto and squeezed. All three rounds found the same target, and the man's head exploded in a cloud of blood, grey, and bone, and he collapsed down on himself like a pile of laundry. The Grenade bounced once beside him and then exploded, just as Ben dropped face-first to the deck.

The concussion and noise knocked the breath from him, but he stayed oriented enough to hear two more things:

FLOOR–MAN—ALI—DEATH—KILL—GOD—KILL

Which all seemed to come as nearly a single word in a foreign tongue that he could still understand somehow, and:

Behind you, Ben.

From flat on his stomach he could not rise and turn in time, so instead he rolled onto his back and raised his rifle in one motion, just as chucks of concrete exploded where his head had been. He sighted and squeezed just as Auger's voice came to him.

"Ben, watch out!"

Then, the three rounds hit the bearded man twice in the chest and once in the throat and he pitched over backwards, slammed into the wall behind him, and crumpled dead to the floor.

He heard two more rifle shots, the sound more like nuclear explosions in the small space and then a moment of silence.

"On your face, motherfucker," came Lash's voice.

A second later came Reed's voice, the words strained and soft, and Ben thought his own heart would stop at the sound.

"I'm hit, guys. Fuck – I think I'm hit real bad."

"Doc," Chris's voice hollered, and Ben heard a panic he had never heard from the officer since he had met him. "Ben, hurry. It's Reed – it's bad."

Ben forced the cloud out of his mind and moved towards the voice, unsteady at first, but then the strength flowed into his arms and legs. He already pulled the blow out kit from his cargo pocket as he knelt beside his best friend.

"Two – Five – are you clear?"

"Two, clear."

"Five, clear."

"One – clear. Three and four are clear." Chris sounded like their leader again, the quiver in his voice gone, and Ben felt glad. "Two, five, secure the crow, and check the bodies."

"Roger, that," he heard Auger say, but he no longer cared what anyone else was doing.

His best friend's right thigh was pretty shredded and bled onto the floor, the skin hanging in thick strips from the exposed muscle underneath. But, that seemed the least of his problems. Ben could see a growing pool of dark blood forming around Reed's left hip where it ran like a small stream from under his vest.

"I can't really get my breath. Oh shit, Ben," Reed said, his voice a loud, rattling whisper.

"I got ya', bro," Ben said and squeezed his buddy's gloved hand. He hoped his voice carried more confidence than he felt.

Ben pulled out his knife and cut away the straps of Reed's harness and the shoulder straps holding his armored vest in place. He didn't see any marks on the vest.

But he did on Reed's body.

Reed wore no utility shirt, but his brown T-shirt had a dark hole just below his left armpit and the whole left side soaked through with dark blood. Ben tore away the shirt with his hands and stared at the small dark whole in the side of Reed's chest and felt his own chest tighten.

"Chris," he called out with a quivering voice. "Help me roll him on his side."

Chris knelt down beside him and cradled Reed's head in his lap and grabbed his shoulders.

"Easy does it, bro," Chris said softly in Reed's ear. The calm, cool voice made Ben feel braver and more confident.

Until he saw the ragged, baseball sized hole on the right side of Reed's back, just past his spine.

Oh, God no. Jesus, please. Please, no.

"Is it bad?" Reed's voice sounded muffled like he spoke through a mouth full of cotton.

Ben shook open a large trauma dressing and packed it partially into the wound and taped it tightly in place. "No biggie, dude," he lied to his best friend in the whole world. "Easy day. We'll fix you right up, and you'll buy the beer in Germany on the way home in a week or two."

He rolled Reed over onto his back. His friend smiled up at him with thin, bluish lips. His face looked so pale, it seemed nearly grey. Ben had his backpack off and pulled more gear out of it and handed an IV set-up to Chris who assembled the tubing and plunged it into a clear bag of fluid. He heard faintly, like background noise, Lash's strained voice calling for an emergency MedEvac. Ben plunged a needle into one of the veins in Reed's forearm and hooked the tubing up to it and quickly taped it in place.

"Squeeze that bag as hard as you can," he ordered Chris. The officer used both hands and squeezed the bag of fluid to his chest.

Reed's eyes were closed now, and his breathing seemed terribly shallow.

I need to put in a chest tube. His left lung is probably down. He needs a tube.

He needs a Traiteur.

The voice sounded like Gammy's, but he knew it was the old man's. Ben held his breath and looked down at the ring on his right hand. The ring was crimson and seemed to glow and pulsate on his hand.

I can't. I don't know how.

Yes, you do, Bennie.

Gammy again, but not really he knew. The old man's voice came to him as its own.

The power is in you, Ben. Not in the ring. Never in the ring. It is in you.

The tingling in his hand moved up his arm and even his chest seemed to pulsate with an almost buzzing like vibration.

Ben looked up at Chris, whose eyes were closed and lips moved, apparently in prayer. He turned and saw Lash had opened his lap top and spoke furiously into his radio, though curiously Ben could hear nothing, as if he watched a movie with the sound turned off. Past him, Auger pulled flex cuffs on the prisoner. Ben raised his right hand, but this time it wasn't the ring that caught his eye.

He watched the golden light that surrounded his hand and his arm to the elbow begin to flicker, like it emanated from a million microscopic fireflies. Ben laid his hand on Reed's chest and watched for a moment as the gold light spread out across his friend's chest and became haloed by a faint and pulsating bluish haze. Ben closed his eyes and felt a heat that came from his chest and pulsed down his arm and out his finger tips with a burning-like pain that was not entirely unpleasant. He became aware of a soft chanting sound and realized the sound came from his throat, though the words were foreign and meant nothing to him.

Even through his closed eyes he could see the sudden explosion of light and for a moment he felt a ripping pain through his chest. He felt certain he had been shot, as well. He opened his eyes in time to see a bluish haze fade rapidly away. He realized he couldn't breathe and heard a bubbling from his own chest. The pain was excruciating and he thought he cried out, certain he would lose consciousness any second. Then another light flashed, and the feeling vanished.

"What the fuck was that? Did you see that light, Ben?"

Ben looked up. Chris still squeezed the IV bag but turned his head left and right.

"Was that lightning?" Lash called out from where he knelt in front of the laptop.

"I didn't see it," Ben lied.

"I think it was lightning."

Reed's voice.

Ben looked down at Reed who smiled up at him. His face looked pink and healthy, though he grimaced a little. "Did it look like lightning to you? Jesus, my arm is cold."

"It's the IV fluid," Ben said. He felt like he floated in a dream. He had the sense that he spoke lines written for him by someone else, like in a play or something. "You can stop squeezing, boss," he said to Chris.

Ben placed a dressing quickly over the smooth unbroken skin beneath Reed's left armpit before Chris could get a look.

"Holy shit, my leg hurts," Reed said. "Hey, man, is that all my blood?" His voice sounded a little panicked.

"Looks like more than it is," Ben said and looked at Chris who kind of shook his head and shrugged.

"MedEvac helo in the courtyard in five mikes," Lash called out, his voice still tight and frightened for his teammate.

Ben stuffed his gear back into his bag and slung it over both shoulders. "Let's get him out to the courtyard." He looked up at Chris. "You want me to go back with him?"

"Maybe," Chris answered. "Let's see how secure we are here. The PJ's can handle him if need be," he said, referring to the Air Force Special Operations Medics aboard the MedEvac helicopter. "If we can spare you I want you with him, though."

"'Kay," Ben said. Across the room, Auger knelt with his knee in the back of the prisoner's neck and strained to see how Reed looked.

"He looks stable, guys," Ben called out to the team. "He's gonna be okay."

"Jesus, I hope so," Reed said with a nervous laugh.

Lash snapped together a stretcher beside them, and the three of them loaded Reed onto it while Auger continued to kneel on the prisoner who now began to cry. Ben's headset clicked with a keyed mike somewhere, and he reached on the front of his vest and turned up the volume. He then clicked the button to allow him to hear the command channel, as well as their team tactical channel.

"Ghost – target secure – four crows."

"Mustang, secure. Five crows."

"Viper, secure," Ben heard Chris's voice and a split second later heard it again in his headset as it bounced back to him from a communications satellite in space. "One crow."

"Yeah, thanks to Rambo over there," Lash chuckled.

Ben looked up at Chris and then shifted uncomfortably under the concerned glare from his boss. He would have some explaining to do later.

But not as much as when he figures out that the lethal holes in Reed's body have somehow disappeared. How the hell will I explain that?

He looked down at Reed who grimaced up at him and squeezed his hand.

He realized he could care less about either question right now. His best friend was alive, and the men who controlled the slaughter on his people were captured or killed – killed if they had been in his line of sight.

The bleeding from Reed's shredded leg had slowed to a trickle and he wrapped a battle dressing around it. Then, he popped a Syrette of morphine into his friend's exposed hip.

You see now the power in you and why our people need you.

Ben ignored the voice and together with Chris lifted Reed in the stretcher and moved towards the courtyard and the sound of the Blackhawk helicopter beating the air into submission.

CHAPTER

10

The burning in his leg had subsided a lot, and Reed found he could relax a little now. Mostly he thought it was because Ben didn't look that worried – at least not about him. His friend seemed lost and far away, but when he came back to the world and looked at him or joked with him, Reed saw nothing that made him think his friend was worried. He felt relief that Ben rode with him in the helicopter.

Reed ran over the strange dream in his head again. The concussion from the grenade blast must have knocked him out for a while. He remembered Chris looking down at him, terrified, and he remembered Ben leaning over him. But so much of what followed seemed a mix of reality and the strange dream that he found it impossible to tell which was which.

"You okay?" Ben's voiced pulled him from his weird thoughts. Must be the dope he'd given him for the pain.

"Yeah," he said, but his voice sounded gravelly, and his throat hurt. "My throat is dry. Can I get water?"

"Sure," Ben said, leaned over him, and stretched the mouthpiece from his camel back to Reed's lips. Reed took a long pull on the warm, rubber-tasting water, but it felt nothing but good on his throat. "Sorry about your kit, dude," Ben said. "Had to cut it away back there. The guys will get all your shit and bring it back."

"No worries," he said. His kit was the last thing he cared about right now. That crazy dream – he had felt certain he would die in only moments back there. He remembered feeling he couldn't pull any air into his lungs and the nauseating, powerful coppery taste of blood in the back of his throat.

"Am I gonna have to have an operation?" he asked and felt a little bit like a kid, but he didn't care. He hated medical shit. It skeeved him out. The thought of going to sleep and having doctors do stuff to him frankly terrified him.

"Nothing big," Ben promised. "They may want to give you some happy juice to clean your leg up, but looks like no broken bones or anything. Just tore up some skin and muscle."

"Oh, is that all?" Reed grimaced.

Thank God Ben is here or I'd be scared and crying like a baby.

In his dream, he felt like he had almost died, but then Ben saved him. Not with medicine and stuff, though. It seemed more like Ben had, well, sort of gone inside him somehow. Like he went inside him and took out the badness. Not fixed it – took it out somehow. He remembered pain and, then, the sense that his chest filled with light and heat. Then the badness disappeared, and he could breathe again. The not being able to breathe – that had been the worst part of the dream. When it went away, he knew he would be okay.

Reed realized his head had begun to feel swimmy. The morphine – he was sure it had to be that. Didn't really feel bad, though. No sir – kind of nice, in fact. He turned his head and looked past the Air Force medic who sat back on a canvas bench. Outside the helicopter, the horizon had just a hint of purple, a little light in the blackness that heralded the dawn. The color reminded him of something, but he couldn't quite grab it. A bluish light somewhere?

"Everybody get off the 'X'?" he asked Ben.

"Sounded like it," Ben answered, pulling the silver thermal blanket up around his shoulders.

"Good," he said. It was always good when they got off target before it got light. He looked up at his friend again and remembered the sight of him wading through the little house, blazing away like a madman from some low-rent action movie. "Dude, you were like crazy shit back there. You just smoked everyone." He didn't mean to bring it up, but the morphine just let the words tumble out of his mouth.

"Yeah," Ben said, and his eyes flashed with a glow or something that gave him a chill. "I'm glad it's all over," Ben said and put a hand on Reed's shoulder.

"Yeah," Reed agreed. His eyes caught the ring on Ben's hand, the one from Christy, and it seemed a little like it glowed slightly, a bluish glow in the dark helicopter. His mind flashed suddenly to Ben leaning over him, his hand stretched out just above his chest. His friend's eyes were closed, and his lips moved as he mumbled something strange – like in French or something. The hand, though – the ring pulsed with an orange light, and his hand sparkled with white light. Underneath he saw a bluish, purple glow – like the dawn outside. Tongues of fire-like light shot out from the finger tips.

Crazy fucking dream.

Reed closed his eyes. He felt safe with Ben's hand on his shoulder. Safe and well.

He drifted into a deep and dreamless sleep.

* * *

Ben opened his eyes when he felt the nose of the helicopter pull up slightly and looked out the doorway. Below him he saw the task force camp rise up towards them – only the second time he had seen it from the air in daylight. He realized he must have slept the entire flight back from the Navy Amphibious Assault ship where they left Reed, only a dozen or so miles off the African coast. The surgeon there, a man only his age it seemed, had promised to take good care of him, but wanted to watch his leg wounds for a few days. He had confirmed what Ben suspected – that although his skin and some muscle looked pretty shredded, there seemed to be no deeper injuries to bone, nerves, or blood vessels. The doc had predicted a full-function recovery. Ben had shifted nervously when they had pulled the battle dressings from Reed's chest to reveal nothing but healthy skin underneath. Ben had just shrugged to the curious looks and said nothing.

The Blackhawk settled gently onto the tarmac with a swirl of dust in the morning sun, and Ben felt his heart rate increase a little. He really didn't look forward to talking to Chris. He knew he had crossed a pretty serious line at the target house. Chris would keep it in the team, but Ben worried more about losing his team's trust than getting in trouble from some higher authority.

As the rotors wound down with a whiny sigh, Ben pulled his pack toward him by a strap, flung it up onto his back, and pulled his rifle back behind his hip. Then, he heaved himself up off the canvas bench and stepped out of the helicopter. He realized he felt completely and utterly exhausted all of the sudden. He could easily drop onto the cracked cement and curl up to sleep right beside the helicopter. He felt a heavy slap on the back.

"Need anything from me?" the Air Force para-rescue jumper asked.

"Nah, I'm good," he said with a smile. "Thanks for everything, dude."

"Shit, I didn't do nothing but ride with you," the young medic laughed. "I should thank you for the free meal on the ship. You Squids eat like fucking kings."

Ben laughed back at the age-old rivalry banter and waved as the man shouldered his own gear and headed towards the clinic, likely to restock a few items from his kit. Ben realized he should restock his kit right away, too.

Not that I'm putting off talking to the boss or anything.

He kept his own stock of medical supplies back in the "box," so he headed towards the barracks. He stopped at the cage where he and Reed kept their gear and stripped off his combat load, unloaded his rifle and pistol, and dropped his radio into a charger that already held a row of radios from the rest of his team.

"Reed doing okay?"

Ben turned to Chris and summoned a big smile. He actually felt pretty glad to see his boss and teammate – the inevitable conversation they would have aside.

"He's great," he said. "Surgeon on the ship says he can come back in a couple of days."

Chris' forehead wrinkled in confusion, though his eyes filled only with relief. "You kiddin'? Coupla' days to get back from that chest wound? Christ, dude, I was terrified he'd die on the flight over."

Ben summoned his best sheepish look. "Yeah, well, about that," he began. "Turns out he didn't really have a chest wound…." He had a lot more rehearsed but Chris interrupted him.

"What the hell are you talking about, Ben?" he asked. "He had a huge friggin' hole in his back. I saw it. I watched you put a dressing on it."

"Hey, I thought I saw it, too, boss," Ben said. "Looked to me like he blew a hole in his back." He took a big breath and dove into the cold water of his lie. "Turns out that a bunch of blood and bits of skin and stuff were stuck to his back from his leg wound. Looked like a hole, and I just covered it up, I guess, without taking a careful enough look. When we looked at it on the ship and cleaned it off, there was nothing there – not a scratch."

"Ben are you just screwing with me or something?" Chris looked genuinely distressed.

"Hey, look, bro, I feel like a complete asshole, but I put a dressing on nothing but blood and dirt. His chest is fine. His leg's a little dicked up, but they fixed it, and he'll be back in a couple of days."

That's my story, and I'm stickin' to it.

"Not a scratch," Chris said to the wall. Then, he looked up at Ben, and his face lit up. "Well that's great news, right?"

"Right," Ben replied.

Chris slapped both of his shoulders in obvious relief. Hell, maybe the good news would soften things for their next conversation.

"Why don't you get your gear squared away, grab a shower, and then you and I can grab a bite to eat, okay?" Chris still looked happy, but Ben knew how serious the conversation would likely be. "Need to talk with you about a couple of things."

Yeah, I guess to hell you do.

"Sure," Ben felt a knot in his stomach like when you heard you had an appointment to talk to the vice principal after school.

"Meet me at the TOC, and we'll walk over to grab some chow."

"Okay, boss."

Chris clapped him on the back again. "Man, I can't believe Reed's okay. I'll go tell the guys."

With that he strode off and left Ben alone with his guilt.

He finished storing his gear, restocked his medical bag and grabbed more ammo to refill his one depleted magazine for his rifle, then squared away his weapons. He didn't obsess too much about the upcoming conversation, but he did dance around memories of what had happened with Reed – each time taking a short look in his mind and then scampering away from the thoughts like a puppy afraid of his own shadow. Towel in hand, he headed out for the shower trailer, careful to move quietly in the dark barracks so as to not disturb the sleeping warriors around him.

Vampires. We really are like vampires.

"Hey, dude," a whispered voice called. "Is it true Reed's okay?"

Ben looked over to see Lash, who peered out from around the poncho liner that hung from the ceiling around his bunk.

"Yeah," Ben said, hoping not to get into any details. "Doc says he'll be back in a couple of days."

"Shit hot," Lash said. "Ben, you are the fuckin' man." The camouflage cloth fell back into place, and Ben stood there a moment, not really feeling like the fuckin' man. Then he headed out towards the showers.

He kept it short, as required to conserve water, but the heat (and the extra minute or two) melted away the knots in his muscles. The tension in his brain seemed to unkink a little, too. Now he stood outside the TOC in the harsh sunlight (harsh to a vampire like himself) and took a deep breath. Just as he reached for the door it swung open, and Chris walked out.

"Oh, hey, dude," Chris said. "Just looking for you. Change in plans – chow will have to wait, at least for you. We got a minute or two, and then I need you to do the medical screen on our crow."

Ben shifted uncomfortably at the thought. It seemed strange that he should do the medical exam on the only one from the target house he hadn't smoked.

"Why me?" he asked, and immediately regretted the tone towards his officer and boss.

"Penance," Chris said simply, not nearly as bothered by Ben's insolence. "You feelin' okay?"

Ben sighed.

Hell, no I don't feel okay. I feel like I'm sleepwalking through a nightmare based loosely on an M. Night Shyamalan movie.

"Sure," he answered. He actually did feel fine physically. In fact, he felt a lot better mentally than he had a half an hour ago. Not just the shower or the catharsis of his killing spree at the target – he believed he had let go of a lot of other confusing shit this morning.

Focus on letting it all go, and maybe you can have your life back.

Chris put his arm around Ben's shoulders and walked him away from the TOC.

"Look, bro," he said as they walked, his voice low but intense. "What happened at the target is unsat – no question about it."

Ben opened his mouth to speak, but nothing came out. What the hell was there to say? It was unsatisfactory. He had killed everything he saw when they had orders to take crows off the target for intelligence purposes.

"No excuse, boss," he said and felt his throat tighten.

Chris stopped and faced him.

"However," he said. "You are an exemplary operator and member of this team. The last few days have screwed with all of us, and I know the massacre at the village hit you particularly hard for whatever reason." Chris paused and watched him a moment, and Ben thought maybe he expected him to provide the reason. Since he had no friggin' idea he just stayed quiet and held his officer's gaze. "Anyway," Chris continued, "we'll keep this in the team. Consider this a counseling session, and get your shit together if you haven't already. Fire discipline is what separates us from them."

That hurt, and Ben felt a knot squeeze tighter in his chest.

"I know, boss," he said. He wanted to say more but didn't know what.

"Shake it off, and let's get back to work," Chris said ending the discussion. "Keep it to yourself until I brief it later, but I just got word we're out of here in a couple of days, so hang tough until then."

"Couple of days?" Ben said. "I thought we had three weeks left."

"Yeah, well the task force commander thinks the hit last night really cut into the bad guys, and he's leaving Charlie platoon, Delta, and the Rangers here to finish their rotation. Guess we're not needed anymore, so home we go."

Home. Home to Christy. Home away from this shithole and the memories of the night in the village. He felt a huge grin on his face, and his cheeks felt hot. This would sure as hell make the conversation with Christy easier in a little while. He would tell her in their own little code – perfected over many deployments – that he would be home soon.

"Head over to the pokey and document your medical exam for the spooks so they can do their interrogation, okay?" Chris ordered. "Then, we can put this whole fucked up thing behind us."

Chris slapped him hard between the shoulder blades and headed off the other way.

"Thanks, bro," Ben called after him.

The SEAL officer responded with a simple wave over his shoulder without looking back.

* * *

Ben leaned back against the small wooden table in the tiny room and tried to figure out why he felt anxious. Hell, he wasn't the one blindfolded and led around by flex cuffs. The thin, middle-aged man that shuffled across the dirt floor, led by the two soldiers on "pokey detail" actually smelled like fear, and Ben was glad for that. So why did he feel anxious?

Just get his vitals, do a quick history through the interpreter, and give him a once over. With any luck this will be the last asshole I have to see before we head home to the beach.

The soldiers guided the man gently into the metal folding chair and pulled off his blindfold. . He looked around anxiously, but Ben could see he struggled to still appear tough and unafraid.

Shocked to be treated like a human being, no doubt.

Ben had seen it a hundred times. The prisoners expected to be brutalized like they would do to their own prisoners and didn't know how to react when they were treated humanely.

Not that you deserve it, you fuck, but no one here will break your knees and carve your tongue out like you did to that poor boy from the village.

He felt a flash of rage flush his cheeks, and he shooed it away. The interpreter came in and nodded. He gave Ben a thumbs-up and smiled, and Ben noted that he still wore the Def Lepard world tour T-shirt that Lash had given him. He had worn that damn shirt every day for nearly a month.

Ben pulled a standard medical form toward him from the table and copied the numerical code off a card handed to him by one of the guards into the space marked "name." There was a flash as a Polaroid picture was taken of the prisoner (which made him jump in surprise), and Ben stapled it to the top of the form.

"Does he have any medical problems? Has he had any surgeries? Does he take any medications?" Ben said to the 'terp.

The interpreter babbled at the man who growled back an answer in a harsh whisper.

"He say dat God be take him to paradise, but all you be dey devils, and one day he piss on you dead bodies."

Ben sighed. Same old shit.

"Ask him again."

The interpreter did and chuckled at the response. "He say you mother be wit a dirty goat, Ben."

Ben smiled and shook his head. He took his pen and under medical history on the form, he wrote "subject unresponsive to questions, but appears well." Then, he heard a whispered voice – not in English but somehow he heard it like English.

If I grab his pencil, I can stab him in the throat before the others kill me. My reward in paradise would be great for taking this devil with me.

Ben looked up and saw the hatred-filled eyes staring hard at him, but no one else moved or seemed disturbed by the words. He looked around to see if someone else had come in.

"Did you say something?" he asked the 'terp.

"I say he say you mother…"

"No, I heard that. Did you whisper something?"

"Whisper?"

Ben shook his head. "Never mind."

He began checking boxes on the form about the patient's, or in this case the prisoner's, overall appearance and level of distress.

Wait for a moment until he relaxes and strike before the others can stop you.

Ben looked up again, this time slowly and directly into the prisoner's eye which continued to burn back at him with unconcealed rage. He realized the weirdest thing was this didn't feel the least bit weird. He thought a message back to the terrorist.

Go ahead, asshole. Please go ahead. We'll cut you down before you are out of your chair, and then I can go and call home. You wanna stab me in the throat? Come on and get some – right here it is. I'll send you to hell where your friends I killed at your house are waiting for you.

Ben moved the pencil towards the man just an inch or two and raised an eyebrow. The man's rage dissipated, and his eyes filled instead with fear. He looked around frantically and, then, babbled again at the interpreter. The interpreter shrugged and looked at Ben.

"He wanna know how you put deh whisper in he head. He say you Mawi Wata—deh serpent – have much bad Ashe – evil power he say." Ben felt a chill at the words. They felt uncomfortably familiar for some reason, and his mind flashed for a split second to a clearing in the bayou where Gammy stood ankle deep in blood. Ben squeezed his eyes shut, and the image went away – another childhood nightmare that followed him even here. "Me tink, maybe he got deh – you know dat word? He got deh crazy head?"

"Yeah," Ben said. "He's got the crazy head alright."

The man in the chair started babbling again, and this time his voice rose to a trembling shout. His balled fists beat the air in front of him. The two rangers on guard duty moved forward and held the man down in the chair by the shoulders as he squirmed and screamed. Ben realized he could hear the words in his head also, softly but still clear over the foreign tongue echoing in the room.

You are the great Satan just as Mohammed wrote. You will be torn from the Earth. You may kill me, but we will find you. You cannot go home and be safe from our reach. We will come again to America, and there we will kill you and your women and your children. You will watch as we rape your woman in front of you and cut the heads from your children in front of you. You will suffer the death of the infidel. You will know…

Ben felt the blue heat spread out from his chest and head and the room turned a purplish tinge as the voice in his head cut off simultaneously with the hollering gibberish in the room. The hatred inside him exploded out of his head and eyes and the room turned from violet to white.

I will keep my people safe from you and all your kind motherfucker.

The explosion hurt his head, the light seemed to burn his eyes, and he heard himself scream in horrible agony. It took a moment to realize the scream was not his.

"What the fuck is going on? Holy shit he's strong."

"He's having a Goddamn seizure or something."

"Doc, Doc – Morvant, do something for Christ sake."

The white light disappeared like the snap of a switch, and the room came rapidly into focus. The terrorist had slid halfway to the floor, his slide stopped by the strong arms of the two Rangers who struggled to keep him in the chair. Blood poured out of his mouth, down over his chin and onto his pale grey shirt. The whole body pitched and shook violently, and there was a sudden and overpowering smell of shit in the room.

The fist at his throat relaxed its grip, and he could speak.

"Let him go," he commanded. "Put him on the floor."

The thrashing body, somehow tossing in every direction at once in a way that looked more like a demonic possession than a seizure, stopped completely just as the soldiers let go of him. The now grey-faced body collapsed to the floor and pitched forward face first with a sickening thud.

"Jesus friggin' Christ," one of the young soldiers hollered and stepped back in revulsion. "What the hell was that?"

"Relax," Ben said with a voice much more calm and control than he felt. He snapped on a pair of black latex gloves. "He had a seizure. Help me roll him over."

Ben knelt beside the body and man-handled it over onto its back. The head made another nauseating thud.

"Oh, Sweet Jesus," one of the Rangers whispered, and the interpreter babbled something that certainly expressed the same feeling in his native tongue. Ben swallowed down the bile that rose in the back of his throat.

The face of the dead terrorist seemed contorted in great pain, the mouth open in a silent scream. Dark blood pooled quickly in the back of the throat and seemed to bubble – as if it boiled – though Ben felt sure it must be from the last little bit of air escaping from the dead man's chest. Dark blood, almost black, trickled out of his ears and nose and steam seemed to hiss out of his nostrils. But it was the eyes Ben suspected would find a special place in the nightmares of all four living men in the room.

The whites of the eyes had turned nearly black and behind the widely dilated pupils Ben could see blood which again seemed to bubble as if boiling. There was a soft pop, and the left eye split open and a small amount of bubbling blood spewed upward and then spattered back onto the grey face. A thin tendril of smoke escaped the ruptured globe with a hiss and then disappeared.

"What– in– the– fuck?" a Ranger asked no one in particular. The interpreter babbled even more hysterically and dashed out of the room.

"You ever see anything like that, doc?" the other Ranger asked in a quivering voice.

Ben shook his head. "I've never even heard of anything like that," he almost whispered.

"Can a seizure do that?" The Ranger bent over towards the body – his shock gone and morbid curiosity seemed to take over. He looked like a little kid, bent over the squished turtle in the road all set to poke at it with a stick.

"No," Ben said simply.

"Some kind of poison?"

"I don't know," Ben said.

But he did know. He had killed the man with his rage somehow. The power the elder had talked about that day in the village, the one beyond the healing power of the Traiteur, had arrived. He felt his hands shake.

"Go get the medical officer," he ordered the young man closest to him. "Get the task force surgeon. Tell him we need him right away."

The Ranger dashed off.

Ben raised his right, quivering hand up and looked at the ring, which pulsed with an eerie orange glow that seemed to beat cadence to the pounding pulse in his temple. Ben sucked a deep breath in to a four count, then exhaled slowly and felt his shoulders sag as the tactical breathing calmed him down. The pounding pulse disappeared, and he watched the ring fade to an innocuous flat, black surface. He dropped his hand to the floor and looked instead at the dead man beside him.

Ben stared at the grey face with the one exploded eye and black blood leaking from every hole. He tried to pull his look away but couldn't.

Powerful Ashe.

He stared at what he had done – at the terror he now seemed able to unleash – and worried mostly about what he would say to the doctor when he arrived. He felt nothing at the death of the evil man in front of him and some quiet part of his mind objected to his lack of regret, but there it was.

It is what it is.

Ben closed his eyes and tried to let his mind drift away – far away to home and Christy and a world without nightmares and dead terrorists and slaughtered villagers. He realized he needed desperately to get the hell out of this room. He heard the voices approaching as the Rangers returned with the doctor and practiced his confusion and surprise in his head.

At home this will all disappear.

He decided to just believe that instead of hoping it was true.

CHAPTER

11

Christy sat with her legs pulled up underneath her on the couch, a soft white blanket across her bare legs. She twisted her brown hair absently with one hand, held the phone to her ear with the other, and listened to the crystal-clear voice of the man she loved. She was used to the strange feeling when Ben talked to her from thousands of miles away despite the phone clarity that made it seem more like he was just a few miles down the road at the base. What felt strange tonight was how distant he felt inside her. She realized what felt so foreign to her was the worry. In all the deployments she had endured she had never really worried. Somehow she always knew Ben would come home to her. Tonight, though, something felt very wrong, and it scared her.

"Are you sure you're okay, baby?" she asked again and then wished she hadn't. Why ask again? Either he didn't know or couldn't tell her (or just wouldn't she supposed). Regardless, the question asked a fourth time couldn't be sillier.

"Promise," said the voice that told her otherwise. "I guess, I'm just disappointed about Jewel. Disappointed and worried."

That could be it, of course, and could explain the weirdness. She had always known Ben would be the father of her children but she had never, ever, heard him talk about being a dad and always assumed he just would when he was ready. She didn't expect he would suddenly be so completely ready and that it would hit him when he was thousands of miles away in Asia or Africa or wherever the hell they were this time.

"Me, too, sweetie," she said and realized she really was. "I'm sure she'll be okay," she said but realized she had absolutely nothing in the universe to base that empty reassurance on. "When you're here in bed with me we can start fresh on our own if you like, okay?"

She expected a chuckle at least and more likely a dirty innuendo.

"Okay," he said instead and the voice sounded so hollow.

Christy forced herself to move the conversation to small talk, the way she had so many times in the past when she could tell he needed to move away from where they were. She talked about their neighbors in the town house beside them and their last drunken party and about her friend Amy and how they were running at least six miles a day now.

"Maybe we can run the Rock and Roll half marathon together," she said.

"You and Amy?" he asked.

"No, you and me, silly," she said. They had talked about doing a road race together for three years, and it had never quite happened – some deployment or training exercise or whatever always foiled their plans.

"I would like that," he said, and his voice told her he really would, but, like her, doubted it would happen.

"I can't wait to see you and hold you and – you know," she said.

"The exercise wraps up in a couple of weeks," he said in a tired voice. Christy heard the words and felt her heart beat in her chest with excitement.

"Wraps up?" she asked. Wrapped up was their code for days, not weeks. "Really?"

"Yep," he said. His voice really did sound happier and full of relief.

"Omigod, that's so great," she bubbled and felt tears on her cheeks. She had expected another month at least. A few days? Holy shit, she had a lot to do to get ready for his homecoming. She looked around their place and saw nothing but projects she wanted to complete while he was gone. "Oh, God, how I miss you, Ben."

"I know," he said. "Me, too."

"I love you," she said. She could tell when his voice sounded like he needed to be off the phone and knew he would never tell her that. "Will you call me when you get up?"

"I don't want to wake you," he said, but he sounded excited at the thought of another call.

"Please?" she asked.

"Okay, I love you," he told her again.

Wow – two "I-love-yous" in less than a minute. Who was this guy, and where was Ben? She smiled warmly.

"I love you, too."

The phone clicked off. For some reason he never, ever said goodbye. He just finished and hung up. She had asked him about it once, and he mumbled something mysterious about his grandmother and Indians and goodbye being bad luck or something. She hugged the phone to her chest and set it gently back in its cradle.

Christy sat on the couch for a while, swimming in one of his many-sizes-too-big-for-her shirts and wept happy tears.

Not like you girl. You don't cry, so what's up? You're a tough SSO.

SSOs or SEAL significant others as she and Amy called themselves – the hint of not being married very much intended for her friend – always knew how to keep an even strain. Maybe it was just the talk of marriage he had sprung on her or the roller coaster of emotions from the almost-maybe adoption of a little girl she had never even seen (hell, she didn't even know what continent the kid was from). Whatever it was, she felt way more emotional than usual. She just wanted Ben home with her. She could feel he struggled with something over there and wanted him here where she could help him.

Christy looked around the family room again and tried to re-prioritize the project list to things she could do in just a few days.

Dreams are the reality that hides from us. You are a Seer, and you know how to find what is hidden.

-The Elder

CHAPTER

12

Ben stretched out his legs on top of his sleeping bag and thought about taking an Ambien CR to get to sleep. He looked at his watch – about five hours to go. Not really enough time. He had too long to go not to sleep but not long enough to dump the drug out of his system before they touched down in Virginia Beach. He fluffed the folded-over sweatshirt he used as a pillow and tried to think again about home and shake away the haunting memories of his time away – memories filled mostly with the last two weeks. Memories of the village, Jewel, the old man, and his ring. Memories of voices in his head, boiling blood, and ruptured eyeballs.

He sighed heavily.

"How you doin', bro?"

Ben looked over and saw Reed had awakened beside him on the floor of the Air Force transport plane, his own head leaned back against a cargo pallet that towered above them in the warehouse-like fuselage of the C-17 Jet.

"Great," he said and thought he pretty much meant it. He felt sure the haunting would end within hours of crawling next to Christy in their bed at home. "Ready to be there, I guess."

"Trouble sleeping?"

"Just excited," he answered. "How's your leg?"

Reed reached absently for his right thigh which remained wrapped in a dressing from ankle to hip. "Feels a lot better," he said, but Ben knew he lied.

"Do you need more pain medicine?" he asked.

"I said it feels better, mom" Reed snapped at him, but he sounded more caught than actually annoyed. "Anyway, that medicine makes me feel weird. You must have given me a ton at the target – it gave me some really fucked up dreams."

Ben let that go. What the hell could he say?

No, I think my penetrating your dying body with powerful Ashe from the ring a dead witch doctor gave me after he healed Jewel's head with magic blue fireflies is what gave you bad dreams, bro.

Ben smiled.

"Wanna watch a movie?" he asked instead.

"Sure," Reed said and grimaced as he tried to shuffle closer towards him. Ben put a hand on his shoulder.

"Just stay still, dickhead. I don't wanna watch you cry. Let me come to you."

He pulled his sleeping bag closer to Reed and pushed himself up into a sitting position against the cargo pallet. He cued up the movie list on his lap top and clicked on *Anchorman* with Will Ferrell without asking what Reed wanted. They had seen it a dozen times, but they had seen all of the movies a dozen times and the last thing he needed was for Reed to pick some action/war movie.

Before the intro credits were over Reed snored beside him, and Ben's mind drifted back to Africa and then way past it to the Louisiana bayou and shadows moving through the woods on a moonless night. He listened to Steve Carrel and Will Ferrell and watched his Gammy stand in a lake of blood, her arms stretched upwards toward the stars and her voice trembling out words he knew but didn't understand.

A few more hours and I'll be with Christy. Africa will fade away, and Gammy and nightmares of the bayou will be safely back in their box in the basement of my brain.

For now, he let the old movie-like memories play in his mind until he finally started to drift off. The voices that called him were far away and easy to ignore, but their whispers followed him into his dreamless sleep.

* * *

Ben thought he would absolutely explode if he had to wait much longer to see Christy as she waited with the other wives and "significant others" in the large conference room at the low brown building that housed their team. Nonetheless, tradition was tradition, and he understood the importance of this one to every one of them.

The old, grey van bounced to a stop at the top of a sand dune at the back of the Little Creek Naval Amphibious Base, and he looked out at the Chesapeake Bay and the long bridge tunnel that stretched across it toward the Delmarva Peninsula. The air was crisp and clean, and after a few months in Africa he realized he really understood what clean air meant, now having something to compare it to. Just out of view to his left sat the town house on the beach where he would make love to Christy in just an hour or so (less if he had his way). The five of them piled out of the van and shuffled down the dune onto the beach.

Ben took the cigar Lash handed him from the dark wood box with a Navy SEAL trident wood-burned on the lid and he drew it across his upper lip, inhaling the rich, powerful smell deeply. Truth be told, he didn't really enjoy cigars that much, but the memory of emotion that now came with the smell of a cigar, the memories of both past celebrations and post-deployment wakes for lost friends, made the traditional post-deployment smoke a very enjoyable cigar, indeed. Ben accepted the cutter from Chris and snipped the end from his before passing it on to Reed.

"Thanks, bro," his best friend said, and he thought he could still hear a strain in the voice that meant pain.

But he's alive. Thanks to the powerful Ashe and the ring.

Ben looked down at the ring which for days now had looked the same – a dull black. He had come to believe the colors and lights he had seen from the ring had been nothing more than his Cajun imagination. Still he had been unable to pull the ring off and leave it in Africa where a part of him thought it belonged.

"Here ya' are, Ben," Auger said and handed him a tin camp cup full of sweet port wine.

"Thanks, man."

Lash leaned in with a lighter turned way up high, and Ben puffed deeply on his cigar as he passed it through what seemed to him a ceremonial flame. The harsh smoke felt familiar and good in his throat.

Port and a good cigar – no way to get more Navy than that.

"To Reed's leg," Chris said.

"Hooyah," they all answered and drank from their port-filled tin cups. Like the cigar, the sweet and harsh wine would normally be unpleasant, but here and with the family these men had become, it was more than enjoyable.

"Auger's ass," Lash said.

"That was last deployment," Auger protested with a chuckle.

"Yeah, but you bitched about it on this one, and doc finally fixed it."

"Works," Chris ruled. "To Auger's ass and to Ben's witch-doctery."

"Hooyah," the team answered and drank. They puffed their cigars again and together they sat on top of the dune, leaned back on their elbows, and stretched out their legs. As always they began the ritual of ribbing each other and started the telling of tall tales that would become a part of who they were as a team.

They laughed and smoked and drank their port, now and again tossing out a toast to particularly deserving memories. Ben felt himself both immersed in the memories and somehow cleansed of them. He had a toast he knew needed to be made and decided it should fall on him.

"The village," he said and raised his cup.

The five of them got quiet for a moment, each taken back to the horror of that day in his own way, a silent tribute to their loss and their failure. Ben watched the slide show in his mind. It began with the old man the first day he met him and ended with his handing Jewel to the woman from her village in the doctor's hutch at their base camp. The show took only seconds, he knew, but felt like a full-length feature film. He felt a warm pulsation in the middle finger of his right hand, but refused to look at the ring. He knew it would glow with some color but had also decided without seeing it that it was his imagination.

The cord between us travels both ways, Ben, and is stronger than the distance you have found. It is powerful and inevitable. It is also eternal.

Ben decided not to argue with the dead man's voice in his head. What would be the point?

"The village," Chris said, and they all quietly raised their port to their lips and drank. Ben then took a long, harsh drag on his cigar and blew out the smoke slowly, trying to exhale the ghosts from the village with it. It felt right, and he dared believe their ritual might actually put the whole confusing and emotional experience behind him for good. He felt lighter somehow.

And, now I want to hold Christy tight and move forward with the rest of my life.

He didn't have to wait long. The five SEALs chatted a little more, the mood more somber than past times on the dunes. Ben sensed he wasn't the only member of the team ready to move away from their failure in Africa, which seemed to overshadow all of their successes.

"To the Commander in Chief, the Secretary of Defense, the Secretary of the Navy, and the Teams," Chris announced with a raised cup to end their ceremony.

"The Teams," the five said in unison, and then Ben swallowed down the last of the sweet but burning wine and stubbed his cigar out in the sand.

"Hooyah," Chris said.

"Hooyah," they answered back, and then the team headed back to the van.

Auger put his arm around Ben's shoulder as they crested the dune.

"Thanks, bro," he said.

"For what?" Ben asked.

"Makin' me better with your Voodoo magic," Auger said and then his voice lowered to a conspiratorial whisper. "I was really struggling, Ben," he admitted. "I was thinking about a medical board the pain had got so bad. I don't know what kind of witch doctor magic you got, man, but you saved my career."

He slapped Ben on the back and moved ahead of him toward the van, apparently having shown all the emotion he could handle at once. Ben watched him go, no hint of a limp or any other pain, and smiled. He caught Chris's eye and his officer nodded and gave him a thumbs up. Ben smiled back but felt more embarrassed than proud. Then another arm wrapped around his neck.

"What're ya gonna do to that pretty lady of yours, huh? Come on, come on – details for a lonely guy."

Ben laughed and pushed Reed away.

"You're a sick puppy, bro."

"You have no idea, man."

They piled into the van and headed down the dirt road, and Ben's heart quickened at the sight of the low brown building where he knew Christy waited for him.

* * *

Christy chatted aimlessly beside the man she loved from the passenger seat of the black Ford F-250 pick-up truck. She had driven Ben's truck, knowing he would want (need?) to drive home the short distance from the base to their town house and that he would much prefer to drive the truck he loved instead of her little silver Audi. Her patter was aimless but not really nervous. She had this quiet introspection every time Ben came home. She wondered why she felt a little detached and anxious for the first few hours. Earlier in their relationship the feeling had lasted a few days – the feeling that she didn't really know the man she held, made love to, and ate dinner with. Over the years the time had shortened to just a few hours. She had never talked to Ben about the feeling (he wasn't exactly competent at talking about feelings) and over time had come to accept it as normal, at least for them. She thought maybe it was just a reaction to not actually knowing anything much about Ben's life during the months that led up to their reunions. There was not much he could talk about, and he talked about even less than that.

The quiet warrior, I guess.

She was unable to stop her litany of stories about which she knew Ben could not possibly care less. She continued her rant about everyday things from home, work, and friends. She figured these were all little things they would chat about daily in their normal life, and somehow catching him up seemed to bring him the rest of the way home for her. She doubted it did much for him, but he seemed to accept she needed it and, God bless him, always feigned interest. So, she finished her story about the rude lady at the cell phone center and the billing error as they turned left towards the beach and their row of town houses came into view.

"Well, I'm sure she was sorry she had been rude once she saw you were much tougher than you look, little girl," Ben said with a patient and convincingly interested chuckle. It took Christy a minute to realize what the hell he was talking about.

Oh yeah, my cell phone story.

"Well, she got an earful of salty sailor talk I learned from my boyfriend, I can tell you," she said with a smile.

"Fiancé," Ben said and squeezed her hand as the truck rocked to a stop in the sand covered driveway.

"What?" she said, thinking she had missed a part of the conversation during her ritual musing.

Ben shifted in the seat and faced her.

"I know this is not the romantic way you deserve," he said taking both of her hands in his, "but, I meant everything I said on the phone to you."

Christy looked into the bluish-grey eyes that always took her breath away.

"I love you, baby," Ben continued and seemed a little nervous – a rare emotion that when she saw it in him made him even more attractive to her, "and I want to marry you. I want to start a family with you and have a white picket fence and grow old together and sit together on a porch fifty years from now and still think of how to get my old bones out of my rocker and on top of you." He stopped and looked down for a moment and then back up at her, his eyes now rimmed with tears for some reason. "Can we get married, Christy?"

She felt tears in her own eyes and threw her arms around Ben's neck. "Of course, Ben," She said. "I love you, too – so very much. Of course, I'll marry you." She kissed him deeply on the mouth and felt a familiar tingle. She realized some of her anxiety was probably just an aching need to be naked and writhing under Ben's touches. She did her best to put that need aside for just a moment more. She looked deeply into those cloudy eyes, the storm that always seemed to brew there a little darker than usual. "What about our rule about not making big decisions when you're deployed or right when you get back?"

He touched her face softly, and she felt a little shudder inside.

"Screw that," he said with a soft smile. "I love you, and if I was smarter I would have married you years ago." Ben took her hands in his again, and she thought she felt a little tremble, though it could have been her imagination. "If you need time to think about it, I understand," he said, "but I want to marry you. In fact, I want to marry you as soon as possible."

She squeezed him tightly.

"I decided a long time ago I would be with you forever, Ben," she said. "If you feel ready to get married, then let's do it. I've always been ready to be with you for a lifetime."

Ben smiled broadly, and the storm in his eyes softened.

"I love you so much," he said.

They kissed deeply. Christy inhaled the smell of him, felt his hands on her neck and face, and realized she had to have him immediately. She pulled away from him before they wound up giving the neighbors a show that would likely prompt a call to the police.

"Take me inside," she said with a quivering voice.

Ben was out of the driver's seat and beside her door before she could hardly blink, and she laughed as he pulled her out and into his arms, carrying her to the door to their home. She hugged her head to his neck as he practically kicked the door open. She wondered if he could feel how wet she was through her jeans.

Ben dropped the keys onto the hard wood floor of the foyer and kicked the door closed behind them. She swung her legs to the floor and kept her arms around his neck, her open mouth finding his, and their tongues exploring each other. Ben grabbed her arm and headed for the stairs.

"Come on," he breathed in a throaty whisper.

Christy was a full foot shorter than her boyfriend (*fiancé!*), but she pulled back on his arm and when he turned to face her she pushed him backwards against the front door with both hands. Then, her mouth was back on his, her hands fumbling between them at his pants.

Stupid friggin' buttons. Who designed these damn uniforms?

His tongue was in her mouth, and his hands already had her jeans open. She wiggled her hips to help him slide them down and then kicked with her feet until she stood against him, naked from the waist down. His strong hand tickled between her wet thighs, and for a moment she thought she might come right then and cried out. She had his belt open but still couldn't quite manage the buttons that kept his cammie pants on over the hardness she felt underneath from her touch. She grabbed his pants with both hands and pulled with all her might. If she didn't have him in her right now she was pretty sure she would die.

She listened to the click-click-click of the popped buttons as they bounced on the hard wood floor as his pants slid down to his knees. She started to drop down to her own knees in front of him, but his strong arms stopped her descent. She looked up at him, and he lifted her into the air and turned them around so that she was against the door. His mouth back on hers, he held her there by her waist, and she screamed loudly as she felt his hardness slide into her wet body. She could feel every nerve light up with electric pleasure as he thrust in and out of her, his own moans mixing with her cries of pleasure. She wrapped her legs tightly around his waist and did her best to grind against him, but mostly she just lost herself in the animal-like thrusting of his body against hers. Then her eyes exploded with white light, and her body spasmed in a crashing orgasm.

"Oh, God, Ben" she hollered and felt his muscles tighten as he pressed her more tightly against the door.

"I love you, Christy," he moaned, as she felt him fill her with his own orgasm. Christy laid her head on his shoulder and lost herself in the feel of his final desperate thrusts as her own electrical storm subsided. He leaned into her as he relaxed and held her that way for what seemed like an eternity, his arms under her knees, holding her against the door as their breathing and heartbeats slowed. Then she unwrapped her legs from his waist and slid her feet to the floor. He held her tight and she heard the un-romantic plop of the product of their uncontrolled lust spattering the foyer floor. She giggled.

"Oops," she said, and Ben laughed.

"Well," Ben leaned back to look in her eyes. "Didn't set any kind of endurance record, did I?" He looked a little sheepish. She kissed him deeply again.

"It was perfect," she said and meant it.

A few minutes later they lay together in sweat pants and T-shirts, arms and legs wrapped around each other in the hammock they kept on the wood deck that stuck out from the back of their town home. They had cleaned up their mess (she wasn't sure what it would do to the wood finish – a very practical, but not very romantic, thought) but still had not brought Ben's sea bag in from the truck. They rocked gently back and forth, held each other, and looked out at the Chesapeake Bay and the Atlantic Ocean not far beyond. Ben turned her face up towards his.

"Can we go get it later today?"

"What?" she asked, totally confused.

"Your ring," he said, "I want you to pick out a ring today."

Christy smiled and hugged him tightly, her head on his chest. "I don't care about a ring, Ben. I don't even need a ring. I'm just excited to marry you."

"I need the ring," he said and kissed her cheek. "Can we go this afternoon?" His voice had a kid-like quality that struck Christy as unbelievably cute. Please, can I have it, Please?

She kept her head on his chest and smiled. "Sure, baby. But not a lot of money, okay? We have lots of better things to spend our money on."

Ben kissed the top of her head and said nothing but she could feel how happy he seemed and realized she felt nearly delirious with happiness herself. Her eyes fell on his right hand which rested on her hip. She had not noticed the ring until now and knew she had never seen it before. In fact, she couldn't remember Ben ever wearing any jewelry before. He took his watch off every opportunity he got.

The ring looked to be made of carved and polished bone-white stone. It shined with a sheen that seemed almost to hold hints of rainbow like color. Christy reached out her own hand to touch it, but her fingers stopped short. She felt suddenly apprehensive about touching the ring that, as she watched, seemed to change color slightly, taking on an almost orange hue – reflection from the sun on the shiny surface as she turned her head she decided. She put her hand down without touching it.

"Ben," she said intending to ask about the strange ring that looked out of place on his hand.

"Yes?" a heavy and sleepy voice said. She knew that voice and pictured his closed eyes above her.

"I love you." She would ask about the ring later.

"I love you, too," his sleep-filled voice said, and his breathing got deeper and more rhythmic.

Christy lay on his chest, watched the dark grey, late winter ocean, and wondered if she had ever been this happy in her life.

CHAPTER

13

Ben walked along the narrow path in his sweat pants and "Duck-Inn Summer Beach Party" T-shirt. He had no delusion this time that this was anything but a dream, but still felt glad he had pulled on a pair of running shoes as he left their wood deck and stepped off into the purple light of the jungle. The sun had set, or nearly so, and the soft remnant of the day did little to illuminate the path, but his eyes acclimated quickly, and anyway he knew the way. What had drawn him out of Christy's arms and back to the jungle he tried so hard to forget? He knew the answer but still couldn't come up with it. Hadn't it been the voice – the child's voice? The words had sounded strange and foreign, but he knew it called to him – an invitation more than a pleading.

So he followed the path he knew would lead to the voice.

To Jewel?

Come see me, Father. We need to tell you something.

Knowing he dreamed did little to curb his anxiety as the smell of cook fires reached him and the brush beside the path thinned. He approached the clearing and the village slowly and prayed it was the village as it should be, not as it had been the last time he had seen it.

Ben pushed through the last few leafy branches and broke into the clearing, the smell of the cooking pots and fire now strong and pleasant. Only a few villagers milled about the clearing, and he could see much better now, the village lit as it was by the glow of several fires. A blur of motion caught his eye.

Father!

Jewel ran to him on wobbly toddler feet, arms stretched up towards him. The voice in his head sounded so much older than the baby girl who weaved towards him. That was just the way with dreams, he supposed. Ben took two long, grown-up steps towards the girl and then scooped her up into his arms. Jewel burrowed into his neck, and the soft, sweet smell of her seemed too wonderful to be a dream.

"Da be doo," she chattered and laughed the music that comes from children in every country.

I missed you, Father. There is so much still to do.

The older voice in his head sounded no less real, which a curious part of his mind wondered about, but mostly he felt happy to hold her. He pulled her face up by the chin so he could see her. She grinned and patted his cheek.

"I missed you, too, Jewel. Are you okay? Are you safe?"

I am safe in our home. We need you.

Jewel squirmed with the universal "put me down" twisting, arms up, that every child knows, and Ben bent and put her down beside him. She seemed so tiny, looking up at him from below knee level, and Ben felt a wave of regret and shame wash over him. He should have done more. He should have found her and brought her home to his life with Christy. His vision of the girl in his dream blurred as his eyes rimmed with tears. He wondered if his Jewel was even still alive.

I am well, Father. We will be together soon.

He looked down at the smiling face and took her outstretched hand. She turned and began to toddle across the clearing of the village, and he went with her, slightly stooped over so he could hold her hand. After only a few steps he knew where she would take him – far to the southwest corner of the village. He felt his pulse pound a loud protest in his temple. Seeing Jewel was hard enough – the rest of it he really needed to be able to put behind him. He needed to leave it behind so he could start his new life with Christy. Jewel didn't seem to care about that and tugged him behind her.

The old man sat squatted on his haunches on the brown mat of woven reeds and prodded gently at a steaming bowl of dark brown mush. He looked at least twenty years younger than the man he had seen in real life, and his head and throat were unblemished by the gaping wounds from before. Ben thought he saw a faint hint of glowing blue light around his head and neck, but it went away when he looked more closely. The Village Elder looked up at him with soft, kind eyes and smiled the broad, brown-toothed smile Ben remembered very well. The little girl let go of Ben's hand and scrambled into the old (young) man's lap.

The man spoke rapidly but softly in the language Ben remembered but still didn't understand, and the girl hugged him, slipped off his lap, and toddled away toward a long, low shack with brightly colored cloth hanging from poles along its corners.

Sit, Ben.

The man motioned with long, sallow fingers and another brown smile. Ben sat down cross-legged on the edge of the mat across from the elder. He felt his hands shake a little and reminded himself again that this was just a dream. His subconscious still must be searching for closure on all of this, and hopefully he could find it in this fantasy. He practiced his four-count tactical breathing and felt his pulse slow.

Dreams are reality, Ben. Gammy taught you that, but you would have known it anyway.

I need to get past this – past you. I need to get on with my life.

Yes, Ben. This is a big part of your life, though, and always has been. You have always known this.

I can't do this. I have to go back.

Ben rose to his feet and looked sadly at the man who still squatted on the mat.

I'm sorry.

The old man smiled again, his eyes light and young.

You have no need. The cycle of the Living Jungle is not something you control, and all is as it must be. You must go back to the beginning, Ben. There you can find the final answers and the path to your destiny.

The beginning? Ben felt his pulse rise again, and his stomach tightened. He could not possibly go back to that morning in the village. He couldn't possibly watch that horror again. He squeezed his eyes shut tightly and with all his might willed himself away from his dream and back home to Christy. He felt the air around him vibrate as he seemed to float and rise up and out of his misty shroud. Far away, below him it seemed, though, with his eyes closed he couldn't be sure, the old man's voice followed him but faded into far away.

When you get there you will find a guide. A face that is familiar and unfamiliar. The answers are there if you find the questions. Look back and ask them, Ben. Then, you will be ready.

The voice drifted farther away and disappeared. The vibrations stopped. Ben slowly and cautiously opened his eyes. He saw trees above him and felt the hammock rock softly beneath him. He reached behind him for Christy and her hand but felt only more hammock. He rolled over.

Ben lay alone and something felt immediately wrong. Why were there trees above him? The smell – the sweet but musty smell of water and rich earth – came to him and, with it, a flash of remembered emotions. He swung his legs out of the hammock and looked around. Right where it should be he saw the ramble shack house with its soft glow from half open windows. He smelled the smoke which, invisible in the dark, he knew curled from the leaning chimney on the roof. He knew exactly where he was.

And when.

This nightmare he knew, and he made no effort to fight it. Years had taught him he would awaken only when released by the power of the dream and so he hopped out of the hammock and walked briskly along the path through the Louisiana bayou. Better to just hurry and get it over with. He followed the worn trail and after a moment the soft glow from the clearing up ahead. He stopped at the edge of the clearing and took a deep breath. Then, he walked boldly into the glow of the camp fire.

No matter how many times he came to this dream it did nothing to lessen the shock each time he saw his grandmother. Gammy – who had bathed him and rocked him to sleep, read him stories and told him Santa made special presents for children of the bayou – stood naked in the clearing. Her bare feet shifted back and forth, ankle deep in the lake of blood, her arms stretched out and upward. Her left hand gripped the handle of the long, curved knife, and blood ran from the bone-colored handle down her arm and across her old and wrinkled breast. In the darkness, the spatters of blood on her face and body looked almost purple. A few feet away the mutilated deer twitched with the last bit of life it had and raised its head to look at him.

The eyes were small and shaped nothing like big doe eyes. They were blue and human-looking and seemed freakishly small and out of place set deep in the deer's face. The tongue that protruded from the deer's mouth seemed thick and swollen and, as always, made the words that hissed out, impossible to understand. This time they seemed weirdly familiar – not from past dreams, but from somewhere else. The blue eyes flashed orange and then turned grey and lifeless. The deer's now dead head fell into the lake of blood with a splash.

An animal scream from his Gammy's throat shattered the night, and then she babbled more unfamiliar words. Then, she dropped her head and looked at him. She stared a moment at him with eyes that glowed red, like the last embers of a hot fire, and she extended a bloody and bony finger towards him and screamed again.

* * *

Ben felt relief that this time the scream he heard in his dream did not come from his own throat, but he snapped his eyes open anyway, his fingers sore where they gripped tightly the rope edge of the hammock. Inches away from his face, Christy smiled at him and reached out a soft hand to stroke his cheek.

"Hi," she said softly.

Ben smiled and swallowed away the remnants of the dream (dreams) and reached up and pressed her hand to his lips.

"Hi, yourself," he said and felt his breathing slow.

"Bad dream?" she asked but they both knew she knew the answer. They had been together a long time.

"Yeah, kind of," he said. Why did he always say that? "What time is it?"

"A little after twelve," she said.

Ben stretched out his back, knotted and sore from the tension of his mystical excursions, and tried to appear casual and normal. He turned to Christy again and kissed her softly on the cheek which brought his favorite smile to her face.

"Wanna go for a walk?" he asked.

"Sure," she said but didn't move to get up. "Are you sure you don't want to nap a little more? You traveled so long and so far."

Ben smiled at her constant concern for him. He used to ask about the paradox – the way she worried incessantly about little things like naps and surfing when the water was too cold, but never said a word or batted an eye about him jumping out of a helicopter into the ocean at night with a full combat load. She would just shrug when he teased her about it and told him she could only control the things she could control, and the other things were just who he was.

"I feel pretty good," he said. "Slept on the plane."

"Okay," she said. He guessed she had learned the futility of trying too hard to take care of him. "Want me to grab two beers?"

"Do we have any champagne?" he asked.

Christy laughed out loud.

"Why on Earth would we have champagne?" she chuckled. "I can't get you to even try red wine."

Ben laughed, too. "Well, if we're gonna be an old married couple, we gotta start drinking old married couple stuff," he said and caressed her face.

"Is that what you think married people drink? Champagne?"

Ben shrugged. "Maybe. Isn't it?"

Christy laughed again and shook her head as she swung out of the hammock. "I'll grab us some beers," she said and disappeared through the screen door. Ben swung out of the hammock, as well, and smiled again. He wondered if he had ever been this happy. For a moment, he flashed on the old man's eyes and the smell of Jewel against his neck, but shook it off.

Maybe that dream will close the chapter. I feel terrible about a lot of what happened, but it is what it is. Time to move on.

"Your beer, old soon-to-be married man," Christy said as the screen door banged shut behind her. Ben decided the dream had been his farewell to the haunting from all that had happened in Africa. He took the cold beer from Christy and then took her hand and led her down the three wooden steps to the beach.

They walked for a while and sipped the ice cold, frothy liquid, the clear sky and bright sun warming their skin against the chill in the air. Ben watched the waves roll gently on to the sand and thought for the ten thousandth time how lucky they had been to find this town house on the beach. He loved these walks together.

And, we'll do them forever.

He smiled and squeezed Christy's hand, and she looked over at him, her eyes happy. He took a swig of cold beer.

"So how do you wanna do this?"

She flashed a seductive smile at him and grabbed his butt after looking around. "Do what?" she asked coyly.

He laughed.

"You're hard to satisfy," he said.

"Nah," she said and sipped her own beer. "Just like to get satisfied again and again."

"I'm talking about the wedding," he said.

Christy squeezed his arm and laughed again. "Who are you?" she asked. "And what have you done with Ben Morvant?"

"I'm serious," he said. "I want to get married like yesterday, but I want it to be perfect for you."

"That's my SEAL," she said. "The decision is made, so it's time to plan the op and execute, right?"

Ben shrugged and laughed good-naturedly at himself.

"I guess that's about right. So do you want a big wedding, a little wedding, church wedding – What?"

"Okay," she said and stopped. She plopped down in the sand and patted the beach beside her. "Let's talk about it then."

Ben sat beside her and took her hand again.

Now we're talking. Let's get this thing organized and move along.

"Okay," he looked at her expectantly.

"Okay," she said and her eyes danced with happiness. "I know you don't want a big wedding…"

Ben raised a hand and opened his mouth to protest, but she cut him off.

"and neither do I," she reassured him. "I don't need a church wedding, but I want a minister to give us a Christian wedding. I would like our friends there, and I want to fly my mom down." Ben looked at her and waited for more, but she just smiled and raised her eyebrows.

"That's it?" he asked.

"That's all I need," she answered.

Ben shrugged. No wonder he loved her.

"I thought women dreamed their whole lives about their wedding day."

"Not this one," Christy took a long pull on her beer. "I have been dreaming for a while about the man I would marry and spend my life with, and you've already given me that."

Ben poked the sand with his feet. There must be more to plan than this.

"Where will we do it?"

"How about the beach behind the lodge over at the Officer's Club on base?" she asked. They had been to a retirement party there a few months before the last deployment. It would be perfect.

"Perfect," He looked at her and squeezed her hand. "What will you wear?"

Christy laid her head on his shoulder and kissed his hand.

"I'll buy a nice dress,"

"A wedding dress?"

"If you like," she said and looked up at him. "It'll have to be on sale, off the rack, and fit perfectly to meet our timeline."

"Which is?" Ben asked. He wanted time to put it together but really would love it to be tomorrow.

"Two weeks?" she asked. "Is that enough time for you to be sure?"

He hugged her tightly.

"I'm already sure," he promised. "I'll barely be able to wait that long. Can we get it all together by then?"

"Sure," she said. "What's to do? We order some food, get my mom a ticket, and tell a few friends where to be." She pulled her head from his shoulder and kissed his cheek. "The rate limiting step will be giving your teammates enough time to get some clean clothes together," she laughed at her own joke.

"We'll do dress uniforms," he said. "Everyone keeps one of those squared away, just in case."

Christy turned away and looked out at the ocean, and he wished he hadn't said that. They both knew what those dress uniforms were kept pressed and in plastic for. They had been to three ceremonies for fallen comrades together since they met. After a moment the awkward silence melted away, and he shooed it farther by taking her hand and pulling them both to their feet.

"Come on,"

"Where are we going?" she asked.

"We gotta go get you a ring," and hugged her again.

"Okay," she said with little girl-like excitement in her voice.

They walked back down the beach at quick pace towards their town house, hand-in-hand.

CHAPTER
14

Reed tipped back the Bud Longneck and wondered if everyone felt this way on the first day or two. That detached feeling – like being the new kid in school, a feeling he knew well after growing up a Navy brat – usually stuck with him for a couple of days and just felt so wrong when he was surrounded by people he loved. And, he really did love these people.

His dad smiled at some joke he had just made, and Reed tried to laugh appropriately and hoped no one could tell how far away he was. They had been close for the last four or five years after a long and bitter period after his mom had given up and left. Reed had been in high school, and Dad had been retired for two years or so. Reed believed now the retirement had been the death of their marriage. Not that it had been great before that, but the time away at sea, and more important the homecomings, had always been just enough to fan the dying embers his parents seemed to have left. But once Dad was home every day – well, he guessed they learned some things about each other and their marriage that neither liked.

The waitress approached, and Reed raised his nearly empty bottle. "Sure," she said. "Anyone else?"

"Another round," Dad said, and three other heads nodded.

"And, some more fried oysters and bread," his brother Carl added. Reed liked Carl a lot more since he had met Caroline, the pretty girl beside him. There had always been a strain with his brother – they were as different as night and day and had been since they'd been little kids. But after Reed graduated from high school and joined the Navy, things had gotten even worse for a bit. Reed always thought it had been because his brother was in college and had become a pacifist of sorts while Reed was training to be a killer in the Navy SEALs. September 11th had changed all that, and Reed would always remember the night his brother had hugged him and told him through tearful sobs how proud he was to be his brother. Reed had just gotten back from Afghanistan.

He shook his head and tried to dial back into the conversation. Dad's girlfriend Jessica, whom he had reluctantly admitted to himself about a year and a half ago that he liked a lot, had said something about the news. Reed looked up but was relieved to see eyes focused on Dad and not him.

Just a few days and the depression and constant emotional reminiscing will go away.

"What do you think, Rocky?" his dad asked.

Reed shook off the twinge of annoyance. He had decided a while ago to not let the nickname bother him. He didn't mind the name, but to him it belonged to Mom. Just as he opened his mouth to sheepishly admit he had no idea what the hell they were talking about, an Aerosmith song chirped from his belt and saved him the embarrassment.

"Excuse me just a second," he said, hopeful he concealed his relief. He snapped his cell phone out of its holster and headed to the door. He felt even more relief to see Ben's name flashed on his phone and not some other non-team person who would make him feel awkward and out of place.

But just for a couple of days. Probably the other guys feel this way, too.

"Whassup, bro," he said into his phone as he stepped out into the chilly air. He stuck his finger in his ear to block the roar of an FA-18 fighter jet that roared in from the ocean across the street, headed to a landing at Naval Air Station Oceana only a few miles away. The tremendous noise drowned out what he thought he heard. "What did you say?"

"Fuckin' fighter jocks," Ben's voice said through the phone. Reed heard a lightness and little boy happiness in the voice that made him feel great. He had been worried about his friend all day, he realized.

"Screw that," Reed said, still unsure what he had heard. "What did you just say?"

"We're getting married," Ben said again with a happy laugh. "We're at the jewelry store right now picking out rings."

Reed closed his eyes and felt a big grin spread across his face. He couldn't have gotten happier news.

"She just couldn't wait for me any longer, huh?' he said. "Tell her I'm sorry – I'm just not the settling down type. She understands, right?"

He heard Ben talking away from the phone, telling Christy what he had said. He pictured her laughing and rolling her eyes, and he realized he might love her almost as much as his best friend.

"She says she's going to try and console herself with a night of meaningless sex with me," Ben laughed, and he heard Christy squeal her good-natured protest in the background. "I want you to be my best man, bro."

Reed felt a tightness in his belly – a good one like when you try and pretend the happy ending of a chick flick doesn't matter to you.

"Of course, man. No friggin' doubt," he said. "You guys got a date figured out yet?"

"Yeah," Ben said. "Two weeks – well, two weeks from tomorrow. You're schedule open?"

"I'll see if I can pencil you in," Reed said, his head whirling a bit. Jesus, two weeks? "Wanna make sure she doesn't have time to change her mind, huh?'

"Something like that," Ben chuckled. "Were you planning some leave for out of town?"

"Nah," Reed said. He had thought about a week of fishing at the condo some of the guys owned together in Hatteras, but that would sure as hell wait. "Where the hell am I gonna go?"

"Right," Ben said. Christy giggled about something in the background. "Hey, dude, as your first official best man shitty job, can you do me a favor?"

"Anything," Reed said and meant it.

"Can you get the guys together for a beer call tomorrow night at Tunaz? Bros and Bras," he said, meaning the team and significant others.

"Yeah," Reed said. "Easy day. How about like eight o'clock. Do it early before the bar gets silly."

"Awesome," Ben said. "Don't tell anyone, okay? Christy and I will announce it together. I just wanted you to know first."

Reed felt a lump in his throat at that.

Stupid, girly, post-deployment emotional bullshit.

"Thanks, man," he said. "That means a lot."

He closed his phone and stood a moment and looked out at the ocean across the street. In the distance, he saw another fighter jet approaching on a magic carpet of black smoke and ducked back into the restaurant before the noise caught up with the image.

Two weeks. Wow, that seemed quick. He knew of no one that belonged together more than they did, though, so why not? He decided he felt more happy than worried now and headed back to the table to try and keep his mind back in the silly conversation and out of the shitty little village full of dead women and children they had left behind in Africa.

CHAPTER
15

Ben had wanted to take her to Aldo's, a fancy and fairly expensive restaurant not far away, but to her it made more sense to celebrate where they would feel at home. Chix Beach Café was a comfortable walk from their house and a familiar haunt where the waitresses knew them by sight if not name, and they could relax and be themselves. She felt a little self-conscious about the ring on her finger – a simple one-carat solitaire in a white gold setting. Ben had picked out a ridiculously large rock surrounded by other stones, but it wasn't really her and it would have taken a decade to pay it off. In the end, she had convinced him it wasn't just the money – she really liked the simple ring better – it was more her. She stole a self-conscious glance at it under the table. She really did love it. She did her best not to stare at it. They knew people here, and Ben really wanted their friends, and especially his team, to hear it from them together tomorrow night.

She looked around nervously and laughed at herself a little – a girl caught trying on her mommy's things. A lot of team guys lived in Chix Beach, and word would travel fast. She kept her left hand under the table and reached for her wine glass. When she looked up she saw that Ben watched her, love and a smile on his face, and she blushed.

"Happy?" he asked.

"More than I could have imagined," she admitted with a smile that almost burst out of her.

She had thought she would be immune to the giddiness of the moment, but the little girl dreams of engagement rings and fairy tale weddings had caught up with her and caught her off guard. She was almost dizzy with excitement.

"Feelin' pretty happy myself," her fiancé said and took a tentative sip at his glass of wine. She had picked a Pinot Noir, thinking a lighter wine might be a better introduction. She had given up trying to convince him that he didn't have to start liking wine just because they were getting married. Ben raised his eyebrows instead of wrinkling his nose – a good sign she guessed. "Hey, that's not bad," he said. "I thought it would be all sweet or something, but that's kind of good."

"You can have a beer, Ben," she stifled a laugh. "Lots of married people drink beer."

"I know," he said with more chuckle in his voice than defense, but still a hint of both. "But you like it so it might be fun if I liked it, too."

Ben had always had a heart of gold – a sensitivity that sometimes seemed out of place in his world. She had come to the conclusion long ago that maybe all of the team guys had a little more of that than they showed in public. Still, Ben was different than his teammates in a lot of ways.

The waitress interrupted her musing with a big tray of food.

"We're all glad you're home, Ben," she said and slid a plate full of oysters, shrimp, and crab legs between them. "Christy is always happier when she's in here with you."

"Thanks," Ben said. She knew how uncomfortable the attention made him. "Good to be back."

"You guys need more drinks?"

"I'll have a beer, I think," Christy said, intent on saving Ben from himself. "Blue Moon?"

"Sure," the waitress – Melissa she thought her name was – said. "How about you, Ben?"

"I'll have another one of these – the red wine," a proud smile crept across his face.

"Sure, it was a Cab, right?"

Ben looked a little uncomfortable and raised his eyebrows at her to rescue him.

"Pinot," Christy smiled back. "It was the La Crema. Actually, maybe I'll stick with wine, too."

"You want to just get a bottle, then?"

"You bet," Ben chimed in loudly. "A bottle of the La Crema."

Christy smiled again as her insides swirled with warmth.

They dug into their seafood and salad and sipped their wine, which Ben really did seem to enjoy (or else he had become a much better actor than the man who had left for deployment). Neither would surprise her. There seemed to be a few things different about her best friend – but all of them felt good.

"So what do you want to do after the wedding?" she asked him.

"Same thing we did this afternoon, but lots more times," he whispered with a little boy wink and smile.

"Well, consider that done, but I meant what after that – like the next day. Do you want to get out of town for a few days? Maybe go to the Outer Banks? We could go to a bed and breakfast up on the Eastern Shore maybe?"

Ben seemed to think hard for a moment, and then his eyes reflected a new thought.

"What would you think about a couple of days in Duck and then a few days in Louisiana?" he asked.

Christy felt a little taken by surprise. Ben had never even hinted at a desire to go home. When she had asked before he had always told her his home was the teams, and he had no one left in Louisiana anyway. Christy had always believed he was a little embarrassed by his very poor and humble background. He had told her a little bit about his Gammy and about what sounded like a shack in the woods where they had lived. She knew his grandmother had died when he was still in school, but she didn't even know how old Ben had been.

"Sure," she said, not sure how to ask more. "I'd love to go anywhere with you."

Maybe he just needed to reconnect with Gammy – whom she thought had really been like his mother – now that he was making a big life change. Like most things, she figured Ben would tell her more when he felt ready.

Ben shifted a little in his seat.

"I thought we could hang out in New Orleans for a couple of days and maybe just drive up home once. Kind of say goodbye to my past or something."

That struck her as a little poignant, and she took his hand.

"You don't have to say goodbye to anything. I want to marry all of you – everything about you, including all of your past. I think that trip sounds perfect." She smiled at him, and he grinned back. "Why don't we just spend our whole honeymoon down there? We can go to Duck anytime – even go for a weekend when we get back." If he needed to connect to home, she wanted to make it as easy as possible and give him all the time he needed. "New Orleans would be awesome in any case."

"Okay," Ben said and seemed a little less tense. He didn't offer her anything more, however.

He lifted his glass to his lips, and Christy again noticed the strange ring on the middle finger of his right hand. She felt certain it had been a shiny whitish color last time she noticed it, but the ring reflected no light back at her this time from its rough appearing, dark blue surface.

"That's an interesting ring," she said, hopeful he would tell her something.

"I got it in Africa," he said and dropped his hand into his lap without looking at the ring himself. He seemed nervous – an emotion she was unaccustomed to seeing in Ben. "It's – well it's kind of a complicated story."

She watched him expectantly. She felt like it was a story he needed to tell her for some reason, but she really wasn't prepared for it.

As they sipped wine and left the food relatively untouched, Ben unfolded his chilling tale. He told her they had been on a mission in Africa (even though she suspected she wasn't supposed to know even that) and some terrorists had attacked and wiped out a village before they could stop them. He told her of an old man, a leader and doctor of sorts, who had been taking care of the injured, including the little girl whom he had later called her about possibly adopting. He told her about the old man giving him the ring to thank him for helping them and how he had been killed shortly after. Ben explained that he wore the ring to honor the old man and the other villagers they had failed to save.

Christy said nothing as he laid out the tale. She knew he left out some details, some for security reasons she guessed and others so she wouldn't worry. He told enough that she knew it to be much worse than what she heard, and the tears that rimmed his eyes told her how deeply it had affected him. The ring made a lot more sense to her now.

"None of our guys got hurt?" she asked.

"No, not really," but his eyes told her something different. She accepted it, anyway. "Everyone is home in one piece. Auger got a scratch in the village, and Reed got his leg tore up a few days later, but he's almost fine now."

"Almost fine?" She felt a wave of concern for his best friend.

"Yeah," Ben said and reached for a crab leg, as much to move them away from the conversation as anything she suspected. "No permanent damage. Just a little hobble for a few weeks."

She nodded her head and thanked God that Ben and his friends were alright. She wondered for a moment if she could live like this for her whole life.

Of course, I can. I love him so much, and this is part of who he is, not just what he does. He wouldn't be Ben if he did anything else.

"I'm so sorry, baby," she said and took his hand again.

Ben just shrugged, like he always did, and took another sip of wine.

My quiet warrior.

They ate for a while in silence. She had learned the importance of quiet when he had moments like this. After a few minutes, he seemed to relax.

"I'm glad I told you."

"You can tell me anything," she said with a smile and not just because she knew there was a lot more to the story than he had shared. Maybe he would tell her more in time, and she would understand the quiet storm clouds in his eyes.

"I know," but he offered nothing more. "We should stay a few days in the Quarter and then maybe drive east and find some quiet beach places to hang out and have a lot of sex," he said, announcing the end of any conversation about Africa.

"That sounds wonderful," and she meant it. "We can get online and make some reservations when we get home."

"After we call your mom"

"After we call my mom," she agreed.

They settled slowly back into the excitement of their big plans and the new life they were starting.

The clouds in his eyes softened, but never really dissipated, and as they chatted she stole another glance at the ring which reflected back a soft rainbow of light from its shiny, bone-white surface.

* * *

Ben woke from a very comfortable sleep with the sense he had traveled somewhere but no memories of anything except a great evening and night in their bed that ended with them falling asleep on sweat-soaked sheets, arms and legs tangled together and faces inches apart. He stole a glance at his feet which stuck out from the sheets as his body searched for cool air and felt relief that they looked clean and unmarked. Then, he felt stupid for thinking they might have been anything else.

He wrapped his arms around the woman he loved, her soft naked body mostly hidden beneath the covers she needed for warmth as much as he needed the air to be cool. He kissed the back of her neck and burrowed against her, the feel of her skin suddenly more important than a comfortable temperature. She sighed in her sleep in response to his kiss.

"I love you," he whispered.

He felt bad he had not told her more about Africa and the ring, but how could he? He had told her what he needed to tell her for her to understand his bond to Jewel, the old man, and the ring on his finger. How could he tell her the rest – the things he wasn't sure he believed himself? She had agreed to marry him, a man hardly worthy of such an incredible woman. It didn't make sense to scare her off with bad dreams, fantasies, and confusing nightmares from a childhood he had tried to forget and bizarre stories of magic rings and strolls through the jungle in his sleep with a dead witch doctor.

It was behind him now, anyway.

Why worry her?

* * *

"Congratulations, brother," Chris said and clapped him hard on the back, his signature Maker's Mark on the rocks swirling in his other hand.

"Thanks, boss," Ben said.

He realized how silly it had been to try and keep things under wraps. He figured as soon as Reed called them and told them Ben had asked for a beer call at Hot Tunaz with significant others, that all of them knew the deal. What the hell else could it mean? Every important announcement they had in their lives took place right here in this bar. Past Chris he watched Christy show her ring to Chris's wife Emily and felt warm inside at her obvious pride and excitement.

"Two weeks, huh? Jesus, dude you don't screw around," Chris said and sipped his drink.

"Can't risk her having time to think it over," Ben said, paraphrasing what Reed had told him when he heard the news.

"Excellent point," Chris chuckled.

"Sorry for the short notice," Ben said. "We'll both understand if anyone can't make it."

"Don't be an idiot," Chris said with a hint of annoyance. "Where else would we be on your wedding day? We're a family, man, anyway, welcome to the club – you should probably be the president."

"What club is that?" Ben asked with a wry smile.

"The Married-Up-Club," Chris winked and then headed off to where Auger and Lash set up a row of shots for the team toast.

Ben felt a warmth pulse up his right hand and looked at the ring on his finger which he had been absently spinning. The surface shined back at him with almost a glow, the orange-gold surface nearly mirror like. The tingle in his finger felt familiar and much less alarming than the first time he had felt it. He thought of all the supernatural significance he had attached to the ring and almost laughed. Crazy, superstitious Cajun.

It's just a mood ring. It turns with my mood in response to temperature or moisture or some shit. I've seen the same damn thing in gift shops at the beach for two bucks.

But not really– not like this ring.

He stopped spinning the ring and for a moment tugged at it gently, suddenly intent on pulling it off and leaving it on the bar. It was time to leave Africa and move ahead. When he tugged, the ring slipped a millimeter and then his finger went cold – nearly frozen. It turned pale and grey next to his other pink and healthy fingers. The ring lost its shine, and as he watched it turn dark grey and then black. It didn't change all at once. Instead, it was as if dark grey clouds swirled across its surface, covering the sun like orange with an angry storm. The grey filled the ring and darkened until the ring looked nearly black – and his finger turned almost blue.

"Best man check," a voice beside him said, and he felt a warm hand on his neck. Ben startled, slipped the ring back into place, and shoved his right hand awkwardly into his jeans pocket. He looked up into Reed's already slightly glazed eyes. "How you doin', bro?" his friend asked.

"Great," He realized his shoulders ached with tension and forced himself to take a deep breath to a four count. "Doin' great, man. How about you?"

"I'm a little toasted," Reed admitted with a crooked smile. He looked around the bar. "Toasted and scopin' the perimeter for targets of opportunity." He raised his bottle and smiled at two girls at the bar who shook their heads, but smiled back. He turned back to his best friend. "You sure you're okay? You look nervous." For a moment his friend's hazy eyes cleared but held a critical look mixed with concern.

"Gettin' married," Ben said and chuckled. "It's my job to be nervous."

Reed laughed back. "Right you are, and my job to either talk you out of it or into not bein' nervous." He belched a little, and Ben realized Reed might be a little more drunk than he had thought. "Haven't decided which yet," Reed chuckled in a conspiratorial whisper.

Then he patted him on the shoulder and weaved his way towards the bar and the two young girls he had toasted. Ben saw he still limped pretty noticeably and made a mental note to check his wounds at work on Monday.

"Ladies!" Reed announced loudly as he sat uninvited at the bar.

Ben smiled. He pulled his right hand from his pocket and looked at his normal, pink finger and the rough surface of the bone-colored ring.

Maybe I'll leave it on a little longer. No sense in rocking the boat.

His gaze swept back to Christy who caught his eye and smiled. From across the room their eyes locked in silent conversation that warmed his heart.

I love you, baby.
I love you, too. I'm so happy.
Me, too.

He winked at her, and her smile widened. Then, he headed over and put his arm around his fiancée.

"Hi," she said.

"Hi, yourself, you havin' fun?"

"Tons," she said and sipped her wine. "I'm getting Navy wife training." She looked over at Chris's wife, and they giggled about some inside joke.

"Well, great," he muttered, not sure what else to say "Anything I should know about?" he asked Emily with a smile.

"Oh, don't worry," she chuckled. "With my help, she'll have you trained up in no time." Again the girls laughed, and Ben realized Christy might have more fun if he worked his way around the room a little.

"Well," he kissed her on the cheek, "I better let you get back to class."

"See you in a bit," she shot him a coy wink that told him this was not her first glass of wine.

Ben sauntered over to the bar and bellied up next to Auger who looked up at him and smiled.

"Ah, the victim himself," he said and then called out to the room in a louder voice. "Rally point, Viper team."

Lash, Chris, and finally red-eyed Reed all sauntered over and one-by-one Auger handed them each a shot glass of clear liquid.

"You, too, ladies," Auger called out to Christy and Emily. Lash's wife Suzanne came over, as well, from a corner table. Auger handed them each a glass. "Present and accounted for, boss," Auger said to Chris.

Chris nodded and cleared his throat.

"To the death of Ben, the demise of freedom, and the newest member of the team," he said and raised his glass.

"Christy," the men all shouted in unison and everyone tipped back their shot glasses.

"Oh, Jeez," Christy coughed. "What the hell did I just drink?"

"The first taste of the pain to come," Reed said.

"Welcome aboard," Chris said and hugged her.

Ben watched with a warm heart as each member of the Viper family hugged his soon-to-be bride. She smiled her beautiful warm smile, and her eyes, rimmed with tears and a little bit of panic, he realized his did, too.

The voices that came to him were soft whispers – not at all like the harsh shouts from the target house, but they were just as jumbled – a collage of unrelated words.

These were in the soft spoken syllables of the people he loved, and he found them easy to push to the background like a radio in another room.

CHAPTER 16

Reed ignored the burning in his thigh and pushed out two more bench presses while Ben steadied the bar above him. A Def Leppard tune blared from the stereo. The pain wasn't all that bad – at least not with the two OxyContin Ben had given him to take. The surgeon over at Naval Medical Center Portsmouth told him not to work out for a while until the skin grafts on his thigh healed, but he couldn't not work out at all, for Christ's sake. Ben had agreed he could just do some upper body stuff. His head felt a little woozy from the narcs, but it still felt good to sweat a little.

"That's enough," Ben said from above him. "You're movin' your leg around too much."

"It don't hurt much," he snapped. "You ain't my mom, bro."

Ben stared down at him with a hard and serious look.

"I am, actually," he said with a stern face. "I'm one of the only guys here who can ground your ass from ops if I think it's bad for your health, so I say that's the last fuckin' set."

Ben tossed a towel on his chest and stepped down off the short stool where he spotted him and grabbed his own towel. His friend ran and swam earlier, neither of which Reed was permitted to do, and didn't lift today. Reed wiped the sweat from his face and felt bad for being a dick. It actually hurt a little more than he thought, so maybe Ben was right.

"Sorry, dude," he mumbled to his friend.

"For what?" Ben said with a knowing smile and handed him a bottled water.

Reed swung his leg painfully over the bench and struggled to his feet. It took some effort not to grimace and prove Ben even more right. He tipped back the bottled water and chugged it down. Ben sat down on the bench next to him.

"How does it feel?" he asked. Ben stared at the bulky dressing on his leg like he had X-ray vision or some shit. Hell, it was Ben so maybe he did.

"Great," he lied, even though they both knew.

"Okay," Ben said. "Let's cool off, and then we'll go to the med shop. I'll have a look at it."

Reed said nothing. He knew better than to argue at this point. He sipped his water and found his mind wandering again to the things Auger had told him about the "Magic-Voodoo-shit" Ben had put on his bullet wound and how it had healed him overnight. Ordinarily Reed wouldn't put much stock in a story like that, but in this case he couldn't help but wonder if there really was some magic. For one thing, Auger told the story, and no one in the teams was more of a skeptic than that guy. For another, it was about Ben. Anything weird about Ben seemed likely to be true. He thought for a moment about asking if he had any of the cream left, but wouldn't Ben use it without his asking if it would help? They were best friends for Christ's sake.

Ben stood up next to him, and Reed watched his face and wondered if he should ask, but decided not to.

"Can I go to the range after lunch or I am grounded from that too, mommy?" he asked. Always the ten year old, but he didn't know how else to be.

Ben laughed.

"Yeah, you can shoot with the team later if you're a good boy when I change your dressing."

They both laughed, and he followed his friend out of the gym and into the cool, crisp air. For a moment, they walked quietly towards the med shop. Reed glanced down at Ben's right hand on a sudden impulse and sure enough his buddy still wore it. The ring he said that Christy had given him looked different now – a dull and almost metallic sheen and greenish-blue color. In his head, he flashed for a moment to the night in the target house and the weird dream about Ben and that Goddamn ring. He remembered it had glowed in the dream – a faint bluish glow – and that blue fire had shot out of Ben's fingers. For some reason the memory made him shudder – or maybe he was just cold. He looked again at the ring. It sure didn't glow now, but it didn't look at all like it had at chow that night he had asked Ben about it. It gave him the creeps, that Goddamn ring. He wished Ben would take it off, now that they were home and all.

"Still wearing your engagement ring, I see," he said. He realized he really wanted Ben to better explain why he wore the ugly thing.

"Huh?" Ben said. He seemed to emerge from somewhere else.

"That ugly fuckin' ring that Christy gave you," he said and gestured to Ben's right hand. "When you gonna stop wearin' that?" He couldn't think of anything else to say so he added "It makes you look gay."

Ben chuckled but didn't look at him. He seemed guilty or something.

"I'm kind of used to it now," he said and twirled it a moment with his other hand.

What the hell kind of answer is that?

"Makes you look gay," he mumbled again, still unable to come up with anything intelligent.

Ben shrugged, and Reed laughed at himself inside.

What the hell do I care? Ain't even the weirdest thing about him. Best friend I've ever had, though.

Ben stopped suddenly and turned to him, his mouth open like he was going to say something, but instead he snapped his mouth and smiled, his eyes sparkling. He squeezed his shoulder affectionately.

"You're a great friend, Reed," he said and then turned and opened the door to the med shop and headed in.

"Thanks," Reed said to his best friend's back.

What the hell was that?

Ben led him into one of the two cramped exam rooms and gestured to the table as he washed his hands at the sink. Reed hopped up onto the table, put his hands behind his head and laced his fingers together, and then lay back with great effort to show no signs of how much burning he now had in his thigh.

"Hey," a voice called from the doorway. Reed looked up and saw the team's Dive Medical Officer, Dr. Brandon West. "How's he doin'?"

"I'm great," Reed answered for Ben. The last thing he needed was the Doc looking at his wound and maybe deciding he needed to stay off the range or, God forbid, go on con-leave.

"He's been doing okay," Ben confirmed. "Just putting a new dressing on." From his voice, Reed guessed Ben didn't want the medical officer nosing around anymore than he did.

The doctor pouted a bit and then nodded "Okay," he said. "Let me know if you need some help."

"Will do," Ben replied quickly.

Reed guessed Dr. West was used to being snubbed a little. The team guys loved their doctors when they needed them, but mostly stayed away from them since they held the power to ground them.

It didn't hurt bad until Ben got to the part where the dressing touched his wounds, and then it stung like hell. The dressing stuck to the healing tissue, and even though Ben poured water on the gauze from a thick plastic bottle, it burned pretty bad when he peeled it off. He kept his hands laced behind his head and showed Ben nothing.

"How's it look?" he asked.

"'kay," Ben looked closely at the skin grafts that covered the huge hole. "Seems like the graft is taking well." He poked at it gently with a gloved finger and with great effort Reed stayed still. He thought again about the Voodoo cream and wondered if he should ask. "Does it hurt?"

"A little," Reed admitted. Maybe if Ben thought he hurt he would offer the magic cream.

Man I could use that cream if it works as well as Auger says.

"I don't have anymore," Ben said.

Reed looked at him a moment, puzzled.

"Any more what?"

"The cream," Ben looked confused. "Didn't you ask me for the cream I used on Auger?"

Did I say that out loud? Man, he is creepin' me out.

Ben stood suddenly upright, and his eyes darted around the small room. For a moment, he looked like an animal trapped in a garage, searching for an exit.

"Let me get some Silvadene on that graft and get you a new dressing."

Reed watched his friend fumble around the small exam room and wondered what the hell was going on with him. He was more than used to Ben's weirdness – hell, they had lived together before Christy – but this seemed more than that. He tried to decide what to say and decided to say nothing. Ben sat beside him on a rolling stool, a big white tub of vanilla-icing-looking paste in one hand and a tongue depressor in the other.

Reed watched him coat his graft with a thick glob of the icing, and then his eyes were pulled to the ring on the hand that gripped the tub. It had turned a deep and angry violet, the surface shiny and almost glowing. Reed felt nearly nauseated now at the sight of that damn thing. He resisted, with great effort, the urge to tear it from Ben's finger. The storm cloud in Ben's eyes didn't help his nausea any.

"Ouch," he said as Ben slapped another thick spoonful of the white paste onto his thigh. His mind had clearly drifted elsewhere. "Easy, dude."

"Sorry," Ben mumbled. Then, he rose and grabbed a roll of gauze and a thick dressing that reminded Reed of a Kotex Maxi-pad, only wider. He watched his friend's face as he wrapped the gauze around his leg to hold the Kotex in place. Then, he taped the end and stepped back.

"Need any more pain meds?" he asked.

"Nah, I'm good," Reed realized he wanted almost desperately to get out of the cramped exam room and, with some guilt, away from his friend.

"Okay," Ben said as if he knew exactly how Reed felt. He snapped off the icing covered gloves and tossed them into the trash. "See ya back at the shop," and then darted out, leaving the door open behind him.

Reed struggled off the table with some effort and then wiped some stray white paste from his black gym shorts.

What the shit is wrong with Ben?

For a moment, he thought about hurrying after him and asking him what the hell was up. But a picture popped into his mind of the ring and behind it a series of images from his nightmare. He again saw Ben, his eyes swirling white clouds and his fingertips glowing with blue light. The image made him shudder uncontrollably. Maybe he should talk to Chris. Maybe he should tell him how worried he still was about Ben. He thought for a moment how he would feel if Ben went to their officer about him without talking to him first and realized he would be pissed to beat the band.

Probably just needs a few more days to get used to bein' home. Hell, home is hard for me for a couple of days after an op, too. He's got a lot going on with the wedding in less than two weeks. I should just do the best man thing and help him out. He'll be Ol' Ben in a couple of days.

He wasn't sure he believed that, but it worked for now.

"How's the leg?" Dr. West asked as he hobbled down the hall.

"Great," Reed answered. He forced the hobble away and walked tall. "Shit hot, in fact."

"Super," the doctor mumbled after him in a voice that said "bullshit" and that he was getting a little tired of being the last to know.

Reed pushed through the glass door and out into the cool sunlight. He saw Ben across the grassy field that separated them from their ops building and watched as he stopped, seemed to consider something, then shook his head violently and continued on, veering at the last minute away from the team building and towards the gym. Reed frowned.

I'll give him a few more days, and if he's still all knotted up, I'll ask him about it.

He unconsciously grabbed the leg of his shorts over his wounded thigh and hobbled towards ops. He needed to get out on the range and shoot away some of his own lingering post-deployment bullshit.

CHAPTER
17

Ben woke from the dreams with a memory of only fragmented images – pictures of Jewel and the old man, of the village as it should be, and how it had been. Just jumbled pictures but no concrete memory, and to him that felt like progress. A picture flashed in his head of Gammy seated at their old table of thick wood. She ate from a bowl, the sides spattered with blood and her fingers pink with dirty nails. Then, the image disappeared with the rest.

He reached for Christy and panicked a little when she wasn't there. Then, he remembered she was with her mom at the Marriott down at the ocean front. She had wanted to spend the night with her mom before the wedding and that seemed fine – more so now, since his dreams tended to wake her up, as well. The twelve days had flown by. He had helped set up the wedding at the gazebo on base, had met with the preacher (a Navy Chaplain assigned to group two, the east coast admin command for the teams) together with Christy to outline the ceremony, had answered questions about food and music and even flowers, and still had time to fill some admin squares at work. In between, he worked out, shot hundreds of rounds at the range, and looked after Reed's wounds which looked great. Reed had tap danced around asking him if everything was okay more than once, but had seemed satisfied with his "I'm getting married" dodge.

Overall, he really felt great. The dreams, like tonight, had been fragmented and left only a slight after taste of fear. He had never been more sure and excited about anything than his wedding (in ten hours he noted with a glance at the clock) – except maybe his decision to become a SEAL.

He ignored his brains "hey, look at this" attempt to make him think about the dreams and instead hopped out of bed and padded barefoot to the bathroom to relieve himself. That mission completed, he checked (for the hundredth time) that his dress uniform looked squared away in its plastic cover and then slipped back under the cool sheets of their bed.

He pretended not to feel the pulse-like sensation in his right middle finger and forced his mind over the big day ahead instead. For a moment, he considered a quick call to Christy, but decided that she needed her sleep and tossed his cell phone back onto the night stand unopened. His eyes felt heavy anyway, so he guessed he would get back to sleep easily, and the four and a half more hours until his alarm went off would help him a ton.

Sleep wrapped around him and he floated down into it – a warm pool of comfortable darkness. He drifted, dreamless, away from home and his troubling thoughts.

"Wakin' up, now boy. We get only dis here minute be talkin' 'bout dat meetin' we get to be havin', know it."

Ben blinked his eyes open and stared up at the half moon, low and bright through the branches above him. It felt like he had fallen asleep only seconds ago, and he closed his eyes again for a moment, thinking he could drift away to a better dream maybe, but he felt a sharp, jarring pain in his side. He sat up and looked to his left.

The man grinned a nearly toothless grin, and the eyes that looked him over seemed strangely young and bright set as they were in a face of a thousand wrinkles. The man was probably the age of the Village Elder, but looked a hundred years older. He set the cane, not much more than a thick, gnarled stick actually, into the ground in front of him and leaned forward on it to support his hunched and twisted frame as he spoke. The accent was thick with home, and Ben doubted anyone who had not spent at least a few years in the bayou would understand a word of it.

"'Ey lookin' bit younger dan 'spected and yo sho' do grow up bigger den me tink, sho 'neff dat." Ben could smell the stale cigarettes and moonshine, and the smell got stronger as the man leaned in so far that Ben feared he might tip over. "Yo' Gammy be right 'bout all dat grow stuff, fo' sho' neff true. Big, Goddammit!" he hacked out a laugh-cough and then spit a big glob of snot into the dirt beside Ben's hammock. The old man recovered from the coughing fit and then went to poke at Ben again with his cane, but Ben grabbed it and held the tip away from his aching side. The old man snatched it away, but laughed a wracking laugh again. "Best be gittin' a move on, Bennie. We got not so much of da' time tin' and we get places for."

The old man turned with surprising balance and headed off down the familiar path in the woods beside the ramble shack house Ben doubted still stood in real life. He swung his legs out of the hammock and dropped his bare feet onto the soft moss of the forest floor.

That the old man moved so quickly came as no surprise – dreams always had their own confusing tempo. Christy had told him once she believed dreams were the mind's way of cleaning house, and he hoped that was true. He had always felt them to be more of a haunting, but maybe some were meant to clear the ghosts out of the attic in his mind, and this kind of felt like that.

The clearing where Gammy usually stood naked, ankle deep in blood, and stark white in the moonlight now held only a wide and irregular patch that seemed strangely devoid of the moss and weeds that made up the rest of the forest floor. The old man looked back at him over a bony shoulder, his eyes a yellow glow, and gestured at the patch of ground with the twisted cane that had left a bone-bruise soreness in Ben's rib cage.

"Strange night, dat, hey?" he said. "Yo' Gammy sho neff' done beat down dem demons dat day, boy." He released a high-pitched squeal of a laugh that again brought on a convulsion of coughing that stopped him and bent him over, one hand on his cane and the other on a bent knee. Ben caught up and put his hand on the old man's back. Through the thin fabric he felt thick sinewy muscle wrapped over brittle bone. He could feel the vibration of the coughing deep inside the man's chest.

"You okay?" he asked and pulled his hand away from the cold body.

The man stopped coughing and turned his head up towards him, the glowing eyes and wide, maniacal smile out of place.

"Been long time far away from okay, sho 'neff dat." He spit a thick wad of blood-streaked snot onto the ground between them. "Guessin' I seein yo' Gammy soon nuff quick. Dat crab been eatin' way dem lungs fas'r'n we hope, guessin' me. Meet yo soon, den next day maybe be movin' dat home place." The man coughed again, this time with more control, then straightened up and leaned again on the cane. "Few mo' tins to be showin' you here, den maybe home, sho 'neff." This time the smile seemed less chilling.

In a blink (because of the nature of dreams?) the old man moved again with animal-like speed through the brush and trees. The cane beat rapidly on the forest floor beside him as he seemed to almost glide through the woods. Ben felt his breathing quicken and a glow of sweat spread across his face and neck. How in the shit did the old man move so fast?

Dreams. Anything can work in a dream, man. Just roll with it, and let it clean the attic.

"Pay da way to here, Bennie Boy," the old man said without turning around. "Yo gots ta findin' dis path you own self, sho 'neff true."

The man had stopped and gestured now with his cane, pointing at a break in the trees like he gave a lecture and it was his pointer. Ben hustled to catch up and stopped beside the small, hunched figure who could not possibly have moved as he did through the woods. The break in the brush was little more than a dark hole, and Ben felt his heart quicken, though he had no idea why.

Because dreams scare you for reasons you need a fuckin' shrink to figure out, and they probably just make their explanations up. Because a dream about a furry bunny can wake you in a sweat with your pulse pounding and a dream about getting hacked to death can leave you feeling nothing. That's just dreams. Roll with it, Bennie boy.

He leaned past the old man's hunched figure and strained to see into the dark, tunnel-like path. He now saw the floor of the path was actually more of a little stream. Thick, black water trickled along in a thin line between thick mangrove trunks that clutched the muddy ground like skeleton claws, digging in hard to suck out every drop of moisture. The mangroves bent inward along the path, forming a twisted ceiling that closed the tunnel completely. Ben felt a cold breeze that sighed out of the path and brought to him a scent – bad and familiar. His brain refused to remind him where he had smelled it before. He knew one Goddamn thing – he had no intention whatsoever of hunching over and goating his ass down this path that seemed to dive downward a few yards in, dropping like a black rabbit hole.

"Yo get to here, and den go alone. Mos' true important, dat, Bennie boy. Alone, fo sho' neff, yeah? Jess you, boy."

Ben peered again into the dark hole in the forest. He had no intention of ever climbing down this wet, woody asshole in the woods.

"I don't think so," he said with a nervous chuckle and pulled back from the clearing in disgust.

"Not now time, dick-hole," the old man said with voice full of annoyance, like he talked to an insolent child who was slow and thick. "You be knowin' when time to go be. Dat udder one tell you, mos' probly like. Dat one like dem old time people but far away."

Ben had no friggin' clue what the old man could possibly be talking about. Was the other one from far away the elder – the giver of the cursed ring that pulsed now with an electric heat on his right hand? He heard a wet rattle, and the ancient, ill man beside him spit again, this time more blood than snot. Then, he laughed that squeaky laugh.

"Yo be knowin' when da need time come, sho 'neff dat. Yo Gammy givin' yo dat shine long, long moons ago, boy." Ben looked into the eyes that no longer glowed and again looked young and bright. "Jess 'member how yo' find dis path here when da need time be get here, 'kay?"

"kay," Ben answered, not sure what else to say.

The old man smiled that crazy smile, and the glow returned to his eyes.

"Be seein' ya few days mo'," he said and then with lightning speed he thrust forward with his cane and struck Ben painfully in the middle of his breast bone.

Ben stumbled backwards over a mangrove root, lost his footing, and felt himself pitch past the point of no return. Before his ass hit the ground, the world turned dark and he fell for longer than it should have taken to hit the forest floor, and he screamed in terror.

He hit the ground – a hard ground not even remotely touched by soft, ass-saving moss – with a crack and felt a jarring pain run up his right hip and into his back.

"Shit," he hollered, interrupting his guttural scream, and flayed out his arms in search of a branch before his head hit whatever rock his rear end had found. His fingers clutched around something soft, and he continued on down, his head smacking hard onto the wood floor of their bedroom. The comforter in his grip floated gently down over his head.

Ben lay there for a moment and then rolled over and pushed painfully to his knees, pulling the blanket off his face. He knelt for a moment beside the bed, his forehead against the edge of the mattress. Then, he struggled to his feet. His breast bone throbbed, and he looked down and saw the tip of a cane shaped welt in the middle of his chest.

Didn't clear out that attic much tonight.

He looked at the clock beside the bed, smiled, and felt the dream anxiety dissipate quickly. The feeling he had from the nightmare was sure as hell nothing new, and he was getting married in only eight and a half more hours to the woman of his dreams. He pumped his leg back and forth and found the painful knot in his hip worked itself out pretty easily – no real damage.

At least I won't limp my way towards Christy.

He flung himself onto the bed, lay on top of the covers, and watched the early, pre-sunrise light paint a peculiar picture on the ceiling. He ignored the memories of the night's dreams and just let himself relax into the excitement of the day ahead.

CHAPTER
18

He literally took her breath away.

Christy stared at him in awe as she walked along the wooden walkway that led across the sand to the gazebo where he waited. It wasn't just how gorgeous he looked in his dress uniform (that brought bad memories, if anything, of the other times he had worn it). She realized what made her body forget to breathe was the absolute perfect look of happiness that lit up her soon-to-be-husband's face when he saw her. She felt her hands shake a little and clutched her small bouquet of flowers more tightly to her chest.

Not nervous. Just perfectly excited.

Christy looked down at her feet for a moment in the hope that a brief look away would let her grab back control over her legs so she could finish her procession to the gazebo. Ben waited patiently for her (though she still couldn't quite look at his face her peripheral vision registered his glowing smile), flanked by Reed on one side and her best friend Amy on the other. She knew that for Amy this must feel bitter-sweet – not only had her best friend pined for marriage her entire life, but she had always had as her singular goal to marry a United States Navy SEAL.

Christy had never defined herself by any man in her life and had only reluctantly agreed (how many years ago now?) to the blind date with the friend of a SEAL (one of many) Amy had been dating. She had never been anti-military or anything, just anti-blind date. Quite honestly, had she not been friends with Amy, she would have had no idea what a Navy SEAL was. Amy had always been incredulous that her best friend had actually grown up in the Virginia Beach area, the heart of all the east coast SEAL teams, and didn't seem to know anything about them. Now she had beaten her friend to the altar and married the SEAL she had met through her. She knew Amy well enough to know that hurt her.

She thought of these things as she walked towards her soon-to-be Navy SEAL husband, and a little part of her felt bad for stealing Amy's dream. But Amy smiled a big, genuine smile as she approached, and she grinned back, mostly because she worried if she looked again into Ben's eyes she might lose it and live her worst fear for this day – crying in front of all these people, especially Ben's teammates and their tough-by-trade Navy wives.

"You look so beautiful," her mother breathed at her as she passed, standing beside her folding wooden chair in the sand. The look on her face told Christy she was sorry for being wrong about the wedding. Most of the past week her mom tried to talk her into a big church.

"What's the hurry, for God's sake?" she had asked, and then covered her mouth at the thought. "Oh Jeez, you're not pregnant are you?"

Christy had assured her that, no, she was not pregnant – just ready. She insisted this outdoor ceremony would be perfect, especially with only twenty or so people in attendance. Her mom's glowing eyes said she had been right. She flashed a nervous (no, excited) smile to her mother. Her mom dabbed at her cheeks with a tissue and mouthed that she loved her.

Christy walked up to Ben, stood beside him, and stared him squarely in the throat. She would look at those storm-filled eyes in a moment when this silly, teen-age wave of emotion past. She felt his fingers under her chin gently tilt her face up, and she stole a look. At once, she felt tears well up, a smile exploded on her face, and all of her worries about embarrassing Ben evaporated. Ben smiled down at her with wet eyes filled with more emotion than she had seen from him in all the time they had been together.

"I love you, baby," he whispered to her in a voice that quivered.

The waterworks spilled onto her cheeks, and she touched his face with the palm of her hand and nodded, afraid if she whispered back her voice would sound like Kermit the Frog, the overwhelming emotion now a tight belt around her throat. She vaguely heard the collective "Awwww…" from the women in the small group gathered to witness their vows.

"Ahem," the Chaplain, Commander Wiltshire she remembered, said to signify they might need to look at him for the next few minutes.

She reached down and took both of Ben's strong, calloused hands in hers. Her mind made a soft note that the ring still held its place on Ben's hand, its surface a soft and glowing orange and so shiny. She guessed she could see herself if she bent over. She turned to face the preacher.

Christy felt like she blinked, and the whole thing was over. She had images etched forever in her mind – the single tear that ran down Ben's cheek when he repeated his vows, the embarrassing stutter she found in her voice when she repeated hers, the hug Amy gave her when she took her flowers, and the inappropriate "Hell yeah!" that Reed bellowed when the Commander announced they were married now (man and wife, he called it). But the rest just evaporated away and even now – just minutes later as they got hugs and handshakes – she could recall almost nothing else from the ceremony. She didn't care. The images she had were hers forever, and the rest didn't matter except that she would wake up with the man she loved for the rest of her life.

Except when he's far away, God's knows where, doing terrifying things – or if he one day comes back draped in a flag.

Christy shook her head and scolded her inner voice that this was not the place or time. She knew the risk of marrying this man, but knew that she would never be happy with anyone else – that he completed her and that made the risk a no-brainer.

"Welcome aboard, sister," Chris said as he hugged her tightly.

"Thanks so much," Christy said and then hugged his wife Emily who smiled broadly.

"Congratulations," she said in her ear. "You guys look so happy."

"Thanks," she said and reached for her husband's hand and squeezed it. "I think we really, really are." The hand in hers felt warm, and she thought it tingled a tiny bit – like a vibration.

"I know you've been waiting for this," Reed said with arms open and a frat boy smile. "You didn't have to marry my loser roommate just to get a kiss from me, baby. All you had to do was ask."

Christy rolled her eyes but laughed at the familiar joke. She kissed their best friend and then hugged him tight.

"Thanks, Reed," she said.

"For what?" he asked, genuinely confused.

"For always being there for him," she whispered in his ear. She knew that kind of thing embarrassed Ben terribly.

Reed looked down at his feet for a moment and arched his eyebrows. When he looked at her again she saw perhaps the first serious face he had ever worn in her presence.

"You got it all wrong there, sis," he said, his voice a low conspiratorial whisper as he cut his eyes over at Ben who hugged Emily and laughed at some joke. "That man of yours is the best friend I ever had, and he's the one takin' care of me."

The words and Reed's soft genuine voice touched something in her, or maybe it was just the surprise at hearing any of these men show real feelings, and she felt her eyes well. "Truth is I wouldn't be here if it weren't for that crazy Cajun."

She hugged Reed again, and he patted her uncomfortably on the back.

"I love you both, sis."

He had never called her sis before today, and now he had done it twice. She liked it a lot and hoped it stuck.

And, then Reed headed off toward the makeshift bar they had arranged on the expansive deck a short wooden path away from the gazebo. Walking the plank they had called it at the retirement ceremony, and the memory made her laugh. She watched Reed a moment, worried about the obvious limp, and then looked over at her husband. His eyes caught hers and sparkled.

Then, Amy was shrieking congratulations in her ear and bouncing up and down and the moment left. But she kept it with her while they drank, laughed, and ate the little wedding cake Ben had insisted they buy.

Amy got pretty wrecked and for a while Christy worried she would hook up with Reed (and with some guilt she worried more that it would suck for Reed than for her friend). Other than that, she took away only happy memories of an afternoon with their closest friends in the world. She had never put much stock in the magic wedding day thing. To her it seemed more like the kick-off for the really good stuff – the life together. So many of her friends had wrapped themselves in the fairy tale of only that first day, and that always seemed kind of sad. So, she felt genuine surprise that this had been the happiest and most fulfilling day of her entire life.

A great start to the long life she intended with the man she cherished.

CHAPTER
19

He loved these men, but not as much as this woman. He realized he really wanted to be alone with his wife and tell her all the things the day had meant to him. Ben grinned at the thought. He must be with the right woman if she could make him look forward to talking about *feelings*.

He watched Reed slow dance with Amy, and they both stumbled around the uneven deck. No one else danced. They had some music playing, but it had been meant as background noise only. "Mood music," Christy had called it. That didn't seem to bother either of their drunken friends as they shuffled around the deck to David Gray's anything-but-dance-music sounds. He saw that each had a handful of the other's ass cheek. Ben took a sip of red wine (he couldn't remember what kind she had told him it was) and leaned over to his new wife.

"Please tell me that is not going to happen," he whispered as they watched their friends. Christy giggled.

"Oh, God, I hope not," she whispered back. "That would be a tough couple of weeks for all of us."

He laughed and looked closely at her smiling face. She felt his gaze and looked over, one eyebrow up.

"What?" she asked and sipped her own wine.

"I love you so much," he said. He couldn't believe how easily those once difficult words now came.

She batted her eyebrows at him.

"Wanna show me?" she asked her hand on the outside of his leg.

"Hell, yes,"

"Rrrrrr," she used best tiger noise. It always made him laugh.

Ben kissed her mouth and took her hand.

"Let's get out of here."

"Agreed," she answered. "One quick pass through the group to say thanks and see ya, but we gotta go consummate this thing now."

That really made him laugh, and he let her lead him by the hand through the group. More hugs and handshakes. Though he ordinarily hated any kind of attention, this didn't bother him at all. He thought maybe the fact that it meant so much to them both made his discomfort fade into the background. He watched her smile, laugh, and thank their friends. He just tagged along – smiling and hugging when it seemed the right time.

Yep, me, too – like she said.

The group followed them down the wooden walkway that led off the dunes and into the parking lot. He would have preferred they just slip away, but not much could really bother him today, he realized. Amy and Reed were conspicuously absent, doubtless still groping each other (or worse) out on the deck, but everyone else stopped at the end of the walkway. There was no rice or bird seed, but lots of waves and cat-calls as they said goodbye again.

"Are you okay to drive?" she whispered to him as they turned from the small flock of friends.

Ben didn't answer but, instead, grinned and gestured towards the parking lot.

The limousine sat with its quiet engine purring, and the driver, complete in black suit and even a black driving cap, hustled around to get the door for them. Christy stopped, and her hand went to her chest. She squeezed his arm.

"Oh, God, Ben, what did you do?" she asked. "I thought we said no more money on the wedding after we agreed to the open bar." But her voice told him *Thank you, baby, this is perfect.*

"You look like a princess or a super model or something," he said. "You should leave like one."

He escorted her to the elongated car where the driver stood nearly at attention, his hand on the door. Ben helped his wife into the plush seat and then walked around to the other side quickly while the driver closed her door. He wanted to get in before the driver tried to get his door, he realized. That might be more than he could take. He slid in beside his wife, and she threw her arms around his neck, kissing him deeply.

"Thank you, baby," she said. "This is perfect."

"Straight to the hotel or drive a bit?" the driver asked over his shoulder as he settled into his seat.

"Drive a bit," Christy answered for them both. "Is that okay?" she asked Ben sheepishly.

"Perfect," he said.

"I'll have you at the hotel in about forty-five minutes," the driver said. "Does that work?"

"It does," Ben responded.

"Alright then," the driver answered. "The champagne is already open and chilling in that bucket, and the glasses are in the panel on your side, sir."

"Thanks," Ben answered and reached for two glasses.

The driver nodded and then disappeared as a dark panel rose up from behind his seat. Then, they were alone. Ben poured them both a glass of sparkling wine, the first glass overflowing over the back of his hand and dripping onto the carpeted floor.

"Shit."

Nice – very romantic.

Christy laughed, obviously unfazed.

He held up his glass.

"To us."

"Hooyah," she shouted, and he laughed out loud at her use of the SEAL mantra.

"Hooyah," he answered back, and they drank.

He decided he preferred the red wine, but the champagne still tasted better than he had imagined. Christy laid her head on his shoulder a moment and hugged herself to his arm.

"Thank you so much Ben. You made this the best day of my life."

She turned her face up, and he kissed her. Her mouth opened, and her free arm snaked around his neck in a passionate embrace. Reed had told him (the only marital advice his best man could come up with) that he should "nail her" in the limo. The kiss nearly made him question his decision to wait – that "nailing her" in the limo might not be the best way to start off his life with his best friend. He stole a glance at the blackened panel between them and the driver and wondered if it was one way glass and the driver watched them at this very moment. The kiss ended, and he chuckled.

"What?" Christy asked with a knowing smile.

"Nothing," he smiled back.

She looked at him coyly and ran her hand up the inside of his thigh.

"We can if you want," she breathed into his ear, and the stirring in his pants said "*Hell yeah*". Fortunately, it was in Reed's voice which just made it funny. He kissed her deeply and then touched her cheek.

"Or we could wait forty five minutes and make the first time as married people last for an hour," he offered.

Christy seemed to consider for a moment and then took a long pull of champagne. Then, she shuffled her way to the front of the limo's cabin and rapped on the black panel. The panel lowered slowly.

"Yes, Ma'am?" the driver said.

"How about you make it more like twenty minutes to the hotel?" she said, looked at Ben, and raised her eyebrows three times in rapid succession.

Ben laughed as she worked her way back to him, her champagne held high and her other hand holding the top of her dress to keep the "twins" from spilling out. She collapsed next to him, her head in his lap, and she closed her eyes.

"Kiss me, husband," she commanded.

"Of course, Mrs. Morvant," and he obeyed.

Seventeen minutes later by his watch (and two more glasses of champagne which, it turned out, got better as you went along) they slid out of the limo as the driver held the door. Ben handed him a twenty and gave him the patented male of the species thank-you nod. The driver nodded back and handed him a plastic swipe card.

"Your room key, sir, and your buddies checked you in, your bags are already in the room, and they upgraded you to a suite...top floor, room eighteen-twenty-two."

"Thanks, bro," Ben said and shook the man's hand.

"I'm supposed to tell you two things," the driver leaned in with a red faced grin.

"Okay," Ben said slowly.

"Well, the first is that your airline boarding passes for the morning are already printed and in the front pocket of your backpack in the room."

"And, the second?" Christy asked with a good-natured smile.

The driver sighed. "The second is from Reed, and he said to tell you 'I knew you wouldn't nail her in the limo.'"

Christy and Ben both laughed, and the driver relaxed a little.

"Thanks," Ben shook his hand again.

A few minutes later they were in the largest hotel room Ben had ever seen (two rooms in fact – a bedroom with a little living room and kitchen). The balcony looked right out onto the ocean, and on the small table sat a huge basket of cheese, cookies, crackers, nuts – all kinds of things. Beside it sat another bottle of champagne with two long-stem glasses on which "The Morvants" had been etched, a vase full of yellow roses, and a card. Ben picked up the card. Christy went for the champagne and started to wrestle out the cork. It popped loudly and smacked into the ceiling as she giggled. Ben flipped open the card.

> *For a long and happy life together.*
> *Best of luck.*
> SEAL Team Two

"From the unit," he said.

Christy wrapped her arms around his neck and stood on her tip toes to kiss his chin.

"They're such nice boys," she nibbled his neck. Ben looked down at her. "Take me to bed, Ben," she said with closed eyes.

He kissed her and fumbled his way into the back of her dress which came off with great difficulty. She stayed in his arms, her mouth locked on his, naked as he helped her tear off his service dress uniform.

They made love for over an hour, all of it slow and gentle. Soft words of love muttered between moans and sighs. Their eyes stayed locked on each other the whole time, no matter how many times they rolled around to new positions. They ended with her on top of him, straddling him with her hands on his chest, his hands on her hips as she finally lost all control and bucked her way into an orgasm that left her crying out, tears running down her cheeks. As she tightened around him in the throes of her own finale, Ben stopped trying to wait and exploded with her, his own cries joining hers.

She collapsed on him, spent and sweaty, her face nuzzled into his neck.

"God, I love you so much, Ben."

"I know," he said and realized tears had run down his cheeks, as well. "I love you, too. Maybe more than you can ever know."

They lay that way for a long time as his hardness wilted inside her. She finally slipped off of him and cuddled into the crook of his arm, her own arm and leg draped across his still tingling body.

* * *

Ben dozed. The nap felt deeper and more refreshing than any sleep he had enjoyed in years – a gentle, dreamless sleep. He woke to a knock on the door and opened his eyes to see Christy lying with her head on his chest, her eyes open and bright. Her hand stroked his shoulder.

"Room service," she said to explain the knock. She let her hand drift downward. "I figured you would need your strength."

Ben smiled, kissed her, and then slipped out of bed to get the door. He looked around for something to cover himself with, and Christy tossed him a heavy terry cloth robe just as he noticed she had one on, too.

"Found them in the closet," she explained. "Rich people must have a truck load of robes at home from these suites."

Ben laughed and pulled the robe around him as he headed for the door in the other room.

"How long was I asleep?" he asked. "What time is it?"

"Time to watch the sunset, that's all I know," Christy called after him.

Ben looked out past the balcony and saw the sky had just begun to turn a soft pink as the sun slipped gently into the Atlantic Ocean. His mind considered a moment his deep – and more luxurious *dreamless* – sleep. It didn't feel like he had returned to normal to have good sleep. He hadn't slept well with any regularity in his entire adult life. But it still felt like a step toward normalcy. If he could have a few bad dreams about Gammy without any demons from Africa intruding, he thought he might feel fully recovered. Strange that familiar bad dreams should define normal for him. He flung open the door and greeted the young lady who stood beside a push cart.

My wife must be hungry.

The cart held five different covered plates and a bottle of red wine.

"Congratulations, sir," the woman said. "Where would you like this?"

"On the balcony," Christy answered for him as she joined him at the door. "Oooh, yummy," she said and rubbed her hands together.

"You sure, baby?" he asked. "Might be a little chilly for you."

"Nah, you'll keep me warm."

The woman rolled the cart onto the balcony. He signed his name on the ticket she handed him, and she left.

"Jeez, what did you get?" he asked.

"Everything," she answered and plopped into one of the two chairs, kicked her feet up onto the balcony rail, and grabbed the wine bottle and a corkscrew.

Ben sat in the other chair and started to pull the silver lids off the oversized plates on the huge cart. Then, he took the glass of wine she offered him and popped a shrimp into his mouth. He suddenly felt half-starved now that he saw the unbelievable collection of hot appetizers Christy had ordered for them. He began to wade with her through the collection of seafood, meats, and cheeses. He took a swallow of the wine his wife handed him which tasted heavier than the others he had tried. He liked it better, he decided.

"That's good, what is that?" He kicked his feet up on the rail like Christy and chuckled at the show they would be giving if they had not been on the eighteenth floor.

"I bumped you up a level," his beaming wife said as she popped a piece of bread covered with tomatoes and feta cheese into her mouth. "You have graduated to Cabernet. Congratulations."

Ben held it up to the setting sun. Darker than the others – just like it tasted.

They chatted and fed, grazing on the food he doubted they would finish but felt no surprise when they nearly did. Ben heard the mumbling voices, a blend of soft sounds like whispers through thin walls. He thought of them as voices, but really they were just soft sounds. They didn't really bother him anymore. He realized they had been there nearly constantly since he got home; now that he let them fade into the background of his life, they didn't distress him at all.

He even began to imagine that perhaps they had been there all along and the events in Africa had somehow just made him more aware of them. Either way, he decided, they weren't worth thinking about anymore. In fact, the less he thought about them the more that proved true. Now and again a sound would stand out above the mumbling whispers as a clear word and grab his attention, but with a little work he managed to ignore those, as well.

"Ben?"

He looked over at Christy who touched his hand and furrowed her brow.

Maybe he had a bad dream before.

That voice was clear as a bell and belonged to his wife.

"What are you thinking about, baby? Did you have a bad dream before?"

Ben took her hand and squeezed it. He gave her his best everything-is-cool smile (easier than ever because everything really was cool for once).

"No bad dreams," he said. "In fact," he took another sip of the wine which seemed to stimulate taste in his whole mouth, "I was actually thinking about the fact that I didn't have a bad dream. That cat nap was the most relaxed sleep I've had in my life, I think." He kissed her chin. "Apparently being married works great for me."

Christy smiled at that. He had found the perfect words, apparently, because her forehead smoothed.

"You are a lucky, lucky man," she sipped her own wine. "Very lucky."

"Very lucky," he agreed. Then he ran a hand up the inside of her robe. "You wanna get lucky again?"

"Maybe," she answered coyly over the rim of her glass and let her legs fall open.

They made love again. This time they started on the balcony and ended up on the floor next to the couch in the sitting room. When Christy's panting slowed to soft sighs, her head on his chest, he shifted around awkwardly to pick her up and carried her to the huge bed. She threw both arms around his neck and nuzzled against his chest, now only half asleep.

I'm the lucky one her voice said in his head, and she hugged him tightly.

He tucked her gently in and slipped under the covers beside her. He set the alarm on his watch to allow them time to get ready and get to the airport for their flight. Then, he reset it for an hour and a half earlier – they might want time for a little something more before getting out of bed, he decided with a smile. Besides, his watch showed it was barely after nine p.m.. He felt either completely exhausted or completely relaxed despite the early hour and closed his eyes, his arms around his wife.

As he drifted off, he felt a strong sense of someone waiting for him, just on the other side of closing his eyes and felt anxious. But whoever it was must have decided to let him alone on the night of his wedding, because he had his second deep and dreamless sleep of the day.

CHAPTER

20

The voices first started to get bad on the flight to New Orleans. Ben sat in the aisle seat, Christy's hand soft in his as she spoke excitedly about the things she wanted to do over the coming week. He found the sounds impossible to ignore. Overnight he had gone from a vague awareness of soft mumbles a few rooms away to suddenly sitting in the dead center of a crowded room at a party. The specifics of the speaker's words were no clearer than before. But the volume had been turned painfully up, and the frequency of recognizable words had also increased. This didn't make the voices any more understandable, of course, just way more distracting and for some reason a little more frightening.

Ben also realized he could now identify individual voices that repeated themselves in the din of competing inner dialogues he eavesdropped on. He heard a young woman, excited about something, perhaps someone she would be meeting in New Orleans. There was one old man (at least he thought of him as old) who seemed terrified, and Ben wondered if he might be sick with something bad, like cancer. Another man, much younger he thought, was just annoyed and angry, though Ben got no sense at all about what had him so pissed off.

He wondered if the close proximity of all the people packed into the confines of their steel tube hurtling above the Earth explained the change. He had noticed a little bit in the airport (which was also quite crowded, of course) but nothing like this. He also wondered if his fear that he might actually meet the old Cajun from his dream in New Orleans could be a factor (assuming the voices really were all in his head –

figuratively not literally). Perhaps his paranoid worry that the man from his dream could be real and waiting for them was worsening his admittedly baseline paranoid musings.

Thanks for all of this, Gammy. Just another crazy Cajun from the swamp.

For a moment, Ben had a short burst of clarity that maybe he didn't really have Gammy to blame. Maybe all of the insane "memories" from his childhood were products of the same chemical imbalance that had created the nightmare fantasy he currently plowed through. Maybe poor Gammy just died from the stress of raising a kid with a serious mental disorder who had now somehow found a way to control his psychosis just enough to barely function.

Ben felt a chill at the thought.

He closed his eyes and with all of his might demanded the voices shut the hell up, at least for a few moments, so he could collect himself. Amazingly the voices did fade a bit into the background.

"Tired?"

He looked over at Christy and felt relief she didn't have her I'm-so-worried-about-you forehead furrow.

"I shouldn't be," he kissed her cheek. "I guess the last few weeks are catching up."

Christy nodded and smiled. "Yeah, you had a hell of a homecoming the last two weeks, huh? Probably got more rest on your deployment, I bet." She patted his arm. "I'm tired, too."

"Best two weeks of my whole life," he told her, and she gave him the grin that melted his heart. "We'll catch up on our rest this week."

Christy laughed. "Yeah, most people think of New Orleans when they think quiet and restful vacation."

"Good point," he conceded. "But we'll only be in New Orleans for two days, right? Then, we head east to the beach?"

"Destin," she said. "It looked great on the Website. I got us a nice quiet place like you wanted."

"Perfect," he said.

As usual Christy had done the lion's share of work planning their trip. Ben had done little more than nod his approval and tell her how great it all looked. He felt like the two days in Louisiana would be more than enough to tell his haunted past goodbye, and then they could start their new life together with a few days lounging on the white sandy beaches of Florida's panhandle. Even Virginia had started to warm up to early spring weather, so he figured the Fort Walton Beach/Destin area of northern Florida would be tropical by now. It really did sound great.

As long as I don't find some big, black bunny hole waiting for me in the woods – Goddamn dreams.

The voices stayed softer but present the rest of the flight, and Ben felt great relief when they left the airplane and the din of cocktail chatter behind. A whispering background of mumbles remained, but the volume returned to a manageable level he again found easy to ignore. He felt his mood brighten immediately as they strolled up the jetway hand-in-hand, backpacks slung over shoulders.

I should kill them both. That fuckin' bitch. And Tony – Goddammit he was supposed to be my friend. I should kill them together while they're fucking in his bed.

"Excuse me," the voice in his head said out loud, and he startled at the sound moving from his head to his ears. The man pushed past them without making eye contact, his briefcase and overcoat knocking into Christy hard enough to make her stumble.

"Hey, watch out, dude," Ben snapped at the man and pushed the black leather briefcase aside.

The man spun on a heel and faced them.

"I said excuse me, asshole," the man said with hot anger, his free hand balling up into a fist. Something in Ben's eyes must have warned the survival center in the man's brain because the fire faded immediately once they were face-to-face. The man looked down. "Sorry," he mumbled and then shot back up the jetway.

Asshole. Wonder whose wife that is he's fuckin'? Who gives a shit? Not worth gettin' my ass kicked.

The man disappeared out the top of the ramp, and the voice evaporated with him.

"What the hell was that?" Christy said, rubbing her thigh where the briefcase had struck her.

"Sorry, baby," Ben said. "You okay?"

"Oh, sure," a smile replacing her irritation. "Guess he took a look at my Navy SEAL and thought twice, huh?" She took his arm again.

"Guess so," Ben wondered if the man's wife and her lover were in real danger or if those had been just angry thoughts that went nowhere. He tried for a second to reach his mind back out to the angry man, but found he couldn't. For a moment a picture of an auburn-haired woman shimmered in his head and then evaporated, but he thought maybe he had just made that up. He decided there wasn't a damn thing he could do either way and pushed the encounter out of his mind.

I'm on my honeymoon.

He took his wife's hand again.

A short time later they exited the airport in their Dodge Charger from Alamo (a man's car he had chuckled to her when they picked it from the row of choices), and he had put the airplane ride and the angry man with the cheating wife out of his head. He followed the directions the GPS called out to him (they decided the feminine, electronic voice should be named Betty) and followed the red line on the colored map. He didn't really need it. Not because he knew his way around New Orleans – truth be told, he could still get around the back wood swamps of the bayou he supposed, but had never really learned the city – but because it was easy to get to downtown or the Quarter from the airport.

His home had been a good drive away, and for poor folk of the bayou with no car to drive anywhere, it could have well been a continent away. When people asked where he was from he said Louisiana, but never claimed New Orleans, though some would argue it was the nearest civilization to their shack in the swamps.

"Feel like home?" his wife asked, as if reading his mind. The thought of her reading his mind struck him as ironic under the circumstances.

"Never did," he said. He looked over at her and smiled. "When you see where I'm really from, you'll understand."

Christy nodded.

He followed I-10 past the fork with I-610 and after only a few minutes headed south, Betty told him to take the next exit. Once off the interstate he was grateful for her help finding Dauphine Street, however, and moments later they pulled into the Dauphine Orleans Hotel. He wondered if they were closer to Bourbon Street than they wanted to be, though Christy had been told the hotel was pretty quiet for the Quarter – at least according to the Website and what she read in Frommer's. Still, the heart of the chaos on Bourbon Street looked to be only a block or two away. Ben shrugged and slipped out of the Charger and pocketed the keys.

"Checking in, sir?"

The man (he actually looked to be a boy barely old enough to drive) looked at him expectantly in what Ben thought to be a silly bellman's type uniform complete with white gloves.

"Yeah," Ben said. He hated to be called "sir." That was a title for officers, not E-Fives.

"Name?" the boy asked, his pen poised above a pad of tickets.

"Morvant," Ben said. Then, he smiled and took Christy's hand as she came around the car to join him, "Mr. and Mrs. Morvant." Christy beamed and wrinkled her nose.

"Very good sir," the boy stopped. "I have cousins named Morvant," his proper language slipped into an accent more familiar to Ben. "They from the wetlands, though."

Ben said nothing, but shifted uncomfortably. A thicker voice left the word *Cajun* floating in his head.

The man handed him a stub torn from his ticket.

"One moment, and I'll get your bags."

"I can get them," Ben said.

The boy shrugged as Ben popped the trunk and grabbed their two suitcases and slung a backpack over each shoulder. Christy smiled, and he thought he saw her shake her head a little.

"Need the keys, sir."

Ben set down a bag and fumbled in his pocket, confused.

"Valet parking," Christy said.

"What's that costing us?" he mumbled.

"Less than parking in the Quarter," the boy chimed in with a smile as he took the keys. "'Specially if you got to pay for the damages to your ride, here."

Ben laughed. "Fair enough."

He didn't mind paying to park. It was their honeymoon, after all. He just felt embarrassed for not expecting valet parking.

A few minutes later they followed the bellman (whom Ben this time reluctantly allowed to carry their bags and walk them to their room) through several quiet courtyards as he told them the colorful history of the hotel. Apparently, it had at one time been a whore house, and they could still see the bordello license over the bar if they liked. Only in New Orleans would such a thing be a source of pride, but Ben had no doubt they would take a picture of it, if for no other reason than to show it to Reed.

They stopped by the bar on the way to the room, and the bellman waited patiently while they cashed in their welcome-to-the-Daupine beverage coupons for ridiculously strong drinks of some sort (Bordello passion the bartender told them, which neither of them could resist). Ben did, indeed, see a framed certificate of some sort which he assumed to be the hooker license from owners past. They sipped the deadly liquid as the bellman led them into their patio room, overlooking one of the courtyards they had toured.

"Wow, pretty nice," Christy said as Ben handed a few bucks to the bellman.

In fact, the room looked much more modern than he expected from the dated appearance of the rest of the hotel, especially the lobby. He tapped the large plasma screen TV and grinned his naughty boy grin.

"Wonder what kind of entertainment we can buy on this?" he asked and raised an eyebrow.

"Probably nothing we can't see for free a few blocks away, if my sorority sisters can be believed," Christy said and wrapped her arms around him.

"True enough," he laughed.

Shortly thereafter, they sipped what was left of their drinks as they caught their collective breath beneath the white duvet cover after "christening the room," as his wife put it. The sex, the too strong drink, and the long flight all crashed on him at once, and he realized he felt half-starved.

"Lunch?" he asked.

"Ooh, yes, by the pool?"

"Perfect."

Ben felt the last of his tension ease away as they slipped into shorts and flip flops. Thoughts of the airplane voices, the angry man with the cheating wife, and then his fears about some crazy old man his mind made up in a dream slipped away with his waning stress.

CHAPTER

21

It turned out Bourbon Street really was only a block away, and Ben wondered if it meant he was getting old that he worried about the noise they might endure when they went to bed later. A short stroll down Court Street from their hotel found them hand-in-hand on the stone streets of the tourist center of the Quarter. They turned right and strolled a block and a half to the Old Absinthe House and found the bar without difficulty. The plaque out front told them they would have their first French Quarter drink in a bar frequented in the past by a bunch of people he had not heard of, though he knew Walt Whitman and Oscar Wilde had been writers.

The bar was far from full, but the dozen or so people there looked to have staked a claim to their stools many drinks ago. The bar itself was covered with business cards, plastered to its surface.

"In 1815 Andrew Jackson and the Lafitte brothers plotted the defense of the city from this bar," Christy said.

"Wow," Ben replied as the middle-aged woman with crazy, wild hair and a soft smile put two beers in front of them. "You really studied for this trip."

Christy laughed and held up the short flyer that told the history of the Absinthe House she had grabbed at the entrance, and Ben laughed with her. They bellied up to the bar on their stools, and Ben tried to lose himself in the Quarter atmosphere, but couldn't quite find it.

"We should walk," he said after a few minutes.

"What about our drinks?" Christy asked.

Ben laughed again. "This is New Orleans, baby," He got up from his stool. "Nobody cares if you drink in the street as long as you don't shoot or stab anyone."

Sho' 'neff true dat.

Ben looked up at the sound of the voice in his head and for a moment he saw the old man, his cane clutched between his bony knees as he sat on the bench seat along the wall, sipping a dark drink out of a tall plastic cup. Then, his lips peeled back revealing tobacco-stained teeth, and he tugged on the bill of the dirty "Purple Haze" baseball cap. Ben nodded back his own howdy before he could resist the urge. Just as his heart sped up the image shimmered and disappeared.

"Getcha some cups?"

Ben looked up at the wild-haired woman behind the bar. She stared back patiently, despite his confused look.

Fuckin' tourists.

"They rather you don't carry them bottles," she said and pulled two green plastic cups from under the bar.

"Thanks," he mumbled as she poured their beers.

Christy either didn't notice his moment or loved him enough to ignore them. She took his hand and led him out of the bar. Ben cast a last nervous look towards the bench seat where he had seen his ghost, but only an empty plastic cup sat there.

Back on Bourbon Street, Christy tugged him northeast toward the bars and restaurants and the more residential Esplanade District beyond. The sun had only just begun to set, the sky above the low buildings behind them glowing purple and the air becoming a more comfortable cool. Already the crowd on the street began to swell and they could feel the energy in the air rise. People moved a bit more quickly (or stumbled already had they failed to pace their afternoon intake), and they heard more laughter, loose and unrestrained. In the distance, he could make out the beat of a saxophone licking through a staccato improv. Just beneath it, Ben heard the buzz of voices pick up as well. But they remained within his ability to push back beneath the surface.

"Hurricane," Christy announced.

Ben looked at her confused. They had seen some remnants of the destruction Katrina had wrought, but here in the Quarter Ben saw nothing to hint at the struggle the city had endured.

"Katrina?" he asked.

"The drink," she answered with a chuckle and a slap on his arm. She pulled a tourist map card from the back pocket of her jeans. "I think it's just a few blocks this way to Pat O'Brien's." She looked up in the direction they headed. "We turn right on Peter Street, and it's like a block down," she was clearly in charge now. Ben enjoyed her enthusiasm. He suspected this was not her dream honeymoon, and he loved her even more that she made it perfect anyway. "I know it's kind of tourist cheesy, but we have to go to Pat O'Brien's, right? I mean to out-of-towners like us, that sort of *is* New Orleans."

"You have a point," he said with a good-natured chuckle. The sighting of the old man at the Absinthe had scared him a little, but why the hell let his crazy Cajun imagination ruin this day for his wife?

They made the turn onto Peter Street just as they polished off their beer, and he tossed the plastic cups into one of the abundant black wrought iron trash cans. They immediately identified Pat O'Brien's by the throng of other tourists that crowded the front, waiting for their turn to buy the famous brain-numbing drink.

Ben and Christy melted into the crowd and enjoyed the 'people watching' as they stood in line in the courtyard by the front bar. They very wisely passed on the trash can-sized "Magnum Hurricane." A rowdy group of boys with UAB Wrestling sweat shirts crowded around one of the huge drinks and sucked the poison up through long straws, laughing and cat calling, their eyes already red.

"That's gonna leave a mark," Christy muttered as she ordered their drink. They decided to share one, and Ben ate the three dollar glass deposit. They left the rowdy bar with their souvenir glass and headed back towards Bourbon Street, sipping the powerfully toxic alcohol slowly as they walked and lost themselves in the people watching and the energy of the Quarter. Back on the main drag, they found a rustic wrought iron bench and sat down to drink and watch the early revelers.

"Are you having fun?" she asked him as she handed him the tall Hurricane glass.

Ben took a long sip. The drink tasted deceptively mellow, but he knew enough to not be fooled.

"I am. I would have fun anywhere with you, but this is actually a wonderful time." He handed the drink back, and they watched two girls, who had to be chilly in their mini-skirts and spaghetti strapped tank tops, who continually peeked back over their shoulders and giggled at the two boys stumbling along behind them. "I wonder what happened with Reed and Amy," Ben said as he watched the drunken pursuit.

"Oh, God," Christy exaggerated her response with a joyful eye roll. "Please, oh please, let one of them have passed out before……Well, you know – just before."

They both laughed.

"Where do you want to eat?" she asked him, her hand warm on his thigh.

"Why, anywhere you like, Mrs. Morvant," he said. "I'm guessing you researched a couple of options for us."

"Jeez, am I that obsessive compulsive?" She smiled and took another sip on their straw.

"Yes," he answered simply, and they both laughed.

"Well," she said with mock indignation. "I'll have you know I planned on us browsing around and just finding something that looked good. We're going to be spontaneous."

"So," he kissed her on the cheek. "You planned out a period of bein' spontaneous in your rigid schedule – is that what you're saying?"

She laughed again and playfully punched his arm.

"Yeah, I guess it is," she said. Then, she kissed him on the mouth, her hand tickling a little farther up his leg. "Are you having second thoughts about your controlling wife?"

Ben looked at her happy face and felt totally content.

"No," he said simply.

"Good," she landed a playful punch on his taunt arm. "'Cause you're stuck with me." She jumped up and pulled him to his feet. "Hurry, I don't have very many more minutes of spontaneous activity in the schedule."

They wandered around, each pointing out particularly amusing individuals among the rapidly growing throngs of partiers in the Quarter that arrived with the night. As the crowd grew, so did the intrusive voices in his head, but he continued trying to force his mind to ignore the cacophony of sounds. After a while he didn't have to think about it at all. The words became dull background, like when you finally stopped thinking about the howling wind outside in a storm.

He saw the old man again at Fritzel's, a small jazz pub with a European feel, where they stopped to share another drink before dinner. The music turned out to be pretty good, even for so early in the evening, and they decided to sit for a while and enjoy the soft but angry melodies of a jazz quartet sitting in wooden chairs on the small stage. They found a table towards the back, but the room wasn't that big. The music filled it nicely.

The old man leaned against the wall, shifting his slight weight back and forth in rhythm to the music. His eyes were closed, and his yellow teeth split his leathery face as he clicked his tongue against chapped lips beneath his battered ball cap. Ben watched him for a moment, and his wife's voice faded into a blur with the ones in his head as he craned his neck to catch the old man's eye.

"What's up?" Christy asked and turned to look behind her at what might have caught his eye.

The old man opened his eyes and saw him. When he did, his grin got bigger. He again gave him the crazy salute with a tug at the weathered beer cap. Ben rose to his feet and headed towards him, unsure what he would say, but definitely done with being stalked. He felt Christy's tug on his shirt but brushed it away.

"Where are you going?"

"I'll be right back," he answered without looking. He weaved through the tight crowd, now and again losing sight of the old Cajun, but then picking him up again as he slipped through the maze of people. The old man had stopped his crazed, trance-like moves to the music, and instead just followed Ben's progress with jaundiced eyes, his stained teeth sending grins of encouragement.

Only a few yards to go and he jostled his way through a frustrating two step with a waitress who carried an enormous tray of drinks on one shoulder. His back and forth dance with the waitress, whose eyes pleaded with him not to knock into her and send her buffet of liquor crashing to the floor, temporarily blocked his view of the Cajun. Finally he stopped, gently took the waitress by both shoulders and stepped around her.

"Excuse me," he said without looking back to see if she smiled or flipped him the bird.

And, the man was gone.

Again.

Goddammit, I know he was here.

Sho' 'neff dat, Bennie boy. We be jawin' 'bout dis tin, jes few minute mo' boy.

The voice sounded crystal clear – way too clear to be real and emanating from the chattering jazz-filled room. Frustrated, he balled up a fist and nearly punched the wall where the ghost of a man had been. Instead, he did his four-count tactical breathing for a few cycles until the pounding in his temple went away, and his fist relaxed and stopped quivering.

He looked back and caught sight of Christy who now stood by their table and their eyes met. She shrugged with both hands up towards the ceiling in the universal "What the hell?" gesture. Ben looked around and spotted the bathroom sign gratefully pointing toward a short hall just past the wall where his imaginary Cajun had taunted him. He pointed to the sign and shot her a sheepish grin. Christy chuckled and shook her head, but she took her seat.

Ben pushed through the battered, glossy black painted door into the men's room. An older guy, his gray and thinning hair pulled back in a desperate-to-not-be-old ponytail, stood at the in-floor urinal, both hands above him where his forearms supported his weight against the dingy wall as piss dribbled slowly out of him, now and again spattering on his sandal-clad feet. Ben strode to the mirror and turned one faucet, which spun loosely and did nothing, and then the other. Clean looking water spit out into his hands. He bent over and splashed it on his face. The cold of it felt good, and he wet one hand and rubbed it across the back of his neck. Then, he raised his head slightly and peered at himself in the mirror.

The face looking back at him didn't look crazy – or at least not any more than the identical face he had stared at every day of his life. The eyes looked intense and put upon – but not crazy. At least he didn't think so (but what crazy person really thought he looked crazy, right?). He blinked hard, and the tap water caused a dull burn in his eyes for a moment.

My sweet goodness, that is a fine lookin' man. I could butter up that ass and eat it.

Ben glanced behind him in the mirror and caught the pony-tailed owner of the voice staring at his ass. The man looked up, saw Ben's eyes in the mirror, and blushed.

"Jess need to wash my mitts," he said with a shrug, holding up soft fingers with long nails and two gold bracelets on his right wrist.

"Sure," Ben said and pulled thin paper towels from the dented dispenser to his right. Then, he stepped out of the way.

He decided it would be awkward if he had to take a leak ten minutes from now and forced himself to pee before he left the bathroom. He stood at the urinal and forced the small amount of urine out of his bladder and alternated between efforts to understand what the hell his hallucination meant and competing efforts to not think about it at all. Neither effort won, and he zipped up and left the bathroom still confused but dedicated to changing the apparent course of the evening.

I'm on my honeymoon, Goddammit.

"Everything okay?" Christy asked as he slipped back into his chair beside her.

For a moment, he looked at her and considered just telling her about the crazy things circling his cluttered mind.

She's my wife now – she deserves to know.

"When you gotta go you gotta go," was all he managed.

"Are you feeling alright?" she asked, and he felt a twinge of guilt at her concern.

"Oh, yeah," he sipped his wine – a little sweeter than the last one. "Just waited 'til nearly the point of no return." He laughed with some effort, and she seemed to relax.

The wine tasted good, and the music sounded great. He slowly relaxed back into their evening, and soon his crazy imagination seemed like an annoyance rather than an emergency. Twice more he considered telling her about it, but never did. Eventually, hunger won them both over, and Christy pulled out her trusty French Quarter map and brochure.

"Authentic New Orleans but not real expensive?"

"Sounds right," he said.

Christy had thought about Tujaques, but the 'E' for expensive on her map and the 'reservations recommended' steered her instead to the 'M' for moderately priced Petunia's. The guide sold them with a promise of authentic Cajun and Creole tastes, and they finished their wine and together chugged tall glasses of water with lemon (hydrate or die his Team training reminded him – perhaps just as true in bar hopping as in conducting combat operations).

They walked hand-in-hand and chatted about nothing. Back on Bourbon Street, they headed west, and the five minute walk to Saint Louis Street provided more entertainment in the form of the alcohol worshippers along the way. Just past Toulouse Street they had to step over the legs of a man who stretched out across the sidewalk, the girl straddling his waist alternating between bending over to kiss him and sitting up to tilt back her plastic cup of disinhibitor. Again, they both thought of Reed and Amy and laughed.

By the time they arrived at Petunia's, just a short stroll north of Bourbon toward Dauphine on St. Louis Street, Ben felt great. The voices in his head were drowned out nicely by those on the street, and Christy's warm hand in his made him feel safe from his walking dreams.

* * *

Compared to the rising din of partiers on Bourbon Street, Petunia's seemed relatively sedate, which felt perfect to Ben. Set in a hundred and fifty year old French Quarter town house, the restaurant delivered what they had paid the brochure company to promise – huge portions of authentic New Orleans cuisine. Together they waded through giant, bowl-like plates of Shrimp Creole and bowtie pasta with seafood and Andouille sausage. They sopped it up with fresh, warm bread and washed it down with more red wine (a Shiraz she told him) and more water to keep the evening from ending in headaches and fitful, sexless sleep.

They talked about the beach, and Christy described for him the ocean perched condo that waited for them at the resort she had booked in Destin Beach a few hours away.

"They have Hobie cats and sunfish at the resort, and we can rent snorkeling gear if we want. They even can arrange some scuba diving for us if you think you want to do that."

"It sounds fantastic," Ben told her over spoonfuls of rich, spicy food. He could tell how excited she was to get there. He wondered if they could check in a day early. Maybe they should get the hell out of New Orleans tomorrow instead of the next day and get on with their real vacation. New Orleans seemed to do nothing for him but conjure up ghosts and nightmares.

"Maybe we should just head there tomorrow," he said and watched her face.

Christy seemed to consider a moment.

"We probably could," She took his hand. "I think we should head up to where you're from after breakfast tomorrow though. I want you to find some closure to whatever that place still holds on you, baby."

Ben looked down, but he nodded. She was right. He had to finish – if only to prove the dreams really were just dreams and that no Voodoo magic waited for him in the swamp. He needed to say goodbye to all that once and for all.

"By the time we go up there and back, it'll be pretty late in the day," she pointed out. "Maybe we just have a nice dinner, spend the evening in bed abusing each other, and get an early start for Destin on Tuesday?"

"That sounds great," he smiled. He loved her so much. He looked at her and saw she looked down at her plate, still half-covered with creamy seafood. He worried she looked distracted. "What's wrong on your side, hon?"

She looked up with a genuine softness. "Nothing at all," but she blushed a little. She took a fork and poked at her food. "There is something I wanted to talk to you about." She looked at him with warm soft eyes that didn't look troubled but held no clues as to what was on her mind.

"Okay," he waited.

"Well," she began softly as if picking her away around some obstacles. "When you were in," she glanced around, not wanting to give away any military secrets he guessed, "you know – when you were away," she continued.

"Yeah?"

It came tumbling out of her.

"Ben, when you called me that night and told me about that little girl and how you wanted us to adopt her – well, I guess that night really got me thinking." Her eyes held his but looked wet now. "Ben, I love you so much, and I know we've only been married for like a day and a half, but – well," she sighed, and her face blushed again.

"What is it, Christy?" Ben asked. He wasn't sure if he should be worried. He did know he had no friggin' clue what they were talking about.

"Okay," she took his hands, holding them softly in her own, and a deep breath. "Ben, when were you thinking we should think about having kids?"

A wave of relief spread over him. "She wants kids" seemed much easier than "'you seem like some kind of lunatic to me." He squeezed her hands quickly.

When did he want kids? He realized Jewel had left him with an ache that felt completely unfamiliar. He had wanted to be a parent to her with everything he held inside him. He knew the circumstances and the situation had impacted those feelings immensely. But he also realized Africa had left him with that yearning – a desire that went beyond Jewel. He always knew one day he and Christy would make babies together. But ever since Jewel, he realized the right time for children from his perspective was yesterday. He loved this woman with all of his heart and starting a family to share that love seemed natural and perfect.

Ben realized Christy still watched him expectantly. He leaned across the table, his shirt nearly dragging in Shrimp Creole along the way and kissed his wife deeply.

"I'm ready whenever you are, baby," He touched her face. "I love you so much that it seems like having babies with you is the next thing. Hey," he chuckled as he sat back down, "we got a license now and everything."

Christy held his eyes.

"Are you sure you don't want to wait awhile? Just be married for a bit?"

"We can," he said. "But, baby, we've shared a life and made a home together for a long time now. I don't need time to see what that's like. I'm ready to move forward, and I think for both of us that means kids, right?"

"It does for me, I know," her face beamed. "I was just thinking you might need time."

"I'm ready," he told her again. He realized the thought of children suddenly seemed more like an immediate need. "We can wait as long as you need, but I'm ready." His mind flashed to little Jewel, her face nuzzled against his neck and her voice giggles and smiles.

"Well," she continued. "While you were gone I stopped taking the pill. Just to give my body a little break, you know?"

He nodded.

"I mean I took another kind of precaution last night and the last two weeks," she didn't elaborate on exactly what kind of precaution, "but I could stop taking anything if you want." She stared at him expectantly and nibbled on her lower lip. He felt her thumb tap nervously on the back of his hand. "I mean it would probably take a little while anyway," she said to fill the short silence, "and I would use something tonight, because, you know, I've been drinking and stuff." She watched his face. "What do you think?"

Ben leaned over again, and this time kissed her forehead.

"I think we should make a baby."

Christy's face exploded with happiness. "Oh, Ben. Are you sure? I mean, I'm sure, but are you sure? Ever since you told me about the little girl in Africa" she stole a look around the room and covered her mouth like she had just given away the missile codes. "Ooohh, sorry," she bounced right back. "Anyway, ever since then, and then when you wanted to get married right away – I just can't stop thinking about it. I mean, God, Ben, you would be such a great dad."

Ben chuckled and waited for her to breathe. She finally gasped inhaled a sharp breath and then sipped her wine again.

"You're sure?" she said.

"I've never been more sure of anything – at least not in the last two weeks, since I asked you to marry me. And, look how great that worked out," he winked.

Christy leaped out of her chair, nearly sending her plate flying off the edge and to the floor, and wrapped her arms around his neck tightly.

"Oh, God, I love you, Ben," she wept sporadic tears across his neck.

Ben realized his eyes felt a little moisture seeping in as well. He touched her cheek and then kissed her again, exploring her open-mouth.

"I love you, too," he said.

They finished their dinner with excited chatter about babies and names and nurseries (the office, they decided, would become the baby's room – she would put a desk in the kitchen). The excitement he felt and saw in her completely drowned out the worries and fears that had haunted him only an hour earlier. He considered just packing up their stuff and running away from Louisiana tonight. They could leave the nightmares of his past far behind and sprint full-force into their exciting future. But he knew he would wonder forever about this place, these feelings, and the dreams that sent him here.

She's right. I need closure.

He smiled at his use of such a girly word as "closure." An old married man already – and barely a day and half into it.

They paid their bill. After a few minutes to consult the magic "Guide to The French Quarter," they decided to walk the ten blocks or so past Esplanade and down to Decatur Street where the guide promised Snug Harbor would offer the best contemporary jazz in the city. The atmosphere presented a concert-like atmosphere instead of what the reviewer called the "messy nightclub backdrop of other jazz venues in the area." That sounded about right to them, and if they kept the stroll brisk they could easily make the ten o'clock set.

They held hands, Christy's other arm wrapped tightly and happily around Ben's. The voice didn't really register at first, drowned out by his happiness, but he heard it clearly when it repeated itself.

Kin be keep dis short. 'Neff bin sayin' and in dat head no how way. Close to dat find out time, Bennie boy.

Ben slowed but didn't stop. He looked around Dumaine Street, the much quieter path they had turned south on to find their way to Decatur Street. A handful of people walked along, but none looked anything like the old Cajun who had haunted him all night. He scanned the small groups of pedestrians for the dirty and beat up "Purple Haze" ball cap, but didn't see it.

He heard the insistent riffs of someone beating on a saxophone and from a doorway up ahead he saw the owner, squatted in front of an open case in which change and a few bills had been tossed. Beside him sat the old man, cross-legged, his thin and frail body swaying with the music.

Ben realized he had stopped breathing and felt Christy's hand tighten on his arm. As he stared the old man nodded to him, then grasped the bill of his cap and mouthed a salute. He felt himself carried toward the doorway, nearly floated really, in a dreamlike way that for a moment made him wonder if this was perhaps a dream. He heard Christy ask something, but the words sounded jumbled and unrecognizable to him. Like the staccato sounds from the saxophone, they also sounded faded and distant.

He stood and glared down at the old man, who made no effort to get up but looked at him with jaundiced eyes and then coughed a deep and rattling cough.

"Lil' days lef me here, boy," he said, and his smile saddened. "Be goin' to dat udder far way place, yo bet dat sho' 'neff."

"What do you want?" Ben asked. He realized he was done with this game. Real or not, he had become tired of the riddle.

"Jes' need be mindin' yo," the man said. "Go time 'e here soon 'neff and yo needin' to hear dat eater of dem dead ones now."

Ben stared at the sunken face that still rocked back and forth to the music beside the man with the saxophone. The musician ignored him, and Ben realized he most probably held a conversation with a hallucination.

That ought to make Christy rethink my passing on my genes.

"Do you know this man?"

Ben realized Christy's words didn't just sound clear, they cleared up something critical.

"You see him?" he looked over at his wife who screwed up her face in confusion.

"What are you talking about?" she asked. He didn't hear any fear, just confusion. "I can't understand a word he says, but I hear him." He felt her hand tighten more on his arm and then slip down to hold firmly onto his hand. "Do you know this man?"

"Yes," he said simply but offered nothing else. He looked again at the Cajun, who grinned back his Cheshire cat smile. "What do you want?" he asked again.

"Hep yo git to dat knowin' place," the man said. "You be mindin' how findin' dat place we be visitin' both us dere? Yo needin' dat place find soon more now, sho' 'neff true dat. Dat dead eater wait no fo' yo dere, but not ever time be dere, know yo dat sho now. Waitin' down way dat bottom. But you be seein' friend long dat hole and also nudder one, sho 'neff true dat. Dey hep'n yo dere and keep yo on dat trail. Mindin' where to go?"

"I remember," Ben said. He realized he would go, if only to prove to himself that the bunny hole had just been a dream. He no longer really believed that lie, he supposed, but either way he would go and then it would be over.

Closure.

The old man coughed again, his frail body shaking hard. He wiped dark blood that spilled over his chin with the back of his hand, and then looked at it and laughed his shrieking laugh from the dream.

"Git down dat hole, Bennie boy. Scaredy sho 'neff dat, but mos portent tings down dere. Needin' dat yo be short time dat now." He spit dark blood onto the sidewalk and sighed. "Git down dey now," he said and then closed his eyes and rocked back and forth again to the sax music, which had moved to a slower and softer tune. The way he moved his head, eyes closed, reminded Ben of the video of Ray Charles, swaying at his piano and singing "Ebony and Ivory."

Ben took Christy by the elbow and guided her away and down the street. She didn't resist; he felt her concerned eyes on him, but didn't look at her – not yet. He stopped suddenly and turned around.

"Will I see you again?" he asked.

The Cajun no longer sat beside the musician, and Ben darted his eyes and head around. He caught a short glimpse, or at least he thought he did, of the small old man in his dirty ball cap just as he turned into an alleyway.

Caint dat be knowin' now. None of us.

The man was gone.

Ben turned and looked at his wife.

"How did you know that man?" Christy didn't looked frightened or worried, just terribly confused.

"He knew my Gammy," he said. He wanted to say more, but had no idea what he could say that wouldn't tip his hand and show how crazy he felt. He watched her instead in silence.

"What did he tell you? What did you talk about?" she asked. "I couldn't understand a word either of you said. It sounded like a different language, but with a French accent. What language was that?"

"He told me that I should visit home before we leave here," Ben said. That didn't seem too much of a lie actually. Ben stopped and considered something. "You couldn't understand me either?" he asked.

Christy shook her head. "You both used that crazy language," she said.

"Cajun talk."

She nodded but seemed uneasy. "That was really weird."

"Yeah," and he tried to sound light. "Totally bizarre. I never expected to see someone from there in the city. Times change, I guess."

Christy said nothing, and they walked on towards the Esplanade, hand-in-hand. Ben actually felt great. Christy had seen him – had heard him even. That meant the Cajun was real. As frightening as what that meant was, Ben realized it felt way less scary than believing you had lost your mind.

Tonight they would enjoy the Quarter. They would drink and listen to jazz, hold hands and make love later. They would talk about the beach and babies.

Tomorrow they would drive up past Chackbay and into the bayou. He would go alone down that fuckin' bunny hole, he knew, and whatever he found there, they would leave it all behind and head to Destin Beach. Then, they would head for home and their new life.

CHAPTER

22

Christy had a lot of questions, but had no idea how to ask them or really even how to put them into words. She sat beside Ben, her hand on his arm and head against his shoulder and listened to the music (which was everything the guide promised). How could she find out if he was okay without making him worry? Whenever she asked about dreams or other things that disturbed him, he always seemed so defensive and upset. She had gotten pretty good over the years at reading him and knowing when to ask for more – which meant rarely at best. Everything inside her told her to let him be and ride it out. The last thing she wanted to do was ruin his night on this very special trip.

Who the hell was that strange man?

No doubt in her mind the bizarre language added to the impression the Cajun had left on her. The fact she could understand almost nothing her husband said made the entire experience even more surreal. But what made it impossible to swallow, she realized, was the circumstances surrounding it.

An old man who knew Ben's grandmother happened to be sitting beside a street musician in the French Quarter, right along their path to Snug Harbor. He and her husband had a short (and apparently heated) conversation, and then they just moved on. Yeah – okay, that could really happen. It bothered her that he didn't tell her more, but she knew asking more would not help either of them in any way. She had asked, and he had likely given her all he was prepared to give right now.

This is not my first day with this complicated man.

Ben looked over with those gorgeous eyes and smiled.

"You need another drink?" he asked.

"I'm good for a bit," she held up her half-full glass. "I love you, baby," she added.

Ben leaned over and kissed her deeply. She breathed in the scent of him and felt her pulse quicken. She loved this man so much, more than she had ever believed possible. What she wanted more than anything, especially any satisfaction of her curiosity, was for him to be happy. Happy and at peace, and while she hoped her husband may have found happiness in her, he still searched for answers. It seemed so much worse after Africa, and she wondered if his deployment and the things that had happened there had opened old wounds or if he now had brand new ones to heal. She knew the story he told her of the village in Africa deeply affected him.

"You like this place?" he asked and pressed her hand to his lips. Just like Ben. He had so much pain inside him and wanted only to be sure she was having a good time.

"It's great," she said. "I love the music so much."

Ben nodded and tugged on his beer. "Yeah, you found the perfect retreat, sweetheart." He kissed her cheek which made her feel warm and safe. "As usual," he added. He went back to watching the five-piece group on a large stage as they completely dominated the piece they pounded out. His eyes still had a storm brewing inside them, however.

Maybe it was just this area. Obviously that didn't really explain the encounter with the old man, but maybe it explained his reaction to it. Maybe it explained how distracted he was and the way he seemed to drift away from her periodically over the evening. She knew his past troubled him, and she suspected there had been at least one particularly bad event that still haunted him. She also knew it involved his Grandmother somehow. She realized it was not in any way important that he tell her what had happened to him as a child – only that he somehow find a way to leave it behind them, to say goodbye to it when they left here. It was why she had so eagerly agreed to this trip and why she still held so much hope for it. She had suspected it might be weird (though the old man encounter way surpassed her expectation), but she felt very strongly it had been the right thing.

Did she have some morbid curiosity about where he had come from? She looked up at his strong face, those sometime hard eyes, and thought about the childlike cries she periodically heard from him at night.

Hell, yeah, she was curious about his home. He had told her so little, but enough that she knew he grew up dirt poor (literally, she suspected) and in squalor in the bayou somewhere. He had talked about his home, which he always described as their shack in the woods, only rarely, but she knew it had been hard and always felt impressed he had made it out. He had found his way to her, as she liked to think of it. She thought for a moment of the Rascal Flatts song she loved and thought of as sort of their song. She certainly felt blessed by the road that had brought them together.

Christy suspected that when she saw it, Ben's childhood home would not seem nearly as bad as he suggested. A part of her wanted to just drag him away from here, to pack the car like he suggested earlier and to lose themselves in honeymoon sex, drinks, and sunshine in Destin Beach. But she knew he needed to find closure, to put this in perspective, and to leave it behind. Running away would get them no closer to that.

She gazed at him again. Though he looked straight ahead, she could see he focused on something far away and in no way related to the stage where the group now brought new life to a song that seemed familiar and brand new at the same time. She wondered where he was right now. She wanted to just hold him and make it better. Christy squeezed his arm, and he startled a little and then looked over. He raised an eyebrow. Christy raised her own eyebrow, tried to look alluring, and hoped she didn't just look silly.

"Wanna head to the room?" she asked. "I would really love to be naked with you, and I think that would go over the line here – I don't care if we are in New Orleans." She gave him her best I love you and want you smile. He lustfully glared back.

"Don't have to ask me twice." He kissed her and then finished off his beer.

They walked home in quiet but Christy had become used to these times. She knew his mind moved rapidly, though through what exact thoughts she had no way of knowing. She suspected it had something to do with home and his past and a lot to do with the old man from the street. She held his hand and let his mind work. She felt a tingle, like the brush of static electricity you feel when you run your hand through your hair on a winter day, and she looked down at his hand in hers. The ring on his right middle finger glowed bright enough to nearly cast light on the flickering passing shadows. The ember red burst looked tinged with orange, but the brightness and the way it seemed to pulsate made her stomach churn. She had an overwhelming need to pull her hand away. She realized the ring didn't just disgust her (it did, and she had no idea why even such a bizarre piece of jewelry would make her nauseated), but it frightened her. She resisted for a moment, but finally shook her hand free of his, and wrapped her arm around his waist so he wouldn't notice her irrational aversion.

She wanted that ring gone. Not just off his hand, but gone from their lives. She wanted it thrown into the sea or, even better, buried deep in the ground. She decided she would have to wait until he finished his journey through his past over the next day. By the time they arrived in Destin, she decided she would ask him to get rid of it. She couldn't bear the thought of it still being on his hand when they walked into their town house in Virginia Beach for the first time as Mr. and Mrs. Morvant.

Not much later her obsessive revulsion of his ring faded (though didn't disappear) as their mouths explored each other on the big bed in their room at the Dauphine. She was aware of the ring on his hand and equally aware that she tried to avoid touching it. As his caressing fingers explored her body she found herself moving around to avoid that damned circled band, but after a few minutes, as her passion and arousal rose, the aversion faded into the background.

A short time later, as she bucked her hips up to meet his, their bodies sweaty and their eyes locked in a loving stare, she thought of nothing except how fantastic he felt inside her and how great his ass felt in both of her hands. They exploded together and only a short time later fell asleep clinging to each other. Her last thought as she fell into a contented sleep in his embrace was relief that his left arm draped across her instead of his right, but this time it brought a sheepish smile instead of the near terror she had felt earlier.

Later she heard the soft but rowdy sounds from Bourbon Street and felt him slip from their bed – presumably to go to the bathroom. She lay half awake and felt something else, too, something inside her. It felt strange but wonderful, but she had no idea what it could be. She never really woke up enough to wonder it through. She did feel like she had forgotten something, but didn't think it could be anything important. She fell back into a deep sleep before he returned.

CHAPTER

23

Ben awoke from the first dream with no memory whatsoever of its content. He felt calm and safe and so for a moment wondered if he had really dreamed at all. He knew he had, but figured the lack of anxiety (and the clean feet that he stole a glance at when the urge finally overwhelmed him) meant maybe it had been nothing more than a normal person's dream. He didn't think he had those much, but his life was better than ever now, he realized with a glance at his sleeping wife. He slipped out of her embrace to hit the head and relieve himself and saw that she stirred only a little.

When he returned Christy had both hands on her belly, just below her navel. For a moment, he worried she might have some abdominal pain or cramping from their food and beverage binging, but the very content, almost angelic smile on her face allayed his worries that his wife might be sick.

He slipped into bed beside her and snuggled close (her familiar, but ridiculously high, skin temperature less important than the touch of her skin) and watched her sleep. Then, his own eyes grew heavy, and he drifted off again before he knew what was happening.

The old man spoke to him from far away and only for a moment – a gentle reminder of the awake-journey that lay ahead of him. Ben couldn't even see him. He found himself seated with his back against a large and gnarled tree trunk, and the voice came to him as if from the jungle itself.

"A many folk be waitin' yo, Bennie boy. See dem fo sho' 'neff down dat dark butt hole in dem woods, heah. Don' lettin' em down be. Bes fo yo also be, wit all comin' for yo' den in dat 'affa time. Dey tellin' yo mo in dat dark hole, sho' 'neff true dat ist 'kay? Yo be memberin' dat way and git down dat hole. Jess yo boy. Leavin' dat woman back fo sho' 'neff. Bes fo her, too. Don fergit dat mos 'portent ting. Alone, boy."

Ben didn't answer, probably wouldn't have had he seen the old Cajun beside him, but definitely not when the jungle spoke to him in that Cajun voice. He knew he would go and needed no reminder in any case. The old man needn't worry about Christy – there was no fuckin' chance in hell he would take her along down that dark hole in the woods. No matter what he did or didn't find there, she would wait behind.

So the voice did little to shake him from his thoughts of where he found himself. He recognized this patch of jungle very well. He was nowhere near the village now, but only a click and a half away from the other village – the one where they had hit the presumed leadership for the Al Qaeda cell that had slaughtered his people. He had managed to put most of that night out of his head these last two weeks. Now, as he sat beside the tree just in from the clearing into which Viper team had fast roped that night, it all crashed back on him. The whispers from the jungle, and the voices in his head on target. His own violent slaughter of the killers in the target house. The feeling of being watched if not guided. And Reed, of course – Reed's mortal wounds that had not killed him. The fireflies from his own hands and the pulsations from the ring.

All of these images flittered around him like mosquitoes, and he unconsciously waved his hand to shoo them away. The images went nowhere, and the emotions that came with them continued to churn inside him as if that night had happened only hours ago. He felt his eyes turn wet at the images of Reed, pale and weak and clearly near death. He remembered how he asked about lightning after Ben had healed his ravaged chest. The thought and feeling of knowing his dead best friend would now survive filled him with happiness.

He felt no guilt at the men he had killed that night. He regretted the task force may have lost some intel, but other than that, the death of those animals left him with nothing – no, maybe there was something – a warm sensation of justice. A feeling that lives might be saved from the death of those bastards.

"You are more than a seer, Ben – more than a Traiteur, if you like. That is part of it, but you have been born to be much more. Your Gammy would call it Rougarou."

That term Ben remembered from his childhood in the woods. It sounded like werewolf, but really meant a protector – someone who hunted down and killed the evil that threatened his people. Like a Sentinel – or maybe like a SEAL. It was a term more Indian than Voodoo, but likely familiar to both.

Ben looked over and felt no surprise to see the Elder squatted beside him and watched as he poked at the ground with a green stick. He looked tonight much like when Ben had first met him – an old man, thin but fit, with a much younger man's eyes. It surprised him to realize he had missed the old villager. He spoke to Ben out loud, and he heard him in English. But somehow he knew they spoke in another language – an ancient language he should not know but realized he always had.

"Rougarou is a fable – a monster of sorts, but one for good – in the minds of children in the bayou at least," Ben told him.

"Yes," the man said and drew in the dirt. "And like all such things, it finds its origin in fact. The Rougarou is the evolution of the Seer – or Traiteur – and only some of us receive that gift. You are one such Seer. Perhaps only once in a few hundred or even a thousand changes of the seasons, does the Living Jungle need such an Ashe, such a power, but that time is now."

They sat in silence while Ben absorbed what the Elder told him.

"Why now?" he asked. "And why me? I share nothing with your people except one horrible night when I failed you miserably."

The old man looked at him, his face split over a jutting mouth of rotting teeth.

"Now is because the dark force returns and seeks to destroy us. Not just my village but all of our people. It uses the men you fight now, but it is greater than them and wants much more." The old man looked at him with eyes that seemed to slip back and forth between old, wise mystical orbs and those of a much younger man. Both held life and power. "The 'You' is beyond us. You were not chosen by me, or the Mami Wata you know as Gammy – you simply are what you are. We are children of the Ginen. We share a lineage, if not of blood then, for sure, of spirit – both descendants of the ancient one – Children of Ginen and sons of the Living Jungle – the Great Vodu."

"I don't know what that means," Ben said, but he thought he partly understood.

"You will learn more from your own Mami Wata soon. The rest maybe you don't need to know – only the Great Vodu can decide."

The old man went back to poking at the dirt with his stick. Ben thought the symbols he made should hold some meaning for him, but they didn't. The Elder continued.

"The Ashe that grows now inside you has been yours always and is focused by the ring, but not from it. You will learn on your own how to use it, and I cannot help you with this, nor can Mami Wata."

Ben felt the world around him shimmer and bow and the sane part of his brain he still clung to reminded him that anything is possible in dreams. The woods around him reshaped – that seemed the only real word for the change – and he recognized the forest it became. Without looking back, he knew he leaned now against a ramble shack house in the bayou that could not possibly still exist. But he believed now it probably did. A new part of his memory clicked into place, and he saw a brilliant fire from the past – a blocked memory that explained why he knew with such certainty that their shack, his home with his Gammy, couldn't be here anymore. Other things from his troubled history tumbled back into place, as well, but he had no time to think about them now. He had to take his very familiar, sometimes nightly over the years, stroll through the Cajun forest of home.

Ben walked along the path in the moonlight as he had done thousands of times. He felt the same anxiety that traveled with him each passing moment and again reminded himself of the dicked-up nature of dreams. Why be scared of a dream that ended the same way night after night after night?

Because you don't choose what you fear in dreams.

Ben came to the clearing and stopped. His Gammy stood naked and pale in the moonlight, head back and arms outstretched. Her quiet voice mumbled words that meant something to him but he didn't know what.

And, then it came.

Not a doe this time, and Ben felt his already pounding pulse quicken more.

The man was thin and pale, his face covered in dirt and stubble, his hair long and unkempt. What looked most familiar were the eyes – the blue, impossibly small eyes from the doe of so many dreams, looked wide eyed on the thin man that walked towards his Gammy as if called. The blue seemed surrounded by yellow, and Ben remembered the man had been sick when he came to Gammy the first time. He remembered, from his bed in the loft of their shack, the shouts exchanged in a foreign tongue, and the fear he had heard for the first time in the voice that belonged to Gammy. He remembered those blue eyes tinged with yellow and how they flashed reddish orange when the man held a long bony finger at his Gammy, the words meaningless to him but the threat clear.

He watched the man with the blue and yellow eyes approach his Gammy, his back arched as if his mind fought against his body as he glided slowly toward her. The face looked expressionless, but the eyes showed the fear trapped inside.

Gammy kept her head back and her mouth barely moved as she chanted, her arms outstretched and hands upwards. The right hand remained balled up tightly, white knuckled, around the handle of the knife.

The man stopped beside her and leaned forward. For a moment Ben thought the man would nuzzle her as the doe had in the dream so many times before. Instead he stopped and then his own head tilted back and upward, his thin neck pale and stretched before the old woman and his red lids closed over the familiar, jaundiced eyes.

Ben knew what would be next and tried to tear his eyes away, but couldn't. He wanted to shout out to his Gammy, to tell her to stop, but his voice stuck in his throat. He didn't want it to happen, didn't want to lose his innocent childhood love for his gentle grandmother.

The flash of moonlight on the steel blade looked the same as it always did, but a scream stuck in his throat because everything else was different. Gammy mumbled loudly as the long, curved blade opened the man's neck easily, the cut in his throat so deep that Ben thought the head would tumble off into the dirt. An explosion of crimson spray soaked his grandmother followed by two pulsing geysers that looked grayish black in the moonlight, but Ben knew would be bright red in daytime. The head fell backwards, nearly striking the man between the shoulder blades, and the now lifeless face stared upside down at him. The tongue flicked in and out of the mouth as if trying to expel some foul tasting shit, and the grey geysers of blood painted obscene patterns across his Gammy's face and sagging breasts as she again raised her hands up at the moon and let her own head fall backwards as she shouted more meaningless words up into the night.

After an impossibly long time the body collapsed at his Gammy's feet, and with incredible speed a huge lake of blood formed as the near headless body drained itself in the clearing. Within moments the blood lapped up over his Gammy's feet. The body gave its last flick of uncontrolled spasm, and the left foot splashed in the lake of death and then lay still, the last nerve now dead. Gammy stood motionless, arms out and up, head back. Red trails ran down her arms and dripped from her elbows and thin streams trickled down her flabby sides and legs.

Ben tore his eyes away at last as tears coursed down his cheeks. He squeezed his eyes shut tightly, tried with everything to force away the terrible image burned into his mind. When he opened them again, the clearing and the horror show it held were gone, replaced by a hammock. The old Cajun sat precariously on the edge of it, scattered teeth gleaming under the ball cap and feet swinging above the moss-covered ground.

"Don' be yo Gammy judge makin' yet now, boy," the old man cautioned. "She be savin' all us kin dat night. She don' chase back dem demons den an like to save allin' us, special mos' like yo', Bennie boy."

The cane flashed out and struck him sharply on the thigh, but Ben didn't flinch. His mind could register nothing except the horror he had just witnessed.

"She sayin' all her on' sef, sho' 'neff true dat. Tellin' yo down ere soon dat."

The old man gestured and Ben looked behind him. The tunnel-like hole in the woods gaped open behind him. It seemed to swell wider, as if reaching out to swallow him, and Ben stumbled backwards away from it, arms up. A foul steam seeped out from the entrance as if it belched the humid smell of rotting death and shit, and Ben felt his stomach heave.

Then, he sensed movement behind him and felt the old man's cane smack onto his ass, and he fell headlong towards the hole.

"In nah, boy!"

The wet heat from the hole engulfed him as he tumbled forward.

* * *

Ben did his best four-count tactical breathing and tried to slow the pounding in his chest and temples. He raised shaking hands to his face and wiped sweat from his eyes as he kicked the Duvet cover and sheet off of his legs. The horrible death-smell from the rabbit hole lingered a moment in his mouth and nose and then disappeared. As his breathing slowed Ben turned his head and looked at Christy, certain he had wakened her and that she would be watching him, forehead furrowed in concern and brown eyes soft with worry.

Christy lay peacefully undisturbed, her face beautiful in the blue light that streamed in from the partially pulled drapes. Her face read nothing but happiness and safety, and he noted her hands still lay across her belly. Ben leaned over and kissed her cheek gently. He watched a moment to see if she would stir, and when she didn't he slipped out of bed and headed to the bathroom.

The heat had dissipated both from the dank, dark ass hole in the bayou and from the lit charcoal briquette he had married. As he splashed cool water on his face, he felt goose-bumps pop up on his naked body and shivered. Ben looked at himself a moment in the mirror, but found he could not hold the stare from the cloudy-eyed, haunted face that glared at him from the mirror.

He grabbed a towel and wrapped it around his shivering body. He decided a hot shower would both warm him and wash the sweat from his body before he crawled back in with his wife.

Ben stood under the hot water and let it melt away his chill as he mulled over the dreams that clung to the back part of his mind. The dream of the Cajun meant very little to him – he knew he would go home and that he would keep Christy safe and no longer needed the old man's encouragement or advice. It was the Village Elder that consumed his thoughts. He contemplated the words, so many of them familiar, the old man had used and rolled his head around under the steaming hot spray to unclench the muscles in his shoulders and neck.

Well, of course, they're familiar, dumb ass. Your mind created the damn dream and found some frightening words from your fucked up childhood at the bottom of your memory barrel. Stop making them more than they are.

Ben knew in his heart he no longer believed that. He knew also his upbringing in the backwoods, the child of a Traiteur, made him prone to accept the supernatural when things didn't seem to make sense. He had tried to work on that his whole adult life, but this went beyond that. Could his mind, no matter how unbalanced from the hauntings of his youth and the trauma of his failures in Africa, really create such vivid and disturbing fantasies? He wanted to believe it could (for the first time the idea of being nuts might be better than the alternative), but he honestly didn't think himself creative enough to pull all of this together.

Ben dropped his chin to his chest and let the hot water wash away the last bit of tightness in his back. Then, he spun the shower off and grabbed a towel. He realized he now felt too hot again, his body replacing the toweled-off water with a new, thin layer of sweat. He looked at his watch on the bathroom sink. He had been lingering in the hot spray for much longer than it seemed.

He stood for a moment in the doorway, his naked body slowly adjusting to the temperature, and tried to figure out what to do next. There was no chance he would fall back asleep anytime soon, and he wasn't really sure he wanted to, since his two old friends seemed to lie-in-wait just on the other side. Of course, the old Cajun had chased him around the Quarter half the night, and he had been awake for all of that, hadn't he? Then, he had a sudden inspiration.

Under the glow of his watch, so as not to wake his peacefully sleeping wife, Ben flipped through one of several guides to New Orleans his wife brought along on their honeymoon trip. He found what he wanted in Frommer's under the "Sights to See and Places to Be" chapter. He skimmed the section of interest and found there was a Voodoo spiritual temple only a few blocks away on Rampart Street. The guide claimed the temple was the real deal and tourists were welcome only if they were interested in learning more about the occult religion and could be respectful of the practitioners there. Ben had no idea whether they would be open at – he looked at his watch – two-thirty in the morning, but everything in his childhood suggested the late hour seemed to be when most of the "occult religion" was actually practiced.

Ben bit his lip and thought for a moment. What the hell would he even be looking for at such a place? Maybe just being there would shake loose something in his head that could answer some of his questions? Maybe someone would know how the Voodoo practiced by some in New Orleans might relate to a primitive people in the middle of nowhere on the dark continent of Africa? He had no idea, but he felt he needed to do something.

Ben looked at his beautiful wife, still deeply asleep and peaceful in their wedding bed. Should he leave her a note? What the hell wound he say?

Had to run over to the Voodoo temple to check on a few things. Back soon – yeah, right. That would work.

He settled on *Be right back* with a big heart underneath it and the letter "B." He just hoped he would be back before she had a chance to read it, forcing him to somehow explain where he had gone. He left the note on the vanity, stuffed the credit card-like room key into the back pocket of his jeans, and quietly slipped out of the room.

The bellman tugged on the bill of his 1920's style hat as Ben left the hotel, and he thought immediately of the old Cajun pulling on the brim of his dirty "Purple Haze" baseball cap. He gave a nod and headed north on Court Street the two blocks to Rampart and turned right. He held his head down, and his brain alternated between scolding him for this foolish outing and searching for some sense he could make from what the Elder had told him. He didn't see the two drunk men weaving towards him on the dark sidewalk until it was too late. He jumped a little, startled from his own thoughts, when the taller guy's shoulder struck him in the chest.

"Hey, watch out, dickhead," the man slurred at him and then stumbled a step backwards.

"Yeah, asshole," the other man said, clearly clueless as to what they were upset about but backing his friend's play. "Yeah, dude, what's your fuckin' problem?"

"Yeah, what's your fuckin' problem, man?" the first one parroted.

"No problem, guys," Ben said. "Excuse me." He went to maneuver around the men, but the bigger one, clad in baggy jeans and a black, sleeveless "Daytona Bike Week" T-shirt, stepped in front of him.

"Is, too, a problem," he said and blinked the impossibly long blink of the shit-faced drunk. He looked at Ben through red eyes. "Is, too, problem," he said again.

"Yeah, asshole," his friend agreed. "You got a problem now." He crossed his arms defiantly across his chest and stepped beside his pal to further block Ben's way.

Ben sighed.

I don't have time for this shit.

Christy waited for him asleep in their room, and he realized all he really wanted was to hurry back to her. He decided his trip was more than unnecessary – it bordered on nuts. He needed to get away from these drunks, clearly upset they had come all the way to New Orleans just to get rejected by a different class of women, and get back to his hotel. He could visit the temple in the morning, if at all. It probably wasn't even open this late.

The two drunks watched him expectantly, foolish smirks on their faces.

"Look, guys," Ben said. "I'm sorry I ran into you. I don't know what else you want me to say. How about I get on my way, and you go crash in your hotel? I don't want no trouble."

"Well, you got trouble, mother fucker," the bigger guy hollered way louder than he probably meant to. "You got a pecker full of trouble, you faggot."

Ben shook his head. He really, really didn't want this. He could feel a heat rise in his chest and creep up his neck. He also in no way needed to get to some tourist trap Voodoo fucking temple. He felt the anger grow larger – as much at himself as these two asshole drunks – and took a couple of four-count tactical breaths. Then, he turned on his heel to head the other way and back to his wife.

"Don't you turn you back on me, faggot," the bigger man screamed. Then he made a giant mistake – he grabbed a U.S. Navy SEAL by his arm and pulled.

Ben didn't expect the hot rage that exploded suddenly inside him. He spun around, using the momentum of man's pull on his forearm, and spun his wrist in a tight arc which forced the man's grip under his own. In a fluid motion, he jerked downward and leaned in toward the drunk to use his weight in the hold. He felt a satisfying crunch of bone as the man's wrist shattered and heard a girlish scream as the pain cleared the man's alcohol-soaked brain. Ben's free hand grasped the man's throat, and he pressed him backwards against the brick wall beside them.

Ben became aware of a tingling in his right hand which spread up his arm as he squeezed tighter and crimped off the whimper in the man's throat.

"Don't ever fucking touch me," he said. "You understand?"

The man tried to nod but couldn't move. His free hand held on tightly to Ben's powerful forearm.

"Leave him alone, dude," the other drunk said and slapped painlessly at Ben's back with an open hand. Ben felt his anger rise more, and the tingling spread farther up his arm. He felt a similar vibration in his chest and behind his eyes. Some part of him watched the ring on his right hand, the one that pinned the drunk to the wall by his throat, turn from pulsating orange to fiery bluish purple and fireflies began to dance around.

The man screamed again – this time in both terror and agony.

"Oh, shit, my head! My eyes – my fuckin' eyes!"

The scream alerted some less primitive part of Ben, which somehow reigned in the homicidal animal intent on crushing the man's windpipe as he boiled his brain and eyes. He immediately opened his hand, and the man crumpled to the sidewalk, clawing at his head. His friend took off at full sprint down the sidewalk away from them screaming "Help! Help!" in a frenzied sob.

Ben looked at the man at his feet and noted the fiery blood red welt marks on his neck which had already begun to raise into blisters. The pain in his neck must have paled beside whatever imploded in his head, because he curled up in a ball on the sidewalk, moaning and pawing at his face and eyes. Ben felt something slip from his right hand and looked down to see a thin sheet of skin hanging from his palm, partially stuck to his thumb by a piece that looked charred. The skin resembled that from a piece of chicken when you flipped it on a grill that had gotten too hot. He flicked at it in disgust, and the long piece of skin tore free and flew slow motion through the air, landing on the back of the man's head and sticking in his long hair.

"My fuckin' eyes," the man moaned. "My eyes are on fire."

Ben opened his mouth to say something at the writhing figure at his feet, but he had no idea what. He snapped his mouth shut.

What the fuck did I just do – and how the hell did I do it?

Ben looked at the ring on his hand as the angry purple faded slowly to a pulsating orange.

Images of the terrorist in the interrogation room in Africa suddenly crashed down on him. How in the shit had he blocked that memory from his mind? He saw him now as clearly as he had that day. The bubbles boiling behind his eyes as his fucking brain turned to liquid. The horrible smell of flesh, shit, blood, and the seizure as the scum died. The eyeball that had popped in its socket and dripped grey liquid down the mottled cheek. He had nearly done the same thing to the drunk at his feet, whose cries had faded to a whimper.

Rougarou – a monster of sorts – but a destroyer of evil.

More than a Seer – more than a Traiteur if you like.

The second voice was that of the Elder.

Ben spun on a heel and walked quickly away, southwest on Rampart Street towards Court Street and home. The pained sobs from the wounded drunk followed him in his head long after he could no longer hear them, and he felt his pace quicken more.

Rougarou.

The Ashe grows inside of you, and you will learn on your own how to use it.

He wondered if he would be able to learn how to control it.

CHAPTER

24

Christy stretched luxuriously beside her husband in the huge bed and wondered if he had perhaps rubbed off on her. She felt like she had drifted through a series of her own bizarre dreams, though she could not really summon any specific memories of them. She immediately felt a flush of guilt at how the thought trivialized Ben's (her *husband's)* nightmares, which she knew, of course, were rooted in childhood trauma.

She threw her arms around him in the bed. He didn't stir at all, and his skin felt cool to her touch. Cool and clammy. Christy chased away the last remnant of sleep and wondered if he had fallen sick over the night. She stroked his face and found that it too felt cool, his short hair plastered to his temples with sweat.

"Baby," she whispered softly. He stirred.

Ben mumbled beside her, his face partially against his pillow, but she felt certain the words would be no clearer even if not blocked by sleep and down.

"Baby?" she stroked his face a little more vigorously. She realized she felt scared, but had no idea why.

Ben's eye's flickered open, and he made a soft moaning noise. She felt her irrational fear slip up another notch. His face under her finger's felt cold. Despite how silly it made her feel, Christy pulled back the Duvet that covered them and looked at the ring on his left hand. It did seem to serve as a mood ring, a barometer of sorts, right? The ring's surface no longer looked shiny, but it still held a soft glow of pale green.

"Baby?" she said again.

Ben's eyes blinked a few times and then seemed to focus. She saw he wore only his boxers, and his legs seemed dirty. He had scattered small scratches, and a large bruise had formed on the outside of his left knee. What the hell? She looked up and saw he smiled at her, returned from wherever his deep sleep had trapped him.

"Hi," he said, his voice still heavy with sleep.

"Hi, sweetheart," she answered softy, the relief that flooded over her as confusing as the anxiety it replaced. "How did you sleep?" She usually avoided this question with Ben for obvious reasons, but couldn't help but ask this morning.

He opened his mouth, probably to say "fine" she guessed, but apparently decided that wouldn't fly this morning and snapped his mouth shut. The storm clouds in his eyes darkened a moment and then he looked at her and answered.

"Restless night," he said.

"Dreams," she said simply.

"Yeah," he said but she sensed there was more – something new.

How could she get him to share more of it with her? Why, after all they had been through together, did he still not seem to completely trust her? She wondered if that was fair. Maybe it had less to do with trust than his inability to face whatever it was himself. She thought maybe denial could be a powerful force for some people. She touched his cheek and decided that loving him unconditionally was about the best she could do – that and being here if he ever felt he could share more.

"Anything you want to talk about?" she asked anyway, unable to resist. A woman's need to nurture, she supposed.

Ben shrugged uncomfortably and then shook his head no. She pulled the Duvet back up around their shoulders and snuggled up into him, intent on letting him know it was okay if he couldn't tell her more. His strong arms wrapped around her, and she felt better.

She also felt different – in a good way.

Another kind of nurturing feeling. I guess, I didn't use my stuff like I said I would, so it really is possible. The timing is right, but…

The thought made her inwardly gasp with delight.

I wonder if it's possible already?

She realized a part of her hoped very much not. She had more than a couple of drinks last night. Was that really the safest way to start it off? She decided to lay off the drinks the rest of the trip – maybe a glass of wine, a short one at that, with dinner, and that would be it. The thought of doing something, no matter how small, to start this new beginning filled her with excitement. She hugged Ben tightly.

"I love you," he said. The voice held a tension that brought back her worry.

Christy kissed his stubbly cheek and stroked his hair.

Stop thinkin' about babies and take care of your husband today. He has a very stressful 24 hours ahead, I think. I may not understand it, but it's real for him.

"I'll be fine," he reassured her and touched her cheek as if he had read her mind. His skin felt warmer, she realized. She decided not to tell him about the strange feeling she had – not today with all that seemed to hang over thoughts. She held great hope their visit to the bayou would really be cathartic for him. She wasn't naïve enough to expect miracles from a day-trip to his childhood home, but maybe it could at least begin some sort of healing process.

"What's the name of the place we're going today – the name of your home?"

She watched those sexy, stormy eyes and even imagined a soft flash of lightning back behind those growing clouds.

"Doesn't have a name," he said and raised his head up to rest his face on his hand and look at her. "I call it the middle of fuckin' nowhere," he said with a smile. "But the closest town is called Chackbay, about a half-hour from our little shack, I guess, depending on the condition of the road."

"Chackbay, huh?" she murmured. "Sounds charming, actually."

"It's not," he said and placed a hand on her bare hip under the covers. "Wouldn't even qualify as a neighborhood in most parts of the country."

His hand slid softly and gently off her hip, across her belly (and whatever might be inside) and then tickled downwards as he leaned over and kissed her neck. Her breath quickened at his touch, and she felt a river of moisture building just past his fingertips. As his mouth worked its way down to her breast, she reached over and wrapped her hand around the already throbbing hardness she found between his legs. She opened her legs a little and moaned.

A half-hour later they stood together under the strong stream of a hot shower and she leaned against his chest, her arms folded between them, as he held her tightly and gently soaped her back. His strong arms and slippery warm hands felt so good that for a moment she thought she might have to drag him back to their big comfortable bed.

My God, he turns me into such a nymphomaniac.

Instead, she just relaxed into his embrace and enjoyed the luxury of letting him wash her. She sighed contentedly and wondered what the rest of the day held for them. She would be very glad when this was over, she decided. She didn't feel any real anxiety for herself, just worry surrounding the impact the day would have on Ben. She truly believed whatever the cost today might bring, it would be emotional payment well spent if it allowed them to move forward and him to start fresh. She guessed the real honeymoon would start tomorrow. She wondered if they should pack up and head to the beach after his visit to his childhood home. Putting as much distance between them and Louisiana might be the best idea, just as he had suggested (though, she thought he had perhaps hoped to avoid the trip to the bayou all together).

She kissed his chest and looked up at him. His eyes were glued to an empty spot on the shower wall, and when she squeezed her arms around his waist he startled a bit. But, then he smiled down at her.

"You look beautiful, Mrs. Morvant," he said.

The name filled her with warmth and happiness.

"What do you think about packing and checking out when we head out to Backbay?"

"Chackbay," he corrected with a smile.

"Whatever it is," she said. "We could call our resort in Destin and try to check-in tonight, even if it's late. Then, we could wake up to our Beach vacation tomorrow."

He stared down at her with eyes that had cleared a bit from the brewing storm.

"That sounds great to me," he said without pointing out he had suggested that and been shot down last night.

What a good husband he is.

"We could maybe even get there in time for dinner if we get a move on."

"Or we can eat along the way if we need to," she said, excited about putting all this place held for him behind them. She handed him a big fluffy Dauphine Orleans Hotel towel and wrapped one around herself, suddenly excited and ready to get going. "Destin is going to be awesome."

Maybe tonight I'll tell him how it feels like something might be growing inside of me – something wonderful and with his eyes.

"We'll get moving right after our free, included-in-our-stay-at-the-Dauphine-Hotel breakfast," he announced as he began to organize things to shove into their roller bags.

That sounded about right. She realized she felt famished.

Maybe I'm eating for two.

CHAPTER 25

He held her hand as they drove out of New Orleans on I-310 towards SR-90 South and tried his best not to look distracted. That proved a real test, since the images of the night before flashed in his head like a slideshow, and the words of the Village Elder drifted through his mind like a sound track. The last thing he wanted was to worry her more than her face suggested she managed to do on her own. He loved her for her concern, but it did little or nothing for either of them.

He saw from the corner of his eye her right hand go again to her belly.

"Are you feeling, okay?" he asked.

"Oh, yeah," she said and patted his hand in hers. "I'm a little nervous, I guess. I'm not sure what to expect." She smiled at him, and her eyes told him it was his reaction she was most uncertain about.

"Well," he mustered to change the subject, "we should at least get you some real Creole food. I'll try and find a Boudin joint in Chackbay for us."

"Boudin?"

"It's a type of spicy sausage," he told her. "It's packed full of tangy meat and rice, and it's totally delicious." He hadn't thought about Boudin in years, but realized that despite gorging himself on free breakfast, he could easily pack away a serious volume of the delicious taste-like-home sausage. Ben's grocery (no relation) in Chackbay, if it was still there, would be a perfect place to score some, as well as coffee.

It would also likely be where he would leave his wife when he headed up to the woods and the possibility that the rabbit hole really existed. He could not take the chance of her being with him if he found what he believed he would in the forest bayou of home. He had also decided not to talk to her about it until they got to Chackbay, to minimize the likelihood she might talk him out of the only plan that made sense. He looked at his watch – with any luck they would be back in the car and headed east for Florida on I-10 by mid-afternoon.

He realized she had said something to him, but had no idea what.

"I'm so sorry, baby, what did you say?"

She smiled but looked worried all over again.

"I said I didn't know you spoke Cajun," she repeated and squeezed his hand tightly. "Isn't that what you and the little old man spoke?"

Honestly, he had thought they had spoken plain English – that was how it had sounded in his head anyway. He knew for certain they had not spoken Cajun French, however. Although he could still understand some of what he heard in that language, he couldn't really speak more than a word or two.

"Creole," he said. "Cajun is a local dialect of basically French with a few English words tossed in." He put on his signal to exit off of 90 South onto Route 307. "Creole is a blended language, supposedly formed from ancient African dialects." He suddenly wondered if that might be the reason the elder's words sounded so familiar – a common language heritage?

We share a lineage, if not of blood then for sure of spirit – both descendants of the ancient one – Children of Ginen.

Ben shook the voice out of his head.

"Anyway, it's mostly thought of as a black language in Louisiana. When you're from a place like where I'm from, you don't really differentiate black from white," he paused as they merged off the exit and onto the now slower two-lane road. "Just dirt poor and folks from somewhere else."

Christy nodded understanding.

"I learned a lot of Creole, and maybe some pieces of other speak, from my Gammy." He was aware his accent had thickened a bit as they got closer to home, but that seemed normal.

They continued on in silence for a while, Christy apparently content to let him alone with his thoughts, her hand in his and her head now soft against his shoulder. Ben's mind wandered between his past, images of Gammy and happy times (there really had been a lot of them) and the bizarre present he felt the past had driven him to. And, the future, of course. He hoped this drive would start him on a new highway that would take them far, far away from the ghosts of his past. Whether his questions were answered, he planned on driving east towards Destin and never looking back again after today – ghosts and nightmares be damned.

They turned at a T-intersection onto route 20 southbound, and things even started to smell of home. A few minutes later they pulled onto the main street (with its two flashing yellow traffic lights) of the tiny town of Chackbay, Louisiana in Lafourche Parish – population barely four thousand and all but a few hundred of that outside the tiny "downtown" itself. A small blue and white sign told them (and any tourist who stumbled on the little village far from civilization) they had just entered the Gumbo Capital of the World. Maybe, armed with that knowledge, the lost tourists would stop and shake off a few bucks here, instead of continuing south to Thibodaux or Shrieves.

Ben's Grocery had gone the way of the Traiteurs, but the old building still stood and now housed "Chackbay Market and Gumbo Café." Below that, like an afterthought in cursive, the sign announced "and Boudin Joint." He suspected if they could have thought of any other buzz words that would make tourists pull into a yellow outlined spot in the uneven parking lot they would sure as hell be on the sign, too. Ben pulled into open parking lot, put the Charger in park, and looked over at his wife who stared at him expectantly.

"Aren't we going up to your grandmother's – house?" Ben sensed she had started to say shack and changed her mind. Her voice in his head confirmed his suspicion.

"It is more of a shack, actually," he said, and she looked at him confused.

Oh right – I'm not supposed to hear people's private thoughts, am I?

"I thought we could go in here and grab a coffee and talk for a few minutes," he said quickly before she thought about his slip too much.

"Okay," she said.

I'm along for the ride. I love him so much. Just be here for him whatever he needs.

Clear as a bell in her soft voice in his head. He smiled.

They chose one of the small round tables instead of the picnic tables and sat down with their fresh steaming coffee. No lattes or cappuccinos on the menu, but fresh heavy cream and real sugar tasted perfect in the strong, dark brew. He took her hands.

"Baby," he started and her eyes held his with no judgment or demands. "I want you to know how much it means to me that you are here with me." He pressed her hands to his lips. "I don't think I could have come up here without you. I needed you – needed us – to make me face my past here and move on. Thank you so much."

She looked at him, and her eyes rimmed with tears.

"I love you," she said simply, as if that should explain everything. He realized that perhaps it did.

"Now," he continued, "I think I really need to go up to the shack in the woods by myself." He watched her eyes, but they gave up nothing.

I want whatever you need. I just want you to be okay.

He stopped himself from thanking her out loud for the thought he heard.

"I won't take long, I just want to say goodbye, I think, and maybe let some old feelings work through me. Then," he squeezed both of her hands in his this time and nearly spilled his coffee, "when I get back we'll sample some gumbo and Boudin, and then we'll get the hell out of here forever."

"Okay," was all she could manage, but he knew it really was okay.

"You'll be okay here?" he asked. "It'll take about a half-hour each way and not too long when I get there – could be as long as a couple of hours." He felt bad about that part.

Christy nodded and smiled her unconditional loving acceptance.

"Of course, I'll wander around a little bit and see what else this metropolis is trying to unload on tourists. You do what you need to do and come back to me."

He nodded and felt his throat tighten again at how much he loved this woman. *Now more than ever.*

"I'll be right back," and rose and kissed her cheek.

"I'll call the resort in Destin and see if we can check in a day early," she pulled out her cell phone, looked at it, then frowned. "One bar," she said and looked up with a tense face. "What if you need to call me?"

Ben touched the side of her face.

"One bar is enough. The reception is probably better outside. And anyway, I'll be right back."

Christy nodded and sipped her coffee. He could see she tried to hide her worry, but the brown eyes and her furrowed brow hid nothing.

"Can't promise I won't need more space in the trunk by the time you get back," she forced smile. "I saw some crafty looking shops back there. We may even need to check bags on the way back."

He kissed her mouth this time.

"No problem, love."

Then, he walked out and forced himself not to look back. He slipped into the Charger and headed west on the main drag and out of town. A half mile out he turned onto a nearly invisible dirt road with weeds that reached the tops of his wheels.

Welcome home, Ben.

He thought the voice in his head was just his own.

* * *

The shack (their shack – Gammy's and his) still stood where he remembered, and he realized he knew it would be there. He had no idea whether the raging fire from his memory was the illusion or the sagging building he pulled up to. One or the other had to be illusion he supposed. He realized it also didn't matter. Not anymore.

Just go for a ride and clear the attic.

Only this wasn't a dream. Now he could be certain of that. This was real – whether supernatural, definitely real. Thirty-five minutes away (the road had been remarkably dry) his beautiful wife and best friend sat and sipped coffee, no doubt with the furrowed brow he felt pretty certain was reserved exclusively for the way he complicated her life.

Today was real.

Dreams are the reality that hides from us.

The Elder's voice in his head felt like a memory, not a new message.

He pulled the Charger, now more grey than black with a thick covering of dust from the twenty-five minutes on the dirt road, up beside the back of his childhood home and turned off the ignition. He couldn't quite get out of the car – not right away – and sat in the growing heat of the driver's seat and stared at the remnants and his past as images flooded through his head. He closed his eyes and took a deep breath of familiar home. When he opened them, nothing had changed except his powerful sense of nostalgia. He slid out of the driver's seat and closed the door with a satisfying thunk.

The tall grass that climbed several feet up the side of the shack didn't look to him like neglect – it had always looked just like this. The roof sagged a little to the left of middle, but again, that was just as he remembered it the day he had last left it – only a few weeks before the fire (if that had even happened).

He walked around to the front and carefully stepped up the three rickety wood steps onto the badly warped porch. From there, he looked out over the yard – more of a clearing in the woods he realized – and for a moment could almost see his Gammy, brightly-colored dresses and bare feet, as she stirred dirty clothes in a giant steel tub over a fire. He felt tears well up in his eyes and realized how much he loved her and missed her.

Past the clearing and the imaginary laundry pot, he saw a short moss-covered trail he knew led in short order to the homemade rope hammock. Beyond were the woods – his woods – the woods he had both embraced and conquered as a kid. Those woods had been at times a refuge for his imagination and, at others, dark and frightening. His woods had been castles he had conquered, forts he had defended from Indians, and his sitting room where he poured through the books Gammy had gotten for him every month from "Dat busy lady in town wit all dem ole books." He sighed and for a moment just let the childhood nostalgia sweep over him in images and feelings. He opened his eyes, and the clearing looked small, so different from six and half feet up instead of through his little boy eyes.

He turned slowly, a part of him reluctant to let go of the warm, bittersweet trip his heart took him on. He knew that Christy, alone and worried back in Chackbay, might think these were the thoughts and feelings that brought him here. He knew that no purging of childhood memories would let him shake off the shackle of this place. He had ghosts to bury, that for sure was part of it *Sho' 'neff true dat*, he thought, and chuckled, but he also had present day demons to slay. Those demons had to die, whether only in his mind or not real, if he wanted to start his life with his new wife. Ben reached out and grasped the knotted rope that served (and always had) as a makeshift door knob.

The only difference was the cold. He walked slowly across the creaky wood floor of the large room he remembered as always being warm, even too hot at times. He knew the frigid air could be easily explained by the now unused large, black pot-bellied stove that had served as stove and central heat (causin' it in da center of da room) that had always glowed with wood fire when he was young, even on sweltering hot summer days. Today the stove looked dark and cold.

Cold here's comin' from more than a lack of heat.

The chill was that of a cave, the wet, cool that breathed out of the dark. He tried to check his imagination and walked to the thick wood table in the corner of the big room. He drew a finger across the surface and shuddered in surprise when it came back without a lick of dust. Except for the chilling air, it was like they had been here, the two of them living their backwoods life, only hours ago. The shudder turned to a shiver, and he rubbed his hands up and down on his arms for warmth.

The ceiling hovered only three or four feet above him, now that he had grown to a strapping SEAL of a man. He felt a little claustrophobic at the nearness that seemed not quite right. The drop ceiling of his little bedroom loft would be a tight fit these days, maybe only a few feet from the real ceiling, but it had never felt small to him back then. He walked over to the homemade ladder he had climbed every day of his child life and grasped the top rung which sat now at eye level. Back then it had seemed an exciting climb, sometimes even a daunting climb when he was young. He could peer now into his little loft without even tipping up on his toes.

The loft looked filled mostly with shadows now – no light from hanging hurricane lanterns today. To his surprise the grey sheet and heavy homemade comforter were there, pulled only partially over his lumpy pillow, the little boy in a hurry to chase dragons through his woods.

Why the surprise? The entire house can't really even be here, and it's the blankets that seem unbelievable to you?

For a moment he was a boy again, rocking back and forth, arms hugged around knees, as he watched his home dissolve in the lapping flames and smoke. And, then he was grown again (all grow'd up) and cold, and he shivered anew as the memory floated away in a smoke of its own.

This time tears spilled onto his cheeks, and he wiped them away in confusion. What the hell was he crying about? As a boy he had dreamed about getting away from here – about getting to the real world. He had wanted to have adventures like the characters in the books he read, to see faraway places around the world. He had found that, hadn't he?

After Gammy died and he had bounced around a few foster homes – first in Chackbay and later in the suburbs of Baton Rouge – he had slowly found his way out. He had discovered television and, through it, stories of soldiers and the famous Navy SEALs. He had escaped like he always wanted to, so what the shit? He never told anyone of the fire or Gammy walking him out of those woods that night – impossible of course since she had been hours long dead by then. He had forced his mind away – to faraway places and the Navy – his own personal life raft.

Ben sniffled as the tears on his cheeks also found their way to the back of his throat. Was this what Christy imagined he would find here? Were these the feeling that would give him the fabled *closure?* He had no reason to feel angry, but he did. Angry at Gammy for leaving him alone in the night while the demons hunted him down, angry at Christy for wanting him to come here (though she had not even suggested it his mind reminded him, jumping to her defense), angry mostly at himself for feeling like this.

The resonating creaking felt, at first, warm and familiar. It was the sound of childhood and meant safety. It meant he was not alone tonight, that Gammy would be home with him.

Creak –Creak – Creak

The sound of Gammy rocking in her chair on the porch.

The realization that the noise meant Ben was not alone now melted away the warmth and replaced it with an eerie chill that made him shiver again. He could almost smell the venison stew on the pot-bellied cook stove, but when he looked the stove remained dark and cold.

Creak – Creak – Creak

Ben walked slowly across the once large and now tiny one-room shack that had been home. It felt more like a tomb and despite the frigid air that raised goose flesh on his skin, he felt sweat pop out on his forehead and temples. One drop tickled its way down his neck.

Creak – Creak – Creak

He reached the door with its rope knob and opened it slowly, the old worn hinges adding their own slow creak, a caricature of a ghost story, he realized. He stepped through the doorway onto the sagging and warped porch with no fear of what he would find. He knew exactly what he would see.

Sho' 'neff true, dat.

Creak – Creak – Creak

Gammy sat in the rocker in her "night time" clothes, the ones that used to mean she would not be home all night, that for a while he would be alone in his loft, alone in their shack in the forest bayou. The grey dress stretched down to her ankles and nearly covered her dirty, bare feet. Her grey hair went every which way, like always, but her face looked like a grandma from an old book, or maybe Mrs. Claus. She smiled at him over stemless glasses that she pulled off her nose and dropped in her lap. She reached out her pale arms towards him.

"My big 'ole boy. Jess look 'atcha now. Come on now 'n givin ole Gammy kisses."

CHAPTER

26

Christy stood outside the Chackbay Market and Gumbo Café and Boudin
Joint in front of a bin full of leathery alligators with shiny marble eyes and
a sign to would-be buyers that these were AUTHENTIC bayou alligator
heads and could be yours for only $9.99. She flipped open her phone
which intermittently flashed back and forth between one and two bars.
She bit her lip, checked to be sure her ringer was on, closed the cover, and
slipped it in her back pocket. That way, even if she set it wrong, she
would feel if it vibrated. She took two steps towards the street, stopped
and turned back. She crossed her arms across her chest and tapped a
nervous foot, then looked at her watch. It had barely been an hour.

*Shit. You best calm down, girlfriend, or you'll have a nervous
breakdown. He's fine – this is the right thing for him, and he is fine.*

Her mind wandered against her will to the doorway on Dumaine
Street in the Quarter and the strange little Cajun man who grinned his
scattered-tooth grin and jived to the saxophone. She thought of those
strange eyes and the stranger language her husband had fallen so easily
into with him and then walked on like nothing unusual had happened.
The thought that more was at work here than just Ben's need to say
goodbye to the memory of his grandmother tugged at her.

*How the hell did that crazy old Cajun just show up out of nowhere and
have a heated talk with Ben. Just what the hell is going on?*

She pulled her phone out again and flipped it open to call him.
Just a quick call to be sure he was okay. Her finger hovered over the

number two, his speed dial number. She shouldn't call, right? She should just let him do what he needed to do up there in the woods. It didn't hurt her at all that he wanted to go alone – she sort of understood she thought. But she did worry more, not being there, not knowing how he was doing or what he might be feeling.

Her finger shifted to the number one, and she speed-dialed her voicemail.

Just gonna make sure he didn't try to leave a message. Reception sucks out here in Deliverance *country.*

Her phone assured her she had no messages (*you—have—no—messages* the annoying bitch told her), and she flipped it closed again, dropping it into her jeans yet again.

She turned away from the diner and decided to stroll around and find something to buy. She had a feeling she would not really want any mementos from today, but she had to do something. For a moment she saw the old Cajun, grinning face, yellow eyes, and "Purple Haze" ball cap, seated on a bench beside a lamp post at the corner. Her pulse quickened, and she felt herself actually gasp, her breath sucked in through clenched teeth. This was no friggin' coincidence.

But then the old man shimmered in the sunlight, like a mirage of water on a hot asphalt road, and disappeared.

My God, get a grip on yourself, girl.

She felt for the phone in her back pocket. Secure it was there, she continued down the street at a tense, trotting stroll. She glanced again at her watch despite her best effort not to.

Four more minutes down.

CHAPTER

27

The terror he expected at the sight of his Gammy – decades long dead now and rocking in her same old rocker, a shaker glass of lemonade in her hand – never came. He realized he had known he would see her today. Perhaps a normal person would feel fear at the sight of a living ghost, creaking in her chair on a warped porch in the woods, but he was a child of the bayou – grandson of a Traiteur (*Sho' 'neff true dat*). Gammy sipped the warm glass of iceless lemonade and flashed again the smile his memory told him meant everything was alright (Awright nah, chile).

Ben approached her and felt a smile creep across his face. This wasn't the Gammy of his nightmares – the Gammy with the long curved knife, dripping blood from her naked body in the moonlight. This was grandma Gammy. The Gammy of bedtime stories and soft songs when he had a bellyache. The Gammy of warm smiles and warm potions on scraped knees and elbows – always with a kiss to "seal dat medicine in yo' knee and heart." The Gammy that somewhere found Christmas presents every year for her dirt poor grandson in the woods.

Just his grandma.

She rose from her rocker with a grunt to meet him.

"Dese ole bones, now," she said.

Just like always.

She wrapped her arms around him in a huge bear hug, undaunted that she now came only to his chest, and he had clearly grown out of that embrace. He fully expected her skin to be, well cool at least, if not cold.

Ghosts were cold, right? But her touch was warm and familiar, and the scent of her was all Gammy instead of the mulchy grave smell he braced for. If not for the powerful memory of her pale and lifeless body, obscene in the simple box so many years ago, he would have been tempted to believe she had never died at all – that he had made some terrible mistake – that and the fact she had not aged a day beyond the old lady from his boyhood.

She pulled out of his hug and looked him up and down. Her wrinkled old face beamed.

"Know'd you'd grow up big, but Christ on a crutch, boy. Look 'atcha!"

Ben beamed back and kept his hands on Gammy's shoulders. She raised an eyebrow at him.

"Lossa questions, 'ey boy?"

Ben nodded and felt like the young child he had been when last they'd talked. Gammy nodded back.

"Lots to tell ya'," she said and looked past him at the sky. "Not much time for the telling, 'fraid." She said. "Sit or walk?"

Just like when he was little and had questions or was afraid (usually from something he heard in the dark when she wore her night time clothes like now). He usually said sit, and they would sit on the edge of the porch. Right now he thought a little distance between him and the shack he last saw in flames might clear his head a bit – even if he was still talking to his dead grandmother.

"Walk," he said.

"Better now," she took his hand and led him down the rickety stairs. "Best be getting' ya on to yo' appointment anyhow."

They walked hand-in-hand through the clearing and started down the moss-covered path at its edge. Ben felt himself drag back a bit as they entered the woods, but Gammy squeezed his hand, and the tension melted away.

Plenty of time for that if I still gotta go down that fuckin' hole.

He realized he still hoped Gammy would say something that could maybe spare him that terrifying journey. They came to a large, moss-covered rock – the moss had overgrown the 'B.M.' he had scraped into it years ago – and she leaned against it and turned to face him.

"Been meetin' dat other Traiteur, ain't ya boy? Dat one from the dark land?"

Ben wanted to be sure he understood everything he heard, even if a part of his mind reminded him – insisted in fact – that all of this was created in his brain.

"Are you talking about the Village Elder? The one I met in Africa?"

"Yep," she said. "Dats da one."

Ben tried to shake away the little boy he felt himself become.

"How do you know about that?"

Because she is inside your diseased brain just like that fantasy.

Except he no longer believed that.

"Dem people is kin for us," she said like that explained everything. It didn't for him.

"What the hell does that mean?"

"Mouth boy," she scolded. As a kid, he'd been allowed to say "shit" but for some reason "hell" had always been a soapin' offense. His face became pensive, and she sighed. "Bennie, I love ya more 'n you could know," she said, "and I wants to tell you everything you needs, but time don' let me. Things is that them people over there is our people. Our spirit kin. We is all one wit dem."

Ben thought a moment.

"All Children of Ginen?"

Gammy laughed the full and deep laugh he remembered, and the musical sound of it tugged another tear out of his left eye.

"We don' call it dat here, but yep – any name'll do it, so sure to dat."

Ben nodded, but didn't really understand.

Gammy looked past him at the sky again.

"Gots to keep tellin' it, honey-boy," she said. "Time keep on movin'."

She took his hand again, and they continued on down the path. Only a few more paces and they passed the rope hammock where he had pretended to be a pirate, high above the sea on the rigging to the main sail, and more lately had awakened in terrible dreams of his beloved grandmother.

"Time was I could jess be Traiteur here around," Gammy continued as they strolled slowly now. Her voice had a sadness that tugged his heart. "Long time like that. Remember dem happy times, Benny?"

He nodded. He had been happy – maybe just a kid who didn't know better or had nothing to compare his life to, but he had been happy enough in their home in the woods. People came by a lot – white, black,

Indian, it didn't matter which – and Gammy made them better or at least feel better. They would give the Traiteur and her young grandson food or blankets or clothes. Once they got a bucket of Boudin so big that even though they salted it, a lot spoiled before they could eat it all. Fruit – he remembered how special it was when her "patients" would give them fruit. The sweetness had seemed almost overwhelming. He smiled at how uncomplicated it seemed. Simple and happy – two good words for those days.

"Then came dat dark one – wantin' cleanin' for dat spirit sickness in him." She shook her head at the thought. "Woulda done it gone, too," she said and looked at him. "'Ceptin' the dark blood got deep in him 'fore I could. May never coulda, I don't know." Gammy stopped and stared off into the woods a moment. "Dat black-blood spirit had him way too tight by then. Sick wit it he was and way too shittin' late." She looked over at him, called back from the memory, and smiled again. "Turn out okay, guessin', right?"

Ben felt a grab on his insides. He had to ask although he knew the answer.

"Did you kill that man, Gammy? The one I saw in the dream who I remembered for so long as a deer – the man that night in the woods?" He held her eyes with his.

He held no judgment for his grandmother. Shit, how many men had he killed in the last few years? If she had done what his dreams told him, it would be for the same reasons – an enemy who had to submit or die for the greater good. As unfair as it seemed though, her answer did matter to him. He knew it would change how he saw Gammy, his gentle and loving grandmother, probably forever.

"Sure the fuck did," she spit back, and the venom in her voice surprised him. "No man, though, not by then. Blood done turned black by then, from dat dark one."

She stopped again and looked at him. Her eyes told him she understood how important the words were to him.

"No could give dat dark one what he wanted and ran out of time to git him gone." The eyes now told him she had done what she had to, nothing more. He wanted that to matter but wasn't sure it did.

"What did he want? The dark one, I guess I mean. What did he want that you couldn't give him?"

Gammy took both his hands in her own and smiled at him with wet eyes.

"Why, *you* chile," she said. "Dark one sent dat black-blooded fuck to take wit him my grandson."

Ben literally reeled at what he heard. His body tipped back on his heels, and he stumbled, catching himself with an awkward jolt or he would have fallen out straight to the ground – like some damn damsel in distress swooning and fainting at a danger she confronted.

"What do you mean?" he cried out and realized his voice, too, had taken on a hysterical high pitch. Did this nightmare begin with him somehow?

Might could be endin' dat own way, too. Sho' 'neff, Bennie boy. Sho' 'neff true dat one.

"What the hell do you mean?" he asked again, his voice more even and his own. "What the hell is the dark one and black blood? What does all this Voodoo shit mean?" He felt angry more than frightened now.

I'm getting pretty sick of this crazy-ass shit.

Gammy again let loose her grandmother laugh.

"More than some tourist shit Voodoo, dis one, Bennie," she said. "Dem 'ole-time Vodu ones, be more like to true. But we all da same, honey-boy. Same kin wit dem dat you met and the ole ones from home."

"What old ones?" he asked, anger now competing with a desperate need to understand.

"The Eaters of the Dead," she answered simply. "We all spirit kin from one same great one – all one spirit family."

Eaters of the Dead. He had heard that enough times now, too. The term brought back nothing from his childhood, but still felt familiar somehow.

"Who are the Eaters of the Dead?" he asked. "I've heard that more than once the last couple of days. What does it mean?"

"You know'n dem Attakapa?" she said.

"Of course," he said. The Attakapa Indians and the Choctawhatchee Indians were the two main tribes of Bayou Louisiana Native Americans. They were also both all but extinct.

"Well, we share more than spirit kin wit dem Indians, Bennie," she said and her face took on a glow that made her look like a young girl. "Share blood and spirit wit dem, you and I." She looked at him and raised an eyebrow like he should know what came next. Then, she shook her head. "Come on, now, boy. Remember nothin' I taught you?" He stared at her unsure what he had forgotten. "Attakapa is a Choctaw word," she told him. "Means 'Eater of the Dead' cause they watch dem Attakapa Indians eat they enemies once they kill'd 'em. They was protectors of the Living Earth, them Indians. Same as you and I."

Ben tried to get a handle on all his Gammy told him. Was she telling him they were somehow descendants of the Attakapa? The poor people of the bayou saw a lot of mixing of blood and culture, to be sure. Hell, that was what the word Creole meant to him. People from a big old mixing pot – mostly because they were too poor to travel beyond walking distance to find a little lovin'. A few generations in the bayou produced the mix-breed mutts they had all become. But, so what? What did that mean to him now, even if he did have some Indian blood in his veins, other than more college scholarship eligibility?

"Why do they eat the dead?"

"They was Rougarou," she said. "Protectors. Eating dat dead enemy prevents the afterlife. Not like some kinda heaven place – no boy. Not like in some story. For dem Indians afterlife meant they could spirit walk back here, back to our world from dat other spirit place, and if them dat come back had the black blood of the dark one, well…." She shrugged like the return of those ghosts held obvious and terrible consequences. She tugged at his arm to get his eyes back on her. "Bennie – honey, boy – you da Rougarou now."

Ben shook his head, tried to make all the dust of this settle into a meaningful pile of something.

"I have no idea what that means for me, Gammy," he said and felt frustration return. "I don't know what any of you want from me."

Gammy touched his face with her warm hand.

"You will, Bennie," she said. She looked again past him at the sky. "Time 'bout up, honey-boy," she said. "Jess remember now – Attakapa is in our blood and spirit, but can be friend or enemy both."

Ben's eyes filled now with frustrated tears.

"I don't know what the hell any of this means," he choked and bent his head down against his Gammy's forehead.

"You will, Bennie," she reassured again and patted his back. "You gots to be learnin' now about controllin' dem gifts' you got, now, darlin' chile. You gots lot more of dat Ashe in you. Don't be scare't now, chile. It's okay, now."

She tipped his head up by his chin and wiped a tear from his cheek.

"I gotta go now, honey-boy," she said, and he felt her hands on him grow light and cold. Her touch became more like a memory. "You gotta go, too. Find dat Indian be waitin' for you, Bennie. More to tell ya." She had nearly disappeared, her touch now gone though he could still see a faint shadow of her hands on his arms.

"What Indian? Where will I find him?"

"You know where, Bennie," she said. "I love you, boy,"

"I love you, too, Gammy," he said, but she had disappeared.

Behind her, behind where she had been, he saw the dark hole in the woods, the hole in his reality. The rabbit hole stared back at him, and he smelled the wet and rotting stench of it. A cold air belched out at him, like opening a freezer in your face in summer time, only with a terrible putrid smell behind it.

Go on, nah, boy. Git in dat dey hole, now. Tings waitin' ya.

Ben realized he had come a long way to this place. He had traveled years, and continents and untold dreams – many forgotten, perhaps – to get here. There was no choice left for him. Maybe there never had been.

Ben hunched down and passed through the green threshold and into the dark, wet hole in the woods.

* * *

He felt the warm wetness of the earth as it squished beneath his feet, and his brain tried to trick him, to let his fear convince his mind that the ground moved a little. He felt as if the tunnel-like hole in the woods might be alive – like he slid down the throat of some living thing.

More like up its ass. When the bayou takes a shit it dumps wherever this path takes me.

The thought that he headed for the place where the magical waste of the haunted woods ended up gave him a tight-lipped grin, but in no way reassured him. But Gammy would never have let him continue on if he was in real danger, right?

The heat felt nothing like Africa or Iraq. Humid didn't even touch it – wet seemed more the word he needed. The air felt thick and heavy, and he found it difficult to suck it in and out of his lungs. The foul smell, like something rotted in the tunnel with him, didn't help his breathing any either. Between his legs, on the tissue-like ground was a thin stream – only a trickle at first – of nearly black water coursing down with him. As he continued downward, the little stream widened slowly until he had to spread his feet apart a bit to keep from stepping in it. He thought perhaps the black water might be the source of the horrible sulfur smell that gagged him and the thought of it soaking through his Keen climbing shoes revolted him.

His impression that the hole dove down a short distance from the entrance had been right on and almost immediately he had to lean backwards to keep from pitching forward face-first down the ever-steepening shaft. He held his arms at shoulder height, ready to grab something if needed, but he greatly preferred not to touch the twisted, grey briar patch looking branches that formed the tunnel in the woods. The branches looked hard and somehow sharp and seemed almost woven together like someone had knitted the hole out of dead scrub. Now and again, a puff of ice-cold air brushed his face and dried, for a moment, the sweat running down his temples and neck.

After only a few minutes Ben felt the pitch shallow out, and the tunnel began to widen rapidly. Just in time, since the little trickle of foul, black water had by now become a full-fledged stream. As the tunnel widened, Ben found he could step to one side of the running water and walk along the edge, so long as he hunched over a bit more to avoid rubbing against the walls and ceiling. He could hear ahead of him a gentle roar he believed could be the tumbling water of a true river, though how the puny little stream could grow to that size so quickly seemed unbelievable.

Yeah – okay. 'Cause the day has been completely fucking believable until now. The black river from nowhere is the only part you can't swallow?

He doubted the foul stench had lessened any, but at least he had acclimated to it and no longer gagged at the smell. As he continued on, the tunnel widened more and shortly he could stand upright which pulled out much of the achy stiffness accumulating in his back and shoulders. He started thinking about what in the hell he was doing, now that he didn't have to focus all of his attention on not stepping in the black shit water or touching the evil looking vines of this damned place.

That Gammy thought he should come here seemed enough. The old Cajun, the Village Elder, even his own sense of calling from the dreams – they all were suspect in his mind. But Gammy – Gammy was different. She had cared for him his whole short childhood and had always protected him, even from her own frightening world. He doubted if he could have gone down this hole if not for Gammy.

So, thanks for that.

He no longer felt like he walked in a tunnel. The walls and ceiling had stretched out to the point where he felt more like he had entered some other world whose low sky had been woven from the dead and sharp-looking brush. The walls now stretched out at angles away from him, ever widening as they disappeared in the distance. Far away, maybe a half mile or more, he saw the black river seemed to flow towards a low, flat rise in the brown and grey horizon – like a squatty building of some sort. Ben picked up his speed to double time, and his right hand unconsciously sought his M-4 rifle in a combat sling on his chest, but of course it wasn't there. He looked at his watch again, Christy ever present in his thoughts. The large face of his Pathfinder flashed the time, but each beat the seconds flashed, the number stayed the same instead of moving forward. He stopped a moment and stared at the watch, then idiotically smacked it with the palm of his hand – the watch version of kicking a generator that didn't fire right away. The watch ignored him and continued to flash:

11:43:05

Each time the seconds flashed, they just repeated. It was still five seconds past Eleven-Forty-Three. Something about this place either made his watch stop working or had actually stopped time. For some reason that made it more real and less dream-like, crazy as that seemed.

Ben continued on.

Guess I don't need to hurry. Seems like I've got all the time in eternity now.

The thought gave him a terrible chill, and he shivered.

A building took shape as he approached and now looked more like ruins of some ancient Incan altar than a real structure. Its surface was half-covered with a sort of moss, only black like the water. A wide opening, about the size of a double garage door, oval instead of square, he thought, opened in its middle and allowed the thick, pasty liquid to flow through undisturbed. At the edges, where the black water should have flowed with subtle eddies of turbulence as it touched the walls it instead moved glass-like and unbroken, as if somehow it flowed through without quite touching the ruins. It looked creepy once he noticed it.

Ben walked slowly up to his side, the right side, of the ruins as he walked along the edge of the black river. As he got closer, the Incan temple feeling of the place increased. The sides of the structure facing him looked now to be more like stairs, partially covered with the black, damp-looking vegetation. The walls angled only slightly, making the steps quite steep, and they rose maybe two hundred feet to the flat top of the square pyramid, and at the top, Ben saw him.

The Indian.

The Eater of the Dead.

He sat cross-legged in the very center, atop the bridge the pyramid-ruins formed over the black river. He watched Ben as he approached but made no gesture, no acknowledgement. His face remained stone. From the distance, Ben couldn't tell if he was young or old, but his body, scantily clad in pants of animal skin and a simple band of cloth around his left bicep, looked young and fit. Ben stared at him a moment and waited for a gesture that he should climb up and join him or that perhaps the Indian would come to him – or meet him half way. The man simply stared, so still as to almost be a statue. Ben hesitated another moment and then shrugged and began to climb.

Came this far – let's see what this guy has to tell me.

The steps were narrow, not even as wide as the length of his feet, and slick as they were covered in perspiring swamp grass. Ben had to be careful not to slip. The last thing he wanted to do was lean forward and touch the steps with their slimy coating of dead whatever, so he climbed with his arms up, his shoulders raised and uncomfortable, and his hand held out like a dainty old woman tip-toeing through a field of dog shit.

With the steep pitch of the stairs that didn't last long, and he felt his legs begin to burn and his shoulders ached. Sweat now poured from his face and body and stung his eyes which he wiped periodically with the back of his equally sweaty arm. As he rose higher above the now cave-like floor of the strange tunnel-world, he felt himself sway a bit.

"Fuck it."

Ben leaned forward began to climb with his arms, as well. His hands now and again grabbed a thick clump of black grass which felt hot and rubbery more than wet. Each time he grabbed a clump, a horrible stench filled his mouth and nose like he had squeezed some primordial fart out of the ooze on the step-like wall of the ruins. He looked up – nearly halfway there – and refused to look down. The arches of his feet now burned from the way he unconsciously grabbed at the steps with his toes, trying to compensate for how narrow they were.

He looked up again and saw the Attakapa still stared down at him, his face impassive and unmoved by Ben's struggle. He doubled his effort and felt his pace pick up a tiny bit, driven forward by sheer will and resolve.

The only easy day was yesterday another SEAL mantra reminded him, this one from his memory and in the voice of one of his instructors from SEAL training. He could almost see him – Senior Chief Perez, hands on hips and blue instructor T-shirt dry and neat – as he and his classmates struggled, filthy and disheveled, through some impossible task.

Ben's arms now burned as much as his legs, but he pushed forward, palms achy from finger-grasping the slick and narrow steps.

I'm not ringing the fuckin' bell.

He was close enough now to see the Indian clearly, but it didn't help him estimate his age. The face was like chiseled stone, and he could have been twenty-eight or Sixty-eight for all Ben could guess. He sat cross-legged and stared at him, hands in his lap.

One more burst of pure spirit and a few minutes later, Ben stepped onto the flat top of the ruins. He immediately bent over, hands on knees, and his chest heaved as he sucked in huge gulps of the thick, wet air. He could feel the Indian's eyes on him only a few feet away, but could not yet straighten up to look at him and instead raised a hand, index finger up in the universal "hang on one fuckin' minute" sign. The Indian made no sound, and Ben sensed no motion.

Slowly his breathing became easier and less painful, and he shook his head to clear the rivers of sweat off of his face. Then, he straightened up with a loud "Whew!" and turned to face the reason for his journey.

From only a few feet away he could narrow the age estimate on the man who sat cross-legged at his feet to perhaps the thirty to fifty range. His dark eyes stared impassively back at him from beneath cropped black bangs of hair. His dark skin seemed barely able to contain the tight, cut muscles beneath it. In another world he could have been a SEAL, Ben thought. They could have been warrior brothers. The grey arm band around his left bicep again struck Ben as remarkably similar to his villagers in Africa. The man stared at him but said nothing. His face told him even less.

"Well," Ben said and his voice sounded to him as far away and kind of dream-like and tinny. The sound echoed off the woven walls and ceiling of the cave like world. "I'm here. I understand you have something you'd like to share with me?"

For some reason that sounded almost hilarious to him, and he barely contained a chuckle. He failed to dissuade the smile that accompanied it. It disappeared when the Attakapa vanished suddenly and then, in a flash, reappeared in front of him, hands on hips and face only inches from his own. Ben startled back a half step and instinctively reached for his M-4 Rifle, which of course did not, in fact, hang in a combat sling across his chest – maybe couldn't even exist in this other world.

"Holy shit," he breathed.

Attakapa is in our blood and spirit, but can be friend or enemy both.

Ben held his Gammy's warning close, but held his ground and the dark-eyed gaze of the Attakapa. He was still a SEAL, Goddammit.

The Indian's face stayed stone, and his mouth remained tight-lipped and locked, but his words floated in the dank air between them just the same.

"I am the protector of the Living World," the low voice said, and the words echoed off the twisted and grey brush sky of their other world. "I am Attakapa and Rougarou. We are from the same circle, you and I, and share both the same Ashe and the same heart. My time passed long ago, but the dark one is here, and so your time is now."

The dark eyes never wavered or blinked, but the lips moved now as the Indian grasped him by the arm just above the elbow in a peculiar embrace.

"We are brothers now. Kin of the same circle of Rougarou."

Ben grasped the Indian's bulging bicep back. The man's dark eyes flashed upwards for a moment, and Ben saw something familiar in the vast recesses. Something he had seen in the spirits of his fellow fighters just before a big operation where enemy fire and bloodshed were fairly certain. The eyes came back to his and seemed to barely conceal a storm behind them.

"We have little time, and I have much to tell you. We will sit."

CHAPTER 28

They sat atop the ruins, cross-legged, facing each other, and Ben felt selfish that his only real goal was to get past all of this and back to Christy and his life with her – a life with babies and dinners on the deck, of long walks and holding hands on the couch. He yearned for that soft life, but the call he felt here seemed familiar and reminded him of the call he answered when he had first joined the SEALs. It had been a call to a hard life of risk and pain, but also one of service and pride – a life of sacrifice with the incredible reward of knowing others were safe and happy because his team was out there on the pointed edge of the spear.

The warrior ethos.

Beneath them the black river moved like polished glass through the tunnel-like bridge of the ruins. Why this felt nothing like an insane dream escaped him completely. The face of the Indian (his brother Rougarou) watched and waited, apparently content to allow him a moment to muse despite his pronouncement that time was short. Ben reigned in his mind, ready now to get to business.

He raised an eyebrow to signal he was ready.

"The protectors have always been among us," the Indian began, his face hard and his eyes unblinking. "Since the beginning of time we have kept the Living Sea, the Living Jungle, the Living Planet safe and protected our people who have, over time, spread out everywhere across her surface." The Attakapa looked off now as if remembering something from long ago. "It is a great privilege to be a keeper of things. It is not from the Mother Earth that we protect our world and our people, though that can sometimes be a part of it. It is from the others – from the dark ones."

Ben shifted uncomfortably on the hard rock surface. He thought back to his Gammy's words – of the dark ones with the black blood. He knew that something so bizarre should sound nothing but crazy to him, but instead it felt familiar. And right.

"Where are these others?"

Give me the coordinates for the target, and we'll get this shit done.

The Indian continued to gaze off into the distance, apparently still lost in some memory.

"For thousands of years they lived among us. Now they live in another place, but times have passed when they try again to come here – to our world – to take from us that which we protect. That is why we need the Rougarou. That time is again here, and the things you see around you in your world – the things that cause fear and suffering – many are brought by the dark ones. The men you fight are often victims of those with the black blood."

Ben's mind reeled around what he thought the Indian told him. Was he supposed to believe that Al Qaeda, the Taliban, maybe even back to Nazi Germany – that those things were instruments of some other-world creatures – of these dark ones? Somalia, Darfur, 9/11…all evil caused by some outside force greater than them?

He didn't buy it –not even a little bit. He had fought against men who had inside them their own evil – and he knew evil existed in the hearts of men. He knew also the Taliban and Al Qaeda fighters he had fought and sometimes killed had believed with his same passion that they were doing what was right. That was what made them so Goddamn hard to beat.

"The evil that is in man is real and has always been with us," said the Indian as if reading his mind. "It always will be with us. The Rougarou fight these men as a matter of routine. Sometimes the dark side of man is nothing more than what it is. Other times it becomes something larger and then it is the work of the dark ones. The Rougarou fight both, but our task is greater and more may be lost when the dark ones are here." He turned his head and looked unblinkingly at Ben with his storm-filled eyes. "You must go back and stop the one with the black blood who inspires evil among those who do harm to our people on the other side of the great water."

Not very mysterious that one. The Attakapa wanted him to return to Africa and face the Al Qaeda assholes who had slaughtered his village. That he would perhaps deploy there again at some point in the next few years seemed likely, but not very important.

"Relax," Ben said and smiled. "I am part of a whole team of protectors. A whole family of Rougarou known as the Navy SEALs. I have friends over there right now continuing the work, so don't worry."

The grip of the Attakapa on his wrist shot flaming spasms up his arm all the way to his chest, and he felt a whimper escape his throat like a little girl. The pain felt like a heat much more than trauma to his wrist.

"They are not Rougarou, and they cannot defeat the dark ones." The Indian's voice had risen in volume as much as it had sunk in tone, and the tremble Ben heard sounded like power not fear. He watched as fireflies began to dance around his arm where the powerful brown hand gripped him, and he wondered which of the two of them the blue light came from. "If the one with the black blood is allowed to arrive, the time for all of our people will be past. There will no longer be a Living Planet, do you understand?"

Ben nodded, more in hope that the gesture would release the grip on his wrist than because he understood. The heat had spread to his chest now, and he tasted metal in his throat.

"We must stop the dark ones where they are or it will be too late."

"By eating their dead?" Ben said and pulled back his arm as the Attakapa released it. He cradled his arm in his lap. The Indian looked past him – perhaps resigned that Ben had not bought all in.

"The eating of the heart of the dead denies the dark ones a vessel to return for their spirit walk here in our world," the Indian said flatly, but his tone told Ben he didn't give a shit what he thought. "The heart holds the part of the spirit that the dark ones may use, and taking it traps them in the dead where they eventually die, as well. The other powers are more important to the Rougarou and to you as the protector of the Living World. You will need the Ashe that grows inside you even now."

Ben thought of Reed and the healing power he had found for him when he needed it. He thought of Auger and his leg and of the thick paste he had used to make that wound disappear. He saw in his mind the hand of the Elder, bathed in blue light and encircled with little fireflies as he had closed the gaping hole in Jewel's head and brain. He knew that these powers were that of the Traiteur, and he knew his Gammy had that power. He also suspected this was not what the Indian spoke of. Again, the Indian read his mind.

"The healer's powers are important, but will not help you defeat the dark ones. The Ashe lets you travel into the minds of others and that can help you. You will not read the dark ones or the one with the black blood easily, but you will find it easy to read the thoughts of men. They will use men to carry out their work. In that way their thoughts are betrayed through the living men they inhabit. The thoughts of those will be open to you even when they are one with the dark ones."

Well, that was sure as shit right. Ben thought of the closed space of the plane and the cacophony of voices that had painfully filled his mind there. He thought of the man with the cheating wife and wondered again if the murderous speculation had ever come to anything. He remembered the voices from the French Quarter and how he had somehow found a way to control it.

"This too will become easier as you grow with the Ashe that is inside you. Eventually you will reach out with your mind into the heads and hearts of others, instead of letting all of their thoughts invade you. Already you have learned much of this. You will also reach out with your mind in other ways."

Ben saw the dead terrorist, his popped eyeball spilling grey, liquid brain onto his swollen face. He thought of the drunk on the street screaming at the pain in his head and eyes.

"Yes," the Indian told him. "These are the weapons of the Rougarou, but you must learn much to be able to control them."

"How?" Ben asked, unable to control the quivering fear in his voice.

"In your own way," the Attakapa answered, which, of course, didn't help at all. "You will use all of these things and more to protect our people and the Living Earth. Our people await you in the jungle and will help you if they can, but you must rely on yourself. You are the Rougarou, and you must return to the fight."

Ben shook his head.

"I'm not sure I'm going anywhere," he said. "It's not really even up to me. I follow orders and go where I'm told." He doubted very much that Viper team would be going back to Africa anytime soon. More likely they would return to Afghanistan.

"The dark ones are in those mountains, also, but the one with the black blood waits in the jungle, and so there you must go." He looked over at Ben and then past him. "Our time is done," he said simply. "All that you need to know is inside you. We may speak again, perhaps, but not here."

And, he was gone.

Ben sat alone, cross-legged atop the tall ruins in the cave-like world at the end of the dark hole in his woods.

Well, this was a wasted fuckin' afternoon.

And then the world around him exploded in white light and screaming noise and his eyes and brain filled with images, some familiar and all horrifying. The images sped through him, and he realized the screaming noise came from his own throat. He grabbed his head in both hands and fell backwards.

He must have been closer to the edge of the flat-top roof of the ruins than he thought because he didn't land on his back, but instead fell through the hot, wet air, legs kicking and arms flailing uselessly as he watched the dead brush woven ceiling fall away from him. He realized where he headed – towards the foul, black water that moved like glass through the tunnel of the ruins. He screamed louder and flailed more desperately at the air around him. The thought of falling into the black, dead, sluggish stream seemed much more horrifying than just splattering his insides all over a hard pavement somewhere.

And then the frothy darkness swallowed him up, filled his mouth and nose with thick, acid-burning stench, and he stopped struggling, letting himself sink down into the murk as his mind faded.

* * *

The heavy emptiness receded slowly, like having a dark shroud pulled away from him an inch at a time and through closed eyes he sensed the world around him had lightened. A cool breeze licked the sweat from his skin, leaving behind itchy salt and a chill that raised goose flesh, making him shudder uncontrollably. It was thoughts of Christy, alone and worried for all of these hours, which finally made his eyelids flicker open.

At first he stared at the woven dead brush ceiling of the hole in the woods, but the branches of the trees were brown rather than grey and between their loosely overlapped fingers he saw sky – an azure blue sky of dry air. He turned his head to the left, gently because of the throbbing in both temples, and he laid spread eagled on the ground in the woods that had once been his home. Something warm trickled down his cheek and into his ear. He raised a tentative and achy arm, wiping it away with the back of his hand and looked at it– blood. He then noticed the metallic taste in his mouth and the burning in his lower lip. He must have bitten it when he fell from the ruins – and pretty deeply from the taste and flowing warm tickle on the side of his face.

You didn't fall from any ruins, you nut job. You're in the woods by your shack – your and Gammy's shack – and you passed out like some scared little girl.

Ben moved both legs, which gratefully worked just fine, and gently raised himself to a seated position on the hard ground, then looked around. He sat at the edge of the clearing in the woods – their yard it had been – right where he had (*imagined he had*) entered the bunny hole. He wiped more blood from his face – this time his chin thanks to gravity– and scanned back towards their shack.

The filthy black Charger sat in the tall grass where he had parked it right beside – nothing. Well, not nothing. One charred corner of what had once been their home remained and across from it a three-foot portion of blackened, collapsed porch, minus the rickety stairs. Between the two sat grey dirt and ash, the rest long ago carted off by others needing wood – or maybe a not-like-new pot-bellied stove. Ben realized that he looked now at what he really last remembered of home.

He struggled to his feet, stopping for a moment at a hunched over half-way point to let the swelling headache subside, and felt fresh tears in his eyes. He thought maybe he cried because he had clearly lost his fucking mind, but after a moment he knew it was for Gammy that he wept – crazy ol' Cajun Gammy and her Witch Doctor ways. God, he had loved her.

But Gammy was gone – as was their home, consumed in fire long ago and with it his childhood. He had no need to come here to see how long ago and far away it all was now.

And no need to come here in my dreams anymore either.

Ben wondered just what the hell his crazy nightmares had meant and what the new ones tried to tell him. He thought now that just maybe his mind wanted to let it go. Maybe the dreams were what he needed to get him to this place, so he could just let it all go.

The image of the Attakapa crystallized in his mind's eye, and the Indian opened his mouth to speak. But Ben dissolved it away before his crazy imagination told him something he didn't want, and maybe no longer needed, to hear.

Crazy nightmares to help you tell goodbye to a crazy childhood. You can wave to it now and move along, back to your life with the best thing that ever happened to you or you can try and embrace it – and be consumed by it.

Biggest no brainer in the world.

Time to say goodbye.

His mind kept reminding him of all it had seen and heard in the last few weeks, especially in the last two days, but it finally snapped closed when his near hysterical inner voice told it to shut the hell up. Maybe he would one day need some help, some professional help, to get all this in order. He kind of thought not, however. He felt himself begin to believe that with Christy he could now move on and forget the bullshit his childhood tried to infect his life with.

Ben looked at his right hand as he shuffled toward the car. The ring looked obscene on his middle finger, and he reached for it – the second time he had decided to pull it off he realized – but he stopped before he touched it. He told himself he wanted to wait, to bury it in the sand like Christy's thoughts had told him she wanted to do. Maybe they could do it together.

That's the reason he gave himself at least. He ignored the thoughts of the mystical water and the ruins and moved his eyes up towards the Pathfinder watch on his wrist – only eleven-forty-eight. He had only been out a couple of minutes from his girly fainting spell, but he had fit one hell of a nightmare into those fleeting moments. He marveled again at the nature of dreams.

Ben slipped into the driver's seat of the Charger, started the car, and backed slowly away from the remains of his house and his childhood and felt a lump in his throat. Then he cut the wheel hard to spin the car around and headed down the bumpy dirt road as fast as he could without risking tearing up the undercarriage and knocking the alignment hopelessly out of whack. With any luck they would be past New Orleans on Interstate 10 and well on their way to a real honeymoon in Destin by early afternoon. Ben felt a gnawing in his stomach as he checked his cell phone for bars (none yet).

Lil' gumbo and some Boudin a' fore we head out, I think.

He headed through the woods towards his wife and their future and away from his troubled past.

CHAPTER 29

The relief she felt as she snapped her phone closed bordered on sexual release. Ben sounded better. No, not just better – he sounded like *Ben*. His voice held the strong confidence of the Navy SEAL she had kissed goodbye several months ago as he had headed off on yet another deployment with his team.

Silly girl – wasting all of that time worrying about him getting hurt instead of worrying about his mind.

She blushed a little at the thought. She never really worried he was crazy of course, but he certainly seemed haunted. Not just by the childhood trauma (which she still knew almost nothing about) but lately he had been haunted by new demons – demons that had hitched a ride home with him from Africa. She knew Ben hated to think of himself that way, but he really was a very sensitive person, and the psychological trauma his team had suffered together seemed to have had a terrible impact on him. Christy suspected that in his case it might be much worse, opening as it did so many doors to his mysterious past.

But that might really be over now and the thought made her unconsciously clap her hands together in utter joy. She felt a little bouncy as she walked up the short main street of Chackbay back towards the little diner. He would pull in a few minutes from now, and she felt very strongly they would step off from here and into a real honeymoon and a wonderful life. The looming specter of deployments and the danger of his job seemed very manageable if they could kiss the ghosts of the past goodbye.

Christy noticed her hand went again to her belly, as if by its own volition. She wondered if the certainty she had about what she felt there was based in truth or just hope. She had always considered herself a very logical realist, would in fact have dismissed this almost premonition like feeling if reported by a friend, but it felt so real and powerful she couldn't easily let it go. Plus, a life with Ben these last few years had definitely opened her to the possibility of senses that might exist beyond simple explanation. Her pulse quickened, and she couldn't keep in the broad smile that filled her face and eyes at the thought.

As she arrived at the corner she looked down at the large paper bag she swung by the built-in cardboard handles, and her grin turned to a subtle frown. The junk in the bag had been meant as a joke – one Ben would ordinarily laugh about she felt sure – but now she had second thoughts. She looked inside at the stuffed alligator head with its cheap marble eyes, the "Chackbay: Gumbo capital of the world" ball cap, and the two "Ragin' Cajun" T-shirts. They were pretty friggin' funny, in fact, but she decided what they both really needed was to drive away from here and never look back. The gag souvenirs she had accumulated over what turned out to be a very short wait now seemed like a constant reminder that her husband probably didn't need.

She dumped the bag into a large green trash can – its black lid secured to its handle with a short chain – and then brushed her hands together ceremonially. Forty-five bucks wasted, but she knew she would never regret leaving the reminders behind.

She stood on the curb and glanced in the direction Ben had driven off only a little over an hour ago. Hell, he probably barely had time to park and say boo before heading back, but that was fine with her. He sounded better, so mission complete, right? "Mike-Charlie" he would say. She felt herself bouncing a little on her toes and realized how excited she was to hug him, kiss him, and drive away together towards Destin and their future – the little 'burg of Chackbay a dusty image in the rear-view mirror.

I think I'll tell him tonight. I'll tell him how it feels like something is growing inside me.

The big, goofy smile returned, and she giggled a little and then concentrated on wiping the give-away smile off her face.

It would wait until tonight. By then she would really know he was okay.

CHAPTER

30

The drive to Destin felt the way a honeymoon should feel. They giggled and laughed, talked about the wedding and about Reed and Amy (Oh God Forbid!), held hands, and grinned at each other almost incessantly. Christy had seemed content with his very brief (and vague) description of his arrival at the burned out shack, his few minutes of reminiscence about Gammy complete with tears (which he did admit to actually – they were married for goodness sake), and his mental goodbye to his past. He left out any hint of supernatural bunny holes in the woods, mysterious Indians atop impossible ruins, black rivers, or special powers. He decided he wasn't really keeping anything from his wife – he simply didn't believe those things himself anymore. Her initial concern over his swollen lip (he had tripped over a root and hit it on the ground – that sounded better than I swooned and passed out like a damsel in distress) seemed more than outweighed by her apparent relief that he seemed okay. Truth was he did feel okay. He felt great, in fact.

Like long drives do when shared by people deeply in love, the several hours flew by in a blur. He had as much fun as if they sat together on their porch holding hands instead of riding along the most boring stretch of highway in all of Florida in a rented car with a crappy stereo. They arrived in Destin close to dinner time (though their bellies disagreed–still distended from gumbo and Cajun sausage in Chackbay). After only a few wrong turns they found their way to the gated entry to the cluster of town houses on the almost blinding white sand beach. The guard checked their name off a clip board, gave them a punch code to work the gate after ten PM and a pink hang tag to put on their rear-view mirror which identified them as guests. Then, they drove down a long road flanked by bright hibiscus, past several tennis courts, and then saw the few dozen townhouses that made up "Hibiscus Bay – a Private community." The town houses sat clustered in three semi-circles behind a huge, resort-style pool, a small putt-putt course ("fun for the whole family" the sign beside a barrel full of putters insisted), and a small picnic area of four tables and six gas grills ("Please don't grill on your deck" another sign implored).

They pulled into one of the two parking spots in front of the tiny box of a building with signs that read "Office" and "Check-In" on either side of the single-glass panel door.

"Locked," Ben announced.

"Oh," Christy said. She rummaged in her purse and fished out a strip of paper. "The lady said they were only here until five, but gave me a code to a lock box that should be….there." She pointed to the black box on a thick post in the mulch-filled garden to the left of the door.

The code worked, and the key to their condo was inside with a little note in cursive welcoming them and congratulating them on their wedding. It was stapled to two sheets of paper, one with rules (like no grilling on the deck) and the other a list of restaurants, an ABC store, and a grocery store nearby. A stack of brochures completed their packet, should they want to rent jet skis, go deep sea fishing, or visit an alligator exhibit. Christy stuffed all of the paper work into her purse, and Ben kept the key. They pulled the car around to the row of town houses until they found 201-D, the last unit on the end of the cul-de-sac to the left. He pulled the Charger into the short driveway and killed the engine.

"It's perfect," Christy sighed as she took his hand in hers and pressed her lips to his wrist.

Perfect was the word he would have chosen, and he thanked God for the ten-thousandth time that his wife had made the arrangements instead of him. The two-story condo smelled of cedar and salt air and looked out from its raised deck onto the Gulf of Mexico. It was only a few dozen yards from the short steps onto the white beach. Ben realized the honeymoon really had begun, and he wasted no time pulling their bags out of the trunk as his wife opened the door with the key he handed her.

He carried the four bags up to the second floor master bedroom suite with its own balcony deck and raised hot tub while Christy slid open the wall of sliding glass doors in the living room to let the cool Gulf Breeze flow through their retreat. He tossed the bags unceremoniously on the bed and headed back down stairs.

"They left us champagne," Christy called out louder than she needed to since he had already come up behind her.

"Who did?" he asked which made her jump.

"Oh, jeez," she said. "That was quick – what did you do, just toss them halfway up the steps?"

"I have other things to do. He wrapped his arms around her and kissed her gently on the back of the neck. "Much more pressing things."

Christy snaked an arm backwards around his neck and pulled his lips tighter onto her flesh and moaned.

"Linda," she said.

Ben stopped and looked at her confused.

"Who the hell is Linda?"

"The property manager," Christy spun around to face him, her hands now pulling at his belt and fly. "You asked who sent the champagne." She pressed her mouth onto his as she pulled his jeans down to his knees.

They made it from the pass through bar of the kitchen almost to the sofa before they gave up and pulled each other onto the floor beside the open doors leading to the deck. They made love with almost violent passion, their grunts and moans carried out onto the beach. Ben didn't worry about the noise they had made until it was over, and they wrapped around each other in a sweaty pile, panting and smiling.

"Well," he said and wiped sweat from his eyes. "We certainly will have made an impression on the neighborhood."

Christy laughed and raised herself on one arm on his chest, looking out the sliding glass door.

"No one out there," she announced.

"No," Ben chuckled. "They all gathered up their kids and took them indoors until the show was over."

They laughed together.

"Well, if we get strange looks at the pool tomorrow, we'll know why," she said.

They lay for a while in each other's arms until the cool Gulf breeze made them chilly. Then, they took their bottle of champagne upstairs. Christy gave a half-hearted glance in both directions before they walked naked onto their balcony and slipped into the hot tub.

They sat engulfed in warm bubbly water, the sounds of the gentle surf a few yards away. Ben let his head rest back on the edge of the tub and closed his eyes. He felt Christy's thigh against his and her hand rested on his knee. He nearly fell asleep, awakened by the near miss as the champagne cork ricocheted off the edge of the tub beside his left ear.

"Sorry," his wife said sheepishly, but with a big smile.

She poured them both a glass of the bubbly wine and then threw her legs across his lap and tossed an arm around his neck.

"I love you, Ben," she laid her head against him before taking a long sip of champagne. She gazed at him. "You seem so much better, baby," she kissed his cheek. "Are you?"

Ben thought a moment. He didn't want to dismiss her concern with a glib answer, but he really was better. He didn't know why a drive to the bayou, a fainting spell, and a crazy nightmare should in any way have made him magically ok, but he felt more whole, somehow. He felt like he had filled in some gap in his mental well-being.

"I really am," he answered honestly. He kissed her back. "Thank you so much for helping me find a way to put the past where it belongs."

"I don't think I really did anything," she laid her head on his shoulder.

He took a long drink of lukewarm champagne. He couldn't really explain to her how just being his wife did more than she could know. Her perfect way of guiding without leading, of encouraging without pushing, really had been the key to his being able to go to Louisiana at all, much less find closure there. He knew the peace he felt was the result of his finding his way toward her as much as away from the bayou.

"You have no idea what your being with me does, baby," he kissed the top of her head.

They sat in their little nest and talked very little, each lost in content thoughts, the cool Gulf breeze letting them sit in the hot water for a very long time.

* * *

He tried to convince himself it was the pizza, which sat like a bowling ball in his gut, and not his creeping fear that if he slept he would dream again. Whatever the cause, he lay awake for several hours and tossed fitfully in the king size bed beside his wife. They had ordered the pizza instead of going back out for supplies, which they decided would best be left for morning. The breeze and the sound of the surf combined with the soft feel of Christy's skin on his (no matter how friggin' hot it felt) should have been the perfect sleeping pill. God knows he felt tired as hell – exhausted, in fact. The emotionally draining day combined with lack of rest from the night before, champagne, a hot tub, a full belly, and (yes that's right) more sex – it should have been impossible for him to stay awake.

Ben turned again in the bed despite all that and flipped his pillow for the tenth time, his face seeking the cool side of the silky case. He sighed and let one leg squirm out from beneath the covers seeking cool air to offset his wife's boiling internal thermostat. He preferred the hot, smooth skin to no contact at all and pulled her sleeping arm across his chest like a security blanket and heard Christy's contented "Hmmmm." He wondered what dream went with the happy sound and thought for a moment about waking her from her peaceful sleep in the hope that (yet another) orgasm might release some magic hormone that would catapult him into the land beyond. He decided his wife needed her shut eye, and if sex didn't get him to sleep the first two times, three was unlikely to be the charm.

The moonlight streamed through the sheer inner curtains and danced across the wall, and he watched the pattern a moment and tried to think about nothing. But, of course, that was like someone saying, "don't think about elephants – okay...start!" His elephant turned out to be Jewel rather than the myriad of other things (delusions and such, he supposed) that he could mull over.

Ben sighed again and slipped out from beneath his wife's hot arm and the cool sheets. He padded barefoot across the wood floor, encountered only one loud creak that didn't evoke so much as a stir from Christy, and then went down the carpeted stairs and out onto the back deck. Just opening the sliding glass door brought a soothing fresh ocean breeze across his bare chest. He stood at the rail in his sweat shorts and stared at the gentle surf of the Gulf as it lapped softly at the beaches edge. The sparkling white sand looked more silver in the moonlight, and he felt a sense of peace flood over him as he stared out. He thought perhaps the relaxing effect would be even stronger at the surf's edge so he hopped down the short steps to the cold wet sand and walked towards the water.

He sat down on the shifting granular surface, arms behind him and feet stretched out to catch just a touch of the teasing water. With about every third attempt the Gulf of Mexico effortlessly tried to creep up the beach towards inland. Now and again one would make it to behind his knees and he would think about slipping back a bit, but then the next two waves would miss him completely. Satisfied with his position, he lay back and let his head drop onto the tiny pebbles. He stared up at the trillions of stars he could see in the low light of the beach despite the brightness of the moon. Not quite the carpet of flickering lights you could expect in the middle of the Iraqi desert, but impressive nonetheless.

He thought of Jewel's eyes. Those eyes laughed more than her mouth when he had snuggled her to his neck, and she had rewarded him with the squealing little "Gah Deh Eh!" He could almost hear the musical sound of her little toddler voice and swore he could smell the sweet little girl smell of her skin. He wondered where (and more importantly how) she was, but didn't let his brain chase the thought too far – afraid of the logical answer.

Those people have survived this and worse for thousands of years. Maybe she's okay. Maybe they found a quiet peaceful place in the jungle, far from the shit heads and the cowboys. Maybe they're happy and content and starting over.

He looked at the stars and tried to make them into a shape, a constellation of some sort, but there were too many, and the images his imagination concocted kept over lapping.

Maybe they don't need a Rougarou or even a Traiteur.

Ben knew better – and not because some Indian told him in a dream or because the dead Village Elder called to him in his sleep. He knew because he had been there and because – well, because he just friggin' knew.

I am well, father. I miss you, but I am well. I am home where I belong. We are waiting for you.

He felt the tears run from corners of his eyes and across his temples. They tickled down into his ears as he stared out into the infinity of the night sky and listened to the surf. He didn't think he could sleep, but he did relax some. Alone on the beach he rested his tired body, watching the stars drift slowly across the vast carpeted backdrop behind the moon that seemed to tug them along, and thought of Jewel and the others.

* * *

He must have slept a little, because he woke up and the horizon to his left had just turned a soft peach color, and his body shivered from the heat it had lost half-naked in the cool night air with the surf lapping at his legs (and now half way up his back). Ben sat up and looked back at the town house, half expecting to see Christy staring after him, a cup of coffee in her hand and a worried scowl on her face. The deck and upstairs windows were empty – to his relief. He shivered uncontrollably and rubbed his hands briskly on both arms to try and generate some warmth. The wet sand on his back and hair, the chill in his skin, and his now chattering teeth gave him a powerful déjà vu of his weeks in BUD/s – the initial training for the SEALs –, his hands so cold he could barely hold anything with his instructor – the King of Poseidon himself – standing over him bellowing "Get wet and sandy, boy!" The memory made him smile.

He struggled stiffly to his feet and felt the salt water from his now soaked sweat shorts run down the backs of his legs. He knew one way to get warm that might also clear his head and would provide a great excuse if Christy discovered his absence from bed.

He struck out down the beach at a stiff-legged jog, but in no time built up to a solid pace. The spongy, wet surface cushioned the pounding of his barefoot run. His body warmed quickly (despite the wet shorts that chafed more than a little), and in no time he felt like the SEAL he was. He let his mind wander as he pushed his body harder. The pale peach smear on the eastern horizon had grown into a reddish pink ribbon, and he guessed that in another five minutes the sun would pull itself up over the water. He pushed his pace faster still, intent on getting as much distance as possible before the sun blinded him and made him turn westward back towards the town house.

He thought again of Jewel, but the tightness that brought to his chest was too much, so he forced his mind around the bend and found his way back to Christy. There was no friggin' way he would let one sleepless night pull him backwards on his path away from the bayou and his recent past in Africa. His strong pull to Jewel should do nothing but show him how ready they were for a family – a child of their own.

Christy's excitement about trying to get pregnant had opened the lid on his own strong desire to have children – and not just because she wanted it. He realized his desire to be a daddy with her had been there for a while, un-noticed until Jewel and then Christy's invitation. The more he thought about it the more he felt his body relax, and his face broke into a smile. This was running towards the future, and if it took him away from his past, as well, then fan-fucking-tastic.

The sun erupted over the flat horizon with sudden and blinding intensity, and he raised a hand to shield his night-accommodated eyes, spinning on a bare heel to head westward toward home. He slowed the pace from what had become a pounding sprint and started a long-stride middle gait. He now felt sweat instead of cool salt water run down his back and legs and moved closer to the water's edge where the sand felt wet and cool on his feet. It was also softer and an ache in his calves surfaced – the good ache of tough exercise.

Maybe they even got pregnant last night. Not impossible right? He had absolutely no idea where Christy was in her cycle. The thought that even now a little cluster of their combined cells might be nestling into a cozy little temporary home inside her made him feel so happy he thought he would laugh out loud. Only his controlled heavy breathing from the hard run kept it at bay. He would ask her about that cycle thing this morning. Might as well give it another go after breakfast, right? Load the boat. He felt pretty certain his little SEAL swimmers would get the job done once the mission had been assigned.

Ben looked and found himself about a half mile from the town house so he turned left and plowed into the cool surf, pushing hard against the resistance until nearly waist deep and then he lunged forward in a flat dive and started a long-stroked freestyle swim for the point on the beach where he had lay and looked at the stars. He pounded the water hard, pulling himself along, but then had to roll onto his back and continue on in a leg-only backstroke while he pulled his shorts back up over his bare ass and tied the drawstring. He then flipped back over and kicked off in a hard sprint. A few minutes later he walked out of the surf, winded and with a stitch in his side, but feeling great. He leaned over, hands on knees, and spit salt water onto the sand. He then stood up and leaned backward, arching his back to stretch out the last kinks and when he did he saw her on the deck, warm in a fleece and sweat pants. She waved and held up a cup of coffee at him. Even from this distance he could see her beautiful smile. He waved back and then jogged up the beach to the deck.

"You are a very crazy man" she said and handed him the steaming cup over the rail. "It is sixty-two degrees out, crazy man, and you are swimming in the ocean?" she shook her head in a mock scold and sipped her own coffee. "Get up here, and let me warm you up."

They sat together on the deck and sipped the murky dark stew she had made from the packets she found by the Mr. Coffee. Not the

Starbucks they both addicted themselves to on and off, but not bad. They drank it black since they had not yet made a supply run for sugar or cream, and they held hands and watched the sun turn the dark ocean into a shimmering blue-green.

"How did you sleep?" she asked, unable to keep a tiny little concerned furrow off her forehead.

"Not great," he answered honestly.

"Dreams?" She looked disappointed. Ben didn't have to read minds to know how much hope she had hung on his trip to the bayou.

"Actually, no, just restless, I guess. Mind spent the day at Disney." That was her favorite way to tell him she had a lot on her mind, and she smiled at hearing it back. She seemed content to let the night go.

"Watcha' wanna do today?"

"You mean in between trips to the bedroom?" he asked with a mischievous grin.

"Or the family room," she gave a wink and a nod.

"Or the kitchen?"

"Kitchen's good," she agreed. "Maybe the deck?"

"Or the beach?" he threw back, and they both laughed. "I was thinking we could rent a Hobie Cat for a few hours," he added. "I saw a place in the stack of brochures they gave us."

"That would be awesome," she sounded genuinely excited. "The water looks so beautiful."

They decided they would make a store run first and then try and find the Hobie rental place later in the morning. Their shower together was preceded by a half hour back in bed when she told him they might as well both be sweaty since they needed to shower anyway. Afterwards he had kissed her belly softly and cupped his hands and in a loud stage whisper said "Go get 'em boys! The egg is your objective for this mission." That got a squeal of excited laughter from his wife, who then lifted her hips and put two pillows under her, elevating her in ways that made him wish they hadn't finished yet.

"What the hell are you doing?" he asked with a chuckle.

She shrugged and blushed.

"Supposed to increase the odds."

Made sense, he thought. His swimmers would be no use to anyone flopping about in a wet spot on the sheets.

They talked about her cycle on the drive to the store where he learned that she was indeed in a "vulnerable window" as she put it. He again wondered if perhaps their baby grew inside her already. He got a few glimpses of thoughts from her that she thought about it to, but tried hard not to invade her mind too much.

They shopped for the rest of the week, leaving a couple of nights open for dinner out, and after they had unpacked it all into the fridge and cabinets they sat again on the deck and enjoyed a late brunch of bagels and fruit. They ate lazily and watched the Gulf and twice returned waves from other couples staying at Hibiscus Bay who walked hand-in-hand along the water's edge. As they cleaned up, he watched a couple their age walk onto the beach with their two kids – both toddlers – and he smiled as the children splashed and giggled in the gentle surf. He could easily picture them celebrating an anniversary here in a few years – a couple of kids in tow.

They were on the Hobie before one o'clock and he felt himself really start to relax. The fatigue from his sleepless night seemed only background noise as they cut the short sailboat through the crystal clear water. Christy stretched out on the canvas tarp while he sailed the little boat back and forth up the beach. He went as far as their condo community a few miles west of the rental company (which had been nothing more than a guy with three Hobie Cats next to a shack on the beach behind the Holiday Inn). The boats looked well kept, the long-haired owner had a genuine persona, and they had no worries renting from him. Now he watched her at his feet, eyes closed and face covered in a happy glow as he tacked back and forth. Now and again she would throw out another name for him to think about.

"Nathan?"

"Reminds me of the Hot Dog store – no."

"Sophia?"

"Old fashioned, but stylish – yes or maybe."

"Brett?"

"Too Yuppie sounding – no."

"Jason?"

"I like that. Yes, it makes the list."

And on it went. When they would heat up in the sun they slipped into the cool water and kissed and groped each other as they held onto the tow line to keep from being left behind should a gust of wind sweep their catamaran away. It was nearly four when they zigzagged back towards the Holiday Inn where Kirk (could have been a yes, but now would always be a beach bum name) waited for them with a Schlitz tall boy in one hand.

"How was it?"

"Great," Christy answered for both of them. "Awesome, in fact."

"You got a lotta sun there, lady," Kirk said, and Ben noticed that Christy's skin had, in fact, turned a slight crimson. "That's gonna hurt later."

Christy pressed a finger to her shoulder and watched a dime size circle blanch white and then turn red again.

"Bummer," she said.

"I'll lotion you up at home," Ben offered as he paid Kirk.

"I'm not fallin' for that again," she grabbed at his hip with a wink.

By the time they walked into the condo the redness had deepened and started to look painful. Ben felt bad for his wife. He had gotten a bit more sun then he wanted as well, but nothing like her.

"I don't know why the hell I didn't think to put on sunscreen," Christy pouted. "We bought it at the grocery and everything. What the hell was I thinking?"

"I really do think I should put a little lotion on that," Ben pursed his lips. Man it looked painful. "Does it hurt?"

"It's starting to," she conceded.

They headed upstairs where she stretched out naked on the bed (obviously planning on more than just lotion) and Ben knelt between her legs and rubbed a thick amount of cool lotion on his hands. He touched her gently and started to rub, but she tensed up a bit.

"Ooooh," she winced.

"I'm sorry baby," he lightened his touch. Then, he looked at the ring on his right hand which pulsed a soft and glowing aquamarine. Ben smiled and stretched his lotion covered hands out over his wife's back and watched as the blue light spread like an aura from his finger tips to his elbows. The little sparkles, what he had come to call the fireflies, followed a moment later, and he spread his filmy covered hands across her back and shoulders. He could feel the hum like vibration in his fingers.

"Hmmmmmm," she sighed. "Wow, that is much better. That feels so awesome. What are you doing different?"

"Shhhh,"

He passed over every sun scorched inch of her skin and then rubbed her neck with one hand while the other awkwardly slid his shorts off. He ignored the fleeting, burning pain in his own shoulders and back that flickered and was gone. He tried even harder to ignore how easily he slipped into the role of Traiteur when his wife needed him. What did that mean about his adamant denial of all that had happened?

Ben shook the thought away and spread her legs farther apart with his knees and then kissed the back of her neck as he slid gently inside her already soaked body. She raised her hips up to meet him and moaned.

They lay together afterwards, wrapped around one another, and she kissed his hands.

"Magic hands," she said. "It might just be my post-orgasm endorphins, but my sunburn feels completely better."

He looked at her shoulders and saw without surprise that the redness had disappeared. Her skin looked lightly tanned and healthy. He kissed her right shoulder softly.

"I'm glad," he stole a glance at his hand again – more of a burnt orange color now. He hugged her tight. "What do you want me to make you for dinner?"

She turned over to face him, and her face literally glowed with contentment.

"Do you know how much I love you?"

"I do," he promised and kissed her mouth.

He spent the rest of the evening happy and fulfilled as they cooked together, sipped wine (only a half glass for her which she nursed all evening on the deck), and held hands. Even during their quiet sunset walk on the beach he managed to keep his mind away from where it tried to sneak. With only a little effort he managed not to think at all about what his ability to heal his wife's burn might mean.

* * *

The rest of the week disappeared, not in a blink, but in whirlwind of building momentum – alternating happy and carefree days of sun, sand, water, and sex and long, pensive, sleepless nights which ended in pounding runs on the beach and swims in the ocean.

Christy marveled on their second day at the miracle lotion that had cured her sunburn, but never brought it up again and wisely slathered on the SPF 30 the rest of the week. They had many times stared at each other and grinned, each wanting to ask the big "I wonder if" – but not wanting to set the other up for disappointment. He did his best to keep his blue light fingers out of her mind, but he knew she hoped almost desperately that they (funny how men had somewhere along the way earned the right to think of it as "we") were pregnant.

The week had been the happiest days of his life, offset only slightly by the long and exhausting nights spent almost sleepless in their bed or on the beach, images of Jewel, Gammy, and the Indian swirling through his mind but held precariously out of reach by sheer will. The short bursts of sleep had been overflowing with dreams of Africa. Always they held Jewel, usually cowering in fear or crying in the dark as evil men with orange eyes did unspeakable things to what was left of their people. He saw the villagers clearly and in rich detail – perhaps twenty of them now that the little band they had rescued had found their way to the others the Elder had told him of.

Always the peaceful scenes were shattered by the violence and bloodshed brought by the ragged bands of Al Qaeda assholes – always with the orange eyes that he somehow knew meant they were possessed by the dark ones and led by the one with the black blood.

His transformation to acceptance of the dreams as prophecy rather than madness or some sort of advanced post-traumatic stress disorder came slowly but surely. By the time they sat on the deck of the Destin town house for the last time, their bags packed and waiting for them by the door, he knew the images were not fantasy. They were a calling. He didn't know what he would do about it – owned as he was by the U.S. Navy – but in the wee hours of the budding dawn of the last day, he had come to accept his new belief in the reality of the calling.

"Whatcha thinkin' about, baby?" He felt her warm hand on his and realized he had felt her eyes on him, as well, but had ignored them in favor of his thoughts. He looked up at her with a sad smile.

"I had the best week of my life, Christy," he said simply. She raised his hand to her lips and kissed it.

"Then, why so sad?"

He shrugged.

"I guess I don't want it to end," he said, and she nodded.

"Well," she rubbed the back of his hand on her cheek, "we're going back to a pretty great life, you know." She smiled warmly. "The honeymoon can go on indefinitely at home if you want." She leaned in and kissed his mouth.

"Oh, I do want," he stroked her cheek.

On the drive to the airport he thought about almost nothing else.

Except of course what he should (or could) do about the calling he felt to Jewel and his people in Africa. He had no idea whether his Gammy, the voices of the Elder, or his meeting with the Attakapa were real. They had felt so real, and he had been so certain of them only days ago, but the insanity of that made it easier to see them as a dream – a last fantasy his mind had created when he had visited his childhood home.

Now, he felt much less sure. A big part of him believed Gammy, the Elder, even the trip down the rabbit hole were, at least, some form of reality. Mostly it just didn't seem to matter much. No matter what the source, the pull he felt to some undefined destiny in Africa could not be denied.

He had a fair idea what he needed to do, and he would have to do it soon if he held any hope of saving his people from the dark ones.

He also wanted to get things done so he could be home in time for the birth of their baby that the magic part of his brain knew grew inside his wife.

CHAPTER
31

She drove home from work and felt the familiar anxiety build inside her. In some ways, Ben seemed worse than ever in the ten days since they had gotten home from their honeymoon. But it was so different from before that it seemed hard to compare.

Instead of dreams that brought him upright in their bed screaming – or sometimes just left him crying in his sleep – he now seemed quiet and brooding in the evenings. It usually started a short time after dinner and lasted most of the evening. She didn't think it had anything to do with them or their fledgling marriage. Whenever she nudged him with a soft touch or softer words he would come back to her, and his eyes filled with the love she had grown accustomed to seeing in them during their time at the beach. He would smile and hold her, tell her how much he adored her, talk to her about babies and names and the future.

He also seemed near exhaustion. She had begun to sleep lightly herself, due entirely to her worry about her husband, and would awaken to see him staring at the ceiling, quiet but awake. He didn't deny he was having trouble sleeping, but he did minimize it a great deal.

She decided it had to be something at work. She had accepted a long time ago there would always be things with the Teams he couldn't tell her. The top secret nature of his job that had seemed so bizarre early in their relationship now felt like just a normal part of who they were.

It must be work. What the hell else could it be?

Whatever was going on somewhere in the world that might inevitably involve a visit by the Navy SEALS clearly had him troubled. She wanted so much to ask him what kept him up at night distracted, but instead dropped subtle hints of her worry in the hope he would share with her if he could.

So far it had not happened.

And, so she felt anxious – not because he kept a secret he must surely have to keep, but because she loved him so much and worried about him. She felt so terribly tired herself. She supposed that sleep lost together, as a sharing of problems even if not discussed, was a part of marriage. It certainly seemed to be a part of theirs.

She steered her way home and felt her pulse quicken with concern as she turned onto their street. But she slowed her breathing when she saw his truck wasn't yet in the driveway. She parked and threw her detail case over her shoulder to free up her hands to grab the grocery bags. She had decided if she couldn't talk to her husband about whatever troubled him, she could at least be a terrific wife and baby him a little.

She had planned a dinner of her Thai Chicken soup, which she knew he loved, and tuna steak from a recipe she wanted to try. She also had a good bottle of Pinot Noir, since Ben now insisted he liked wine better than beer. She might not have enough security clearance (or any, in fact) to give him someone to talk to about what was on his mind, but she could sure as hell cook up a great meal and give him a back rub (and maybe a little something more) to take his mind off of it.

She got excited about taking care of her man and rushed inside to get their dinner started before he got home. Her mind also wandered to the purple and white box labeled "E.P.T." that she knew lay buried in the groceries. Another week or so and it would be time to pee on the stick and see if her sixth sense was right. She wanted to believe it with all her heart.

CHAPTER

32

Ben sat in his truck – his official orders to join the "Joint Special Operations Task Force-Africa" in his lap – and stared out at the Atlantic Ocean. He had no doubts about his decision – he knew, in fact, it was not his decision at all so much as fate or destiny or some such shit – but he had some wicked serious misgivings about having to tell Christy he would be heading back over in only a few days.

He had just returned and should be on a shore cycle for at least three months, and she would know that. She had a pretty good understanding of how things worked, a knowledge all "SEAL Significant Others" developed very quickly. She would also know, of course, that such things were never set in stone, especially since that fall day in 2001 when the deaths in Manhattan, D.C., and a Pennsylvania field had changed all the rules forever. The Global War on Terror had always kept the shore/deployment schedule pretty dynamic, but those few months right after a deployment had stayed relatively sacred. Ben didn't worry she would be angry – just sad and disappointed. And worried, of course (he could almost see her brow furrow as he told her).

He looked down at his watch – nearly six-thirty. He really needed to get going. She had taken to trying to have dinner ready when he got home lately – to him a definite sign of her concern, considering her work days were every bit as busy as his. He needed to either get on home or give her a call that he was running late. He looked at the papers in his lap and sighed.

Getting the orders had been pretty easy, actually. The JSOTF in Africa stayed undermanned, and his dual training as a medic and a sniper made him pretty valuable. The hardest part had been talking to Chris to get his approval, which was required to release him from Viper team to take additional assignments. Chris had pursed his lips and rubbed his chin.

"Everything okay at home?" he had asked.

Ben had assured him everything was great – perfect, in fact. He just had some things that felt unfinished over there. Chris had nodded but then told him he doubted another forty-five days in Africa would do anything to erase that feeling.

"I know," he had told him. "I just need to do it."

To his credit the Officer had said nothing more – just sighed and signed his chit.

And in a few days he would join a team of west coast SEALs who had taken over for them in Africa. Many of them he would know – the SEALs were a small and very close-knit community – but it would still feel very strange being there without the rest of Viper team.

And, just what the hell did he think he would do over there? He had no choice but to admit that he had no friggin' idea. He did know, however, that the sense of destiny had grown terribly strong. He no longer doubted at all that he had to go back. He hoped it involved Jewel in some way. He feared it involved the dark ones – the ones he saw during his rare snatches of sleep – somehow living inside the Al Qaeda cell that operated over there. It wasn't just the short dreams. He heard the voices now even when awake.

He didn't see the old Cajun as he had in New Orleans or the Indian he had sat with atop the ruins in the rabbit hole in the woods. But he did hear them – soft voices he recognized calling to him, urging him forward to his fate. The Elder's voice had fallen silent, but he had heard his Gammy a time or two, soft and gentle, telling him only to "Lissen to dem boys, now chile. Lissen up." The voices blended with the thoughts he now heard much more clearly from those around him. Gratefully, he had also shored up his ability to control those intrusions. It seemed almost like a filter at times and at others more like just adjusting the volume on the TV to take a call – you could still hear the TV, but it faded into the background and became easy to ignore.

He thought about the terrorist he had killed – boiled by his anger – and of the poor drunk in New Orleans. He wondered with a shudder of fear what he was really being called to do. He wondered also if he would know how to do it. He felt the power inside him, but worried about his ability to control it.

He turned the ignition key and fired up the big pick-up truck, put it in reverse, and looked over his shoulder. For a moment, he saw a flickering image of the Attakapa in his back seat, but he felt certain *that one at least* was just his imagination. He spun the wheel to the right to head left toward home only a few blocks up the beach from where had brooded the last half hour.

Home to the love of his life and the difficult news he had to share. He knew he had no hope of making her understand it since he didn't understand himself. He also knew she would support him unconditionally – as she always had.

That won't make it any fuckin' easier for her, though.

He felt nothing but tired and disgusted with the thought that, once again and maybe this time for real, this might finally put it all behind him, and they could start their life. He would go over, close the circle, and come home knowing he had done everything he could possibly do.

And, then I'll really come home. Home to my wife and new baby boy.

*   *   *

Reed sat outside the door to the large warehouse-sized equipment room divided into bathroom-sized cages where the SEALs kept their deployment gear and where he and Ben shared a cage. He packed a thick wad of dip into his lower lip from a fresh can of Wintergreen Kodiak and leaned back against the wall, uncertain what he would say to his best friend. Not that it mattered much now – they had all made their decision, and he knew it was the right one.

One for all and all for one, right?

No big deal for him, of course. Nothing held him here. He had no girlfriend even (and he and Amy had vowed never to tell Ben and Christy about the four wild days after they had left for their honeymoon – it would just make it awkward for all of them). His father and his new lady were already down in Florida again. His only real family was Viper Team.

"Hey, bro,"

Reed looked up and saw Ben approach, his face confused.

"Whatcha doin'? Thought you were still at the Roost."

Reed had been at the Roost – the condo on the beach in the Outer Banks where the team hung out when they could – when Chris had called him. They had all met together to decide what to do. Reed had been very clear – no matter what the other guys decided, he was going with Ben. He believed he owed him that, and he felt his best friend just might need some looking after. He had not been surprised by the response of the rest of the team.

And, as his best friend I should tell him.

"Came back this morning," Reed said and tossed the can of Kodiak to Ben. "Thought we ought to do gear check together."

"You didn't need to come back to help me with my gear," Ben said. He looked genuinely sad Reed had interrupted his trip. "Obviously, you heard from Chris." He packed a dip into his front lip, and then he tossed the can back. His eyes were distracted, and he looked tired. Reed got to his feet.

"Yeah, well I don't trust you to check my shit, bro," he said and opened the door and followed Ben inside. They walked down the first row, between the rows of black barred cages full of gear – summer, winter, dive gear, parkas, ammo packs, back packs. Some were woodland green, others desert cammie. All the cages were packed to the top.

"What the hell are you talking about?" Ben asked. He looked around for something, and Reed handed him the Gatorade bottle he had brought for him. Ben spit dark brown tobacco juice into the bottle. "Where the hell are you going?"

They reached their cage, second from the end on the left, and Reed spun the combination into the lock on the gate (sixty-nine, sixty-nine – not very original. He imagined two thirds of the cages had the same combination). He popped off the lock and looked up at his best friend.

"I'm goin' with you, bro," he said simply.

Ben's mouth opened, he made no sound, and then it closed again.

"Guess the boss figured out you're not really worth a shit without me," he said with a laugh and clapped Ben on the shoulder.

Ben clenched his jaw tightly and a pained look spread across his face.

"Reed," he said softly and looked at his feet. "Dude, I'm not trying to drag you into anything here. I just," he stopped and stared off, and Reed wondered just what the hell his friend saw when he did that. Ben's eyes refocused. "I just have some things I feel I need to finish over there, you know?"

Reed pulled a black bag off a low shelf that held his kit – body armor with pouches for ammo and other gear, his helmet, knee pads, gloves and other junk.

"We all got unfinished business back there, Ben," he said and pulled a second bag off a higher shelf. "I was there too, you know. You ain't the only one that feels like shit about them villagers." Reed felt his emotions start to rise and struggled to pull them into check. He sighed and looked at his friend. "Ben, I wanna go. No just for you, for me too."

A wall of light broke into the dusty dimness of the warehouse-like building as the door opened at the other end of their row. Reed peered past Ben and saw what he expected. He gave Chris a nod, and Ben turned around.

"Gentlemen," Chris said as he, Auger, and Lash approached, "and I use that term quite loosely."

"Boss," Ben said with a nod. "You knew about this, I guess – about Reed going back to the Task Force with me?" Reed thought he heard something other than just guilt in his best friend's voice. Not fear exactly, but something.

"Yeah, of course," Chris said and gave a nod to Auger who already opened the cage next to them. "And, of course, nobody could expect you two jokers to perform at even marginally acceptable levels without proper supervision." He slapped Ben on the back.

"One for all, and all for one," Lash said from a cage across the row. He had pulled down a long rifle case he used for his sniper gear.

Reed thought he saw Ben's eyes turn wet, but his friend turned away before he could be sure.

"You guys do not have to do this," Ben said with a tight voice.

"Yes, we do," Chris said. "This whole team has some unfinished business back there."

"I'm bored, anyway," Auger said with a grin. "Just how much beer can one guy be expected to drink?"

"Yeah," Lash agreed. He had opened his case and inspected the sights and other optics inside. "I can't stand watching any more women shoot Reed down."

"Amen to that," Chris agreed.

"Anyway," Lash said. "There is a war going on you know? Maybe you heard about it? It's kind of a big deal."

Viper Team laughed and set about the task of organizing their gear for deployment. Reed wondered for a moment how Christy was doing. He thought maybe he would invite himself over for a beer tonight and make sure his little sister was hanging in there.

He looked over at Ben who knelt beside his own kit changing batteries in all of his electronics. He worried about his friend. He didn't like that he wanted to go back so soon after the wedding or that stormy look he had in his eyes again.

And, he hated that goddamn ring he still wore. He would see if Christy could talk him into getting rid of that damn thing.

Maybe when they got back.

CHAPTER

33

The C-17 cargo plane had a few round, porthole like windows scattered about, but he and Reed had stretched out their sleeping bags and gear campground style on the aft cargo ramp so he couldn't really see any of them from their dark and cave like perch.

Ben thought watching the coastline disappear behind them as they headed east towards the dark continent might erase the dream-like quality he felt envelope him. What he didn't feel was anxious or frightened. In fact, he felt remarkably at peace as if the act of returning had finally stifled the many voices that demanded his journey in the first place. He wondered if he would feel so confident if his teammates were not spread out all around him.

"What's it gonna be, dude?" Reed asked as he opened his lap top and unzipped his DVD case.

"Anything not set in Africa," Ben replied. His throat tightened with the thought that he ought not complain – that, if not for him, Reed would be drunk at the beach instead of heading back to that shit hole and certain firefights with those Al Qaeda dick weeds.

"You got that shit right," Reed said with a laugh, obviously not as bothered as Ben by the hypocrisy.

He popped in "3:10 to Yuma" and they began to watch a young used-to-be-batman-cowboy limp around his ranch.

Ben's mind slipped inevitably to Christy. She had not reacted with any of the emotion or frustration he had feared, but then he really knew she wouldn't. She had maintained the even strain of the perfect Navy Wife. The fact he would be back in only six weeks helped a lot he felt certain. He doubted he would have gotten the Christy-style unconditional support had he been courageous enough to tell her he had volunteered for this trip. He had no idea how to explain it to her without her thinking he had lost his mind completely, so he had allowed her to believe that orders were orders.

She had wanted to tell him something earlier that morning, but had changed her mind at the last minute. It didn't matter – he knew her thoughts even without the strange new gift. He knew her like a husband knows his wife. Christy believed she might be pregnant.

And, she's right. Should I have told her? How would I have explained how I know?

The pregnancy test she had tucked behind the spare rolls of toilet paper in their bathroom cabinet would give her the answer soon enough – and he would be home to share the excitement soon after. They would be together for most of the pregnancy. In fact, he had all but decided to ask Chris for some home time after this – some protected shore time until after the baby got here and they got through the first year or so. Maybe a training billet or something.

On Reed's laptop, Batman was trying to explain to his wife how tough it was to lose a leg and still be a man. Ben closed his eyes and reached out behind them, out of the plane and back to the beach.

I love you, baby. I will be home soon, and it will be my turn to support you. You and our little boy.

He felt her tears as she sat on their deck back at the beach. Above it he heard the soft whispers of the Indian, the Elder, and more clearly the voice of his little girl.

"*I have missed you, father,*" Jewel said in his mind. Little Jewel, who in real life was probably a year away from being old enough to talk in even her own language. "*I have missed you, but I will see you soon.*"

He decided to try and focus on the movie. There was no friggin' way he would be taking any Ambien on this trip. The last thing he needed was to not be able to wake from some dream he couldn't control.

* * *

For a moment Ben's voice sounded so real and clear in her head. It didn't speak to her but about her. She knew it had to be her imagination because his voice talked about their son and about being there with her for her pregnancy. Even if she could hear his thoughts from so far away, he couldn't possibly know what she only suspected. She had decided to wait until he got back – by then she would know for sure and would even be toward the end of the tentative first trimester. They could relax into the excitement of their coming baby. The last thing he needed was more to worry about, especially doing what he would be doing – wherever the hell he would be doing it.

She wiped the tears from her eyes and blew her nose in a tissue. When he got back, they would be sure.

She looked out at the dark Atlantic Ocean and then up into the sky above it, wondering what her husband was thinking.

You are the Rougarou, and you must return to the fight.

-The Attakapa

CHAPTER 34

Ben walked beside his teammates with hands in his pockets and his thoughts far away. He had re-acclimated to their vampire-like lifestyle very quickly, having been away from it for only a month or so. He missed the warm feel of afternoon sun on his skin, especially with Christy beside him holding his hand, but the chronic malaise he always felt when exposed to only the last few rays of setting sun quickly became familiar background noise. For a SEAL he knew that darkness was just another tool.

The problem was he hadn't seen his enemy yet. They had been on ops every night since they arrived, Viper team usually just one piece of a larger operational puzzle, and they had certainly had contact with Al Qaeda. The resistance had not been much, and they had taken a handful of bad guys off the targets each night. None of these assholes had what he searched for, though. He had reached into their minds (had become quite expert at controlling that part of it at least) but had yet to feel the presence of the dark ones. Even as he thought about it, he felt ridiculous. This evening, despite the same dreams as the other nights, he had awakened with a deep-seeded feeling he had made a terrible mistake – that he had left his wife behind and dragged his team back into combat in the shittiest place on Earth because of a simple chemical imbalance in his brain that had left him with insane delusions he could trace back to a disturbed childhood.

A part of him actually wanted to believe that. The thought of being crazy no longer seemed the most terrifying thing he could imagine. If he wasn't crazy, the reality led by his nightmares and the voices in his head certainly held a shit load more terror than needing a good shrink and some psychotropic drugs.

Ben slipped into the back seat of the windowless white pick-up truck, one of a fleet of beat up and rusted hulks lined up beside the low brown building where they lived. The base they were on now was much more comfortable than the condemned airfield they had occupied last month. This base actually housed the "host country's" militia and, in fact, bustled with activity. The host country had only a small number of troops on the base, in fact, but a large number of NATO troops were deployed here. The airfield was always bustling, mostly shuttling in foreign troops, such as his team, many of whom continued on by helicopter to some other forward outpost. In general, Special Warfare types shied away from crowds, but at least the crowds usually meant great living conditions.

"Which one?" Reed asked from the driver's seat in front of him.

"The big one," Lash said as he crowded nearly on top of Ben to make room for Auger beside him in the back seat of the tiny Japanese truck. "I want that stir fry bar."

"Small one has a better salad bar," Auger griped.

"Sweet Jesus, you guys got soft quick," Chris chided from the front seat beside Reed. "Next you'll be expecting back rubs."

"You offering?" Lash asked as he packed a dip in his lip and tossed the can to Ben.

"You wish," Chris chuckled.

"I vote stir fry bar," Reed said. "And, I'm in the driver's seat," he added, settling the debate. He put the truck in gear and headed for the gate to their small compound tucked in the corner of the airfield. Together with their Army counterparts and the aviators that toted them around in their specially equipped helicopters, they lived apart from the rest of the base behind the twelve-foot fence and double rows of concertina wire – a base within a base. Ben hopped out to unlock the combination lock on the gate and then hopped back in once the truck had pulled through and he had secured the gate behind them.

Reed drove along the edge of the long runway, their beat up little truck pulling a tail of dust behind it, and skidded through the gravel to make the sharp turn which would take them down the hill and into the main area. In unison, Ben and his fellow SEALs grabbed on to the frame of the truck to keep from toppling over, but none said a word – they had all ridden with Reed before, and the bruises were just part of letting him behind the wheel.

Ben stifled a yawn and rubbed his face as they settled back level, bumping out of the dirt onto the narrow road. His restless nights (well, days) seemed greatly magnified by the busy tempo of their current operations. His muscles ached with a fatigue that felt almost like the flu. He wondered if being tired made the images seem more real, his exhaustion-numbed brain becoming even more delusional, or if it was just being back in this shitty country that made everything so vivid.

"Trouble sleeping?"

He looked over at Chris who twisted around in the front seat to evaluate his teammate.

"Yeah," Ben said holding his gaze but trying to look less tired than he felt. "Still getting the rhythm." It often took a few days to get into a groove at the start of a new deployment. Of course, they had been here longer than a couple of days.

Chris pursed his lips but nodded and said nothing more.

To make matters worse, the dreams held no useful information. He had assumed the voices would become incarnate in his sleep and somehow fill in the gaps of just what the hell he should be doing. Perhaps the fact that he drifted in and out of sleep prevented that, he couldn't be sure, but unlike the long walks with the Village Elder or his Gammy he had experienced before, he instead woke from fragmented dreams that told him nothing. He dreamed often of Jewel and, in fact, felt her presence even when awake, but of course that was easily explained by his emotional tie to her and the heavy rucksack full of guilt he carried with him everywhere. Still, if not for the pull he felt towards little Jewel and the undying sense he would somehow see her again, he would have felt much more certain he had made a terrible mistake. Along the way managing to fuck his teammates – all of whom should be at home right now, enjoying their families or drinking beer and chasing skirt at the beach.

And, you should be at home with your beautiful bride, you dumbass.

Reed skidded the truck to a stop in the gravel-filled parking lot beside the flat aluminum building that clearly did not fit in with the rest of the cement block base. NATO troops loved their chow, and this had clearly been added when the troops had arrived. The rest of the parking lot held mostly Humvees and green trucks with a variety of insignia, but the blue NATO flag predominated. Only a few other scattered vehicles were beat up, unmarked civilian looking trucks like their own.

"Let's eat," Reed said as he cut the motor. He winked at Ben in the rear view mirror and then hopped out.

They all walked together down the cement path, showed their military IDs to the local militia in their green uniforms and silver dome helmets, and entered the busy chow hall. The long tables were mostly empty, and the few diners sat clustered in small groups. They spotted another group of Special Operators – mostly Army and two of their fellow SEALs – and returned the customary nods. Ben followed Reed and Lash to the stir fry bar where dark-skinned foreigners (Ben guessed Pakistani) tossed together ingredients handed to them in little cups which "customers" filled from the buffet line. Reed rubbed his hands together.

"I think I eat better here than at home," he started to fill two cups with meat and vegetables.

"None of your calories here come from beer," Lash pointed out.

"That might be it," Reed chuckled and handed his cups to the cook who tossed it onto a griddle, sprayed it with oil and some sort of sauce from squeeze bottles, and began to mix in brown rice.

A few minutes later, they slid their trays in beside Chris and Auger with their burgers and fries.

"Healthy," Lash said. "I thought you wanted a salad."

"Probably no more fat than that oily crap you're eating," Auger countered. He took a huge bite of greasy burger. "And, the salad bar sucks at this one, I told you that."

The two bickered on, but their voices faded into the background as Ben lost the battle to keep his mind from wandering.

"So whaddya hear, boss?" Auger asked. "We out again?"

That brought Ben back.

"Well," Reed said "I hope we got something better tonight." He lost some rice down his chin as he talked around a huge bite. "We sure ain't done much to redeem ourselves so far." Ben felt his friend's eyes on him. "Not that I mind bein' here," he mumbled.

"Gonna all change tonight," Chris said. "Sounds like we got a real deal in the works."

"No more corporals?" Lash asked, referring to the mostly low-level shit heads they had encountered so far.

"We'll hear more at the brief," Chris said. "But I think we got some guys from the list lined up tonight."

Ben felt his pulse quicken, not with fear but with excitement. It was high time they did something that mattered. The list referred to intel's list of "management level" Al Qaeda in the area they deemed worthy targets. The last few weeks the task force had mostly missed listed targets. He knew every crow they brought back added a piece to the intel puzzle and brought them closer to a high-value operative. Even if this didn't fulfill his sense of prophecy and calling, taking out some big time bad guys would make him feel a hell of a lot better about dragging his team out here.

Be careful, Rougarou. The dark ones are closer than you think.

Ben looked up at the voice in his head. He felt no real surprise or anxiety at the sight of the Attakapa seated at the end of a long and otherwise empty table just across from where his team ate. The Indian sat bolt upright, his arms stiffly at his sides, hands clasped together in his lap. Their eyes locked a moment.

The time is close. We can guide you, but the rest is up to you. Use the dark ones to find the one with the black blood. Remember what you have been told.

The image shimmered a moment and then evaporated. Ben realized that didn't surprise him either. He had either accepted it as real and had seen it enough to no longer be amazed or he really had lost his mind, which he clearly couldn't fix. Either way – fuck it.

And, just what the hell had he been told? That he would have to figure this shit all out on his own? Very fucking helpful. He had learned a lot from his time with Gammy about where he had come from and maybe who he was. He had sure learned a lot about who the hell she was. He wished he could fill in the missing pieces of that night. He now knew that it was no deer he had watched her slaughter, and he thought maybe he understood a little about what had happened – but not much more than that. He still felt there was more. He remembered a fire, and he remembered walking out of the woods that had been his home – alone and crying. Where had Gammy been? What had caused the fire?

Ben shook his head. He had been told nothing that would help him. He had learned about the Eater of the Dead and why he did what he did. He learned the term *Rougarou*, which he already knew, and had been filled with more questions than anything.

He dug into his steaming plate of food. Maybe the nightmare would become real tonight. He had seen what Gammy could do and that was sure as hell real enough so why not this? He definitely would be fighting Al Qaeda tonight, dark ones or no dark ones. He had the sense that either way he would need his strength.

CHAPTER 35

Ben moved quietly through the rapidly thinning brush of the jungle. Ahead he could see the whitish glow through his NVG's that meant Viper Team approached the camp higher authority had targeted. From the brief, he knew there would be a single building at the far edge of the compound, but they would encounter numerous fighters stationed in the clearing around it – protectors for the handful of upper-level terrorist leaders inside.

The dense jungle prevented a decent uplink of real time data from the predator that flew high and quiet overhead, but the break in the jungle canopy over the area had allowed a few glimpses and had confirmed "ten to thirty" enemy combatants. Not a very useful estimate, but they at least knew someone was home.

Ben had no trouble focusing on his job for the moment, the dreams and voices completely pushed aside, and his mind now that of a career professional soldier. He glanced over at Chris who indicated with hand signals he wanted them to fan out a bit so he moved left and then dropped to his belly. Ben shimmied the last few yards to the edge of the brush and looked at the target. The clearing was full of light from lanterns and two camp fires, as well as harsh white beams from corners of the house powered no doubt by the large generator he heard grumbling and rattling from that side of the camp. Ben flipped up his no longer needed NVGs.

He saw perhaps twenty fighters, mostly young and all of them relaxed and casual. Only about half of them even had their weapons, and those that did either slung them over their backs or dangled them from their hands as they smoked and laughed. Clearly they did not expect any trouble.

Not even remotely a professional or disciplined fighting force – again.

He looked for vests. Many times the senior leadership would surround themselves at important meetings (such as the one intel told them went on now inside the little mud hut) with suicide bombers. They would run at attackers and then detonate themselves, taking as many as possible with them as they headed off to paradise and their flock of virgins. From the look of this group, most of them would see their first naked woman in paradise – many looked less than sixteen years old. Gratefully, he saw no vests.

"Viper Team – set," Chris's whispered voice said in his earpiece.

He listened as the three other team leaders checked in from their positions in the circle they had formed around the camp.

"Hold Chevy two-one," a much clearer voice commanded from many miles away back at the operations center. "Two minutes. On my call."

The JSOTF commander must be getting some new info or else watched something that bothered him from the predator feed. Whatever gave them the eternally long two minute hold made Ben curse under his breath. Nothing felt worse than a hold once you were in position. He shifted his weight back and forth and tapped a finger on the side of his M-4. He did his best four-count tactical breathing and felt his heart rate slow.

As his body relaxed, he probed out, into the camp, with the blue light of his mind – gently searching for thoughts that would help him in the assault and more importantly for signs of the dark ones. At first the voices came in a confusing burst of mixed thoughts, but he slowly filtered them out – like fine tuning an old radio. The voices were predominately in a foreign tongue, but he found he could understand them in his head anyway. After only a moment it was as if he heard them in English. But they held no real clues. The men in the camp thought mostly about food, about women, and about when they would get the chance to kill the infidels. One voice stood out for a moment as important but before he could tune it in the commander's words in his headset broke his concentration.

"Chevy two-one – go on my mark," the voice said, and Ben tightened his muscles for the leap to his feet – a sprinter in the blocks. He pulled a concussion grenade free and pulled out the pin, then raised his rifle to the ready position. "GO, GO, GO!"

Ben lobbed the concussion grenade gently into a group of four bad guys that stood in his little sector of the battlefield. Only two had weapons – AK-47s which their elbows rested on like walking sticks – and all smoked and laughed. When the grenade rolled into the middle of them they simply stared at it in shock as if they could not possibly believe what they saw.

Ben entered the clearing at a brisk jog, weapon up and aimed at the group. The non-lethal concussion grenade went off and drove three of the four to the ground, hands over their ears. The fourth dropped his cigarette and tried to pull his rifle to his shoulder, but he faced the wrong way and Ben dropped him with a single shot to the temple. The other three screamed in terror, their voices high-pitched frightened children.

I don't want to die today.

Please don't kill me, please don't kill me.

Why am I not at home with my mother and sisters?

The voices in his head sounded like English in his mind, and he advanced quickly on the group of teenagers as their older friend dropped dead in the middle of the fray.

If you stay still and put your hands up in the air, I won't be forced to kill you.

He sent the thought out as he placed a boot between the shoulder blades of the nearest terrorist, and all three shot their hands into the air. Other concussion grenades exploded nearby. But he stayed focused on his task though his eyes swept his immediate perimeter while he kicked rifles away from the now crying boys. Then, he knelt beside them and quickly flex-cuffed them together, their hands behind their backs.

If any one of you moves at all my teammates will kill all of you.

He tuned out the sobbing thoughts and turned to his right, rifle up again, and moved deeper into the clearing.

"Viper Three…Three crows southwest corner."

"Viper Lead, Roger that—break – Viper Two, on your left," Chris's voice sounded even and professional as always, and the crack of Lash's rifle followed the warning.

The low building appeared through the smoke about seventy yards ahead. Viper Team would clear their sectors and then form a perimeter around the building as the breachers from their sister team of SEALs went in and took down the real targets. They would keep the perimeter and take any squirters that tried to escape.

Two men, older and clearly more seasoned, moved across his field of fire from right to left with weapons up. He squeezed off four rounds that dropped them both and sent them sprawling face-first in his path – dead before they hit the ground. Ben leapt across them like a hurdler and scanned right for stragglers from that direction and saw one just as a pink puff of blood erupted from the back of his head. He dropped straight down into the ground. Lash gave him a head nod from behind the dead terrorist as if they had just run into each other at the mall and then moved off right for his own assigned corner of the house.

Ben saw three Al Qaeda at the front of the crumbling structure with weapons drawn, clearly more hardened and professional than the mob of children strewn out in the clearing. They fired into the smoke at the rapidly moving force of American infidels. As he drew down on one Ben watched as they both dropped to the ground in lifeless heaps as Viper Team converged. Ben adjusted fire left and fired at the remaining terrorist who screamed his last breath, his rifle dropping beneath him.

Don't move asshole, or I'll drill a hole in the back of your head.

He sent the thought directly into the mind of the enemy fighter as he moved in on him. Motion to his left made him tick his eyes briefly in that direction where his mind registered Reed converging on the fallen Al Qaeda fighter with him.

"I got him, bro," Reed said and placed a foot on the back of the man's neck, his rifle trained at the back of his head.

Ben moved in, but he knew something was wrong. He wanted to get the man flex-cuffed quickly and clear him of weapons. He knew he wasn't dead from the thoughts that flooded him.

The Great Satan must never win. We must protect the plan at all costs. Allah will reward us richly in paradise.

Ben slung his rifle on his chest and pulled a flex-cuff from his kit as he knelt down. The man's face looked pale, and a second voice suddenly joined the first one in his head. The two flooded his mind in unison, making it impossible to make sense of either, though he felt certain both voices somehow came from the man beneath him.

My the mission one is chosen clear by my the God light is great here, and he my must family not will be allowed to proud find to the I Dark succeed Heart lose Kill or the I our nothing time in will the be service lost of for God another and thousand it years is Kill an the honor ROUGAROU to KILL die THE in ROUGAROU his KILL service THE I ROUGAROU will kill the infidels and my reward in paradise will be great they will all suffer the wrath of our one great God.

Ben jumped back at the sound of the name he shared with the Attakapa, and he gasped when the terrorist's eyes sprung open. He stared into the glowing red coals. The fire seemed to shine an orange light into the dirt beside the dying man's head. Ben felt himself stumble backwards from his kneeling position in surprise and fright.

"Dude, what's the matter?"

Reed's voice blended with the voice in his head, now unopposed by the dark one, and he realized the terrorist had both hands tucked beneath his body.

Praise be to God. Praise be to God. Praise be...

"Reed – get back," he screamed at his friend. He knew the terrorist would explode any moment and take them both with him.

Ben reached out his right hand, and the ring glowed a fiery red as his fingers erupted in blue light which spread to his elbow. The sparkling fireflies appeared in a cloud around him, and his vision became hazy and mixed with orange – like he looked through a glass full of glowing red liquid. He vaguely heard the terrorist scream out in pain and terror as Ben felt heat spread out from his chest and down his arm until it seemed to burst out of his fingers. His eyes registered a cartoon-colored image of the Al Qaeda fighter's head exploding. Then he felt a real heat – a heat from outside his body – like he had lit a grill with his face to close to the coals. He fell backwards on his ass, and for a moment the world went dark.

Ben scrambled to his feet and pulled his rifle up to firing position, his eyes blinking rapidly to clear the burning pain and the tears that ran down his cheeks and blurred his vision. He felt a hand on his arm and heard Reed's voice. It quivered with something not quite fear but not far from it.

"Dude, I'm pretty sure he's dead."

Ben blinked again, and his eyes finally focused.

He looked over the rifle sight at the charred rubbish that had been a man only moments ago. Several little wisps of blue flame still danced off the back of the charred black corpse with little spinning cyclones of greenish smoke rising above each. The corpse ended at the shoulders and pool of grayish liquid boiled for a moment in dirt and then evaporated in a cloud of steam with a soft hissssss. The blue flames winked out and left only a headless, charred body which still smoked into the wet air. The smell that filled Ben's mouth and nose caused his stomach to heave, and he lowered his rifle. He looked up, and Reed stared into his eyes, his own face still full of fear. Ben caught a few short words from Reed's confused mind and realized the fear was directed at him, not the dead terrorist.

"What the fuck was that?" Reed asked, his voice a low and conspiratorial whisper.

"I...Uh," Ben could think of nothing else and dropped his gaze to the ground – Reed's look more than he could bear.

"Three – Viper Lead–Everything ok?" Chris's voice sounded tense but professional.

"Sector secure," Ben managed in a tight-throated voice.

"Roger," Chris said.

"Two secure."

"Four secure."

Reed's voice followed a short pause, and he heard it in the air a moment before in came into his ear from his headset – a strained voice that still quivered slightly.

"Five."

"Viper Team secure." Chris announced.

Ben felt Reed's eyes on him but didn't look over. Instead, he tried to get his head back out of his own ass and focus on the mission before they all got killed.

"Phantom team – Go, Go, Go," another voice said in his headset and seconds later he heard the breacher charges fire as the assault team blew the doors and windows to the house. Ben focused on scanning his sector, but his mind saw nothing but the smoking, headless corpse. He swallowed hard and shook his head to clear the image. Moments later he heard a smattering of small arms fire as Phantom took down the house and secured the Al Qaeda leaders inside.

The eating of the dead denies the dark ones a vessel to return to our world. It destroys the dark one and traps him in the other world.

Ben stole a glance at the corpse. The black, leathery arms ended at the wrists leaving nothing but twigs of black bone where the hands had been.

Fuck that.

There sure as hell would be no eating of the dead here today. Not a fucking chance. He would leave that little trick to the Attakapa.

A soft breeze swept over him and gratefully pushed the smell of the corpse in the other direction. He looked over at Reed who also scanned the clearing, his face now more controlled. Ben thought about probing his friend's mind, but decided against it. He knew basically what he would find. He considered planting a thought there – something that might give some comfort – like a possible explanation for what Reed had seen.

Like what?

He squeezed his eyes shut for a second, and the thought passed between them.

Suicide bomber gone bad. The blast blew his head off, and he burst into flames instead of killing us somehow. Damnedest thing.

Ben listened to the shouts from the house as the bad guys were secured and a moment later heard his headset crackle again.

"Phantom secure – Five crows and two KIA – ready for exfil."

"Viper secure with three crows."

He listened to the voices in his headset, grateful they weren't in his head, and waited for the order to pull back to the clearing they had marked as the landing zone for extraction. He definitely needed to get the hell out of here.

* * *

Reed did his best to keep up his scan of the clearing, but he found his eyes pulled repeatedly to Ben and his bizarre vision of blue light and lasers shooting out from his best friend's fingers, boiling the terrorists head until it exploded and he burst into flames. But that was crazy, right?

Suicide bomber gone bad. The blast blew his head off, and he burst into flames instead of killing us somehow. Damnedest thing.

Of course, that was what had happened. It made the most sense. An explosive device the terrorist had strapped to him had somehow malfunctioned, and he had killed himself instead of them. He shuddered at the flood of memories that engulfed him. Memories of the nightmares he'd had in a haze of morphine and shock after his injury. Images of Ben, his eyes swirling clouds of milky white as blue light and sparkling pin points had surrounded them both. In his dream, fire or lasers or something had come out of Ben's fingers, as well, hadn't they? And that fucking ring – it had pulsed with orange light just like today.

Well that's the explanation, dick head. You're having some weird post-traumatic stress thing. This is your first time back in combat, for shit's sake, and it brought back them weird ass dreams. That has to be it, right?

He looked over at Ben who scanned his sector, M-4 at the ready – the perfect SEAL. Shit, he should be on a Goddamn poster. Sniper, medic, SEAL – maybe a Cajun witch doctor of sorts – but he sure as hell didn't just melt some dude's head and set him on fire with lasers from his fingertips.

His eyes caught the ring on the middle finger of his right hand which supported his rifle by the rear grip. The ring – that damn creepy ring– glowed a soft bluish-green. God, how he hated that friggin' ring.

Ben's face remained set in stone as he cleared their sector.

"Phantom is clear to the exfil LZ," a voice said in his headset and pulled him back to the job at hand. Across the clearing Auger led three teen-aged boys, all flex-cuffed together by the wrists, towards them. He urged the boys forward with his rifle.

"What in the holy fuck happened here?"

Reed looked up and saw Chris who stared wide eyed at the still smoking, headless corpse. His eyes then caught Ben's, but his face gave away nothing. His friend clenched his jaw and shrugged his shoulder.

Suicide bomber.

The voice was Ben's but his mouth never moved, and Reed just shook his head.

"Shit if I know, boss," he said. "Suicide bomber gone bad, I think. Crappy job of riggin' his shit, maybe. Blew off his own head and set his ass on fire, but Ben and me didn't get a scratch." His mind replayed the explosion of steam and the pool of boiling grey water when the terrorist's head had evaporated more than exploded.

"Never seen nothin' like it, bro," Ben said. "Guess Reed's right, but holy shit, man."

Reed looked at his friend who shook his head and looked away. Chris looked at both of them, then down at the steaming body and back at them again.

"Well, shit if I ever saw anything like that, man," he said. "Assholes are gettin' dumber and dumber."

Chris moved off toward Auger who strained his neck to see past the officer.

"What in the hell happened there?" he asked.

Reed moved away from the corner of the house and toward his two teammates, suddenly unable to stand being near the corpse. He also realized he wanted a little distance between him and Ben, but immediately felt like an asshole for the thought. In any case, Ben held his position at the corner. Lash approached them from the far side of the house as Phantom's six-member team marched five hooded men in long grey robes out of the house their hands secured behind their backs with flex cuffs.

"Everyone okay?" Chris asked the group.

"Hooyah," they answered in unison.

The SEAL at the end of Phantom team's train of bad guys looked past Ben and pursed his lips.

"Who's the crispy critter?" he asked.

Reed felt his chest tighten and for a moment felt a little dizzy. He brushed past Phantom team and their conga line of senior Al Qaeda assholes and then past Chris and Auger. He just needed a minute.

So this is what PTSD feels like. I feel like a damn teen-aged girl goin' all weak kneed at sight of a road kill. Christ Almighty.

"You okay, Reed?" Chris called after him.

He waved his hand over his shoulder and then gave a thumbs up. The last thing he needed was the team worryin' about him.

* * *

Ben took the rear behind the column formed by Viper Team and the three teen-age terrorists he had captured. He hoped the restraint he had displayed with the group of bad guys had shown Chris he had the fire discipline he had been counseled about on their big hit of the last tour. He realized that op, their last before heading state-side and his wedding, felt like years and years ago. It couldn't really have been more than six or seven weeks he realized. He shook his head.

Father.

The voice sent a chill of both fear and excitement through his chest, and he looked over to his right. Jewel sat cross-legged on the floor of the jungle between the out-stretched legs of the Elder. She smiled, and he smiled back. Just as he raised a hand to wave, the image shimmered, turned silver, and disappeared. He squeezed his eyes shut, and when he opened them he saw he had fallen a few paces behind the group. Ben scanned the jungle around him for Al Qaeda and ghosts and then continued on, catching up in a few long strides.

"Hear somethin'?" Lash asked.

Ben just shook his head.

As he looked up he saw the Attakapa, statue still and balanced precariously on a huge gnarled tree branch several feet above the team as they passed beneath him.

The dark one you battled was not consumed. Little matter. Soon they will lead you to the one with the black blood.

Ben refused to let his eyes glance upward as he passed beneath the Indian, but his peripheral vision registered the silver shimmer as the dark-skinned legs evaporated into space.

Leave me alone. I'm working here for God's sake.

Ben concentrated his gaze on the back of the teen-aged terrorist's head at the rear of the line and kept his eyes away from the jungle around them. Not the best way to clear their route of other dangers, but he just couldn't take it anymore. He heard the rumble of approaching helicopters, a low deep rattle of the huge Chinooks instead of their favored sports car-like Blackhawks. They would need the extra space for the eight bad guys that accompanied them out.

They broke into a clearing as the first helicopter touched down briefly, and the Special Operators moved swiftly in through the already lowered back ramp. Seconds later the twin rotors beat the air back into submission, the helicopter was airborne again, and the next helicopter already flared for its own landing.

In less than forty five seconds three helicopters cleared all of the teams out of the jungle, and Ben sat on the hard metal floor across from the terrorists whose hands had been secured to the metal D-rings usually meant to secure cargo pallets in the massive helo. He sighed and leaned back. His helmet tipped forward over his eyes as it impacted the wall of the aircraft. Ben left it where it ended up, obscuring his vision, and sighed again. He felt complete exhaustion – his mind, as well as his body. He knew he wouldn't sleep today though, and the thought nearly made him cry. He knew he should think about all that had happened – all that he had seen and heard – and search for clues that might end this insane crusade.

I can't. Not right now. Not yet.

He snapped off his NVGs, and the green light disappeared leaving him in total darkness. Ben closed his eyes and felt tears trickle down his cheeks.

I miss you, Christy. I love you so much, baby, and I miss you. I promise I'll be home very soon.

CHAPTER

36

Christy yawned, squeezed her eyes shut, and then opened them wide. The last thing she needed was to get in a wreck on the way home from work, but good Lord was she tired. She had awoken as she always did these days, after only an hour or so of sleep, and tossed and turned as she thought about her husband. She knew it was a mistake to do the time difference math in her head, and now she awoke at about the time she assumed Ben would be waist deep in the shit of his job. She would then spend the rest of the night mostly awake, worried the phone would ring and instead of Ben it would be another voice – a sad voice of a friend with horrible news about her husband.

As she turned off of Shore Drive and onto Pleasure House Road toward the ocean and their Chicks Beach town house, she laid a hand across her belly and gently rubbed it. She needed to be careful and get better rest. It wasn't just about her anymore. She smiled a tense smile at that thought. It would be so much easier to be excited when Ben got home, and she knew he would stay safe.

It was still a little too early for an E.P.T., but she had convinced herself it was really just a formality at this point. She no longer had any doubt at all that their child grew inside of her. It wasn't just the PMS-like symptoms or the tender breasts either. She was certain she could *feel* the baby within her. She turned into their driveway and stifled another big yawn. Then, she sighed. It had become so hard to go into their home and be alone. She felt she had so much she needed to share with her husband.

I miss you, Christy. I love you so much, baby, and I miss you. I promise I'll be home very soon.

The words were so clear and so real she actually looked over into the passenger seat. But, of course, Ben did not, in fact, sit there with a loving smile on his face. She saw him in her mind's eye anyway.

"I love you, too, baby, and I miss you more than anything," she said, in case the words in her head really were from her husband. Fantasy or not, she did feel much better having heard them and thought maybe tonight she would really sleep.

He sounded fine, he loves me, and misses me.

Christy gathered up her detail case and her take-out Chic-fil-A sandwich and headed inside.

CHAPTER

37

Sleep did come, but the initial welcome relief proved short-lived. He had collapsed into his rack in the small three-man cubicle he shared with Reed and Auger, his weapons and kit on the floor beside him. His dirty cammies and boots were still on. It felt he had slept for either a few minutes or a few days when the soft voice stirred him awake – well, not really awake he supposed, but wherever he went on these little journeys. The tiny voice filled him with warmth rather than fear.

I have missed you, father.

Ben opened his eyes and found himself curled in a ball on the soft moss floor of a clearing somewhere in the jungle. The smell of the cooking pots made him realize how hungry he was. His eyes focused on the little bare feet in front of him, and he followed them to the tiny hands folded neatly in her lap.

Jewel sat like the young toddler she was – legs in front of her crooked at the knees and bent slightly forward at the waist to keep from tipping over backwards. Only the gently folded hands gave her the illusion of age – that and the voice in his head from a baby too young to talk yet, especially in English.

Grandfather said you would come and find me. He said you would keep us safe. And, now you are here.

When her lips finally moved, they simply smiled and said "Deh, Deh Da Eh," which apparently meant something funny in toddler speak because she squealed a little giggle and then reached for his nose.

Ben sat up and crossed his legs Indian-style and reached for her. Jewel climbed eagerly into his lap and snuggled against his neck, and he felt his eyes moisten. Until he felt her and smelled her, he hadn't really known how much he missed her – and loved her, he decided.

"I love you, baby girl," he said and hugged her as she tugged at the chain that held his dog tags around his neck beneath his dirty brown T-shirt. "I'm going to bring you home, Jewel."

But I am home father. I'm where I belong, and now you are with us.

He breathed in the sweet little girl scent of her, and tears spilled onto his cheeks. He wanted the dream to be real and knew on some level that it was – at least in some weird way he hadn't really figured out yet. If he did nothing else in Africa, he wanted to find his little girl. He wanted to make her safe and bring her home to Christy – and to the rest of their family that grew inside her.

They are all your family. Not just the little one, but all of them.

At the Elder's voice Ben opened his eyes and saw for the first time the small band of villagers that stood in a loose circle around him. At the sight of him opening his eyes, his people smiled and nodded their heads. He felt a warmth of kinship as he looked at their smiling faces. Or maybe not kinship so much as responsibility. He wondered if that came mostly from the guilt about the massacre they had not just failed to stop, but had likely caused.

The small circle parted, and the Village Elder strode towards him on the strong body of a much younger man than his old face suggested. Like his stride his eyes were full of youth. He smiled down at Ben a moment and then joined him on the ground and folded his legs beneath him.

You have encountered one of the dark ones?

Ben thought about the glowing eyes of the terrorist at the target. He thought about the second voice that had blended with the Al Qaeda fighter – the voice that commanded the man to kill the Rougarou. He knew that voice came from another world.

"I think so," Ben answered. "He's dead. I killed him. He won't hurt our people anymore."

The old man shook his head, and his young eyes looked sad. His lips stayed pursed tightly as he spoke in Ben's head.

You have killed the man but not the evil. The dark ones can travel quickly from one vessel to the next. The Attakapa know a way to stop them in the moments after the death of the vessel, but it is no matter. The dark ones are dangerous to our people but it is the one with the black blood who threatens not just the Living Jungle but the Living Earth. He must be stopped before his power grows beyond us. The dark ones can lead you to him. Only you can stop him now. You are the Rougarou.

Ben knew the truth when he heard it and chuckled at his fantasy that his mission might be only to rescue his little girl. He felt suddenly afraid – not for his own safety, but of failure. He knew he really didn't understand any of this, but the magnitude of it seemed almost in his reach.

"How will I know him? What will he look like?" For a moment Ben had an image of the demon-like creature, the burnt orange skin taunt over rippling muscles and the animal face, snarling over fang-like teeth. The eyes were yellow and cat-like. He doubted his M-4 would do much more than piss something like that off.

That image is not far from the truth. The one of the black blood is much like a demon, a monster that inspired legends over the thousands of years since he once walked in our world. He will appear as a man – a leader. You will know him to be of the other world by his eyes, much like his army of dark ones. But it will be his thoughts that will reveal him to you, Ben. His thoughts will tell you, and you will know. He must be stopped before he can cross over to our world and become the creature you imagine.

The old man looked up at the break in the jungle canopy and seemed to read the stars like a watch.

The time is quite short, Ben.

Ben felt Jewel's chubby hands tug on his cheeks, and he hugged her tighter to his chest.

Tonight I will see you father.

"Goo, Da da, eh."

You must come to us tonight, Ben. There is no time left to wait. Tonight you will battle again with the dark ones and their numbers may be greater. Then, you must leave your friends and come to us. You will need our people to guide you to where the one with the black blood hides.

"How will I find you?'

I will send you a heart message when the time comes. That will guide you to what is left of the keepers of the Living Jungle. From there we can lead you to your prey.

Ben startled at the Elder's use of the word, but that was right, wasn't it? He was, indeed, a predator.

Jewel kissed his cheek softly with an exaggerated "Hmmm Mmmuh," and then crawled out of his lap. She struggled to her feet, teetered a moment, and then toddled over to the Elder. Ben felt his eyes grow heavy but sensed he had one more place to go.

He rose on fatigued, achy legs, and the villagers parted for him to pass through the circle. He left the clearing, walked only a few yards before he smelled the familiar smells of home, and saw the light from two lanterns on the sagging wooden porch that hung off their shack like the after thought it had probably once been. Gammy sat in her rocker, a warm glass of sweet tea in her hand and another on the railing. She waved to him and smiled.

"Hurry it on now, chile. You be needin' some rest more dan a long goodbye."

Ben climbed the three creaking steps, moving to the left side to avoid the cracked board he knew was in the middle of the second one, and kissed his Gammy's chubby cheek. He then grabbed his jelly glass of tea and took his seat in the wooden chair beside her. She took his hand and held it as they both sipped a moment in silence.

"Guessin' dis be goodbye fo' now, boy," she said. Her voice sounded sad, but she turned and looked at him and smiled. "Be seein' you 'gain, though, Benny, don' worry'n none 'bout dat. Jes gots to wait a bit now – least I hope so." She chuckled at some inside joke and then squeezed his hand. "Proud o' you, Benny boy," her voice sounded tight. "Hope I gave you enuff, is all. But I sho' is proud of my Benny."

She looked out over their yard and sipped her tea. Ben squeezed her hand back. For a moment he saw her face surrounded by raging flames – her voice screaming in pain and urgency and directing a much younger grandson what he must do and where he must go. The memory evaporated again before he could make sense of it, and he realized he would need another time to chase it down.

Got enough on my plate, for sure that.

He sat and sipped tea and held hands with his grandmother.

* * *

Ben leaned back against the edge of the door and felt the cool wind whip his face. The familiarity cleared his head more than the wind. His NVGs were flipped up and he stared at total darkness. He knew the jungle slid by only a hundred feet below. But the blackness was so complete he might have floated anywhere – over the ocean, in space, anywhere. He listened to Toby Keith in his headset from the iPod in his kit, but for a moment the song about a big blue note was interrupted by a static-filled voice in his ears.

"Weapons test," a cool deep voice said.

He lowered his head and a few seconds later the fifty caliber machine gun mounted in the front of his doorway coughed out a dozen rounds. Ben felt the spent casings bounce off his helmet a moment after the long tongue of flame disturbed his dark mental security blanket.

"Left."

Another burst from the other doorway. This time he couldn't see the flame but the glow lit up the inside of the UH-60 Blackhawk for a moment.

"Right."

"Weapons clear."

And, then the darkness returned. He leaned his head back against the doorway and again felt the wind on his face. He tried to keep his mind far away from dreams and thoughts of dead Indians and grandmothers. Jewel kept coming back to him none the less – Jewel with her big eyes and chubby little hands tugging at his ears. He knew now beyond more than a little doubt (the strange hope that maybe he really was just crazy) he would see her – if not tonight then before the sun set again. He tried not to think too much about how that must mean he would not be riding home with his team from this op.

He listened to his music and forced his thoughts back to the mission as it had been briefed. He still had a job to do no matter where the rest of the night led him on his crusade. Viper Team – his friends who were more like family – needed him to be at his iced best. He would do his job the only way he knew how, the way he had trained and executed since his days in SEAL training. Ben reviewed the operational plan in his head as they hurtled through the darkness in the Blackhawk. The half-hour sped by like mere minutes, and then another voice broke into his music, this time cutting off one of his favorite Credence tunes.

"Five minutes," Chris's voice announced.

He flipped his NVGs down and checked over his gear in the green-grey world they opened up for him. He checked his rifle last, confirmed (again) that a round was chambered, and then tugged his gloves to make sure they were tight.

"One minute."

A few moments later, he lay prone in the brush and scanned his sector quietly through his NVGs as the thumping sound of the helicopters faded into the distance. At the sound of Chris's one-word command, he rose silently, rifle up and ready, and began the forty-five minute trek to the target. He knew from the brief the fighters that waited at this camp would not be the children they had fought the night before. They had been told to expect a smaller but heavily armed and seasoned fighting force.

They anticipated a second perimeter farther out from the camp and scouts patrolling the area. Fortunately, they had the support of a predator drone orbiting high above, this one equipped with infrared heat signaling. They would have real time data on anyone alive in the jungle around them. They may not know who they were, but they would see them. They would assume anyone moving about at two o'clock in the morning in the middle of the jungle and in proximity to an Al Qaeda command post were bad guys.

Their first contact came from the Task Force commander in the form of relayed information from the life-saving predator.

"Viper Two – Viper Three – two targets fifteen meters left and moving towards you." The calm voice in his headset dropped Ben down into the brush.

He scanned through the bushes to his left, the green-grey world in his NVGs so far devoid of motion.

"Viper Two – target just past you and is moving away – Viper Three – target now only a few meters and heading right towards you."

He crouched lower into the dense vegetation just as the man came into view. The Al Qaeda terrorist moved slowly and deliberately toward him, and his head seemed to move side-to-side. He had one hand on the grip of his rifle, and the other held something to his face. Ben recognized the hand-held night vision system and sunk lower. The terrorist also had a radio. Ben closed his eyes a moment and reached out with his mind, but he heard nothing that made him think the man thought American soldiers might be hidden in the jungle. He seemed to want only to return to camp and get something to eat.

The man turned suddenly and looked behind him at the same moment Ben heard the quiet sound that he knew meant Lash had taken out his partner. Ben took advantage of the man's distraction.

He leapt to his feet and sprinted forward, drawing his SOG knife from its scabbard on his vest as he did. The man heard him, but way too late, and Ben threw an arm around his neck as the terrorist turned toward him. He shifted all his weight to the right, pulling the man off his feet by his head just as he plunged his combat knife into the soft spot at the base of his skull. He instantly went limp in his arms, and Ben lowered him gently to the floor of the jungle.

"Viper Three, clear," he whispered into his microphone. He knelt beside the body and scanned the dark jungle around him but saw nothing else that concerned him.

"Viper Two, clear," Lash's voice told him in his earpiece.

Ben looked down at the lifeless body beside him. The Terrorist stared blankly at nothing.

Can't breathe– can't move– can't breathe!

Ben shut off the voice in his head quickly, not wanting to hear the last terrified thoughts of the man who died slowly beside him as his brain screamed for more oxygen – the message never reaching his body through the now severed spinal cord. Ben saw the lifeless eyes held no orange light, and he heard only the single frightened voice in his head – no dark one here.

He waited another few seconds and then continued his quiet movement towards the objective. The Operators monitoring the predator feed from the operations center warned them of nothing else, and in a few more minutes he again lay prone at the edge of an Al Qaeda camp.

Unlike the night before, this camp had no real clearing, just a slight thinning of the jungle, so the dozen or so terrorists that sat beside two open fires in front of three large tents would have plenty of cover during the attack. He also grimly noted they had a fifty caliber machine gun in a trench dug beside the corrugated tin shack where the true objective would no doubt be found. The weapon was not manned, but he had an inkling any attack would immediately drive several trained gunners to the efficient weapon. That would have to be the first order of business.

"Viper Lead – Two – you see the fifty?" Lash must clearly be in place and had seen the gun nest, as well.

"Rog– Two, that's your target."

"Two."

"Three in position," Ben whispered into his mike.

"Four."

"Five."

Only a few moments of silence passed that as usual felt like an eternity. Finally, Chris's voice came over the headset.

"Four and One are the breachers now – Two on the Fifty – Three and Five secure the camp. Smoke and bang on my mark."

Ben pulled out a smoke grenade and a concussion grenade and waited.

"Viper Team, go."

He tossed both of his grenades into the center of camp just as others lobbed in from what would appear as all directions to the bad guys. Unlike the children from the camp the night before, these fighters reacted instantly. They quickly scrambled to their feet and raised their weapons as they moved in all directions away from the grenades which rolled around on the jungle floor. Two men sprinted towards the machine gun as they all hollered at each other. Ben heard the spit of Lash's rifle and watched the two collapse to the ground before they had made it two paces. Ben sighted in on his own targets from the fighters who scattered like rats and began to fire.

Moments later all but two of the dozen or so of the enemy lay dead, the tents had been torn down to clear them of additional fighters, and Viper Team moved toward the tin shack beside which Lash sat at the fifty and gave a grin and mock salute. The two wounded terrorists crumpled through the door to the building and slammed it behind them. Chris and Reed were already there as it closed. Reed pressed a shaped charge around the door knob then plunged wires into the charge and flattened himself against the wall.

"Fire in the hole," he hollered, and the door disappeared in a flash of white light and smoke. Immediately, he and Chris entered the shack, and Auger followed a split second later. Two cracks of M-4 fire were followed by Chris's voice yelling commands in English. Then, he heard Reed's voice.

"Squirters out the back – three of them!"

Ben sprinted around the corner and saw three figures in grey robes and high-top tennis shoes tear off into the jungle. He fired his M-4 on instinct, and the tail-end Charlie in the group pitched forward face-first onto the ground. Ben was on him in a second, a knee between the man's shoulder blades as he scanned the jungle through his rifle sight.

"Two are still on the move," he hollered. "I got one."

"Hold," Chris commanded from inside the shack. "We have both of the primary objectives." Apparently the big fish had been captured.

The Rougarou is here. We must warn the master.

Ben grabbed the terrorist by the hair and pulled his head up off the ground. The eyes opened and looked terrified, but they clearly were not the eyes of a dark one. Ben probed the man's mind and found only a single voice, full of disjointed fear and pain – but alone. He had not been the source of the new voice who knew him as the protector and hunter he had become.

He stood up, shifted from a knee to a foot keeping them man pinned to the ground, and scanned more intently the ten or so yards of jungle he could see. He had to get the two squirters – at least one of them was a dark one and could help him find his own primary objective. He wanted only to do what fate had decided he must do and get the hell home. He felt his heart pound at the thought of losing the trail of the escaped terrorists. A hand fell on his shoulder.

"Nice work," Lash said as he looked at the bad guy under Ben's boot.

"You got him?" Ben asked.

"Sure," Lash said but looked confused.

Ben sprinted off into the jungle. As he moved swiftly through the brush he searched through his NVGs, but also sent out the blue light of his mind. If he could hear their thoughts again he could track them. He slung his rifle across his chest so he could move more quickly and use both hands to clear the brush ahead of him. He wouldn't need it now.

He had other weapons at his disposal.

Chris's voice in his headset demanded that he come back – that they had completed their mission. Ben pulled the earpiece out of his ear, and let it bounce against his kit as he moved swiftly, tracking his prey.

CHAPTER 38

"What the hell do you mean he's gone?"

The boss sounded highly pissed as he led two Al Qaeda leaders out of the shack, their hands bound behind them. Reed followed with his own prisoner.

"He took off after the squirters," Lash said as he pulled plastic cuffs onto the terrorist he knelt over.

"Didn't you guys hear me order a hold? We got what we came for," he said and gestured to the two prisoners who both stared at their feet. Lash shrugged.

"Maybe he didn't hear you," Reed offered.

Chris shot him a look that kept him from saying anything else.

"Goddammit," he mumbled then reached up to key his mike. "Viper Three – this is lead. Return to the camp. We got 'em, Three. Return to camp."

There was a long, awkward pause while Viper Team looked off and waited for Ben to check in that he understood and would be there in a minute. The pause stretched out longer, and Reed cursed in his mind.

"Three, this is Viper Lead – how do you read?"

Another long pause, and then Chris repeated his call. The officer rubbed his temple with a gloved hand.

"Did you hear any weapons fire?" Chris asked.

Lash shook his head.

Reed felt a tight band around his chest. Where the hell was Ben? Had he been hurt or – oh, Jesus no – killed? Maybe his radio was dicked up. That made the most sense. Ben would never ignore the radio calls, and he couldn't be dead, right? Reed ran through all of the ways you could kill a man without firing a weapon. Still, he found it hard to imagine these shit heads could kill a fully armed SEAL, especially Ben, without shooting him.

He peered into the greenish-grey jungle through his NVGs. Any second Ben would come into view, likely leading two prisoners and with a shit-eating grin on his face. But he saw no movement at all.

Reed listened as Chris called again over the radio, but again got no response. Then, the officer looked over his team.

"Alright," he said. "Reed and Auger stay with these assholes." He turned to Lash. "Lash, come with me – we'll do a quick search."

"Hey, I need to go help you find him," Reed said and grabbed at Chris's sleeve.

"No," the officer said. "Stay with Auger and guard these guys. We'll be back with Ben in a minute."

The Team all nodded, and Auger herded the terrorists into a little circle and forced them to their knees all facing its center. Lash and Chris headed off into the jungle on divergent paths in the general direction Ben had headed.

Reed kept his rifle trained on the circle jerk of bad guys, but he couldn't help but scan the edge of the camp. Where in the hell was Ben?

"He's alright, don't you think?" he said to no one in particular. Only Auger was there to hear, and he shrugged and said nothing. But his tight-jawed face said enough. Reed shook his head. "He's alright," he announced as if saying it would make it true.

He had to be alright. Reed didn't think he could even go on being a SEAL if he lost Ben. He had lost friends before, but this was different. Ben was his family – him and Christy. The thought of Christy at home at the beach made Reed wince.

"He's alright," he announced again and continued to scan the jungle, knowing his best friend would emerge at any moment.

CHAPTER 39

Ben knew in a few more minutes a claim of radio problems would fail to keep his ass out of wicked serious trouble. Even with his earpiece bouncing on his chest he could hear Chris's desperate calls to him. At this point, they would assume he was injured or killed – or God forbid captured – and the thought of the fear and worry he caused his team tore at him.

Nothing I can do about it this second.

He knew in his heart the best thing he could do for everyone was to track these fuckers down and find out where their leader hid from the *Rougarou.* That was the mission he came here for, and he now believed completing it not only would be his ticket home and back to real life, but might really save the world as he knew it. Like most SEALs, Ben had never thought of himself as a hero and even now thought only that he really had no other option. An image of the giant demon-like creature flashed in his mind. He could never let the power and destruction he thought such a creature would have unleash itself on his world or his family.

It's for Christy as much as anything – Christy and Jewel and our unborn son.

The voices he heard now were those of the Al Qaeda terrorists and no longer the dark ones who lived inside at least one, if not both, of them. The voices provided no clues as to where they were going other than a picture he flashed on briefly of the remains of what looked like an ancient ruin of a building which the jungle seemed to have nearly swallowed up. The voices, however, seemed to work almost as a beacon – the clarity improved when he felt like he moved in the right direction. The volume got louder when he felt like he got closer. All of that could be total bullshit imagination, of course, but he had nothing else to go on.

Ben pushed back some thick jungle grass that came nearly to his chest and tried to pick up the pace. His gaze fell briefly on his hand as it pushed the brush aside and he saw the ring. It had turned a strange combination of colors – an almost lime green at the outside which faded to a bright yellow in the middle. The yellow part seemed to pulse gently, becoming brighter and then fading again to a soft glow. He also noticed the very faint blue light around his hand and forearm.

Good. Nice to know that's still there if I need it.

The thought didn't keep him from tapping his M-4 with his other hand to make sure it was in position for a quick draw to firing position. He also checked that his nine millimeter pistol rode in its holster on his right thigh.

He broke through the grass and found himself on a rise over a deeply cut ravine with several rocky outcroppings which he used as steps of sorts to drop swiftly from the top of the hill. As he did, he caught a glimpse of two grey-robed figures dashing madly up the other side of the ravine that some rainy season gone by must have created. The two were maybe sixty yards ahead now and seemed oblivious of his presence.

Ben felt his right hand tingle and knew his blue light would be brighter now. He had no clue if that power could work over any real distance – had never had a chance to field test this particular weapon. He definitely knew something that would, however, and as he jumped the last four feet to the bottom of the hill he pulled his M-4 up. The two had been slowed down by a giant tree trunk that blocked the exit to the ravine, and Ben took the opportunity to cut the distance in half. Then, he flipped up his NVGs and sighted through the night vision optical sight mounted on his rifle, saw the infrared dot appear on the first man's back, and squeezed.

A small pink cloud with a dark hole in its center marked where the high velocity round tore through back of the terrorists neck. He started to pitch forward, but gravity won. Instead, he tumbled backward and then slid a meter or two head-first back down the incline. Ben had already sighted in on the other man, thought briefly about trying not to kill him, and then instead squeezed his trigger again and watched as the right side of the man's head blew apart. He fell over the far side of the tree trunk over which he had already partially scrambled.

Ben watched through the scope for movement, and when he saw none, he dropped his rifle back down to a ready position. Then he flipped his NVGs back into place with his left hand. The jungle returned to its eerie greenish-grey, and Ben walked slowly towards the terrorist lying head down on his back on the upside of the hill. He kept his rifle partially raised and at the ready just in case.

The man's eyes were partially opened, and his cheeks were wet with tears. He didn't look at Ben directly, and he decided the dying man must be in shock. He still kept his rifle cautiously trained on him, however. With his left foot Ben stepped on the man's right hand to keep him from reaching for the AK-47 that lay between his arm and chest, still attached by a black sling. With his left hand he frisked along the man's sides, looking for other weapons. The glazed eyes ticked a moment in his direction, never quite seemed to focus, and then closed. The chest rose slowly, and the breaths seemed quite shallow. Then the man shuddered, and his breathing stopped. Ben reached down cautiously and felt for a pulse in the neck – he felt it – weak, but there.

The man's eyes sprang open suddenly, which caused Ben to stand up and stumble a step backward as his mouth opened and a horrifying, animal-like scream tore through Ben's head. It seemed to almost vibrate the jungle around them. The eyes had turned to the now familiar fiery orange, but through the NVGs glowed out at him as a pale white, and then two hands grabbed his left ankle with incredible strength – enough to cause him to wince in pain.

Instinct took over, and Ben aimed and squeezed the trigger of his M-4. Both rounds impacted the middle of the terrorist's forehead. The jungle grass and moss puffed out around the dead man's head as the back of his skull exploded out into the jungle floor. Ben watched as the glowing eyes faded slowly and then appeared grey and dead – unfocused and turned up at the jungle canopy above.

Ben did a few slow tactical breaths to calm his heart rate and get rid of the fine tremor he felt in his hands. He squeezed his eyes shut and opened them again, staring at the man at his feet. A large pool of blood, black in the night vision optics, had formed around the blown out head.

That dude is dead.

Ben reached out with the blue light of his mind anyway. The terrorist's thoughts were gone, but the dark ones thoughts were still there.

The Rougarou is among us. The brothers must know so they can protect the Great One. The Rougarou must be stopped.

Another voice, or at least a vibrating sound, filled his head suddenly and brought a pain he thought might blow out his temples. The message in the sound was lost on him, and he registered nothing but torture, a vibration of some sort, and explosions of white light behind his eyes. Some other part of him sensed movement, and he forced his thoughts to focus.

The dead terrorist moved his arms slowly and then raised his legs at the knees to push backwards away from Ben. The glow in the eyes had returned and, in fact, was nearly blinding in his NVGs. By the time he reacted, the dead man had flipped himself over and was pushing himself up to a kneeling position – impossible, of course, because from this new vantage point Ben could see the entire back of his head was missing. The skull was now a ragged empty cavity, the brains having been made a permanent fertilizer for the mossy jungle floor.

The words of the Attakapa flooded into his mind, and Ben unsheathed his combat knife. He threw himself onto the back of the dead man. In one powerful stroke he sliced through the neck from behind, down to the spine, and nearly decapitated the already walking zombie. The body collapsed again, now face first, onto the ground. Ben watched, his breath coming in painful rasps, and saw the corpse's fingers flicker and then slowly close into a fist.

Ben flipped the corpse over and let out his own animal-like scream as he plunged the foot long blade into the base of his throat. With strength he couldn't possibly have he pulled the knife downward, split the man's breast bone, and opened his belly almost to the navel. He felt the hot spray of blood across his face and neck and felt it soak into his shirt. With both hands he grabbed the edges of the split sternum and tore the man's chest open like he gutted a catfish.

The heart lay still in the center of the man's chest, and Ben stared at it – grey and lifeless in infrared. Then, a white glow returned to the sightless eyes, and the heart quivered. It squeezed tight a moment before it began a rhythmic beating in the splayed open chest.

Ben reached into the split opening, grabbed the muscular organ, and tore it from the ragged cavity. Strands of tissue dangled from the eviscerated organ across the backs of both of his hands.

He brought the heart to his face. Without any hesitation he opened his mouth wide and crammed the bloody thing between his teeth, bit down, and tore a giant piece of thick, sinewy flesh away. He chewed the heart muscle with reckless abandon, oblivious to the gore that poured down over his chin and dripped onto his knees as he hunched over his feast. He swallowed the bite, which stuck for a moment in his throat, and then opened his mouth again.

CHAPTER 40

Reed tapped his hand nervously on his leg which burned like hell from his old injury. It had been no easy task to get the command surgeon to clear him for this deployment, but despite the pain he had no doubt he was right where he belonged. He watched as Chris rubbed both temples, like he always did when he made tough calls.

"Gather up," the officer said. Reed thought that sounded stupid since they already stood in a tight circle, except Lash who now guarded the shit heads. He decided not to point that out.

"What's up, boss?" Auger said. His voice said a lot more. None of them had any intention of leaving this target without Ben – alive or dead they would all leave together. It was their code.

"I need a secure satellite link on the computer," Chris told Reed. "I want to get some help to exfil the crows, and then we can concentrate on finding Ben."

"What if they say no?" Lash asked from a few yards away where he held is rifle at the ready, trained on the nearest prisoner who kneeled like the others and bent his head forward into the middle of the circle.

"They won't," Chris predicted. "But if they do, they can find these fuckers later in a shallow grave. Then they'll have to find us, too, because we are not leaving here without Ben."

The other three gave curt nods, and Reed knelt down, then pulled a laptop out of his back pack. He spread open a small, collapsible dish antenna and used his compass to point it roughly at two-hundred and forty-five degrees – the approximate direction of the satellite that would link him to the Task Force commander. He would fine tune the direction with the help of the computer. He fumbled with the cables and realized his hands were shaking.

Please be alive, Ben.

He took a deep breath and tried again to hook up.

CHAPTER

41

Ben stripped off his back pack and vest and then pulled his cammie shirt over his head. He used the one clean sleeve to wipe the sticky gore from his face and neck and then pulled his T-shirt off, as well. He soaked it with water from his camel back using the hose that secured it to his vest and then cleaned the dried blood left behind on his face and chest. He felt better already.

He forced himself not to look at the mutilated body of the former Al Qaeda terrorist and threw his ruined shirts onto the ground and then pulled his kit back on over his bare and sweat-streaked skin. He needed to check the other asshole who lay dead on the other side of the fallen tree. Ben picked up his rifle and stepped over the now dead-for-good corpse without looking down.

Mike Charlie – mission complete.

Ben didn't like the scramble over the tree trunk, which left him vulnerable with both of his hands tied up, but he didn't want to waste any more time either. From the fallen tree he saw the other terrorist prone on the ground, the right side of his head mostly missing from his high velocity gunshot wound. Ben pulled his rifle up and then jumped the five feet to the ground a couple of yards away from the body. He dropped to a crouch immediately, dissipating the energy of his leap, and trained his M-4 at the corpse. Two months ago he would have felt like an idiot being this careful about a man who clearly lay dead, but his reality had changed a lot in those two months and even more in the last ten minutes.

No sense in taking any chances.

As he got closer he slung his rifle and again pulled out his combat knife. Just as he reached his hand out to flip the body over, the corpse's arms shuddered violently and the dead man rolled onto his back, reaching for him. Ben stumbled backward onto his ass as he slipped from the grasping hands clutches. The eyes again glowed with the fire of the dark ones. Before he could act the corpse's mouth opened impossibly wide, and a brilliant light poured out like the powerful spray from a fire hose right at his face. Ben instinctively raised his arms, but just before the spray hit him in the face it made an impossible bend and arched skyward.

Ben fell the rest of the way over onto his back as the high-pitched scream he had heard from the other dead man filled the air – this time it seemed to emanate from the tube of blinding light and seconds later the last of it fled the corpse's mouth. Ben saw the mouth had been torn open much farther at the corners, the opening now a ghoulishly bloody smile. He thought for a moment of a Jack-O-Lantern. Then, the body pitched forward back onto the ground face-first and lay still.

Ben sat a moment, caught his breath, and waited for the spots to clear from his eyes from the eruption of light and his ears to stop ringing from the scream. He blinked a few times and then rose to his feet. He stared at the dead man. He wasn't certain (of anything he supposed), but he believed he had been too late this time. He suspected he had just seen the dark one leave the body of the dead terrorist.

Shit. Maybe I'll get another chance to send that one back to hell.

Ben slid his knife home into its sheath on his vest and then stood there a moment. He scanned the jungle around him and saw nothing. He had no idea which way to go or even what his destination was supposed to be.

You need to come to us, father. Come home, and let us help you.

Jewel's impossible-for-a-can't-talk-yet voice felt good in his heart – like maybe he wasn't alone and crazy in the African jungle. The Elder's voice followed.

Come to us, Ben. Time is dangerously short, and we can help you find the Evil. Come to us.

Where? How will I find you?

There was a short pause, and then the Elder's voice gratefully came back.

You have the power to find us, Ben, but no matter. I will send you a heart message to guide you here quickly.

The voice was replaced with something else – just a feeling, but he knew it was real. He felt drawn to his left, turned that way, and started through the jungle. As he did another voice came to him.

"Viper Three – Viper Lead – do you read me? Three, are you there, Goddammit?"

The pain in Chris's voice gripped his throat, and he stopped for a moment, turning, and looked back the way he had come.

There is no time, Ben. Trust me to keep them safe. I can guide them as before and keep them from harm. I can have them meet you at the end, but you must come to us. There is no time left.

Ben sighed heavily and then snatched the earpiece out of the radio which rode in a pouch on his vest. He tossed it to the ground and continued in the direction his heart message told him would lead him home. The jungle was painful as it pawed at his now-bare arms. The feeling got stronger, and he moved more swiftly toward the help he knew his people would provide.

* * *

Christy sat on the edge of their bed in her robe and tapped her foot nervously against the night stand. She looked again at the clock – another minute to go. She kept her hand wrapped tightly around the white plastic she held. She refused to look at it until the time had completely elapsed. She had all the uncertainty in her life she could stand right at the moment.

She let her mind drift to Ben. Where was he now? Was he safe? She felt her eyes fill with tears, and the glowing numbers of her alarm clock went blurry. She blinked them clear and left the tears in place that spilled over onto her cheeks. She couldn't free up a hand and risk a peek at the pregnancy test she clutched – not until the time was up.

The message she had received felt so real – *sounded* so real seemed more accurate. His voice had sounded so clear and true in her mind. Could Ben really send thoughts to her from eight thousand miles away? She suspected he could and felt no surprise that she believed that. Ben had changed a lot of firmly held beliefs and skepticism for her since they had met.

Her sports watch beeped, and she looked over at the clock in time to watch the numbers change. She had added a full minute to the time the box told her it took for the test to work – just to be sure. Still she couldn't quite bring herself to look. She closed her eyes and then opened her hands, which had turned white from her tight grip on the plastic test kit. She started a slow count to thirty.

She had convinced herself somehow the test was a formality – that she knew with such certainty that even a negative test would not shake her belief. Since the moment she had dipped the strip into a plastic cup of her own pee, however, that feeling had evaporated completely. She now felt the little test kit held great power over her and her future. It felt suddenly that the answer she got from the eight ball-like prophet in her hands contained information as real for her as the mouth of God.

Christy opened her eyes slowly and for a moment could not focus on the tiny window of truth. She realized she must have squeezed her eyes shut with incredible strength because little black dots filled her vision as her eyeballs gasped at the release of pressure. When they did focus they relayed the information they collected for her impassively. For a moment she had to search her mind to remember what the two parallel lines meant – but then a smile spread across her face so wide it almost hurt her cheeks. She didn't care. She gasped, covered her mouth, and stared again at the window. She felt a little laugh escape her.

She had a sudden terrifying thought that maybe she had read the directions wrong. She set the revealing plastic stick gently on the nightstand as if it was a fragile, ancient relic and then sprinted on bare feet into the bathroom. She dumped the contents of the wastebasket onto the floor, her hands too shaky to reach inside. She smacked away the scattered balls of tissue paper, most streaked with black mascara, and snatched the E.P.T. instructions from the middle of the mess. She scanned them quickly, tearing them nearly in half as she flipped them over to look at the results section.

Christy let out a little scream, jumped up and down like a game show contestant, and then ran back to the bedroom. She picked up the test and stared at the window again. Then, she collapsed backward on the bed, hugging the pee-stained symbol to her chest as she laughed and cried again.

She wondered if Ben's power worked both ways. She hoped it did. She squeezed her eyes shut tightly again and sent a message out to her husband with all the concentration she could muster.

I love you, Ben. I love you so much, baby. I miss you, and I love you, and I am SOOOO happy right now. Please, tell me you love me. Please tell me you're okay.

She kept her eyes closed and listened in her head. She listened with all of the "hearing" she thought her mind could muster. She listened and listened, but she heard nothing except her own racing thoughts. She tried to will Ben into answering – but she heard nothing.

Christy rolled onto her back and slowly opened her eyes again. She suddenly felt so very alone. She laid one hand across her belly and with the other held the test to her chest. She lay there a long time, crying alone in their bed.

* * *

Ben felt no surprise at all when the brush thinned out, and he broke into the clearing he knew must be there. It looked exactly as in his dreams and just like his dreams he saw Jewel immediately – arms stretched out and toddling towards him from an old woman who bent over awkwardly and kept hands on either side of her in case she toppled over.

"Gah, Deh, eh!" she squealed at him. Her face beamed with delight when Ben knelt down and opened his arms to receive her.

He scooped her up and breathed her in. He felt his eyes fill with tears again and hugged her tight. For a split second it scared him that this felt so exactly like his unreal world – might that mean he was dreaming now? The feeling evaporated immediately. He knew the difference with certainty. He was a Traiteur for God's sake – a Rougarou.

Ben shifted Jewel to one hip as a tall and muscular man came forward from the small throng of villagers that had surrounded him – perhaps a dozen people, mostly women and young children he noted with some concern. There were perhaps three men who could be thought of as warriors – the other one seemed far too old. The man, whom he now recognized from before – he had been among the survivors – bowed his head and placed both his hands open palmed on Ben's chest.

That won't do. Where I am from men great each other like this – especially warrior brothers.

Ben shifted his hip to support Jewel and extended his free arm, hand spread. The man looked up and smiled and then stretched out his own arm and grasped Ben's at the elbow, the grasp identical to the Attakapa, Ben noted. The man smiled and spoke. His words sounded like gibberish to Ben, but he heard them again in his head where they were quite clear.

We serve the Rougarou that serves the Living Jungle and our people.

The man signaled behind him, and two women brought clay jars which they set at his feet. Then they scurried backwards, their eyes never leaving the ground. Ben spoke again to his new partner.

Tell them I come to them in service and not in power. They act like they've met royalty, but I'm family. This is not how you treat family. They are my sisters, not my children.

The man smiled broadly at Ben and nodded. He clearly liked him. Ben hoped he would fight with him the way his brothers in the teams fought. The man spoke quickly to the people around them, telling them what Ben had said. The words were greeted with sighs of relief and giggles from the women who now smiled broadly and nodded eagerly, their eyes bright and holding his.

Ben reached down and picked up one of the jars which held a pale green liquid, the color of green tea he thought. Jewel tugged at the jar as he tipped it to his lips. The liquid tasted sweeter than he expected, and only after he took his first deep swallow did he realize how thirsty he had become. He chugged down the entire jar and then reached for the other. The small crowd reacted with chattering excitement – clearly glad this first family gathering seemed to be going well.

The jars empty, Ben followed the crowd, which tugged at his arms and vest. He kept Jewel in his arms, but away from his rifle which he had shifted over to hang on the other side. They led him to one of two low, thatched roofed huts. Ben had to stoop down to enter the tent-like building. Inside he saw a bed of sorts – more like a nest almost – made of soft leaves and surrounded by grey cloth. He chuckled a moment at the sudden thought of how much it looked like a dog bed. Beside it was a flat dish full of steaming brown meat mixed with green and brown plants that looked more like roots than vegetables. Ben turned around and saw that only the man he had spoken with had followed him and Jewel inside.

Thank you. I'll eat the food, but then we need to go. We have to find the bad guys – the dark ones – and we need to go quickly.

Ben realized his haste was motivated as much by a desire to get back to Viper Team – to let them know he was okay – as by the very real urgency to find and destroy the evil he felt growing stronger by the minute.

You will rest a short time first, Ben. You will gain strength from the food and a brief nap. Then, your two warriors will lead you where you must go.

He knew immediately the voice belonged not to his new friend, but to his mentor – the Elder who had so far not led him wrong. He nodded and wondered if the man beside him heard the Elder, too.

The man nodded with a big smile and then left the hut, pulling a leathery looking cloth over the entrance. Ben sat on the soft ground and Jewel clambered into his lap, one hand still clinging to his shoulder. He pulled the platter of food toward them and began to scarf down the sweet-tasting meal with slightly bitter roots or whatever the hell they were. After every few bites he broke a small piece of the savory meat away from the large chunks and fed it to Jewel, who smiled and opened her mouth in the "yes, please" way babies must do anywhere in the world. Then, she would gum the soft food and smile at him.

The food disappeared quickly as Ben found his surprising hunger rivaled his enormous thirst. He felt content and full, slopping up the last bit on a finger and splitting it between himself and Jewel. Ben stripped off his backpack and body armor vest. He put his rifle on the far side of the little nest-like bed and left his pistol in place in its holster on his right thigh. Then, he curled up on the surprisingly soft bed and put an arm across Jewel as she burrowed in beside him. He fell asleep almost immediately, vaguely aware of her soft, deepening breath on his arm.

CHAPTER

42

Higher authority had granted their request, of course – how could they not? Leaving no one behind was the very heart of their brotherhood in Special Operations, whether Navy SEALs, Army Rangers or Green Berets, Marine Recon – it was all the same. The helo had arrived within fifteen minutes, coming only from the staging area where they had waited to exfil the team anyway. The Air Force Para rescue specialists, Special Operators themselves, had taken custody of the Al Qaeda prisoners and told them another five-man team of SEALs would be there to help them very soon.

A Quick Reaction Force of Army Rangers stood back in reserve ready to infil immediately if needed. Reed knew they assumed the same thing as Viper Team – Ben had been captured. Alive or dead, a U.S. Navy SEAL operating in secret in Africa would be a terrific propaganda tool for Al Qaeda. Reed shuddered at the image of the American journalist beheaded for the world to see, the video posted on the Internet. Dear God, please don't let that be Ben. It would be better if he had just been killed.

Reed forced the thoughts from his head. Ben was alive, and they would find him. Maybe he was wounded and hiding, just waiting for his teammates to rescue him. Why not? His radio damaged in a fight, maybe even now he waited for the cavalry to come over the hill. Reed decided he would cling to that for a while at least.

He continued his slow, sweeping trek through the jungle. He realized the world through his NVGs had lost some green and taken on more of a grey color. He stole a glance around his goggles. The jungle had grown lighter – he could make out some shadowy shapes – and in the distance, the sky seemed a light purple above the canopy of trees. He realized in a very short time the Special Operators biggest enemy would arrive – daylight. Would Chris let them continue the search when the sun came up or would they hide in little burrows and tree trunks until the comfortable cloak of night returned?

He'll let us keep looking. Fuck the daylight. This is Ben we're talking about.

"Lead – Viper Four– boss you gotta come see this." Auger's voice sounded tight and choked, and Reed knew they all thought the same thing. He couldn't help the breach of radio discipline.

"Is it Ben?" he asked, his voice cracking.

"No," Auger replied immediately. "It's not – it's not Three." Reed thought Auger had nearly repeated his gaffe and also used Ben's name. "I think it's a bad guy, but – you guys need to come up here."

"Position, Four," Chris said tersely.

"Thirty yards up at your two o' clock. I'm in a shallow ravine." Auger sounded like he had regained his composure.

"Viper Team, rally on Four," Chris commanded.

Moments later, the team stood in a loose circle around Auger's horrifying discovery. Reed had seen a lot of terrible things in war over the last few years, but nothing that prepared him for what he stared down at now, slack jawed and with trembling hands.

"That's not Ben, right?" For a moment he imagined a little cluster of laughing shit heads with a camcorder, recording the mutilation of his best friend for later broadcast to the world. He knew immediately it was not, of course. The face was still mostly intact and had a thin beard with dark dirty hair.

"No," Lash said, but his sigh of relief told Reed that he had the same initial, terrifying thought.

"Do you think an animal did this?" Auger asked. His voiced sounded tight, like maybe he struggled to keep his generous, big-base dinner where it belonged. "A tiger or something?"

"I don't think there are tiger's here, right?" Lash asked.

"I think there might be," Reed said. "Tigers live in Africa, right?" He felt pretty sure tigers lived here.

"It's not an animal," Chris said, and the team turned to look at him. "There are no slashes or tearing injuries like a mauling. His chest looks like it was opened with a saw, right down the middle. Notice anything missing?"

Reed looked with a heaving stomach at the open chest cavity where large flies now darted in and out for their turn at the feast, their wings vibrating the air. Lash knelt down beside the corpse –

One tough motherfucker.

– and waved a hand to shoo the flies away.

"The heart was cut out," he said.

"Torn out," Chris corrected.

Auger turned away, and Reed thought they would smell vomit in a moment to add to the delightful bouquet of the rotting corpse. Just that thought knocked him up a notch closer to losing his own dinner.

Fuckin' animals. What the hell did this guy do wrong? He sure as hell pissed his buddies off.

"Some sort of ritualistic killing?" Lash asked. Reed saw he grimaced a little. Maybe Lash was mortal after all.

"I don't know," Chris said. "Fan out and search the immediate area."

None of them needed to say what they looked for. Reed struggled with the thought that Ben may not be okay after all.

"Hey, boss," Lash said from only a few yards away. "Guys, look at this."

Reed turned and saw that Lash held something black that dangled from his gloved hand by what looked like a shoe lace. Reed flipped his NVGs up – there was unfortunately more than enough light now. As he approached Lash, his chest tightened.

"Earpiece from Ben's radio," he said. No one pointed out that he stated the obvious.

"Guys," Auger said and now his voice really trembled.

The team hustled back to the corpse where Auger squatted down just a few yards away. He held his find up for all of them to see.

The sight of Ben's brown T-shirt and cammie top would have frightened him enough. The fact that both appeared soaked with blood and that they were beside a mutilated corpse were more than Reed could bear and he turned away, his eyes filling with tears.

"This is really fucking bad," Lash said.

Chris called out to Reed.

"Get the lap top up and send a secure message," he said.

Reed stood motionless, tears streaming down his cheeks.

"Reed," Chris called and he turned to face the officer. Reed saw that Chris's face registered the same terror, but his voice remained controlled. His teammate put a gloved hand on his shoulder and squeezed. "We don't know what happened. We don't know if he's alive or dead or even if he has been captured. He could be hiding nearby for all we know." Reed resisted the sudden, almost overwhelming need to holler out Ben's name to the jungle. "We don't even know if that's his blood, dude. Get the laptop up and send it. Tell the Head Shed we found some gear and clothing we believe to belong to Viper Three. Don't tell them yet about the corpse."

"What if they tell us to make a hide and pick up the search at nightfall?" Reed asked. He knew they had to find Ben soon.

"Then tell them 'Roger that' and then we'll keep fucking searching. Got it?"

Reed nodded and peeled off his backpack and quickly unloaded his computer and fanned out his little satellite dish. Maybe they could re-task the predator. Maybe they could see more in the light and, even if not, they could use the thermal imaging– if Ben was alive and hiding somewhere, maybe they would still find him.

CHAPTER

43

en knew he slept – could still feel Jewel on his arm and hear her soft little reathing – as he sat cross legged and faced the Elder. He felt no anxiety, no ar. He breathed in deeply and smelled nothing but the sweet smell of his ttle girl.

"You must rest, Ben. I will answer the questions that keep your sleep ght and then you must rest. The end is near, and you will need your trength." The old man's young eyes held his and sparkled with power and omething else – love maybe.

"How many dark ones are there?"

"There are many, and they are everywhere," the old man said. "But ney are not your concern. The power you have is much greater than theirs, nd they fear the power of the *Rougarou*. They can come and go and for the nost part pose only a slight danger more than the bad men who serve as osts."

Ben nodded. The Al Qaeda terrorists were danger enough. He was one rmed SEAL helped by a couple of unarmed men who might have time-varped here from two thousand years ago. He understood his power now etter than ever, but he was one man against how many? And how many of nose were helped by the dark ones who possessed them?

The Elder seemed to read – if not his thoughts, then surely his oncerns.

"The dark ones will all be defeated when the One with the black blood s stopped. Defeat him, and the others are gone."

Okay – sure – but what about the hosts? Would the terrorist hosts remain or die with their possessors? The Al Qaeda he had fought so far were pretty well armed.

"As are you. The power you have is much more powerful than the tools you bring with you. Rely on them, not your primitive weapons."

Ben chuckled at the irony of the thin old man, clothed in animal skins, smiling at him with brown teeth, and sitting cross-legged in the dirt in the jungle calling *him* primitive. He had found a trust in the power he had gained – or maybe just finally mastered – but he would be taking his rifle into this fight nonetheless.

"The victory will be great as the powerful One with the black blood possesses a man who is very evil in his own right," the Elder continued. If he sensed Ben's rebuff of his assessment of his weapons, he at least politely ignored it. "The One with the black blood is incarnate with the leader of the men your people fight."

"What do I need to defeat him?" Ben asked. He thought of the powerful voice he had sensed – the vibration in his head had felt like his skull might explode.

"You will know," the Elder said.

Ben realized he was pretty friggin' sick of that answer. He knew there was no point in asking for more and sat silently for a moment.

"And then?" he asked. "When this is over, I need to come back for Jewel. I need to bring her home." He realized this had always been a part of the mission for him.

He looked up and realized he now sat alone.

She is already home. You know this. She is a part of the living jungle. She cannot be a part of your other world, Ben. You know this. Just as you know she will forever be a part of your heart.

Ben realized he had known this all along. He lay down then, already asleep.

Ben thought for a moment about Christy. He thought of her alone at home and of their child inside her. He wondered if she knew about their son yet. She had suspected before he had even left. He wondered if she knew for certain yet.

Ben sent a quick heart message out to his wife and then forced his mind back to the task at hand. He needed to finish his mission to have any hope of getting home to her – of ever meeting his son. Even if he had to make the ultimate sacrifice to complete this mission, he had to succeed. He had to ake sure his family would be safe and his child could grow up free from the rror he thought would come with the demon he had seen in his mind.

He closed his eyes (he knew they were already closed, of course) and lt himself lying flat in the comfortable nest, his arms around Jewel. He let his ind drift from thoughts of demons and dark ones and into a warm blanket of pe for his family.

* * *

They had not been told to stand down – a surprise that Reed still uldn't quite believe – but they were directed to sweep only their immediate ea again and then wait for more intel from a predator pass. Reed now sat unched over his laptop and looked at the information they had gained from at pass. With a few clicks of the mouse pad he actually looked for himself at e real time thermal imaging data from the unmanned aircraft that circled ove them even now.

"So, nothing in our area?" Chris asked as he leaned over Reed and oked at the lap top screen. They had all hoped they would see the yellow-red an shaped glow of Ben hidden nearby in a fallen tree or ditch he had nverted into a hide.

"No," Reed said in response to the rhetorical question. "But he has to there, right?" He pointed at the cluster of thermal images less than two lometers from their position as he tapped his finger on the mouse pad to ake the image widen and pan out. "There are no other human-looking hits r over twenty kilometers. He can't have gone that far – not even close."

He left the thought that Ben might be dead unspoken. But even if so, s killers couldn't have traveled that distance either. Whether they found Ben e answers to their questions could only be found in the cluster of thermal nages one-point-eight kilometers northwest of them. He turned and looked at e boss and raised his eyebrows. Chris nodded.

"We'll wait a minute to see if they give us orders, but then we head off wards that group," he said. "We can keep radio com if they need us after at."

Reed liked that answer. They all knew that time would run out quickly if they had any left at all. A text box blinked on in the middle of his screen, bstructing the predator feed. Reed smiled.

"Chris," he called after the officer who had started to walk away wards the other two remaining members of Viper Team. "You'll like this," e said.

Chris leaned over and read over Reed's shoulder. Then, he slapped him on the shoulder.

"Fuckin' A," he said. "Tell them we'll be there and pack up." Chris turned and walked briskly over to Lash and Auger. "Movin' out, guys," he said.

Reed typed a short reply and verified the landing zone, or LZ, and rally points. Then, he quickly packed up his gear and flung his pack onto his back. He re-slung his rifle and joined the team and together they moved out towards the northwest.

CHAPTER

44

Christy had fallen into a restless sleep. She didn't know if the nausea and malaise she felt were related to her pregnancy, her worry about her husband, or both. Either way, the decision to call in sick had not been a tough one – she felt pretty certain that if she hit the road to make sales calls she would be kneeling beside her car in her business suit, barfing on the shoulder of the road in less than an hour. She had not called in sick a single time in four and half years, and her call to her district manager had been met with real concern.

"You sure you're okay?" Steve had asked. "Is Ben okay?"

"Everything is fine," she had reassured him. "Just got the damn flu or something."

She lay now on their bed – on top of the covers instead of under them as she couldn't quite stand to be really in the bed without him right now. She had covered herself with a worn blanket from the linen closet and left her robe on. Every time she woke from her fitful sleep – it felt like every few minutes, but she refused to keep looking at the clock – her mind went first to Ben and then to the positive test she had placed in her drawer.

She had decided she would wrap the test kit as a gift (as gross as that kind of sounded – she had peed on it for goodness sake) and give it to Ben when he got home. She felt stupid for being so wracked with worry just because she had tried to squeeze a thought out to her husband across eight thousand miles of space and he had not answered. She might have come to believe in these sorts of things when it came to Ben, but did her faith in it carry enough weight to literally worry herself sick? Even if her beliefs were true, she had no idea if she could send little thought notes to him just because she thought she could receive them.

She tossed over on her other side and tried to get comfortable and then let out a little, "whoa," at the wave of nausea that came after. This had to be the pregnancy. She gripped the covers until the churning feeling subsided.

Lord, please tell me I don't have nine months of this.

She rode out the nausea with her stomach contents where they belonged, and not on the rug beside the bed, and let out a soft sigh. Christy sat up slowly and waited for another wave to hit her, but it never came. Relieved, she headed towards the stairs. She had read somewhere that crackers and flat ginger ale could help with pregnancy upheaval. She knew they didn't have ginger ale in the house, but surely she could dig up some crackers – stale or not. Maybe she would make some warm tea. She was half way down the steps when his voice came to her.

I love you, Christy. I love you, and I'm okay. Soon, I'll come home to you, I promise – home to you and our son.

Like before, the voice sounded so clear and so real she felt Ben stood right behind her and even turned a little to look over her shoulder. Then, the tears came, and she slid down onto the steps, pulling her robe around her legs. She sobbed with both worry and happiness.

Ben was okay. Not only that but he knew – he knew about their baby. About their *son*? She touched her belly, and for some reason that felt right. She decided she believed – she believed she heard her husband's voice, and she believed he might be right about the sex of their baby. She started to laugh – or at least mix in some laughter with her tears. Then, another wave of nausea swept over her.

I love you, too, Ben. Come home to me, baby. Come home soon.

She pulled herself to her feet, stood still a moment until the wave passed, and then headed downstairs on her quest for soothing sustenance.

Ben was okay. He was okay, he knew about the baby, and they were going to have a little boy. All the sickness in the world couldn't steal away her joy of that moment.

CHAPTER 45

Ben thought of the Elder as he checked the additional magazines for his rifle. He had stripped his gear to almost nothing, and his vest felt strangely light as he pulled it back on. He left his radio, his night vision goggles, and various other electronic equipment in a pile with his spare gloves, extra batteries, signaling mechanism and a variety of lights. No damn wonder he felt so light.

He slipped his additional magazines into pouches on his vest, checked that similar magazines for the pistol on his hip were in place, and then picked up his rifle and slipped his arm through the harness. He tossed his helmet into the refuse pile and turned, looking at the two villagers who waited patiently.

The contrast struck him first as worrisome, then as funny, and he found it hard to stifle a laugh. The two warriors were basically naked except for skins that covered them from waist to knees and the grey cloth tied around their arms. Each held long, thick staffs – like oversized walking sticks – and nothing else. Ben thought maybe he was laughing not at them but at himself. He had been told – and wanted to believe – that all he needed was inside him – that he was the *Rougarou*. He believed that.

I sure as shit wouldn't be here if I didn't.

He couldn't quite take the leap of faith needed to set out without his rifle and handgun, however. He also had a couple of grenades. If that was just a security blanket, then so be it. Ben chambered a round in his rifle and turned to his two warriors.

"Alright, guys, let's hit it. This op has a green light."

The two smiled at him and looked at each other. He knew they had no clue what he said.

We will go now. We must find the powerful One with the black blood. Do you know where the ruins are?

Both looked at him quizzically. Ben thought them another message where he tried to describe the ruins he had seen in his head, the ancient structure that seemed to be swallowed by the jungle. The warrior on his left, the one he knew from before – from the massacre and the base – suddenly nodded.

I know where the ancient place is. It is a sacred place of those long ago from a time before the dark ones. I can lead us there.

"Great," Ben said. Then he gestured ahead towards the edge of their small encampment. "You have point."

Lead on. We should move swiftly but must be quiet. Surprise will be a great friend to us. I expect many bad people to be waiting for us.

Ben looked again at the two nearly naked men and felt a wave of doubt and fear. He felt a tug at his sleeve and looked down.

Jewel reached up at him with both arms in the universal "pick me up" signal. He smiled and scooped her up. As he did, he thought about his unborn son and wife back in Virginia.

He knew there was no turning back. He had to finish this and find his way home. He kissed Jewel's cheek, and she grabbed at his ear.

"I'll be right back," he said and prayed a moment that he told the truth.

Then, he followed the two barefoot villagers westward into the jungle.

* * *

Reed stayed low and quiet, listening to the thump-thump of the lone Blackhawk helicopter fade rapidly as it headed to a staging area he hoped was fairly close. He had a feeling when they were ready to leave they might be in a bit of a hurry. God, how he hated the daylight. Without the cover of night he felt a hell of a lot more like a target than a hunter. After a few minutes of silence – during which he diligently scanned his sector and saw nothing – he heard Chris's voice in his headset.

"Ghost – Viper – are you clear?"

A moment went by during which he assumed Ghost team checked in on their own frequency, and then he heard "Ghost secure – where ya at, Viper?"

Reed and his teammates rose slowly and then watched as the five members of Ghost team seemed to materialize out of nowhere and stood hip-deep in the jungle grass.

God, I love being a SEAL.

His brief revelry disappeared when he realized how many times he had heard Ben whisper that to him over the years. He tightened his jaw. They would find him – he had become sure of that for some reason. And not dead, either – Ben was alive. His brain told him he just felt the power of hope and denial that he may have lost his best friend, but there was something very real in the feeling that Ben was okay.

And nearby.

It was just the kind of thing he would have ridiculed Ben mercilessly for, but the sense Ben was nearby felt tremendously powerful – and very real. Maybe there was something to that Cajun bullshit. He didn't know, but he knew as sure as he stood there that Ben was okay.

The nine of them huddled up like a football team and came together with a quick battle plan. They couldn't possibly tell from the thermal imaging just who clustered together a kilometer away. It could be a dozen Al Qaeda fighters or just a small camp of hunters or villagers like they had met on their last deployment.

"We can't just kick in the door and come in all balls to the wall is the point," Chris said. The leader of Ghost – Curt Malloy, Reed remembered from somewhere – nodded. "We'll set up a perimeter and then take a quiet look. Even if Ben is there, they may just be helping him for all we know. We need to be careful, and I don't want to hurt any good guys. No collateral damage, okay?"

Both teams nodded agreement, but Reed suspected the thought of not hurting innocents might be a little more personal to Viper Team. Wasn't that guilt what got them into this fucking mess?

They briefed a plan that would put Lash and a sniper from Ghost – a Senior Chief whose name Reed didn't know – into high positions where they could pick off anything they didn't like and watch the team's back. They would then surround the camp, see what the hell was there, and improvise based on what they found.

Pretty loose plan, but flexibility was the key to their world.

Reed found it hard to concentrate on his sweep of the jungle as they moved quietly, but quickly, towards the cluster of glowing humans from the thermal imaging and cursed himself repeatedly for his inattention. His mind drifted continually to Ben and then to Christy, his new little sister back at home. He absolutely had to bring Ben back to her. He knew that time was very much against them. If Ben was severely wounded, then he could be bleeding to death as they moved through the jungle towards the objective. If he wasn't wounded then he must be either dead or captured – both very bad.

He may not be in this fucking village at all. He could be dead in the bushes back where we came from, and we just never saw him.

Reed's training and operational experience both told him the chances of Ben being recovered alive were nearly non-existent, but his heart still insisted he could feel him out there somewhere and that he was okay – at least for now.

He took up his position at the ten o'clock point of the circle they had made around the village and watched through his binoculars as he waited for a call from Chris. What he saw filled him with a glimmer of hope. The small camp looked to be a miniature version of the village they had encountered on the last deployment – the start of it all, he realized. The villagers, mostly women and a few children and an old man, milled about casually and tended to the business of the day – stirring cook pots and caring for the little ones. Reed wiped away sweat that threatened to dribble into his eyes. The sun had brought with it heat and the muggy air felt stifling.

He saw no sign whatsoever of Ben.

"Ghost – Viper," Chris said in his ear.

"Ghost," came Master Chief Malloy's short reply.

"Looks quiet. No obvious hostiles. I want to move in with four of us from four corners. Sniper cover and then four in reserve. Peaceful search. That okay with you?"

"Perfect," came the SEAL team leader's response.

That sounded right to Reed. He realized he desperately needed to go, but resisted the overwhelming urge to radio his request to the boss. He had violated communications operational security enough for one day when he called out Ben's name over the air. Instead, he waited and bit his lip.

"Viper Five – Lead – you and me on my call. Slow and peaceful."

"Five," he acknowledged with relief.

I'm coming, Ben. Hang in there, buddy. If you're here, I'll find you.

"Ghost Three and Four – lead – you join them," came Malloy's voice.

"Three."

"Four."

On the go signal, Reed rose slowly and walked into the clearing. He kept both of his hands on his rifle grips, but pointed it at the ground rather than up at the ready as they normally would. He watched as his three fellow SEALs entered the camp from three other corners.

Yeah – we don't look at all fucking scary. Just four peaceful tourists in full combat gear.

After only a moment, the first villager noticed them – a woman who held a toddler on her lap – and she called out to the others. With some relief, Reed saw that she smiled and then waved at him. He raised an awkward wave, and then re-gripped his M-4 rifle. The toddler struggled out of the woman's lap and started a teetering run towards Chris, but the woman snatched her back up.

"Gah, Deh, Eh," the girl said and for a moment he thought it might be the little girl from the village slaughter. He quickly dismissed the thought as ridiculous. Kids all looked the same to him anyway, he realized.

The villagers began to congregate together and moved slowly towards the center of the clearing which the SEALs converged on. Chris raised a hand in a sort of greeting and looked to be trying his best to smile. Then, he pointed at Reed and one of the Ghost team members, pointed to his own eyes with two fingers and then at the two low huts at the periphery of the clearing – an order for them to search the huts. Reed nodded and headed toward the first thatched shack. Chris keyed his mike.

"Eagles," he said – a call to the snipers – "Two guys searching the huts. You got angles to cover them?"

"Viper Eagle," Lash said in his ear, "I got 'em."

"Ghost Eagle has them, also," the other sniper said.

That made him feel better, but Reed raised his rifle to the ready position as he approached the doorway. A dark cloth of animal skin flapped lightly over the entrance, and Reed used the muzzle of his rifle to pull it a few inches open and peered inside. He saw no movement in the low space and pulled the cover the rest of the way open with his left hand and advanced into the room, clearing the corners as he did.

Then his eyes fell on the little pile of gear beside a nest-like bed against the far wall. For a moment, he couldn't find his voice and then he fumbled, unable to find the button to key his radio.

"He's here – I mean he's been here. B..." he stopped himself before screwing up on the radio again. He took a slow quivering breath and started over. "Viper Lead – Five – you need to come here. Looks like Three has been here."

"On my way," Chris said in an excited voice. "Hold cover, Eagle."

Reed squatted down and let his rifle fall onto his chest by its combat sling as he reached out a gloved hand and poked at the small pile of equipment. The radio looked completely undamaged, though the earpiece and microphone were missing.

Well no shit – we found them by the mutilated corpse.

That could explain why Ben hadn't responded to the radio calls. But where the shit was he? The gear in the pile looked undamaged and unbloodied. He picked up the helmet and looked inside – no blood or damage. The electronics, his lights, batteries, radio, helmet, and gloves – but no weapons and no magazines. What a strange assortment of shit. He looked at the "B.M." stenciled on the helmet liner, but he knew it was Ben's gear before he saw it.

"Whataya got?" Chris called over his shoulder. "Shit – is that Ben's stuff?"

"Yeah," Reed answered.

"Where's his kit?" Chris asked, and Reed wondered how the hell he thought he would know. "And, where the hell are his weapons and ammo?"

Reed looked up at the officer.

"Why would only this shit be here?" he asked.

Chris rubbed his face in standard Chris fashion.

"If he was captured, the shit heads would have taken his weapons," he offered.

"But not his electronics?" Reed said, and knew immediately that he too asked obvious but un-answerable questions. "And why leave any of this shit here? These villagers are like the others – they ain't Qaeda, and I don't think they would help them."

"No blood or sign of a struggle," Chris pointed out.

"So, what the shit?" Reed asked.

Chris simply shook his head. Together they gathered up the gear and headed back to the center of the clearing. When they got there the villagers just smiled. Chris held up the helmet.

"What happened here?" he asked slowly and deliberately, like that would help. Reed wished like hell they had brought an interpreter, but even if they had he might not speak whatever the hell language these folks spoke. The villagers looked at each other and then back at them, but their faces registered nothing but confusion.

Chris sighed and turned to the Ghost team SEAL beside him.

"Any of you dudes know some magic way to communicate with these people?" The SEAL just shook his head. Chris keyed his mike. "Ghost leader – village is clear – bring it in. Eagles – hold position and watch our asses."

"Ghost leader."

"Viper Eagle."

"Ghost Eagle."

Chris turned back to the small group of villagers who watched him intently and continued to smile. Reed thought they sure as hell looked like they would love to help if they had any idea what the SEALs needed. Chris pointed vigorously at the helmet and then passed his hand across the village and shrugged, hands upward in a sort of "What the hell?" gesture.

The old man nodded his head and spoke some gibberish and then pointed off into the jungle in a roughly westward direction. The rest of the adults, all women, seemed suddenly to understand and joined the man, the whole group pointing west.

"No shit," Reed said under his breath. "You think he's a prisoner?"

"They seem awfully fucking cheerful for a group who just met with Al Qaeda terrorists who captured an American Soldier," Chris said. "You remember what those assholes did to the last village? I don't think these guys'd be smiling if Al Qaeda dragged a captive Ben through here."

"Especially Ben," said Auger, who had just joined the group.

"What's up?" asked Malloy as he joined them, as well.

Chris quickly filled him in and then turned to Reed.

"Set up a sat call to the Head Shed and see if you can get some more thermal imaging data from the pred," he directed.

Reed frowned. The jungle had heated up very quickly. He doubted that they could get much useful data now – at least not thermal data. He set up his gear quickly anyway and made contact with the operations center. After a few minutes he turned to the boss.

"They say they'll re-task a predator, but the temp is gonna hurt us," he said. "But they also said they tracked three people leaving the village westbound not too long ago. They tried to contact us, but couldn't get you on the secure frequency."

Chris cursed and checked his radio. Then, he shook his head.

"Tell them what we know and where we're headed," he said.

"Where are we headed?" the Ghost team leader asked. "We have no idea where those three went or who the hell they are. We sure as shit don't know where they're going, and it is awfully fucking light out here. Where are we gonna go?"

"After my friend," Chris said and tossed Ben's helmet back to Reed. "You can stay here if you want." Reed smiled.

Fuckin' A, right.

Malloy shrugged and turned to his men who all nodded.

"Shit, we'll go with you," he said. "Got nothing else to do."

They called the snipers out of the trees, briefed a quick search and recovery mission, and headed westward out of the village. As they entered the jungle again they fanned out.

The voice Reed heard in his head sounded so crisp and clear that he turned around, weapon drawn.

Ben will need you very soon. He has nearly completed his task here, and then he will need you very badly.

There was no one behind him, and he lowered his weapon and scanned the surrounding jungle in a quick circle – nothing.

I'm losing my fucking mind. I blame you, Ben Morvant, and you owe me a big fucking drink when we get home.

* * *

Ben moved swiftly behind the half-naked man that led them through the jungle at a stiff pace. Despite his great condition, he felt sweat literally pour off of him, and yet the warriors beside him seemed barely to glow with perspiration and smiled each time he looked over. Ben felt complete amazement at the total silence with which the villagers moved and he winced each time his booted foot would make a soft "crack" on a rare piece of dry jungle wood.

Bare feet must be the key.

He had started to regret his impulsive tossing of his headset. At the time, he needed to shut off the calls of his teammates, and he guessed he needed the "No Going Back" finality of losing the gear. But now that he felt his target close he had begun to wonder just how in the shit he would get back to his team once he finished his mission. The ultimate goal in his mind still remained getting home to his family, and he had made that tougher with an impetuous act.

Ben thought again of Christy and his son inside her. He had heard her thoughts, or at least he had convinced himself he had (he didn't want to admit it could as likely have been imagination fueled by desperate hope). He knew he had to keep such distracting ideas out of his head and focus on the mission, but he had no clue what to think or how he would handle it – no understanding of what was expected of him or what power would be needed to defeat the powerful One with the black blood. So, he found it difficult not to let his mind drift. He thought also, with a great deal of guilt, about his team. He hoped and prayed they were safely back at the JSOTF base, but he knew that would not be the case. His team would never leave without him (or at least his body) any more than he would leave one of them behind. All he could do for now was pray for their safety and complete what had to be done. Then, they could all finally be secure.

Ben heard the soft rumble and realized what it was a moment after his imagination made it something much scarier. He listened to the sound of rapidly moving water and tried to pinpoint it as ahead of them or off to the side. Either way, he realized the ground beneath his feet had become softer and boggier. By the time the warrior ahead of him raised his hand to stop (Ben marveled at how like the SEAL team hand signal it appeared – he guessed warriors had been the same for thousands of years when it came down to it) the sound had increased to a roar, and he suspected the moving water must have come from some elevation, though through the dense jungle he could get no sense of whether the terrain rose ahead of them.

But it must, obviously.

He crouched beside the two villagers and the point man touched his lips and his left ear, which Ben thought meant they should be quiet.

We must be close.

Ben doubted that anyone could hear them over the loud roar of the river he could not yet see, but he moved forward slowly now anyway, his body in a combat crouch and his ears straining to hear past the echoes of the tumultuous water. He realized he came equipped with more senses than that though, and closed his eyes a moment – his mind reached out ahead of them in a soft blue light.

He heard several voices which fought over each other in his head. He felt there might be seven or eight men total. He realized that if some were the voices of dark ones inside the Al Qaeda fighters then it might be a few less, but there might also be a couple more that he just didn't separate from the others.

Call it ten to be safe.

Nice. One SEAL (though well trained and somewhat well-armed) and two unarmed, primitive and usually peaceful villagers against nearly a dozen heavily armed terrorists. Perfect.

What could possibly fuckin' go wrong?

He followed the lead villager, the three of them now belly crawling so he knew how close they must be, and in his mind he counted out the bullets in his spare magazines as he often did to keep relaxed. Then, the villager gently parted the thick jungle grass and moved aside so Ben could peer through.

Ben felt a chill at the familiarity of the structure. The river was clear blue water instead of the flat and black mirror he had seen down the bunny hole. It ran over the top of the ruins instead of through it and formed a waterfall as it fell off the top of the heavily overgrown, squared off arch. The river itself seemed to defy physics – it ran with great speed and volume and yet beyond the ruins he saw no rising terrain– not so much as a little hill much less a mountain – to provide the gravity force to push the water.

Nonetheless there it was, seemingly appearing out of nowhere, pouring over the archway and onto the jungle floor, and then veering off to the left in a rushing flow. The parallel steps that formed the sides looked much shorter than the building he had sat atop with the

Attakapa. It seemed more the essence of the ancient structure that looked familiar.

It sure as shit smells better.

This river still has the life of the Living Jungle – the river you visited before is on the other side, the death side.

Ben dismissed the Elder's voice since it seemed to hold information irrelevant to the task at hand – but tucked it away just in case.

Ben saw four bad guys, two on either side of the waterfall at the base of each of the stepped walls of the ruins. They stood just inside of the falling water and seemed relaxed, but Ben could sense they all held the thoughts of dark ones, as well – and he knew those fuckers might just be able to sense him, too – so he kept the blue light of his mind in his own head.

No sense letting them know we're here until we have to.

He realized he had no idea if it worked that way. He was completely making this up as he went along. Still that *felt* right, and he had nothing else to go on, so screw it. He strained his eyes to see past them, to see into the dark and cave-like interior of the ruins, blocked by the curtain like waterfall. He saw only shadows – but he knew his target was there. He didn't hear the One with the black blood in his head, but somehow he knew he was there. He pulled back from the parted grass and took a deep breath. He needed a minute.

The villagers lay beside him in the jungle grass and watched. They had done their part by delivering him here, he suspected. Now, it was his show.

You will know what to do.

Yeah – right.

Ben did his four-count tactical breathing and then slowly parted the grass again, this time with the barrel of his rifle. He suddenly wished he had his sniper rifle with him instead of the shorter range and less powerful M-4. He ignored the whisper of the Elder in his head telling him he needed neither.

Tough shit. My show – my way.

Ben peered through the long range sight and drew down on the terrorist on the right side of the river fall, closest to the water – the most difficult target. He felt no wind, but corrected in his head for the distance and raised his sight up slightly above his intended target. He knew if the dark ones were inside these assholes then shooting them wouldn't stop them. But his very limited experience told him that it would slow them down a few minutes and gain him hopefully enough time to get past them and into the objective and find his target.

No time to stop for a snack – which seems to be the only way to actually kill them for good.

His stomach turned slightly at the thought (memory), and he forced it out of his head. He sighted again, took a slow, deep breath and then held it at the end of the exhale.

Ben squeezed the trigger back and watched through the sight as the terrorists head erupted in a cloud of pink and grey. He immediately pulled his rifle left and sighted on the inboard target on the right side of the waterfall. This target now moved rapidly and Ben led him slightly to correct and then fired again.

CHAPTER 46

The rifle shot sounded completely unmistakable to Reed, and the second and third shots that followed it confirmed what he knew – it was the sound of an American-issued M-4 rifle.

"Lead – Five," he nearly shouted into his microphone.

"I heard it, Five," Chris answered curtly. "It had to be his, but we don't know who has it and is firing. Viper – Ghost – move quickly and spread out."

"It was fucking close – just up ahead," Auger called.

"Radio discipline," Chris chastised.

Reed moved quickly, his rifle up and ready as he scanned around him through the holographic sight. When he broke out into a clearing suddenly, he nearly tripped in an effort to stop his forward momentum. Instead, he capitalized on the stumble and dropped himself into a prone position as his mind tried to make sense of what he saw.

The rocky outcroppings on either side of the waterfall slowly made sense to his brain as stone stairs rising up on either side of the river. His mind had tricked him at first, because the stairs were nearly completely overgrown by jungle moss and grass. Only a few patches on either side were clear of the encroaching vegetation, maintaining the look of the man-made structure they had once been – hundreds if not thousands of years ago he guessed.

Then, his mind finally registered something else – something no less unexpected and hard to believe.

The figure that stood up over the body of the fallen terrorist had a short rifle raised in a combat stance and scanned over it. Then, he saw the muzzle flash and a split second later heard the retort of the M-4. The figure wore cammie pants and a body armor combat kit over an otherwise bare torso covered in sweat. He looked through his sight at the figure's uncovered head just as he disappeared behind the water fall.

Ben – holy shit it really is him.

Reed pushed aside the obvious and disturbing "what in the fuck is he doing here?" thoughts and keyed his mike.

"Lead – Five – I have Three in sight."

"Where?' Chris's voice came back sharply. "I don't see him. Where the hell is he?"

"Just disappeared behind that water fall," Reed said. He felt his voice find some sort of calm center. "I'm going after him."

"Negative, Five, Stand by One," Chris commanded.

Too late, boss.

Reed sprinted across the short clearing towards his goal, his rifle up and ready, and his head on a swivel.

"We've got company – up on the top," Auger's voice came. "Shit, it looks like a bunch of them."

Reed looked up just as he arrived at the base of the steps to the right of the river and saw at least a dozen figures move along both sides of the water above him.

"Set up a better perimeter," Chris commanded. "I need Eagles up also – snipe anything with a weapon that didn't come with us. I'm going after Five and Three."

Reed peered into the dark behind the waterfall and saw that it masked the entrance to a long, wide tunnel. He looked down at the dead terrorist at his feet and kicked the AK-47 clear of his grip just in case.

"I got two KIA's here, Lead," he said into his mike. "Looks like a tunnel of some sort, just behind the waterfall. I'll wait at the entrance for you."

The officer might have thoughts of court martial in his mind for him, but they might as well do the breach correctly anyway. His radio began to fill with chatter as the Viper and Ghost teams both started to call out targets and engage the enemy above him. He heard the sound of both M-4s and the AK-47s of the bad guys and the occasional deeper, throaty spit of the sniper rifles. A moment later Chris put a hand on his shoulder, and Reed peered back at him.

"Ben went down this tunnel," he said. "He looked like he wasted another bad guy over there," he gestured with his eyes to the other side of the tunnel, "and then he went inside."

Chris pointed at a wide blood trail that snaked into the dark opening along its right wall.

"Looks like one of the shit heads didn't die on cue. Looks like he went after Ben."

Reed nodded and then waited for his boss to make the call.

"You take the left side of the tunnel, and I'll take the right. Shoot anything except Ben."

"Roger that," Reed said with a tight smile.

Together they entered the constricting tunnel, and Reed flipped his NVGs back into place, turning the air an eerie green and the wide blood trail black. He doubted that whoever left the bloody remnants would be much threat by the time they got to him – it looked like he had left most of his bodily fluid on the floor of the cave.

Reed scanned back and forth over his rifle and watched the infrared dot paint a pattern of parallel red lines on the walls. Then, he moved deeper into the dark and strangely quiet cave.

* * *

Ben moved as quickly down the tunnel as he dared and cursed himself again for not bringing his helmet and NVGs. He had flipped his rifle sight to night vision mode and held his face close to the sight, but the small field of vision made it difficult to scan the wide tunnel as he moved. He could hear whispered sounds behind him and over that another sound – like a wet bag being dragged over dry concrete. He suspected one of the dark ones had pursued him. The whispers were something different, but he dared not reach out with his mind for fear that the powerful One might hear him coming.

Don't be an idiot. He knows you're coming – has probably expected you all along.

Still – no sense in risking it. He would deal with the voices behind him when he had achieved his objective – if he were still alive.

The persistent scraping crawl seemed closer though, and over that he now heard a rattling grunt with each pause.

Grunt – drag – grunt – drag

It was unnerving in the dark, and Ben tried to pick up the pace. Ahead of him, in the night sight of his rifle, a soft whitish glow began to appear. Ben looked around his rifle to see the source. He strained his eyes and thought he saw a soft, reddish light, but it looked too faint to be certain. Still, the glow in the sight seemed real enough so it was probably not his imagination. He continued on, scanning the murky air through the laminating scope. The whispers had stopped, but the dragging noise seemed even louder.

Grunt – drag – grunt – drag

Ben spun around and scanned the black tunnel behind him through the scope–and there he saw it.

The corpse had only half a face – the left side of the jaw bounced up and down on the right shoulder, and the ear had flopped over upside down on the side of the neck where the high velocity round from his rifle had torn through the head. Ben's second shot had blown through the groin and nearly severed the right leg, which had spun around, the foot facing behind the rapidly advancing dead man.

The corpse leaned against the right side of the tunnel wall with his arm to compensate for having only one good leg and dragged the mangled and bloody leg behind him. The eyes glowed yellowish green through the night sight, but he knew would look more orange to the naked eye. Ben sighted the red dot of his infrared night targeting system in the middle of the mangled face, and his finger tightened on the trigger.

What the hell is the point at shooting again at a man you already shot to death?

Ben dropped the rifle and felt a now familiar tightening in his chest and a warm vibration that ran up both his arms. He had no time tear out the creature's heart, but he thought he could probably make the corpse a much less threatening tool for the dark one inside.

The tunnel took on a soft bluish glow, and he felt and saw the dancing little fireflies all around him. Then, he let the feeling in his chest run rapidly down both arms and flung his hands out, fingers extended, and watched as two bright balls of bluish light exploded out of his hands and tore down the tunnel towards the zombie like creature, parallel fire trails dragging behind them.

The balls of light smashed into the corpse's chest and a horrible scream escaped the brutally disfigured mouth. Ben watched an explosion of light shoot out in all directions, and then the dead man burst into flames. The corpse bounced around on its one good leg a moment, the horrible wails warbling in time to its obscene dance. It then fell over in the tunnel consumed. The body twitched a moment and then lay still. A second later the scream returned, and Ben watched as the spray of light erupted from the mouth, tearing the jaw the rest of the way free to careen towards him. The charred and bloody pieces of skull bone skidded to a stop at his feet, and the bright light shot down the tunnel back towards the entrance, careening impossibly off the walls as it did. The high-pitched noise followed it and faded with the light as both disappeared back the way he had come.

He stood in the now quiet, soft glow of the few wisps of blue flame that danced off the blackened remains of the corpse. Those winked out a moment later and he was left again in darkness, alone with a horrible smell and white spots in his eyes from the sudden burst of light.

He may not have destroyed that dark one, but it sure as shit wouldn't be using that corpse to pursue him anymore.

Ben turned back towards the slight red glow deeper in the tunnel and raised his rifle again. Guided by the night sight, he continued towards his objective and whatever waited for him there.

* * *

They had seen the light – a soft glow of blue that to Reed seemed somehow familiar – before they heard the scream. The horrifying shriek sounded in no way human, and Reed felt his pulse pound in his temple at the thought of what it might be. He gripped his rifle tighter and scanned the direction of the blue glow but saw nothing. He was about to ask Chris what the hell he thought the sound had been, but before he could speak the tunnel ahead of them exploded like a boiling sun. The sudden burst of light in his NVGs blinded Reed. He tore them away from his eyes which knocked his helmet sideways just as the shriek grew louder and he thought his eardrums would explode. He dropped to a crouch and tried to keep his rifle up, but he could see nothing to shoot at through his burning eyes.

A glowing tube of light streaked suddenly over top of them, and he fell to his back on the floor, rifle raised, his own scream stuck in his throat. The terrible animal sound echoed off the walls as it seemed to pass with the luminescent trail and then faded away as the tunnel returned to blackness.

"Reed," Chris hissed at him from nearby. Reed could still see nothing but the glowing light burned into his retinas which danced around in the darkness as his eyes darted back and forth. "Reed – dude, are you hurt? Are you alright?"

"I'm okay," Reed managed and struggled to a kneeling position in the dark, his right arm against the wall of the tunnel. "I'm okay, but I can't see shit. Are you okay?"

There was a pause while his teammate assessed himself.

"I think so," the quivering voice said. "What in the holy shit was that?"

"I don't know," Reed answered, but his mind went to another bluish light that had exploded near him recently. That light had come from his best friend's hands and moments later the terrorist at their feet had been burned beyond recognition. What the fuck was going on? "I don't know," he said again.

Reed had convinced himself the light at the target house had been his imagination – that the terrorist had, indeed, botched a suicide bombing. But now he wasn't nearly so sure. He blinked a few times, and the spots in his vision seemed to fade. He straightened his helmet and then with some trepidation pulled his NVGs back into place.

The tunnel, green in the NVGs, now held scattered black spots from the explosion of light that had scarred his eyes temporarily, but he thought he could see well enough to continue on.

"Can you see okay?" he asked Chris.

"I think so," Chris answered. He heard his officer take a few slow deep breaths. "Let's get moving," he said, and Reed heard him struggle to his feet.

Reed continued down the tunnel, his right sleeve along the wall, as he scanned back and forth. His vision improved rapidly, and a few minutes later seemed nearly normal, though he could still feel tears which ran in little streams down his cheeks.

"What's that?" Chris whispered.

Reed strained to see ahead of him in the tunnel. A few yards forward he saw a heap of something, and at the same moment a horrible smell filled his nostrils, gagging him. The mound slowly took on the rough shape of a man, though the head seemed to be missing and the corpse was badly charred. Again the images from the target house returned to him.

"Jesus," Chris whispered in the dark.

The voices in his headset, which had become like background noise, now sounded more urgent.

"Viper Lead – acknowledge."

Auger's voice sounded tense, but the transmission also seemed slightly garbled, and his earpiece sounded full of static.

"Say again, Viper Four," he heard Chris say.

Again the message seemed broken up, and he assumed the tunnel interfered with good reception.

"can......explosion......okay?"

"We're okay," Chris said. "No injuries."

"......toward you.......two......tunnel......"

"Say again, Four," Chris said, but they heard nothing but static. Chris tried again, but still no reply – at least not that they could hear. They listened together for a moment more. "Did you get any of that?" Chris asked him.

"No," Reed said. He doubted from the tone of Auger's voice that it had been anything good, however.

"Let's get Ben and get the hell out of here," Chris said.

They stepped over the charred corpse and continued down the dark tunnel. Reed thought he saw a faint glow of yellow-white in his NVGs, but it seemed subtle and he thought it might just be the residual effects of the explosion on his eyes. He kept his right elbow against the wall and moved deeper into the tunnel.

Then they both jumped at the sound of another rifle shot, followed a moment later by four more shots in rapid succession.

"Keep moving," Chris commanded.

* * *

Ben moved smoothly and without pause down the tunnel towards the rapidly growing red beacon. As he neared the source at the tunnels end, the eerie reddish hue provided enough light that he no longer looked through the night scope mounted on his rifle, but he continued to hold his weapon up in the ready position. A few yards farther, and the source became apparent – the tunnel dead-ended ahead and the left wall opened in a garage door sized opening, beside which stood a single Al Qaeda fighter armed with an AK-47.

Ben fired once – a head shot that dropped the terrorist like a bag of laundry. He had no chance to see if the eyes glowed, but he assumed a guard posted so near the powerful One with the black blood would most certainly be a dark one. He moved swiftly over the body and fired four additional shots to each arm and both knees, shattering all four extremities.

That'll slow the bastard down if he comes back.

Ben stepped over the heap of flesh and entered the large room.

The red, glowing light didn't seem to illuminate the man so much as emanate from him. The terrorist leader sat at a single table-like desk on which rested a laptop computer with cables that disappeared into the wall behind him, a wide variety of radios, scattered papers, and a pistol – a large revolver which he made no move to grab as he watched Ben approach. He wore the same long and flowing robe style shirt over grey pants that most of the Al Qaeda he had encountered in Africa wore. His feet were clad in red high top tennis shoes. The bearded face parted in a slight grin.

The eyes of course glowed back at him with a harsh red light.

It took you a long time, Rougarou.

Ben hunched into a combat firing stance, leaned in, and squeezed his trigger four times in rapid succession.

Four dark holes appeared in the man's face, three in the forehead and one to the right of his hawk like nose. Blood and gore spattered the glowing wall behind him. The head jerked back with each hit, but then the smile returned, even as blood trickled out of each hole. The one near the nose began to blow little bubbles. For a moment the man's face seemed to shimmer, and Ben thought he saw the demon from his nightmares replace the man's features. Then, the shimmering stopped, and the face returned to the grinning bearded terrorist, now full of holes.

The mouth opened and a growling roar escaped, filling the room with heat and a sulfur-like smell. Then, Ben saw the hands rise from the desk. Fireflies flickered from the fingers to the forearms and then two red fire balls exploded from the hands, crashing into Ben's chest. He felt himself driven backward until he slammed into the wall, crumpling to the floor. The heat felt like he was burning to death from the inside and he tasted blood in his throat. Ben shook his head to clear the stars and looked up in time to see the terrorist rise calmly from his seat, moving around the desk to face him. His body seemed relaxed, and his hands pulsed with red light. The fireflies now flickered around his arms all the way to the shoulders.

Ben concentrated with all of his might and felt a new and familiar aura replace the pain in his chest, and his own hands began to tingle. He squeezed the feeling out of his chest, down both of his arms and two balls of blue light exploded from his fingers. The terrorist/demon raised his arms, and the fireballs glanced off of them, bouncing around the room a moment before they fizzled out harmlessly.

The man opened his mouth and laughed. Dark blood escaped his throat and poured into his thick beard. Again, he seemed to shimmer and for a moment the figure was replaced by a horrible monstrosity, with a long face full of razor-sharp teeth, the bald scarlet head covered in knots that looked like horns and arms extending in impossibly long fingers – more like claws than hands. The shimmering stopped, and the creature turned, its leathery skin covered in black sticky liquid, soaking into its clothing. The hands started to pulse again, and Ben tensed for the next, probably lethal, shot.

You are unprepared, Rougarou. You don't know how to tap the power you need and you have failed.

Ben tried to raise his arms, in protest if not in defense, but the two fire balls smashed into him before he was able. He felt himself engulfed in heat, the energy from the powerful One lifting him from the floor as he smashed painfully into the rock wall several feet above the ground. Ben felt and heard the snap of several ribs as he crumpled to the floor.

The bloody faced terrorist laughed uncontrollably. Ben saw its facial image flicker between that of the wounded man and the oppressive demon. Its long teeth and lizard like face contorting between its false bravado and the reality of what the beast really was.

"I've failed," Ben mumbled and felt hot tears on his cheeks. How could he possibly have believed he had enough power to defeat such a creature?

It resides within you, Ben. It is in your soul and not the Ring. The power comes from who you are, from all around you. From your teammates, from your family here in the jungle, from the heart of Jewel and the spirit of both Christy and your son inside her.

GET UP.

He thought the second voice was his, but couldn't be sure. Ben squeezed his eyes shut and felt something manifest inside. With a burst of power he didn't really think he had, he exploded onto his feet.

The sound of shouts from the tunnel was followed by gunfire which echoed off the walls of room. Ben recognized the sounds of AK-47s and the return of M-4 fire.

"Chris – behind you."

The voice sounded like Reed, and Ben felt a belt tighten around his throat.

Then, he heard the burst of an AK-47, short pain-filled screams – and then silence.

The heat that built in his chest felt so powerful that he thought at first he had been hit again by fireballs from the demon who stood in front of him. But the terrorist still looked out towards the tunnel, and Ben could think about nothing but his friends.

"The power is in *you*, Ben."

He didn't know if the voice belonged to the old man, the Indian, or maybe himself, but he knew it was true.

He saw Christy's smiling face in his mind and felt the heat spread from his chest, down his arms. This time the blue light burned brighter as it burst from his fingertips.

The sparkling spheres of energy pulsated into the raised arms of the demon in front of him as a horrible scream echoed in the cave like room. White light exploded from the center of demons chest and it dropped to one knee– its legs turning into a horse-like limbs with a cloven hooves.

The demon sprang forward on the animal legs and raised its long, clawed arms above its now lizard like head. The long teeth dripped blood and spit onto the floor, its arms pulsating with red light.

"You are too late, Rougarou." The words came from the horrible demon like mouth which seemed no longer to move. There was no longer even a flicker of the man-like terrorist from before.

"Fuck you," Ben screamed. Images of Reed and Chris – perhaps dying now in the tunnel and just out of reach – fueled the heat in his chest to a higher level. A single ball of blue light shot from his hands and smashed into the creatures head, this time with enough force to drive it backwards into the wall.

Ben knew his moment had now arrived and pressed his advantage. He thought again of Reed and Chris and squeezed his eyes tightly closed

Images of Viper Team, Reed, Christy, Jewel, and his unborn son played rapidly in his mind's eye. With each image the pressure and heat inside him grew larger until he could no longer contain it. He felt he would explode into flames from inside. Instead of tingling down his arms, the vibration this time climbed up the back of his throat and Ben opened his mouth.

Again the demon creature appeared as the terrorist leader, the face bloody and the back of the head missing. He dropped both of his hands to his sides and felt his entire body tense as the energy surged out of him. He felt every joint stretch and even his flesh seemed to pull away from the muscles underneath. Ben thought his eyes would explode as the fire-blue light erupted out of his mouth and struck the terrorist mid-torso. For a moment blue fire spread out over the man's body, his red glow replaced with blue. But then a huge circle of white grew in the center of his chest, and the blue column of flame-like light burst out his back. An enormous hole formed where the light had struck him. Ben could see, with what little vision he had left, the wall of the room through the gaping hole in the center of the man.

As the blue light spread over him, the man's flesh began to melt, falling to the ground in huge chunks. Ben watched from some faraway place as the bloody, bearded face slid off like a fleshy, hideous mask and landed in a steaming pile on the floor. A moment later, the terrorist shed like a burning snake the rest of his outer shell and the red-skinned demon creature stood before him, thrashing violently under the unleashed power of the *Rougarou*.

Ben felt anger, hatred for the creature that twisted in the blue light in front of him, and love – love for his team, for his wife, for Jewel – for his son. The emotions churned, coursing through his body. It seemed like gasoline on the fire of the blue light that poured from him with a ferocity that made him feel like he might explode in fragmented pieces. A bat-like shriek echoed off the walls from the wide open, snarling snout of the creature. Then, the red skin of the lumpy head and face began to smoke – and then boil – a moment later the creature evaporated in a cloud of smoke and foul smelling steam. The scream echoed down the tunnel and was gone.

Ben collapsed forward and caught himself painfully on outstretched arms. The world spun around him in a terrible vertigo, and he tasted blood and bile in his throat. Then, the room went black, and he felt himself slip away.

CHAPTER 47

"What the hell was that?" Chris's voice sounded tense but not afraid, and Reed spun around to the sound they both heard behind them. He aimed his rifle carefully, placed the red-dot center mass in the terrorist's chest, but just as he started to squeeze the trigger, the image came into real focus and for a second he froze.

The terrorist had only one arm – the left arm had been torn away a few inches below the shoulder – except for half of a foot of ragged bone that ended just above where the elbow would have been. He also had a gigantic hole in his chest through which Reed could see the grayish-green heart convulse periodically in some sort of spastic beat. The man's throat had been torn out, and his head ended in a bloody hole just above his eyebrows – the rest blown away, likely from a high-caliber round from the snipers.

It took Reed less than a second to take the image in, and then he re-sighted his rifle at the man who could not possibly be alive. Before he fired, he heard Chris's rifle explode and drown out his teammate's "What in the fuckin' hell?" Then, Reed squeezed his own trigger twice.

One round tore away the right side of the terrorist's remaining face, one hit him in the stump that remained of his left arm, and the third blew away the bottom portion of the spastic heart in the chest. In response, the man dropped to one knee, steadied himself with the rifle in his remaining arm, and then slowly stood back up. Reed felt his mouth drop open at the impossible sight and felt his rifle drop towards the ground. His shocked mind was no longer able to send the proper signals to his body.

"I'm dreaming this," he whispered.

"What the shit?" Chris screamed.

And then the corpse raised the AK-47 just as Reed finally noticed the second, equally mutilated, corpse beside the first. Both AK-47s erupted, their muzzle flashes blinding in his NVGs, and Reed felt the hot rounds tear through his body. His last thought before the world turned grey was that gunshot wounds hurt like shit, unlike what he had heard before and remembered from his last injuries.

Reed felt the world tilt violently back and forth and worried he would vomit and then choke in his own puke. He tasted blood and something else – bile maybe – and stared at the hazy image a few inches from his face. It took a moment for his brain to identify it as Chris's boot. He saw it looked covered in blood – black in the green world of the NVGs which somehow were still in front of his eyes. Reed tried to push up with his arms, to get his face out of the dirt, but he found with a sort of detached interest that his body would not do anything he told it to do. He felt like he still breathed, could hear a bubbly kind of noise that he thought might be his breath – though it could have just as likely been Chris, he supposed. He turned his head slightly and focused slowly on a tennis shoe-covered foot. As he did, he felt with some sort of sixth sense that the terrorist's rifle was aimed at his head.

He felt incredibly calm and sort of not really there.

I guess I'm dead. Isn't that a son of a bitch? I hope Ben is okay.

Then he felt the cold metal of the rifle barrel against his temple, and he closed his eyes softly.

Fuck me.

There was a brilliant flash of blue light and a horrible scream which he assumed was the rifle shot and his own last dying gasp – except that he still felt, well, *everything*. He felt the burning pain in his chest and belly and a coldness in both feet. Then, he heard a wet thud and tasted dirt in his mouth. Reed squeezed his eyes shut to clear the tears that blurred his vision, and then registered the mutilated face of the terrorist, the top of the head still missing. As he watched a faint orange glow faded in the milky eyes and winked out.

Then, the world really did turn black.

* * *

Ben opened his eyes and his first thought was of Reed and Chris outside in the tunnel. He scrambled painfully to his feet as every muscle in his body screamed in protest. He had heard of horrible muscle pain in victims of electrocution, and he imagined it felt exactly like this. He also had a nasty, charred wood taste in his mouth – as if he had taken a big bite of the ash in the bottom of a fireplace. He guessed the taste may have been the source of his thoughts about electrocution. His eyes were drawn to a black circle in the middle of the room (which now had a soft blue glow instead of red). The charred circle was all that marked what had happened and looked like the remnants of a bonfire but with all the wood and soot removed. He did see one red, high-top tennis shoe lying on its side at the periphery of the charred circle. A thin tendril of bluish smoke rose from the otherwise empty shoe.

Ben shook his head and then limped towards the entrance to the room and out into the tunnel. The sight that greeted him squeezed his chest and throat, and he struggled not to vomit.

Reed lay face down, his head turned away from Ben and his arms at his sides. He lay in a lake of his own dark blood. Chris lay on his back at a ninety degree angle to Reed, his booted right foot only a few inches from Reed's face. His cammie pants were soaked and glistening with blood, but more terrifying was the round hole in his forehead just above his left eye. A mutilated – and now clearly lifeless – terrorist corpse had crumpled on top of Chris, what was left of the head across his right thigh. The one remaining eye was open and held no orange glow. A few yards away lay the discombobulated heap of another body – another bad guy he saw with some relief.

Ben raced to Reed's side and gently rolled him over. His best friend's eyes flickered, unseeing. His mouth opened and closed like a guppy spilled out of its bowl onto the bathroom floor. Ben heard a sob escape his own throat.

"Reed – Oh, God, Reed, I'm so sorry, buddy. I'm so sorry, Reed." Then, the tears spilled out of his eyes and he cried uncontrollably. He felt Reed's shoulders tense rhythmically as he struggled for breath.

Ben lay his friend back in the dirt and stared at the unseeing eyes that moved back in forth beneath grayish lids. Then, he reached out and placed both hands on Reed's chest. The familiar warm vibration began immediately, and he saw the ring turn to a pulsating orange. Then, his vision blurred with a milky white halo, and he closed his eyes tightly.

He could feel the heat in both of his arms and a moment later his mouth turned coppery with the taste of blood. He felt an excruciating, ripping pain in both sides of his chest. He felt suddenly unable to breathe as his chest got heavy and his lungs filled with the murky liquid death. He fought away the dizziness and kept both hands on his best friend's chest, intent on taking all of his pain and all of his wounds.

Blood filled his mouth and, unable to find the strength to spit, he opened his lips, letting it pour over his chin. He felt the warm and sticky wetness spill over his chest. He felt the world tilt and became aware that his hands had lost contact with Reed, but he couldn't stop the momentum and fell painfully on his side next to his friend.

Ben could hear his own moaning and the bizarre vibration throughout his entire body. But he could think only about his painful, desperate need for air. He heard a bubbling sound each time he strained to suck in a breath and would have screamed, if only he could get some Goddamn air.

Slowly the heaviness began to ebb and just as his consciousness started to fade he felt a little puff work its way into his chest. He pushed it back out with all of his might, and then sucked again and this time felt a much bigger gulp slowly expand his burning chest. It took great effort – like trying to breathe through a three-foot long straw, but eventually his lungs filled with sweet oxygen. He again squeezed down to force it back out as he felt his mind clearing. The next breath came easier – and the next – until he breathed almost normally, a throbbing headache replaced his dizziness.

Ben opened his eyes and shook his head. He found his face to be only inches from Reed's, and although his friend's eyes were closed, he saw his skin now looked pink and healthy. His breath went in and out of his open mouth with normal ease. Dried blood caked on Reed's face, but no longer bubbled out of his mouth. He struggled to his knees on the hard floor of the tunnel next to his best friend.

There were four black holes in Reed's vest and Ben tore apart the Velcro flaps that held it in place. Beneath the body armor the same four holes looked back at him from Reed's Cammie shirt and beneath that his T-shirt. Both were completely soaked in reddish death. Ben tore the T-shirt away.

The skin of Reed's chest beneath his clothes was also soaked in blood, and Ben smeared it away to get a better look. He stared in joy and disbelief at the smooth, unblemished skin beneath the bullet holes in Reed's clothes. The chest rose and fell slowly and softly, with apparent ease.

I did it. I fuckin' did it. He's gonna be okay.

Then he turned and shuffled on his knees over to Chris. He pushed what was left of the corpses head off of the legs of his team mate and looked him over. From the waist down, his cammies were soaked in blood and Ben saw two bullet holes on Chris's right hip where the high velocity rounds had torn through his pelvis, no doubt shattering it and his hip joints. God only knew how much damage they did on their way through. Those injuries would be devastating – he doubted if he survived he could ever again walk – but they were the least of his problems. Ben stared at the dark round hole in his friend's forehead as he felt for a pulse in Chris's neck – there was none.

Ben felt the tears flow down his cheeks. Chris should be at home with his wife – not dead in some dirty tunnel in the middle of nowhere thousands of miles away. Ben realized with great pain, that if not for him, that was exactly where Chris would be.

He's dead because of me. I killed him as sure as if I'd shot him myself.

Your destiny was no longer yours to choose, Ben.

He turned and looked at the old man who squatted on the floor beside him.

"Fuck that," he hollered. "These men are my family, and Chris is dead because of me. How do I fix that? How?" He wiped the tears violently from his face. "Can I heal him? Can I heal him even if he is dead?"

The spirit is still in your friend, and the life is not gone yet from him, so it is possible. It is not likely you could survive, though. You are weak already from healing the other, and it would take time to replace the life energy you have used.

Ben looked back at Chris and for a moment thought of Christy and his son, still inside her. Then, he thought of Viper Team and how they had all come here with him. None had even understood why he had to be here, but they had come anyway.

I love you, Christy. I love you, and I love our son.

He concentrated with all his might, and once he was sure the heart message would make it to his wife, he reached out and placed his hands on Chris. Again the world took on a milky white blurriness and he took a long, slow tactical breath and closed his eyes.

* * *

It took Reed a moment to remember just where the hell he was, and when he did he sat up. With one hand, he frisked his body for wounds and with the other snatched his rifle out of the dirt. He sensed more than heard movement to his right and spun in that direction, raising his rifle to a firing position just as his heart beat accelerated at the feel of warm, sticky wetness on his bare chest. The memory came exploding into his head – the zombie-like corpses firing their rifles at him and Chris.

He saw Ben.

He kept his rifle up in a one-handed grip and scanned a circle around them as his left hand continued its search for the holes in his flesh that had to be there. He remembered the bullets tearing into his chest, and he was covered in blood. But he found no holes.

And, I'm awake and standing here for Christ sake, so let it go for now.

There was no one in the tunnel except him, Ben who knelt over Chris's body, and the now-motionless corpses. Had he dreamed the whole Goddamn shooting? But then why was he covered in blood ,and why the shit was he naked from the waist up?

"Ben?" he called out.

But Ben stayed kneeled over their officer, who Reed now saw was unmoving and covered in blood. His best friend seemed to moan as he rocked back and forth but as he listened the soft moan sounded more like a chant in some strange language he had never heard. He felt a weird sort of déjà vu.

He walked around his teammates, his rifle now limp in his grip. As he circled around to the front of Ben, he saw his friend's eyes were open. Even in the soft bluish light, which he now noticed seemed to actually emanate from Ben, he could see their milky-white appearance. It was less like a film over his eyes and more like Ben's eyes were filled from the inside with a white smoke that swirled around behind his corneas.

Ben's hands rested on Chris's chest, and Reed saw the flickering beams that seemed to dance around his hands and arms, pulsing from his fingers.

He knew that Chris was dead. The dark hole in his forehead and unseeing eyes told the whole story, and he felt his throat tighten at the loss. He thought for a moment about Emily and how her world would unravel when she found out her husband had died in the service of his country. He had seen it too many friggin' times.

"Ben," he called out softly again.

His mind went suddenly to the dream – the dream of Ben with his hands glowing blue, surrounded by flickering white light. He remembered the ring – that damn ring – glowing orange and the energy that came from his fingertips.

He watched Ben chant, his eyes swirling with the white smoke, his hands glowing, the ring pulsating orange, and he knew. He knew it had not been a dream.

Or else I'm dreaming now.

But he knew that wasn't true. He knelt beside Ben and began to cry.

"Please, Ben," he whispered. "Please save him."

As he watched the little firefly lights seemed to fill the hole in Chris's head. He saw they danced around the back of his skull where the huge exit wound almost certainly dumped blood and brains into the dirt behind it. Reed gasped as the hole in his team mate's head began to lighten, and the edges pulled together, filling in.

He excitedly slapped Ben on the back, but his smile disappeared when he felt warm stickiness there. Reed looked at his hand which was covered now in bright red blood and watery grey gore. He leaned left, and to his horror saw a large gaping hole in the back of Ben's head. As he watched the hole grew, and blood poured out onto his best friend's neck.

"Ben," he screamed, this time in terror.

Then, Ben pitched forward face-first into the dirt.

* * *

Ben raised the warm glass of iceless lemonade to his lips and waited for his Gammy to speak. He felt a crushing sadness at what he had left behind, but he had no regret. He had done only what he had to. He was a SEAL. He was also a Traiteur.

There had really been no choice to make.

Gammy patted the back of his hand and sipped her own drink. She turned to him and smiled the way he remembered from his childhood. It was the smile that said your scraped knee hurts now, but it's gonna be alright, chile, and you gonna be jess fine. He smiled back.

"No room for no sadness now, chile. Gammy's as proud as can be now. You done been turn inna one helluva a man." She patted his hand again. "You done been a sight good Traiteur, too, no doubt dat."

"What about my family?" he asked and felt his eyes swell with tears. "Who will look after them?"

"Look affa them yo' own self, I expect," his Gammy said patiently.

He sighed a pain-filled sigh.

"Is that how it works?"

His Gammy said nothing, but patted his hand again and then sipped her lemonade.

"I did what I had to do," he said and sipped his sweet, warm drink.

"Did whatcha had to do," she agreed. "'Course now you always did, chile. Ever since dat night, dincha?"

Ben thought a moment. He didn't really know.

He saw the fire – saw it swallowing up his home and could almost feel its heat. He could also feel the tears on his young cheeks as he stood there alone in the woods. He remembered the figures in the fire, flames consuming them as still they grappled with each other. And, he remembered her voice – soft and gentle as always, a grandma's voice – telling him to run. She told him where to go, who to find, and what to say.

And, he had never been back after that, not even in his mind until just a few weeks ago he realized. He had never even wondered.

"You saved me that night, didn't you?" he asked and looked at her wrinkled and beautiful face with the grey, but sparkling, eyes.

"Oh, my, shit no, chile," she said and squeezed his hand and laughed. "Done saved yo' self dat night. Saved yo' self and one whole lot more. Same as always I expect. Proud dat night, too."

For a moment he saw it – through his own little boy eyes – the demon-like yellow orbs of the creature and his Gammy screaming for him to find something he was supposed to have inside. Then, the heat in his little chest had grown, and the glow around his small hands had pulsated. The fire shot from his little body, and then he listened to the shrieks from the creatures as the fire consumed them – and his Gammy, too, he supposed.

And, he had left his home in the woods and never looked back.

"Done been dat man since yo been a boy, huh, chile?"

She patted his hand again.

"So," he said and looked out from their porch on the woods he now remembered he loved. "Now what? We just sit here on our porch forever? Is this supposed to be Heaven?"

His Gammy laughed a big belly laugh.

"Might jess sit a bit my own self," she said. "But you gots stuff to be doin' I think, now. No time to be jess sittin'."

"Might just sit a minute," he said, and leaned back and sipped his lemonade. "Just a minute."

"Okay," she said. "But jess a minute, chile. Gots no more time den dat."

CHAPTER 48

The light blinded Reed as they burst out of the tunnel behind the waterfall, and he squinted, unable to raise an arm to block the intruding sun. Both his hands were busy pushing down rhythmically on Ben's chest just as he had been taught.

I think Ben actually recertified me in CPR.

The irony didn't seem particularly important right now. The Air Force PJ's, the special ops medics extraordinaire, had slipped a tube down his best friend's throat and periodically squeezed the green plastic bag they had attached to it.

"Helo is on the ground," Auger hollered at them. "This way, this way," he shouted and dashed off to the left.

The SEALs and two Air Force medics struggled to keep the stretcher level as they started down the rough terrain leading off the ruins, and Reed struggled to keep up the chest compressions without losing his footing and falling to the ground. The hole he thought he had seen in the back of Ben's head –

I did see it – it was there, and then Ben – wherever he is, or was – somehow healed it. He's trying to make it back.

– had mysteriously disappeared. But the round hole in his forehead remained, and blood soaked his body below his waist. His right leg flopped around like it wasn't even attached to his body, and his left leg had turned around nearly completely backwards.

Come on, Ben – please don't do this. Please don't leave us. Christy needs you – and I need you.

"Come on – let's go, let's go," Chris hollered out from the head of the stretcher as they approached the helicopter whose rotor still spun overhead, ready to take off as soon as the patient was secure. Chris looked completely unharmed except his pants were soaked with blood from the waist down. He walked without so much as a limp.

They slid the stretcher into the helicopter, and Reed started to climb up after him. One of the medics inside put a hand on his chest.

"We got him from here," he said gently.

"I need to go with him," Reed said in a trembling voice and felt tears spill onto his face. "Please. He's my only real family in the world."

Chris took him by the shoulders and pulled him gently back from the doorway.

"They'll take good care of him, bro," he said softly.

Reed watched as one of the medics took up the chest compressions he had been responsible for. On an impulse, he reached inside and took Ben's right hand a moment and squeezed. Then, he slipped the dull, bone-colored ring off of his finger.

"Gunshot wound to the head," one of the PJs from the tunnel said.

"Oh, Jesus," the medic inside responded, and then pushed the microphone from his flight helmet to his lips and started to talk to someone far away.

"He's gonna be fine," Reed screamed up at them as the helicopter spun and began to hover just above the ground. "He's my family, Goddammit, and he is going to be okay. You hear me?"

The medic in the helicopter gave him a halfhearted thumbs-up as the helicopter lifted off, and Chris held him by the shoulders as he began to sob. Reed wiped the tears from his face and looked down at the ring. It lay in his hand, a pale grayish white ring of unpolished stone. He slipped his dog tags over his head and slipped the chain through the center of the ring and let it slide down on top of his tags. Then, he slipped them back over his head. He turned to Chris.

"He's going to be fine."

"Okay," Chris said, but Reed knew he didn't believe it. They watched the helicopter fade to a speck in the distance, and then Reed grabbed his rifle and headed back to the team of SEALs and the small group of flex-cuffed bad guys who knelt in a circle at their feet.

"He's going to be fine," he mumbled again to himself.

CHAPTER 49

Christy sat in the large wicker chair on their deck and looked out at the Chesapeake Bay as she stroked the hair of the baby in her lap who fought valiantly against sleep. It had started to turn cold again after a short early summer weekend, but the beach was still busy with the hard-core beach bums who wore sweatshirts over their shorts. A group of them tossed a Frisbee back and forth and laughed and drank beer from red plastic cups. She missed that, she realized.

You'll have it again. And anyway, look what you do have.

She hugged little Jason to her chest and pulled the soft blanket around him. For a moment he looked up at her with his grey and stormy eyes. Then, he sucked harder on his Binky and gave up, his eyes closing as he snuggled against his Mommy's warmth.

Totally worth it. Besides, life is getting more and more normal every day.

She had everything she needed in the world right here in this house. She wondered if she would ever know the truth of what happened to her husband in Africa. He sure as hell wasn't talking now was he?

Her thoughts were interrupted by the bang of the front door and heavy footsteps in the house. Then, she heard the screen door creak open.

"Hey, Reed," she loud-whispered over her shoulder.

"Hey, sis," he said back softly and kissed her on the back of the head before settling into the chair beside her, two beers now evident in his hands. He twisted the top off one and set it on the rail in front of her and then opened the other and took a long swig. "How's everything in the Morvant household?"

She smiled a genuine smile. "Better all the time," she said and reached for the beer slowly, careful not to jostle her now sleeping son. "You look great," she added.

"Only member of Viper Team to escape without a scratch – well, me and Lash, but he's not really a mortal as you know."

She held the bottle up, and Reed clicked his bottle against hers. "To Ben," he said.

She smiled agreement. "To Ben," she said and took a long swig.

She watched as Reed stared out over the beach to the bay and sighed. She noticed the pale, bone-colored ring still hung from his dog tags, but wasn't surprised. It had been over a year, after all. Why would he suddenly take the ring off now? Maybe he needed it – needed the reminder for some reason.

"Boy, do we miss him over at the team," he said absently.

"I know," she said. "He misses you guys, too."

"Sometimes it feels like he's still – I don't know – sort of looking over us, I guess." He took another long swig of his beer.

"Maybe he'll be back soon," Christy lay her head for a moment against Reed's shoulder.

"That's up to the Navy," Ben's voice said from the door behind them. "I'm ready."

Christy turned and her face felt warm with the love she had for her husband. She watched as he maneuvered painfully through the doorway and onto the deck, his hands gripped tightly on the handles of the two canes. He did seem to walk with so much more strength, but she hated the grimace of pain in his face as he limped towards them.

"Where the hell's my beer, dickweed?" he asked Reed.

"Hey, dude, you're interrupting a date here," Reed answered. He got up and hugged his best friend gently, then clapped him on the shoulder to remove any testosterone inhibition the hug might cause. The man-ritual always made Christy laugh, and she smiled broadly but kept the chuckle in. "I'll grab you one," he said and headed towards the house.

She watched as her husband eased himself painfully into Reed's chair, but resisted the urge to help him. She wanted to ask if he had taken his pain medicine, but she bit her lip instead – she didn't need his scowl, and anyway the number of pills in the bottle in their bathroom hadn't changed any in weeks. So, she had her answer.

Stupid, pig-headed SEALs.

She put her hand on his arm and wondered how he had managed to walk at all with his pelvis basically pulverized by bullets.

"How you doin'?" she asked – not capable of asking nothing.

"Great," he smiled and put her hand to his lips and kissed it. "I really am great, baby. I got everything I need right here."

"I know you want to make it back, Ben," she looked down at their sleeping son. "I want you to make it back, too, but if – you know– if you can't – I mean if you take the medical retirement and just stay home with us – that wouldn't be so bad, right?"

Ben smiled at her and his beautiful grey eyes lit up and melted her heart.

"That wouldn't be so bad at all," he promised.

She watched him stare out at the bay and wondered what had really happened over there. She guessed it didn't matter – he made it home to them just like he promised, and their family was together. She knew he thought about Jewel and all the other things that had happened if Africa, but she knew also that he seemed truly happy now. And free – he seemed free and really happy for the first time since she had met him. His eyes still held the steel grey, but the storm in them seemed gone.

Whatever really did happen over there, her husband seemed to have finally been released from the iron grip of some sort of haunting. Maybe it was the past or maybe it was something else, but all that mattered was it seemed to be gone, at least for now. And the ring – that damn ring – at least it was finally off of his finger. She traced the back of his strong, worn hand with hers.

Jason stirred, and she looked down to see him looking up at her with a big, toothless baby grin. His blue-grey eyes – Ben's eyes – held some of the storm clouds she remembered from her husband's. She smiled.

We're in for a rough time from this one, I bet.

"Here ya go, bro," Reed said and handed a beer to Ben. "Hey, cool – my little nephew is up." He reached out his hands, and Christy smiled. A few months ago Reed had been afraid to hold Jason, and now he couldn't seem to get enough.

"Just remember," Ben said smiling, "we're very glad he doesn't actually have any of your genes in him."

"Yeah, yeah," Reed lifted Jason from his mother's arms and held him up over his face for a moment. "Don't worry, big guy. Uncle Reed will teach you all the stuff your Daddy doesn't know."

Little Jason cooed and reached out, grabbing Reed's nose which made them both laugh.

"Nice grip," Reed said.

He pulled the baby to his chest and hugged him.

Jason reached out for the dog tags that hung from Reed's neck and grabbed them playfully – no doubt intent on pulling them into his mouth like everything else he got his hands on. As Christy watched, her baby's chubby little hand grabbed the pale, bone-colored ring.

A chill went through her as she watched the ring turn suddenly smooth and then change color to a soft bluish-green as Jason held it in his chubby fingers, cooing his happiness. The ring almost pulsed with glowing light, and for a moment she thought she saw tiny, sparkly fireflies glimmer around his little hands, but then they disappeared. She held her husband's hand, watched the storm clouds rise in her baby boy's eyes, and shuddered again.

She shook her head and blamed the cold.

CPSIA information can be obtained at www.ICGtesting.com
Printed in the USA
LVOW041713120912

298542LV00003B/72/P